WIDOW MAKER

A NOVEL OF WORLD WAR II

E. R. JOHNSON

Llumina Press

ISBN: 978-1-62550-490-6

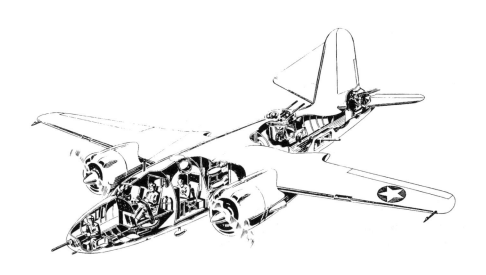

U.S. Army Model Martin B-26B-10-MA Aircraft

DONEGAL BAY

IRELAND

IRISH SEA

NORTH SEA

LIVERPOOL

CARDIGAN BAY

ENGLAND

NORWICH
SNETTERTON HEATH
BOXSTED
GREAT DUNROW

HIGH WYCOMBE

LONDON

IJMUIDEN

AMSTERDAM

HOLLAND

ENGLISH CHANNEL

BRUSSELS

NAMUR

COLOGNE

BELGIUM

LENS

GERMANY

ROUEN

PARIS

FRANCE

AREA OF OPERATIONS

Dedication

This book is dedicated to the memory of my father, Col. E. R. Johnson, Jr., USMCR (ret.), who, as a citizen soldier and military pilot, flew combat in the Southwest Pacific Theater during World War Two, then answered the call to fight again in Korea in 1950-1953. My father taught me that warriors are mostly ordinary men who are called upon to perform extraordinary deeds.

Acknowledgments

Special thanks must be given to Mr. Roger J. Piazza of Boling-broke, Georgia, who, as a U. S. Army Air Force Lieutenant, flew fifty combat missions as a B-26 bombardier-navigator attached to the 455th Bomb Squadron, 323rd Bomb Group (Medium), 9th Air Force. Roger not only provided a wealth of photographs and documents, but spent many, many patient hours with me detailing medium bomber operations and relating his personal combat experiences.

In the course of my research, one of the best resources I found on B-26 operations in general was the book by Maj. Gen. John O. Moench, *Marauder Men: An Account of the Martin B-26*, Malia Enterprises, Longwood, FL, 1989. Much of the technical information I used came from the *Pilot's Flight Operating Instructions for Army Models B-26B and B-26C Airplanes,* AAF Manual No. AN 01-35EB-1, Pittsburgh, PA, 25 December 1943 (known to pilots simply as the "dash-one") and Frederick A. Johnsen's excellent reference, *Martin B-26 Marauder, Warbird Tech Series Vol. 29*, Specialty Press, North Branch, MN, 2000.

PROLOGUE:
A PLANE A DAY IN TAMPA BAY

October 17, 1942, U.S.A.A.F. Headquarters, Washington, D.C.

Brigadier General James H. Doolittle walked briskly down the hall of the Army-Navy Annex, curious why General Henry H. Arnold, Commander of the U. S. Army Air Forces, wished to see him on such short notice. Doolittle, who had recently been promoted and given command of a newly-formed air wing scheduled to participate in the upcoming invasion of North Africa—secretly known as Operation Torch—couldn't fathom why General Arnold would want to discuss any of the planning with someone at his level. When he reached Arnold's outer office, a middle-aged secretary, who recognized the diminutive brigadier, instructed him to go on in, the General was expecting him.

As Doolittle stepped through the doorway, General Arnold, a somewhat moon-faced man in his mid-fifties, looked up with an enthusiastic smile, then got out of his chair and walked around his paper-laden desk to pump his visitor's hand and squeeze his arm in the manner of old friends.

"Jimmy! How in the world are you?"

"Fine, General...kind of up to my ass in alligators getting this new wing ready to go overseas...but otherwise I can't complain."

Lowering himself to one of the easy chairs in front of his desk, the General looked at his short, balding friend and pointed to the other chair. "Congratulations on the promotion and the new job, Jimmy. Both were well-deserved."

"Thank you, sir."

"But funny you should mention alligators," the General said with cocked eyebrow, a smile on his face. "How would you like to take a short trip to Florida?"

"Sir?" Doolittle gave him a puzzled look.

"I know you're busy right now...getting your new command shaped-up and so forth, but..." the General's smile disappeared "...I've got an urgent problem on my hands, and I want you to take care of it for me."

Doolittle's gaze became curious.

"You've probably heard we're having problems with the Martin B-26," the General continued, "bigger problems than we normally have with a new airplane. This year alone, over two hundred pilots have been killed in training accidents. *Killed!"*

Doolittle had heard about some of the problems with the airplane but was stunned by the statistic the General had just shared with him.

The General paused and exhaled noisily. "And this airplane—you know this already—was the first one we ordered right off the drawing board without extensive testing. Well, the operational accident rate makes it look like we've screwed up royally! And you know what the damned newpapers are calling it?"

"No, sir, I don't get the chance to read the papers much."

"They call it the *Widow Maker."*

"And that's not the bad part, Jimmy." Arnold's voice became confidential, and he leaned closer to smaller man. "Let me tell you about what's happening here in Washington: the Senate Committee on Military Procurement, the so-called Truman Committee, is running my ass ragged over this airplane. Take a guess what those civilian yay-hoos want to do with it?"

Doolittle continued to stare at the General without comment.

The General made a cutting motion across his throat and rasped, "The sons-of-bitches want me to cancel Martin's contract and shut-down the whole B-26 production line!"

The revelation shocked Doolittle.

The timbre of the General's voice lowered again. "God help us, Jimmy," he murmured. "We're gearing up to start major offensive operations in this war, and they want me to stop—*stop!*—production of a combat aircraft."

The General sat back and closed his eyes for a moment. Doolittle noticed the strain and weariness on the face of General Henry H. "Hap" Arnold. They'd known each other for over twenty-five years, were contemporaries in fact, but Arnold had remained in the Air Corps while he'd gotten out. Doolittle had only returned last year, as a major. The General's appearance was alarming: he looked old, tired, and his hair had turned snow white. The war was only ten months old, and Doolittle predicted that it was going to be a very long haul for both of them.

"Sir, what do you want me to do?" Doolittle finally asked.

The General seriously regarded the small man who was one of the best-known fliers in America. "Jimmy, you understand airplanes as well as any person I know. You've flown practically everything...you've got a doctorate in aeronautical science. I trust your judgment."

Doolittle appreciated the flattery but kept his expression blank.

"I want you to go down to MacDill Field in person and find out what's wrong with that airplane." The general's expression was pained. *"Find out why it's killing so many of my pilots!"*

Fixing Doolittle with a grim stare, the General said, "You'll have the authority of my office to investigate anything...*anything* ...you think is relevant. I'm going to put the technical people from Martin at your disposal, too. We'll eventually need a full report in writing to give to the Truman Committee, but I want you to report back to me in one week."

"One week!" Doolittle exclaimed, bolting up in his chair. "That really only gives me five days to sort this thing out!"

The General looked at Doolittle and gave a dismissive wave of his hand. "Jimmy, this won't wait...I needed it done yesterday. The politicians I told you about...they want answers *now.* I'm sorry, old friend, but one week's the most I can give you. Your temporary orders and travel vouchers have already been cut."

End of conversation.

Exactly one week later Doolittle strode into General Arnold's office at 0800. He'd left MacDill Field the previous afternoon, arriving back in Washington around midnight. The same middle-aged secretary looked at him tiredly and waved him into the General's office.

The General, glancing up from a stack of papers on his desk, stood to greet his visitor. "Jimmy, nice to see you again." He motioned to the chair. "How was the flight from MacDill?"

"Fine, General, no problems." Doolittle noticed that the General's drained appearance had not improved from the previous week. He wondered how early the man had gotten to his office or whether he'd left it at all.

"I suppose you flew the plane back yourself?" The General knew that Doolittle rarely rode in airplanes but flew them every chance he got.

"Not all the way, sir, just the leg from Raleigh."

Doolittle was utterly exhausted and looked it. In addition to conducting the B-26 investigation at MacDill, he'd been on the phone many times each day, trying to maintain control of things at his new wing. Looking down, Doolittle extracted a file from the flight bag sitting at his feet.

"General," he said, matter-of-factly, "there's nothing wrong with the B-26." Pausing a few seconds to allow his superior to absorb the generalization, Doolittle continued, "The chief cause of most of these crashes, as I see it, is bad training. There have been some serious maintenance problems, for sure, but those things have been largely resolved by the technical people at Martin. The real problem is with pilot training." Doolittle rocked forward on his knees to emphasize his point. "Hell, General, the instructor pilots don't even know how to fly the airplane, let alone checkout student pilots fresh out of advanced training."

The General looked at him with a steady gaze.

"You're an experienced pilot, too, sir...you know that most high-performance airplanes have some bad habits; and this one...the B-26...has a few that will kill you if you're not properly trained to fly it. My investigation revealed that most of the crashes involved losing an engine on either takeoff or landing. I took Captain Vincent Burnett down there with me...you probably remember him...and we put the B-26 through a full flight evaluation program. You know about the wing loading, of course...highest of any aircraft in our inventory?"

The General coughed and nodded.

"This wing loading gives the airplane a highly critical range of single-engine control speeds. The problem is simple: if you get behind the plane after you've lost an engine, *you're dead*!" He mimicked the motion by rotating his hand upside-down and smacking it against the top of the desk. "I'll tell you one thing, sir," his tone became grim, "if Burnett and I hadn't been experienced multi-engined pilots, we'd be dead ducks right now.".

"*But*," Doolittle's said the word with great emphasis, "neither do I believe the B-26 is the deathtrap its critics claim it is. Other than what I just mentioned, the flight characteristics are above-average, and it's an extremely rugged airplane that'll carry 4,000 pounds of bombs almost 1,000 miles at a cruising speed of over 200 m.p.h. There's no question that the other medium bombers in the Air Corps inventory are more docile and easier to fly, but none of them...*none*...can equal the speed, range, firepower and bomb-load of the B-26."

Doolittle looked thoughtfully into the General's weathered brown eyes. "Sir, I think, with proper training, our pilots can be taught to safely fly the B-26. Captain Burnett is in the process of re-writing the entire training syllabus and will stay down at MacDill to re-train the instructor pilots himself. After these new pilots and co-pilots have completed the B-26 conversion course, I'm recommending comprehensive changes to the operational training phase, too."

Doolittle gave the General the file in his hand and said, finally, "Sir, if you can deal with the politicians and bureaucrats, and save this airplane, I believe we will see better results with the crews."

"Thanks, Jimmy, I'll see what I can do."

Minutes later, the General watched the balding little man disappear through his doorway. Hap Arnold appreciated Doolittle's enthusiasm and his level of conviction, but he knew that time would be the final judge of this airplane, and *time* was something he was fresh out of.

PART ONE:

CRADLE

CHAPTER ONE

November 27, 1942, MacDill Field, Tampa, Florida.

The B-26 smoothly lifted from the runway at 120 m.p.h. indicated airspeed and started climbing into the cloudless Florida sky. It was a B-26A-1, an early short-winged version that had been relegated to training duties. The two Pratt & Whitney 1,850 horsepower R-2800 engines were delivering their throaty song as the big bomber struggled to gain altitude in the humid air. The pilot, First Lieutenant Theodore J. Shaw, U. S. Army Air Corps, called out, "Gear up, flaps up!" as he reached down and moved the twin throttles and propeller controls to climb power.

Everything was copasetic.

The instructor pilot in the right seat, Captain Robert M. Armistead, U. S. Army Air Corps, a native of Greenville, Mississippi, who also acted as co-pilot, acknowledged, "Gear and flaps comin' up." At the same time, he reached down and pulled the mixture lever on number two engine to the idle-cutoff position and phlegmatically said, "I think you just lost number two."

Shaw, without looking at the instructor, simultaneously moved the throttle and propeller control on number one engine to full power, dropped the nose of the airplane and added full right rudder and enough aileron to counteract the tendency of the airplane to corkscrew into the dead engine. Almost in the same instant, he shouted, "Feather two! Secure fuel and ignition to two!" Noticing the airspeed stabilizing at 150 m.p.h., he reached above his head and began winding in rudder trim to ease the pressure on the right rudder pedal.

Armistead indifferently replied, "One feathered, fuel and ignition secure." In recent months, the young Captain had earned a reputation as the toughest check-pilot at MacDill.

Shaw reached down to the control pedestal and closed the cowl flaps and oil cooler shutter on the dead engine. Satisfied that the situation had stabilized, he eased back the manifold pressure and propeller

RPM on the good engine and rolled-in a little elevator trim to re-establish the climb.

Armistead observed the look of intense concentration on the young pilot's face. No panic, he thought, *not yet*. "Nice recovery, Lieutenant," he said matter-of-factly. "You already got some multi-engine time in B-18s, I believe?" He had inspected Shaw's logbook before the flight.

"Yep," the young pilot grunted without looking at his instructor. He was completely preoccupied with the task of flying a B-26 on one engine.

"Well, the B-18's a real old lady's airplane compared to this 'un, ain't it?"

"Yep." Shaw noticed the altimeter passing through 2,000 feet and began mentally coaching himself for the next simulated emergency the instructor might throw at him.

Armistead interrupted his thoughts. "Lieutenant, you're in a situation where you just lost an engine and need to land this airplane sometime. What you gonna' do next?"

Shaw replied almost automatically, "I'm going continue the climb to 5,000 feet and maintain this course over the bay until we reach a position to dump fuel, then I'll turn around toward the field."

"That's right, Lieutenant, except we sure as hell ain't gonna' dump any of the Air Force's high octane gas into the ocean. You just turn this airplane around and get ready to enter a downwind leg for a landin' on two-seven, got it?"

"You want me to re-start number one?"

"Did I say that? I'll damn well tell you if I want you to do somethin' else."

Shaw thought about the injunction, *never turn a B-26 into the dead engine*, and simultaneously eased the bomber into a shallow left turn to reverse course. In the middle of the turn, he suddenly remembered that they had taken off from runway three-six, and an approach to two-seven would require him to land in a direct crosswind! *Crosswind with a dead engine!* The thought of it gave him the urge to urinate. He strove to calm himself as he silently reviewed the steps he would have to take to get this airplane on the ground—-in one piece. Shaw didn't believe in luck; he thought pilots, especially the dead ones, made their own luck. To his way of thinking, flying this B-26 or any other airplane was a feat of acquired skill. As he stared through the windscreen at the sapphire water of Tampa Bay, he felt himself relax. There was still some tightness in the pit of his stomach, but his mind was clear. He knew what to do.

The instructor's voice interrupted his thoughts again. "I'll handle the radios," Armistead said, "while you set up the approach, got it?"

Shaw simply nodded and said, "Roger."

Armistead studied the demeanor of the boyish pilot, noticing a determined set to his face, but not the wild-eyed fright that frequently overwhelmed some of his students at this point.

As the airfield drew near, Shaw eased the throttle back slightly and advanced the propeller RPM to start a gradual descent to a pattern altitude of 1,000 feet. In part of his mind, he heard Armistead call the control tower and advise them of the intended landing on two-seven.

His earphones crackled again. "Army two-one-two, wind is from one-six-zero at fifteen," the tower reported. "Altimeter is twenty-nine point six...you are cleared to land on runway two-seven."

After resetting the altimeter, Shaw reminded himself of another injunction: *a B-26 will not maintain level flight on one engine with the landing gear down.* At least that's what the book—the pilot's manual—said, and it was true. But the book, he knew, did not define all possible solutions. The easiest, he thought, was not always the *best*.

The solution was clear.

Banking the bomber to intercept the downwind leg of the runway, Shaw glanced to his right and noticed the instructor-pilot was tightly cinching-down his shoulder straps. He wondered what Armistead expected him to do. *Probably not what he had planned.*

"I'm going to fly the downwind leg out a little further at this altitude," he announced to the instructor-pilot, "curve around base into a long final, then begin my descent. You be ready to lower the gear and flaps on short final, as fast as you can...I'll tell you the amount of flaps I want." Shaw rolled the bomber into a gentle left bank until he was lined up with center of the runway.

Armistead wasn't sure what was on his student's mind, but he was no longer detached; he was watching Shaw closely. Noticing the airspeed had stabilzed at 150 m.p.h., he looked out the windscreen at the runway and said, "Don't you think you're kinda' high and fast for a landin' on two-seven, Lieutenant?"

"Nope," Shaw replied, "I think we're all right." Reaching down to the control pedestal, he eased the throttle back on number two engine and felt the airplane begin to sink. The needle on the rate-of-descent indicator settled on 1,000 feet per minute. In one minute, his solution would prove itself—one way or the other.

Armistead was about to order full power for a go-around when

Shaw suddenly turned and screamed, "Gear down! Thirty degrees of flaps, NOW!"

Whatever else was on Armistead's mind, he acted with the instincts of a long-time pilot, responding without thinking, "Gear coming down, flaps coming down to thirty!"

Releasing the levers, Armistead glanced to his left.

The young pilot's face was taut with concentration, his mouth a compressed slit. But the calm, steady gaze of his eyes told the story. Armistead noted with unspoken admiration that Shaw wasn't man-handling the controls but caressed them lightly, moved them with fluid motions. The instructor-pilot had been forced to take the airplane away from many of his students at this point. This time he watched, holding back.

Shaw added a touch of power on the good engine to keep the bomber's nose lined up with the center of the runway and rolled-in "up" elevator trim until the airspeed stabilized at 135 m.p.h. He screamed again, "Gimme full flaps!"

Pushing the lever to its stop, Armistead yelled, "Full flaps!"

The B-26, which has about the same sink rate as a Pullman Car, plunged down to the end of the runway like a falling elevator. Nearing the threshold, Shaw began to ease the bomber's nose up to check the descent rate, glancing at the airspeed indicator and feeling the positive pressure of the seat-pack parachute on his buttocks. The airplane flashed over the large runway threshold numbers at 125 m.p.h. The young pilot slowly reduced power to the good engine, simultaneously feeding in right rudder and left aileron to compensate for crosswind drift. With the good engine reduced to an idle, the B-26 floated a few feet above the surface of the runway, slightly wing low. Shaw, the control yoke held in both hands, increased back pressure, whispering to himself, *"hold off...easy."*

Seconds later he felt a gentle bump on the seat of his pants and heard the *chirp-chirp* of the main wheels making contact with the runway. Tracking the plane down the centerline with small inputs of rudder and aileron, he held the nose up so the wings would act as airbrakes. When the airspeed dropped below 75 m.p.h., he gently lowered the nose to the runway's surface and began to apply the brakes. With the B-26 slowed almost to a walking pace, he turned onto the taxiway that intersected the middle of the runway and braked to a stop. Removing his hands from the controls finally, he flexed his shoulders and turned to look at the instructor-pilot.

"Captain, do you want me to re-start Number One?"

"Huh?" Armistead looked at him trancelike.

"Do you want me to re-start the engine?"

The unconcerned expression returned to Armistead's face. "Yeah...start it up and take the plane back to the ramp," he said.

"Back to the ramp, Captain?" A feeling of alarm began to wash over the young pilot. "Is the check ride over...I mean, have we covered everything?"

"We'll talk about it in a minute, Lieutenant." Armistead picked up the microphone and said, "Tower, two-one-two is off two-seven on taxiway Baker and will proceed to ramp, over."

"Roger, two-one-two, you are cleared to the ramp."

Shaw started number two engine and taxied toward the tarmac where the other B-26's were parked. As he pulled into the parking area, he watched the ground crewman giving hand signals to guide the aircraft into the its assigned parking place. When the man gave him the "cut" signal—a slashing motion across his throat—Shaw reached down and yanked both mixture levers to the idle cutoff position. The large four-bladed propellers milled to a stop, replacing the noise with a conspicuous stillness.

Shaw slid back the window on his side and listened to the gyros spool down and the tinkling of the engines as the metal cooled. To his right, Armistead was busy writing notes on a form attached to a clipboard.

Completing the last entry with an exaggerated flourish, the instructor-pilot turned and gave him a cold look. The young pilot's elation over the smooth landing dissolved instantly.

"Lieutenant," Armistead drawled sourly, "you really got some balls...puttin' the gear down on final with a dead engine. The way you set up that approach ain't 'zackly the procedure prescribed in the pilot's manual, huh?" The question sounded like an accusation.

"No sir."

"Then *what* 'zackly is the prescribed procedure, Lieutenant?"

Shaw recited the litany: "To attempt a belly landing while maintaining sufficient power on the good engine for a go-around."

"Uh-huh, then what was on your mind, Lieutenant, when you *ordered* the gear down and turned this B-26 into the world's heaviest glider?" Armistead leaned closer, awaiting the answer.

Shaw felt foolish. There was obviously not an acceptable response, but he said, anyway, "Captain, I saw a B-26 belly land one time here in training...it came apart and burned."

"You didn't seriously think ah was goin' to allow you to belly land?"

Shaw measured his words. "No, sir, but I thought it would be better to set up a committed approach..."

Armistead interrupted him, "Committed? You mean a *no* go-around approach, don't you?"

"Yes, sir, a no go-around approach, but watching the descent rate... carrying enough power on the good engine to make a safe touchdown."

"Safe you say!" Armistead snorted. "Lieutenant, if you'd been just a coupla' seconds too soon or a coupla' seconds too late on your landing flareout, me, you and this airplane would just be a lot of flamin' trash scattered all over the Florida countryside!"

Shaw steeled himself for the final humiliation.

Armistead relaxed in his seat, crossing his legs and pushing his cap to the back of head. The expression on his face was devoid of any emotion. Looking at the clipboard, he said in a matter-of-fact tone, "Ah'm giving you an overall 'pass' on the check ride and rating you as an aircraft commander."

Shaw was struck speechless, returning the instructor's gaze with a blank stare.

Armistead inclined toward him, smiling for the first time. "You got an uncommon touch for this airplane, Lieutenant, real uncommon. That was one of the smoothest engine-out recoveries ah've ever seen." He tapped the clipboard with his pencil. "And that crosswind landin' on one engine...well, that was a real piece of work! You practice that before?" he asked.

"Actually, no." the young pilot answered.

Armistead waved the clipboard at him. "Ah signed-off the rest of the check-ride report...just routine stuff. Ain't much else ah can teach you about flying this airplane."

Feeling the tension finally drain from his body, Shaw surveyed the cockpit with his eyes and inhaled the pungent odor of leather, hot metal, ozone, and hydraulic fluid—airplane smell. It made him tingle. The young pilot loved flying the B-26, loved everything about it: loved the streamlined, powerful look of it, loved the resonant thunder of the twin R-2800 radial engines, and loved the solid feel of the big airplane in his hands. It sometimes amazed him that the Air Corps was paying *him* to fly it!

The truth was that Shaw had had a love affair with every airplane he'd flown: the Piper J-3 Cubs in Civilian Pilot Training; the Boeing PT-13's in Air Corps Primary; the North American BT-9's in Air Corps Basic; the North American AT-6's in Air Corps Advanced; and even the lumbering old Douglas B-18's in multi-engine bomber training.

In fact, Shaw couldn't remember when he hadn't wanted to fly. As a boy, he'd read *G-8, Popular Aviation, Flying Aces,* and everything else about flying he could get hands on. He'd gone to see movies like *Wings, Hell's Angels,* and *Ceiling Zero* over and over again. At age fifteen, at a small grass airfield in his hometown, Big Spring, Texas, he took his first plane ride. The ride in the two-place, 37 h.p. Aeronca C-3 had lasted ten minutes and cost two dollars, a lot of money in 1935. For Theodore J. Shaw, son of a small cattle rancher, it had been a life-changing, life-shaping experience. Neither he nor his family had had enough money for flying lessons. The Depression had been hard on the cattle business. But, every time he could save enough money, he'd hustled out to the airfield for another brief ride in the Aeronca C-3. Once, during the county fair, for three dollars, he'd gotten to fly around the local area in a big Ford Trimotor for over fifteen minutes. Afterward, he'd known that he wanted to fly big, multi-engined airplanes, and the best way to achieve this goal, he learned, was to join the Army Air Corps. They would train him and pay him at the same!

Toward this end, Shaw had seriously applied himself to his high school studies, graduating as the salutatorian of his class and receiving a partial engineering scholarship to Texas Technical College in Lubbock. He'd never intended to finish college but felt he needed at least two year's preparation before applying for the aviation cadet program in the Air Corps. While studying mechanical engineering, he'd worked at various odd jobs to make up the rest of his college expenses. Because of this and a steady girlfriend at home in Big Spring, he'd virtually ignored the limited social activities of the college. At the end of his first year, in 1939, his father had been seriously injured and as an only son with three younger sisters, he'd been forced to take a leave of absence to go home and help with the ranch.

By the fall of 1940, Shaw's father had sufficiently recovered for him to return to school and resume his studies. By this time, he'd felt an even greater sense of urgency about getting into the Air Corps because of the recent trend of the war in Europe. Unlike his one-time hero, Charles Lindbergh, Shaw had thought it only a matter of time before America would be drawn into the conflict on the side of the Allies.

That fall, shortly after his return to school, Shaw had learned of a new government program called Civilian Pilot Training, which provided free flight instruction to qualified applicants. He'd immediately gone to the local airfield in Lubbock and applied; three weeks and five flying hours later, he had soloed a Piper J-3 Cub. Through the balance of the year, he'd learned the rudiments of theory of flight, aircraft systems, aerial navigation, and meteorology, and had managed to accumulate a total of forty flying hours. By the Spring of 1941, he'd taken his Private Pilot check ride and earned his Airman's Certificate. Shaw's instructor had told him he was a natural pilot, but he'd never developed the cocky, bullet proof attitude that afflicts—and occasionally kills— many new aviators. While Shaw loved flying with an unbridled passion, he nevertheless viewed pilots as professionals, not daredevils.

At the end of his fourth semester in college, in 1941, Shaw had applied for admission into the Army Air Corps Aviation Cadet Program located at Randolph Field in San Antonio, Texas. After passing a series of aptitude tests and physical examinations, he'd finally received a letter ordering him to report for training no later than October 1, 1941.

"Lieutenant?" Armistead's voice shook Shaw from his reverie and brought him back to the present. The lanky instructor patted him on the arm and said, "Let's check this bird in and go get a beer...ah'm buyin'!"

February 4, 1943, Big Spring, Texas.

"Ted, I told you to stop, now please let me up!" The girl promptly sat up and slid to the other side of the battered divan.

"Aw, Mary Beth," Shaw pleaded, almost out of breath.

Mary Beth Wainwright regarded Shaw's flushed face as she smoothed the wrinkles from her clothes. He wasn't exactly what you would call matinee-idol handsome but possessed strong, even features, framed by clear gray eyes and crew-cut, sandy brown hair. At a lean five foot eleven, he towered over her diminutive five foot two. She had set her cap for Ted Shaw over six years ago, when he was a junior at Big Spring High School and she was in the ninth grade. He was never like the other boys his age, who were prone to rambunctious showing-off and clownish behavior. Always polite and reserved, he rarely acted on impulse. The only time she had honestly seen him lose control of himself was during their necking sessions.

Right now she was exasperated. "All of this is your fault, Ted, you know that! I want it as bad as you do, but you...you said we can't get married until the war is over." She pointed her finger at him accusingly. "You know I'm not going to..."

Shaw cut her off, "Yes, honey, I know." They'd had this conversation many times before.

"Ted, I really don't understand you...lots of girls are getting married to boys in the service right now. Why can't we? Why?"

Shaw looked fondly at this russet-haired girl whose hazel eyes were flashing at him right now. Most people would classify Mary Beth as "cute as button," but something about her petite, pixyish looks had powerfully attracted Shaw from the first time he noticed her. And by the time she'd reached the ninth grade, Mary Beth Wainwright had become exceptionally noticeable. The old idea that opposites attract was never truer than in the case of these two. Shaw was methodical and analytic, planning most everything he did or said down to the last detail; Mary Beth was vivacious and spontaneous—utterly unpredictable. The differences were normally complementary.

Not today.

Shaw struggled for the right words. "Mary Beth, you know how I feel...you know I want us to get married and settle down, but this isn't the right time, honey, not in the middle of the war with me getting ready to go overseas sometime..."

"Ted, don't give me a speech about getting killed and leaving me a widow!" she interrupted. "You've already told me a million times not to worry about that!" He'd once confidently told her that flying for the Air Corps was "safer than farming." She knew better.

"Let me finish, Mary Beth, will you?" He gave her an impatient look. "Did I say anything about getting killed?" Leaning toward her, he grabbed both of her hands. "If you'll let me finish, honey, I'll try to explain. In one week I'll be reporting in at Barksdale as an aircraft commander. That makes me responsible for five people I haven't even met yet..."

She interrupted him again, "You've already mentioned that, and I really don't understand what it has to do with getting married."

Shaw grimly looked at her, trying to keep his irritation under control. "Because, Mary Beth, this crew's gonna' be a big responsibility." His voice became solemn. "The way I do my job can make the difference in whether they live or die..."

She could see the disquiet in his eyes, something she had rarely seen.

"I've given this crew thing a lot of thought, honey." He squeezed her hands as if to emphasize the point. "What I'm trying to say is that I can't be responsible for them and you at the same time...not right now. Can you understand that?"

Mary Beth's expression had softened. "Ted, I understand... at least I think I do, but don't you think you're putting too much on yourself?"

"No," he answered her gravely. "Like I said...I'll be dealing with other people's lives. It's important."

She yielded to his reasoning but wasn't willing to let everything go. "Ted, I can live with us not getting married right now or even real soon, but I don't want to wait until this damn war is over." She seldom cursed. "When you finish this tour, I want us to be married, war or no war."

Shaw regarded her for a moment, then smiled. "We'll see...that's a long way off."

Mary Beth knew he would think about it.

He asked her to turn on the radio to see if there was any good music playing. Switching it on and rotating the tuner, she stopped on a station playing the powerful, rhythmic tones of a swing popular swing band. She lay back on the divan with her eyes closed and started swaying from side to side in unison with the beat.

Shaw cocked his head and listened to the rich harmony of the horns and woodwinds. "I like that tune...what's the name of it?" he asked.

"It's Duke Ellington's newest number, *Take the A-train.*"

When the song ended, Shaw stretched and looked at his wristwatch. "You want to go the movies?"

"What's playing?"

"*A Yank in the RAF* with Tyrone Power, I think."

She looked at him questioningly. "Didn't we see that a few nights ago?"

"Right," he said as if he'd just realized it. "Don't you want to see it again?"

Incorrigible, she thought, then said, "C'mon flyboy, get your coat and let's go!"

February 15, 1943, Northwestern Louisiana.

Second Lieutenant Luciano E. Clementi, U. S. Army Air Corps, brooded as he stared out of the train window at the monotonous Louisiana farmscape. Because the crops had been harvested and the fields turned over, the view offered only a brown nothingness, which compounded his gloom. For the umpteenth time, he asked himself: *why* did I volunteer for flight training in the first place? Temporary insanity was the only explanation that came to mind. He'd never been crazy about flying, in fact had never flown in an airplane until his orientation flight in primary training, which had scared him and left him scared of every flight since. He flew well enough, possessed the needed coordination and aptitude to operate an airplane, but the desire was not there. At several points, he'd seriously thought of quitting the program—all one had to do was 'un-volunteer'—yet he never did.

With his business background, Clementi considered that he could quite easily have gotten a commission in the Finance or Quartermaster Corps. But damn his pride and vanity: the Air Corps had seemed adventurous and exotic—he would become a dashing flyboy like the ones he'd seen in the movies. The girls would sit at his feet! The people of his Brooklyn neighborhood would be awed!

But the reality of flight training seemed to have rolled him up like some kind of inescapable, forward-moving force: one moment he was taking his initial instruction in a Fairchild PT-19 and nine months and 205 flying hours later, they were commissioning him and pinning silver wings to his chest! Despite his growing competence as a pilot—albeit mediocre—he'd never shed his underlying uneasiness.

At the end of advanced training, he'd requested the conversion course for multi-engined transports, C-47's probably. But his orders had defied belief: Martin B-26 training at MacDill Field in Tampa, Florida! It was the last thing he would have chosen. Everybody knew that B-26 aircrews didn't have to worry about combat—*they got killed in training!* He'd almost quit then and there, but knew if he had, they would have sent him straight to the infantry as a buck-ass private! And as if to confirm it all, he'd barely squeaked through the B-26 course at MacDill. The instructor-pilot who had given him his checkride had gravely stated that his handling of the airplane was "marginal," but had cheerfully added that he would get the hang of it later—after a couple of hundred hours as *a co-pilot*. Now, he was on his way to Barksdale Field to join the 333RD Bomb Group (Medium) and be assigned to an aircrew. Whoever they were, Clementi hoped they had their shit together. He didn't.

February 16, 1943, Barksdale Field, Shreveport, Louisiana.

As he made the last stroke with his Gillette safety razor, Second Lieutenant Michael B. Grattan, U. S. Army Air Corps, looked in the mirror at the cheerful, ruddy face that stared back at him. Premature baldness had cost him much of his reddish hair but the expressive green eyes were still unlined and clear. Donning a clean, starched khaki shirt, he carefully knotted the tie and tucked it in below the third button. He wanted to look sharp when he met in a little while with the rest of his crew. The shimmering reflection of the navigator's wings pinned to his chest caused his broad features to crease in a wide smile. A little less than a year ago, he'd been teaching English at a parochial high school in his hometown of Philadelphia. Funny, he thought, the way things turn out. At age ten, he'd yielded to the call to become a Catholic priest. Following religious confirmation, he'd become an altar boy, and after graduating from a Catholic high school, he'd entered seminary training. Then three years later, he'd met Madeline. Her aggressive sexual prowess had overwhelmed him, like being caught up in an all-enveloping maelstrom from which there was no escape. But, almost as quickly as it had happened, it was over, and Madeline had abandoned him for a new quarry.

Nothing had been the same after that. Nothing.

After re-assembling the pieces that had been his life, he'd applied for and obtained a position teaching English at the Catholic high school from which he'd graduated years before. A year later, he'd started dating Eleanor, the headmaster's secretary. They'd been married now over two years, and Eleanor was expecting their first child soon. She was no Madeline, but he was utterly, irrevocably in love with her.

When war had been declared, Grattan knew he must join the service, not because the draft would compel him to do so, but because it was the right thing to do—to serve his nation and its people. He truly wanted to do something important, and from what he'd read and learned, he believed this war would be decided by air power. Mild astigmatism in his left eye was sufficent to rule out pilot training, so navigator's school had seemed the next best option, and he'd excelled and finished near the top of his class. Upon competetion of the course, he'd requested heavy bombers, B-17s or B-24s, for no particular reason, but was content with the assignment to B-26s. He didn't believe much of the hyperbole he'd heard about the airplane. Because of the dual crew requirements for the B-26, he'd gone direct from the navigator's course to radio operator's school. Grattan cheerfully looked forward to the forthcoming crew assignment. At twenty-six, he knew he'd probably be the oldest member of the crew—he hoped he'd fit in.

At the same time Grattan was putting the finishing touches on his uniform, a female clerk who worked in the base personnel office was taken aback by the striking good looks of the young lieutenant she was waiting on. He reminded her her of a younger version of the actor, Robert Taylor: tall and dark with penetrating blue eyes. Many women, old and young, were affected this way by Second Lieutenant Joseph H. Glowgower, U. S. Army Air Corps, son of a prosperous Louisville, Kentucky rug importer. He wasn't wearing the rumpled and often ill-fitting khakis that adorned most aircrews but a sharply-creased gabardine shirt and trousers, which looked tailor-made. The clerk noticed from the wings pinned to the elegant young man's chest that he was a bombardier. Glowgower's looks had always opened doors for him—until he washed-out of flight school.

Glowgower picked up the file and headed out the door to the crew meeting he was by now late for. His day had already become chaotic and confused—a condition which seemed to follow him ever since he'd joined the Air Corps over a year ago. Before then, life had been easy, and he'd never been induced to work hard for anything. At age twenty, he'd left the University at Lexington after three semesters and entered flight training, as an Air Corps Cadet. Boredom with college and the fraternity house social scene rather than patriotic fervor had been the chief impetus for taking this step. When he started pre-flight training, he'd been disagreeably surprised by the difficulty of the academic material and the stress on military discipline. His greatest shock, however, came soon afterward in primary flight training when he'd washed-out at the end of the first two weeks. The instructors had unsympathetically reported: "Cadet Glowgower apparently lacks the coordination and depth-perception sufficent to fly an airplane as contiually reflected by his inability to properly control the craft in most attitudes of flight." The humiliating words still burned in his mind! He hadn't even been allowed to solo.

Afterward, a non-flying captain in Technical Training Command had strongly suggested that he apply for bombardier training, where he would still gain his wings—bombardier's—and an officer's commission. Without really giving it much thought, he'd signed the application. Twenty-one weeks later, despite his indifference toward the classroom work and boredom with the flying in the Beechcraft AT-11s, he'd managed to finish the course somewhere in the middle of his class. Only toward the end did he fully comprehend what he'd got himself into: *a sure assignment to bombers in a combat theater*! His naiveté and arrogance had blinded him to the dangerous—potentially fatal—aspects of joining the Air Corps. Then following bombardier's school, the worst had happened: assignment to Martin B-26 operational training at Barkesdale Field and eventual movement to a combat theater—a virtual death sentence! What ever happened next, Glowgower gloomily hoped it would swift and painless.

CHAPTER TWO

February 16, 1942, Barksdale Field, Shreveport, Louisiana.

The room, although full of hearty young men wearing khaki uniforms, was strangely quiet because most were strangers to each other. Each one was an officer, either an aircraft commander, a co-pilot, a navigator, or a bombardier. Only the wings pinned to their shirts told them apart. The expressions on the youngful faces varied: some were cheerful, some were apprehensive, some were bored, and a few were suffering from evident hangovers. All of them were present for the same reason: to be formed into operational B-26 aircrews.

Shaw, seated near the front, felt a mixture of excitement and apprehension. Though he'd never been on a blind date, he thought the waiting must be something like this. His attention was suddenly shifted to the front of the room as a middle-aged, non-rated major walked to the podium and asked for everyone's attention. In a stentorian voice, the older man instructed them, "Stand up when you hear your name called! When your assignment is complete, you may leave the room and assemble outside!"

The crew rosters were alphabetized according to the last name of the designated aircraft commander. After what had seemed like hours but, in fact, had been only twenty minutes, the Major, his voice becoming hoarse, bellowed, "First Lieutenant Shaw, Theodore J., aircraft commander!" Shaw ungracefully bolted up from his seat to listen to a staccato announcement of names: "Second Lieutenant Clementi, Luciano E., co-pilot; Second Lieutneant Grattan, Michael B., navigator;" and "Second Lieutenant Glowgower, Joseph H., bombardier. Next!" Shaw got no more than a fleeting glimpse of the men who were about to come under his care before they disappeared out the back door of the room.

In the middle of the room, Clementi, however, noticed Shaw when he stood up. Looks like a hard-case, the co-pilot thought, probably all balls and no brains. Grattan, from his position, saw both men and the obvious contrast of their facial expressions: Shaw, hopeful and expectant; Clementi, gloomy and nervous. Glowgower, lost in his own thoughts in the back of the room, failed to pay attention to anything other than his own name being called and was forced to go up to the front of the room and ask the Major to repeat the name of his aircraft commander.

As he stepped off the back stoop of the building, Shaw Shaw forced himself to stroll at a nonchalant pace. Although his initial nervousness had left him, he didn't want to appear over-eager. Seeing two of the men he vaguely recognized standing to one side of the gravel path, he stopped and smiled. "I'm Ted Shaw...I believe I'm your new aircraft commander." He extended his hand first to a slightly-built, dark-haired man who introduced himself as Luce Clementi. Shaw wondered why the man seemed so tense. Standing next to the skinny co-pilot, a balding, strongly-built man offered his bear paw of a hand and cheerfully anounced himself as Mick Grattan. The big fellow's twinkling green eyes and open expression gave Shaw a good feeling. Releasing Grattan's hand, he asked, "Where's our bombardier...wasn't his name Glowgower?" But before the question could be answered, the three of them were held momentarily spellbound by the extraordinary good looks of a sleekly uniformed young man approaching them, who halted and asked, "Is this Shaw's crew?"

"You're Glowgower?" Shaw held out his hand, then introduced Clementi and Grattan. "You go by Joe?"

Glowgower thought a moment. "That's what they call me at home, but everybody in bombardier school called me Glow."

"Glow," Shaw echoed. "Sounds good to me."

Lighting a cigarette and offering his pack to the others, Shaw said, "I was told that our enlisted crewmembers would get here in three or four days. The four of us have been assigned a four-man room in the BOQ. They'll give us room keys as soon as we can get over there...so let's pick up our gear right now and meet back at the sign-in desk." Shaw noticed the manila envelopes each of them had tucked under their arms. "Before I forget," he said, pointing to Grattan's envelope, "let me have your 66-1 files...I'll turn 'em in at group personnel after I've had a look."

Clementi and Glowgower both shot him uneasy looks. Even though looking at the files was part of his prerogative as an aircraft commander, Shaw didn't want them to feel coerced. "Listen fellas," he said in a quiet voice, "there shouldn't be any secrets between us..." He qualified the statement. "I mean the kind of stuff that has to do with our ability to function as an aircrew. None of us is perfect...we all got our good and bad points, right?"

"Sure," Clementi said without smiling. Glowgower gave him a curt nod.

"Besides," Shaw added, holding up the envelopes, "this is just between us, o.k.?" He glanced at his watch. "I'll see you at the BOQ in a little bit." As Shaw was beginning to leave, Glowgower stopped him.

"Uh, I might need a little help with my gear."

Shaw looked at the bombardier curiously. "What've you got?" he asked.

"Besides my B-4 bag, I've got two trunks."

"Two?" Shaw looked surprised. "What's in 'em?

"Uniforms mostly."

Shaw started to say something about having too many uniforms when Grattan interrupted, "Not to worry, Glow, I'll give you a hand." Shaw shrugged and left.

By late morning, the four young officers had managed to get themselves moved into their new quarters. When they had finished putting their things away, Shaw said, "I've got some business to take care of here, but you guys go to lunch and meet me in the briefing room assigned to our bomb group at 1300."

As the other three filed out the door, Shaw sat down at the tiny desk furnished with the room, lighted a Lucky Strike, and removed Clementi's file from the envelope. This was the first time he'd ever looked at someone else's records and it gave him a strange feeling. Getting past the general information, he noticed that his co-pilot had attended C.C.N.Y. night school for two years, taking mostly business courses. Under "previous occupation," Clementi listed himself as a "management trainee" with a bank in New York City, one of the big ones Shaw thought he'd heard of. Clementi's scores and evaluations in all three stages of flight training had been consistently average, except where he'd busted his first instrument check ride. For pilots, average typically meant marginal, because below-average pilots were washed-out. Shaw frowned at the negative comments made on Clementi's B-26 check-ride. He wondered why they passed him. Was this the Air Corp's standard method of dealing with pilots with confidence problems—turning them into co-pilots?

Laying Clementi's file aside, he picked up Grattan's and began to leaf through it. Shaw's eyebrows arched suddenly when he read that the big navigator had studied three years for the Catholic priesthood, then for some inexpicable reason, became a schoolteacher. Reading on, he uttered a low whistle when he came to the information on Grattan's performance since joining the Air Corps: number one in his class in both of the service schools he'd attended; unqualified praise from those who had taught and commanded him. This reinforced the good impression Shaw already had.

He opened Glowgower's file and briefly glanced at the the general information when something caught his attention: the letter "H" beside "Religion." Shaw thought about it a moment, remembering that it stood for Hebrew, a classification for the Jewish faith. Did this have something to do with Glowgower's apparent uneasiness? Doubtful, he thought, because the Air Corps was a non-traditional, performance-oriented service that paid scant attention to a man's religious affiliation. In flight training, Shaw had known a lot of people from Jewish backgrounds who had fit in like everybody else. Turning to the training data, he immediately discovered why Glowgower might be so touchy about the file: he'd washed-out of flight training and taken the bombardier's course as a booby prize! The information was puzzling: Glowgower's Air Corps entrance scores were excellent, indicating above-average aptitudes in most areas, but his marks in the bombardier's course had been monotonously average. There were other comments in the file like "not working up to potential" and "indifferent toward military authority." Shaw wondered how he would deal with these problems. His review of Clementi's and Glowgower's records had generated more questions than answers.

Replacing the files in their envelopes, Shaw felt his stomach grumble and looked at his watch. Damn! It was almost 1300 and he'd forgotten about lunch. Remembering there was a Coke machine downstairs, he reached into his pocket to see if he could find a nickel. After briefly inspecting himself in the mirror on the back of his locker door, he left the room. Five minutes later, half-finished Coke in one hand and flight bag in the other, Shaw entered the briefing room and walked toward the three recognizable faces seated toward the front of the room.

Grattan saw him out of the corner or his eye and snapped, "Atten-HUT!" Clementi, Shaw noticed, seemed to rise from his seat in slow motion; Glowgower's expression was bored.

"Take your seats, fellas'," Shaw said briskly, removing his cap and pulling a chair in front of them. "As far as I'm concerned we can skip the military crap from now on, o.k.?" He finished the Coke and lit a cigarette. "Let's stick to first names except in the plane...where we'll use crew postions, like pilot, navigator and so on." Shaw hadn't really

considered what he was going to say to them but could read the antici-
pation on their faces. After pausing a moment, he asked, "You guys
find the chow hall o.k.?" They nodded in unison. "How's the food?"

"Crap," Clementi said flatly. "I'd rate it as edible crap."

"I've eaten a lot worse," Grattan offered.

Shaw exhaled a puff of smoke and said, "I'm told it's a lot better
than the dehydrated shit they're feeding the Army ground-pounders."
Grattan laughed but Clementi and Glowgower remained expressionless.

Pulling a small notebook from his flight bag, Shaw said, "Let's get
down to business. There're a few things we need to do before we can
fly." He looked at Grattan. "Mick, you can go pick up the charts for this
area and any other navigational dope we're gonna' need." Shifting his
glance to the bombardier, he said, "Glow, try to find out something
about the bomb practice schedule." He gave the handsome man a
knowing look. "You're the only one of us who's really dropped a bomb
on a target." Turning to his co-pilot, he said, "Luce, let's find us a B-26
and work on cockpit drill, all right?"

Clementi responded with a frown. Cockpit drill during time
off! This confirmed his impression that Shaw must be some kind
of hot-shot.

Shaw ignored the co-pilot's sour expression. "I know you guys want
some time to settle in," he said seriouly, "but Group's not going to give it to
us. Fact is, we're flying tomorrow morning, briefing at 0630."

Clementi and Glowgower both groaned, but Grattan looked genuinely pleased. "What will we be doing?" he inquired.

"Just a local familiarization hop, I think...do some air-work, shoot a
few landings, you know, get the cobwebs out."

Great, thought Clementi, *two* hot shots.

After Grattan and Glowgower left the room, Shaw looked at the
brooding visage of his co-pilot. "Luce, I've looked at your 66-1." He let
the information sink in. "What you did in flight training or in the B-26
course is yesterday's news as far as I'm concerned. What matters to
me...really matters...is how well you do from this point forward. You
understand where I'm comin' from?"

"I quess," Clementi replied noncommittally, looking at his fingernails.

"Mind if I ask you a few questions?"

The co-pilot shrugged, still looking at his hands.

"Smoke?" Shaw pulled the green Lucky Strike pack from his shirt
pocket and offered it to the co-pilot.

"Thanks." Clementi said, extracting one from the pack.

Shaw produced a Zippo lighter from his pocket and lit both cigarettes. After exhaling a puff of smoke, Shaw leaned forward on his el-bows, made eye contact with the co-pilot, and asked calmly, "Luce, you got a problem with being assigned to a B-26 outfit?"

Clementi hesitated. "I think the airplane's a friggin death-trap, if that's what you mean."

Shaw paused, unsure of what to say. "Listen to me Luce...the air-plane's not a death-trap."

The co-pilot scowled at him and murmured, "What're you? Some kind of expert?"

Shaw tried to ignore the challenge and keep his voice calm. "No, Luce, I'm not an expert, but I've got some flying time in the airplane."

The co-pilot shrugged and muttered, "Whatever."

Cooly meeting the co-pilot's gaze, Shaw persisted, "You want to know why I don't think it's a death-trap?"

Giving him a petulant look, Clementi replied, "I guess you're going to tell me anyway."

"The airplane's got some bad tricks...I won't kid you about that...but once you learn 'em, you won't have a problem. All it takes is a little practice."

"You make it sound simple...too simple," the co-pilot answered scornfully.

"It is simple, Luce, simple as this: do you want to believe all the bullshit you've heard about the airplane or do you want to learn how to fly it?"

Clementi didn't answer the question but his hostile expression said, *is this over with yet?*

Shaw seemingly indifferent to the co-pilot's implied jibe, got up from his chair and said, "Let's go find us a B-26."

Later that afternoon, as they both headed from the flight line back to the BOQ, Clementi thought about the time he'd spent with Shaw so far. The pilot had been very patient with him during the cockpit drill and hadn't talked-down to him like most of the in-structors in flight training. Clementi had been impressed with Shaw's knowledge of the airplane and had to admit—to himself at least—that he'd even learned a few things. Maybe, he thought, the guy isn't a total horse's ass.

A captain in the back of the hall called, "Atten-HUT!" Amid the scraping of chairs and shuffling of feet, a short, stocky Lieutenant Colonel strode briskly to the front of the room. It was exactly 0629:59.

After stepping up onto the low platform, he momentarily surveyed the assembly of young men in flight gear and said, "Seats! Gentlemen, for those of you who don't know me, I'm Lieutenant Colonel Robert Ridley, commander of the 333RD." He motioned toward the other men on the platform and said, "This is Major Vincent Spinelli, deputy-commander, Major Chester Edrington, our operations officer, and Captain James Blackwell, my adjutant. You'll get to know them and the rest of the group staff as we move through this training phase. I know all of you are interested in where we are going and what we're going to do when we get there. There's not a lot I can tell you today, but sometime in the near future, we'll be picking up new planes and moving overseas. But in the next few weeks, gentlemen, we've got the opportunity to get ready for combat—that's what operational training is all about. We're going to practice everything: bombing at different altitudes, gunnery, formation flying, and long-range navigation. We are in the process of organizing the group into squadrons and flights. The rosters will be posted this afternoon.

"There won't be another Group level briefing until next Tuesday, the day after New Year's. We'll all be on stand-down Monday, and I suggest you get some rest...you'll need it. Any questions?"

A young Lieutenant in the back of the room raised his hand and said, "Colonel, is there gonna' be any leave between now and the time we go overseas?"

"I don't know yet, the Colonel replied, looking around at everyone, "it depends on a lot of things, mainly how much progress we make between now and shipping out time. Anything else? If not, I'll turn the briefing over to Major Edrington, who'll fill you in on what you're going to do today. Major?"

The Major, a tall, skinny man whose hair was flecked with gray, looked a little old for his rank. He had weathered skin and deep crow's feet around his eyes which were the result of thousands of hours spent in open cockpits. "Men," he said, "we're going to keep it simple today and do some local practice flying. You'll each be assigned a practice area and an altitude to be maintained while in the area. When I say maintaining altitude, I don't mean one foot lower! The first cowboy I catch flat-hatting is going to be on the next train out of Shreveport, probably to Fort Polk for infantry training! Understand?"

He waited a minute for the warning to sink in and continued, "Most of B-26's we'll be using here are A and early B models that have come back from the Pacific theatre. Most of them aren't equipped with bombsights, but when you do fly missions to the bomb range, you'll be assigned a plane with an operable N-2 sight. In case you're curious about what's in the rear bomb-bays, that's 500 pounds of sand ballast, designed to give the B-26 a little more aft C.G. and to give you some practice flying a heavier plane. Now remember this...as part of your pre-flight, make sure the shackles are free...because if you lose an engine, you'll need to drop the ballast, quicktime!"

Clementi and Glowgower, sitting in the middle of the room, both winced at the Major's warning.

When the briefing concluded with a local weather advisory from the meteorological officer, Shaw and his crew stood in line to receive their assignment. At the table in front of the platform, Shaw and Grattan both looked at the area chart which was divided up into practice grids. The big navigator marked his own chart, and the pilot noted an assigned altitude of 7,000 feet AGL. Their airplane number was six-one-niner. Shaw pointed to the door and told them, "Let's go draw our chutes and find the plane."

Fifteen minutes later, as they walked across the tarmac toward the row of parked B-26's, Shaw said, "You don't have to wear your chutes after we take-off, but never, I repeat *never,* let them get out of reach while we're flying."

Glowgower momentarily balked at this remark and asked, "You really think we're going to need them, I mean, you're not going to do anything dangerous, are you?"

Shaw was a little annoyed by the question. Didn't they wear parachutes in bombardier's training? He answered Glowgower's question in a flat voice, "The answer is *no* to both questions, but you never know when you'll need it, o.k.?" Walking under the wing of the plane assigned to them, Shaw told Clementi to crawl up into the cockpit and bring back the pre-flight checklist.

Clementi faced him and said defiantly, "Why are we doing it...aren't the mechs supposed to pre-flight the planes?"

Shaw became livid. "Because *my* life might depend on it!" he snapped. "If something goes wrong, we're the ones who'll auger in, not the mech who did the preflight! You got that?"

Clementi, startled by the pilot's swift outburst, quickly turned away and disappeared up the hatch through the nose wheel well. He was back in a minute with the checklist in his hand.

Shaw turned to the others. "Mick, you climb in and set-up the nav station; Glow, you get in and check the ballast shackles and get any loose gear you see squared away." The previous incident already forgotten, Shaw turned to Clementi and said calmly, "Luce, you read, I'll check." As they proceeded through the checklist, Clementi watched the efficient and methodical manner Shaw used to complete the checks. Shaw did things quickly but never seemed to be in a hurry. Oddly enough, this made the co-pilot feel less anxious about the flight.

With the pre-flight completed, Shaw climbed in the plane and settled in the left-hand seat. After strapping-in, he scanned the cocpit of the B-26 for anything out of the ordinary. The airplane smelled strange. Must be some kind of mold brought back from the Pacific, Shaw thought fleetingly. Sliding back the side window to allow some of the stink to escape, he smiled. For the first time in days, he felt at home. Plugging-in his headphones, he switched the battery to "on," then listened for the crackle that indicated the interphone was working. He keyed his microphone and said, "Pilot to crew, interphone check, how do you read?"

"Navigator to pilot," chimed Grattan, "five-by-five."

About thirty seconds passed before Shaw said, "Pilot to bombardier, do you read me?"

Shaw waited a few moments longer, turned to his co-pilot and said, "Luce, stick your head down there and tell Glowgower to get his ass plugged-in!" Clementi unstrapped, got up, moved his seat back, and yelled down into the nose, "Hey, Glowgower! You plugged-in?"

Shaw and Clementi heard scuffling and felt the movement below their floorboard.

The intercom suddenly came alive. "Uh...bombardier checking in, you need me for something?"

"Pilot to bombardier, *how do you read me?*"

"Uh, o.k., loud and clear, I mean."

"Use proper interphone procedure, dammit!"

A short pause, then evenly, "Bombardier to pilot, I read you five-by-five."

"Pilot to bombardier, come on up to the nav compartment for start-up and take-off."

After Glowglower wiggled through the flight deck and Clementi got back in his seat, Shaw turned to the co-pilot and said, "Luce, hand me the start-up checklist, will you? You check, I'll read." As the pilot read off each item, Clementi responded with either "check" or "set" or "on" or "off." With this task completed, Shaw leaned forward, turned-on the master switch and fuel boost pumps, then commenced the starting sequence for number one engine: cracked the throttle open about one inch, toggled the primer button, and switched the magneto to "both." Watching the ground crewman standing to one side with a fire extinguisher, he stuck his head out the side window, yelled, "CLEAR!"

then moved the starter switch to "energize." When the large four-bladed Curtiss propeller had turned through five revolutions, the 18-cylinder radial engine emitted a huge gout of white smoke and rumbled to life. Advancing the mixture lever to the "auto-rich" position, he watched the RPMs stabilize and heard the engine settle down to a steady bass din. He repeated the procedure to start number two.

With both engines running smoothly, Shaw tuned the radio to the tower frequency and said, "Barksdale tower, this is Army B-26 six-one-niner at the ramp, radio check, over."

"Army six-one-niner, tower reads you five-by-five."

Shaw continued, "Tower, six-one-niner is ready to taxi, over."

"Ah, six-one-niner, surface wind is out of three-five-zero at fifteen, altimeter is thirty point two. Hold short of runway one-eight and wait for a green light."

Shaw moved the bomber across the tarmac to the taxiway and braked to a stop short of the runway. Turning to Clementi, he said, "Get on the brakes with me while we do the runup." The throttle to each engine was advanced independently, after which the magnetos were checked for RPM drop and the controls to the propellers were cycled from high to low RPM. With the engines back to idle RPM, the plane wiggled slightly as Shaw moved the flight controls back and forth to their stops to check for freedom of movement. After he uncaged and set the gyros, he announced, "Take-off check complete," and shifted his attention toward the tower. A half a minute later, the green light blinked, and Shaw moved the bomber onto the runway, keyed his mike and declared, "Pilot to crew, prepare for take-off!"

Shaw halted the B-26 on the runway centerline and looked at his co-pilot. "We're light and have lots of runway...so we'll take-off with the flaps up." Clementi nodded. "Stay on the throttles with me until we're airborne...be ready to get the gear up fast. Start calling off airspeeds at sixty ...here we go!"

Moving the throttles up to full military power, Shaw listened to the echoing thunder of the engines and the piercing reverberation of propeller tips as they went supersonic. To uninitiated occupants like Grattan and Glowgower, the noise level and vibration seemed incredible. An unconscious grin appeared on Shaw's face as he released the brakes and felt the big airplane move forward. Behind him in the nav station, Grattan shared the pilot's tingle of excitement. Glowgower, already stupefied by the noise, felt the bile rise in his throat as the acceleration pressed him into his seat.

"Sixty!" Clementi announced as their speed increased, then

"seventy!" then "eighty!" then "ninety!" When the co-pilot called out "one hundred!" Shaw eased back the yoke and lifted the bomber's nose from the runway. Moments later, the rumbling of the wheels ceased and the B-26 was airborne. "Gear up!" he shouted over the noise, continuing to hold the nose down until he saw the airspeed climbing past 145 m.p.h.

"Gear coming up!" Clementi responded.

As Shaw heard and felt the wheels thumping into their wells, he he eased the throttles and propeller controls back to climb power and immediately rolled in elevator trim until the rate-of-climb stabilized at 1,000 feet per minute.

Clementi shouted over the noise, "You always do that, I mean, hold off until it reaches one-fifty?"

"Yeah!" Shaw loudly replied. "As long as you don't have any obstacles to climb over, that's the fastest way to get the plane up to single-engine control speed. Once you're there, you don't have to worry as much...even if you lose an engine."

The interphone crackled. "Navigator to pilot, stand by for course to grid."

That was fast, Shaw thought cheerfully.

"Navigator to Pilot, turn left to a heading of three-one-one."

Shaw banked the bomber onto the new course and watched the altimeter swing through 4,000 feet. Behind him, Grattan plotted the distance and time to the grid, came back on the interphone. "Navigator to pilot, we'll reach the grid in twelve minutes at present speed."

"Roger, twelve minutes," Shaw repeated, then said, "pilot to bombardier, go ahead and take your station in the nose."

"Ah, y...bombardier to pilot, roger," came the uncertain reply.

"While you're up there, keep a sharp lookout for any other aircraft operating near our grid. If you see anything, let me know, o.k.?"

"Roger." The co-pilot unstrapped and stood up while the bombardier awkwardly crabbed through the space on the right side on the instrument panel.

Leveling the B-26 at 7,500 feet, Shaw moved the throttles and propeller controls to cruise power, then dove to 7,000 feet to put the airplane on the imaginary "step." A small adjustment to the elevator trim wheel yielded them an indicated air speed of 200 m.p.h.

Five minutes later, Grattan announced they had entered the grid and would fly out of it in seven and one-half minutes on present speed and course.

"You fly it for a while, Luce," Shaw said, holding up both of his hands.

Clementi reached for the yoke and said, "I've got it."

"We'll practice some basic maneuvers first, o.k.? Turn right, 30 degrees of bank, to a heading of one-four-one, maintaining altitude...start your turn now."

As Clementi rolled the bomber into the turn, Shaw noticed the nose creep up and watched the airspeed fall off. "Get the nose down, you're climbing! You have to stay ahead of it...feed in elevator while you're turning...that's better." Clementi overshot the course by a few degrees but quickly brought the bomber back to the correct heading and eased it back down to the proper altitude.

Over the next fifteen minutes, Shaw ran the co-pilot through a full series of level turns at various angles of bank then repeated the process while and climbing and descending. After a while, Shaw decided that Clementi wasn't a totally bad pilot. He seemed to be learning. Shaw glanced out the window then looked at his watch. "Luce, you ready to try some engine shut-downs?"

The co-pilot flashed him a look of uncertainty. He was tired of flying the airplane.

Ignoring the co-pilot's reluctance, Shaw shrugged. "This is one of the tricks I was talking about, Luce. We'll both practice it until we can do it in our sleep."

Clementi reluctantly nodded.

"You stay on the controls," Shaw continued. "I'll shut the engine down and feather it." Shaw pulled the mixture lever to number one back to idle cut-off, waited for the manifold pressure to drop, switched the mag off, and stabbed the feather button. When Clementi attempted to respond by slamming on full power to the good engine, the nose reared up sickenly and the bomber began to career steeply to the left, a situation that could become critical in a hurry. Fighting the urge to rip the controls away from the fumbling co-pilot, Shaw kept his hands in his lap and rapidly barked a series of commands: "Get the nose down smartly! Kick the right rudder all the way to the stop! Use your ailerons to keep that left wing down! Watch your airspeed...don't let it get below one-fifty!" The co-pilot's face, Shaw noticed, was a mask of fierce concentration, his shirt saturated with perspiration.

Behind Shaw and the sweating co-pilot, Grattan looked out his small window with eerie fascination at the stationary propeller on the left engine. When the gyrations of the plane had settled somewhat, he consulted his watch and said, "Navigator to pilot, we need to turn around in thirty seconds to stay in the grid."

"Roger, nav." Shaw glanced at the nervous the co-pilot. "Luce, tell me the most important rule of maneuvering a B-26 with a dead engine?"

"Never turn into the dead engine?"

"That's right. Now, start a gentle right turn back around to a heading of three-one-zero, nice and easy."

After they turned around, Shaw ordered Clementi to practice three more engine shut-downs, and the co-pilot's response became a little smoother with each try. While Clementi wasn't enjoying the exercizes, it was obvious to Shaw that the co-pilot was not only improving but also becoming less nervous. "O.k., Luce, I'll take it," Shaw said as he placed his hands on the yoke. "We'll practice this again on our next hop, you and me both...fair enough?"

Clementi gave him a weak nod.

Shaw flexed his fingers on the yoke then called on the interphone, "Pilot to crew, everybody strapped-in tight?"

"Navigator, roger."

"Bombardier, roger."

Sounding like a ringmaster announcing the next act, he said, "Pilot to crew, hold on for evasive maneuvers!" Shaw moved the throttles up and pushed the bomber's nose down until haw saw the airspeed reach 300 m.p.h., then, using coordinated imputs of aileron, elevator, and rudder, rolled the nose around the horizon in a neat barrel roll to the left. Once level, he pushed the bomber's nose down again to gain airspeed and smoothly applied right rudder and aileron to enter a steep, direction-reversing chandelle. Behind the pilots, his face sagging with the G-forces induced by Shaw's maneuvers, Grattan grinned boyishly at the chalk-white face of the bombardier whose eyes looked wide with fright. His mirth turned to concern. "Are you all right, Glow?"

Glowgower, taking deep breathes, uttered, "Yeah, I'm fine."

"Everybody o.k.?" Shaw asked a moment later.

"Navigator to pilot, we're o.k.," Grattan answered as he stared curiously at the unsmiling bombardier.

Clementi had been surprised, if not exactly frightened, by the manuevers. "I thought you weren't supposed to roll a B-26," he questioned.

Shaw gave him a conspiratorial wink and replied, "You're not." Then looking at his watch, he announced, "Pilot to crew, we're headin' for the barn!"

After lunch, they returned to the flight line and flew the same old B-26 back to the assigned grid. Shaw and Clementi practiced various maneuvers and simulated emergencies, including engine shut-downs, and the co-pilot shot several touch and go landings on the way back in. Shaw verbally coached his co-pilot during the first two landings but forced himself to remain silent on the third, which turned out to be the smoothest of the three. Clementi's handling of the airplane was still somewhat awkward, Shaw judged, but his overall coordination had definitely improved.

The following day they were assigned a new practice area north of the field. Before they took off, Shaw told them that he expected each man on the crew, officers at least, to be familiar with the other's crew duties. After the B-26 had been in the grid for about thirty minutes, Shaw told Clementi to vacate his seat and tell Grattan to come up to the flight deck. When the big navigator arrived, Shaw instructed him to strap-in to the right seat. "How much actual flying have you done, Mick," he inquired, "I mean, with you on the controls?"

"On the controls...none," the navigator replied.

"I want you to get a feel for the ship in straight and level flight, and then we'll work on some turns and some climbs and descents."

The big man smiled expectantly. "You just tell me what to do."

"Get your feet on the rudder pedals and hold the control yoke with your right hand." Shaw gave him a thumbs up gesture. "All right, you've got the airplane. Just hold her steady." Shaw watched the big navigator's face broaden into a wide smile as the big plane obediently responded to his movement of the controls. Pointing out the windscreen, Shaw told him how to establish a visual reference point between the nose and the horizon to keep the plane in level flight. The pilot talked him through some gentle turns in both directions. "That's the way, Mick," the pilot coached, watching the horizon move lazily across the windscreen, "once you establish the bank, just hold a little back pressure on the yoke...see there...the nose'll stay right where it's supposed to be." For someone with no previous flying experience, Shaw felt that Grattan had a nice touch with the airplane. After a few more minutes of flying, Shaw questioned him, "You know why you need to learn this?"

The big navigator considered the question and replied seriously, "If you and Luce get hit in combat, somebody's got to fly the plane...right?"

"Exactly." Shaw shot him a grim look and added, "Let's hope it never happens."

Shaw showed him how to use throttle movements to cause the big plane to climb or descend. When they were again level on their as-signed altitude, he gave Grattan a friendly pat and said, "Good job,

Mick...go ahead and unstrap," then called Glowgower, "Pilot to bombardier, come on up to the flight deck."

By the time Grattan had returned to the nav station, Glowgower appeared next to Shaw, crouching between the pilot's seats. Pointing to the right seat, Shaw said, "Get yourself strapped-in."

"Why?" the bombardier inquired with a frown.

Shaw was running out of patience with the churlish bombardier. "'Cause you need to get some stick time on this airplane, that's why," he snapped.

Glowgower reluctantly strapped himself in and sat rigidly in the seat, keeping his hands away from the controls. Noticing the bombardier's wooden expression, Shaw said, "I'm just gonna' show you some basic stuff."

"I'm a bombardier," Glowgower said in a plaintive tone. "Why are you making me do this?"

"Let me ask you a question, Glow." Shaw leaned closer so he wouldn't have to shout. "You ever think about who's gonna' fly if the rest of us get hit?"

Glowgower went absolutely white. The situation had obviously never occurred to him and brought to mind a scene from hell.

Noticing the stark horror on the handsome face, Shaw wondered if his question had been overly dramatic. "Not much of a chance it'll ever happen," he said dismissively, hoping to mollify the shaky bombardier, "but it doesn't hurt to be prepared, o.k.?" Shaw pointed to the control yoke and nodded. "She's already trimmed for level flight...take the controls."

Within moments after Glowgower grasped the yoke, the B-26 was bobbing and weaving all over the sky like a drunken beast. The bombardier's knuckles were white with tension as he sawed the controls back and forth in a death grip. Shaw watched the horizon weave around in front of the windscreen.

"Easy, Glow!" he barked. "You're over-controlling, try to relax." In the nav station behind the flight deck, Grattan and Clementi looked at each other quizzically. Compared to Glowgower, Clementi mused to himself, I fly like a bird.

Despite Shaw's efforts to coach and calm the struggling bombardier, the drunken ocillations of the airplane continued as before. Minutes later, Glowgower shouted in a hoarse voice, "Can I stop now?"

"O.k.," Shaw conceded, taking the controls back. The big airplane immediately settled down like an old beast recovering from a momentary fright. It was plain to Shaw why the bombardier washed-out of flight school—absolutely no feel for an airplane. "Go ahead and un-strap," he told him. "Tell Luce to come back up."

Glowgower looked at him with undisguised resentment. It was bad enough that Shaw had seen the contents of his file, but humiliating him in front of the others had filled the bombardier with a smoldering anger.

Returning to the traffic pattern over the field, Shaw and Clementi took turns shooting touch and go landings. When they had climbed back to pattern altitude from their last take-off, Shaw leaned toward his co-pilot. "Let's practice a single-engine approach." He pointed to the yoke. "Stay on the controls with me...get ready to put the gear and flaps down on my command, got it?"

Clementi gave a stiff nod.

Instead of fully shutting the engine down, Shaw allowed it to run at slighty above idle RPM. This would simulate the problem but still give them the ability to effect a quick go-around. As the airplane descended, Clementi rested his hands and feet lightly on the controls, marveling at the manner in which Shaw flew the airplane, like it was on rails. Half way down final to the runway, the pilot called for gear and flaps. Clementi continued to follow Shaw's smooth control inputs. Floating across the threshold, the wheels softly kissed the runway, one at a time.

Shaw slowed and turned the bomber off the runway, then flashed Clementi a huge grin. "Piece of cake, huh?" the pilot chortled.

Clementi gave him a half-hearted wave. Though the co-pilot still had serious misgivings about flying, he had more or less decided if he had to be someone's co-pilot, he'd rather fly with Shaw than some jerk who could fly a B-26 little better than himself. He'd also concluded that Grattan, while a little bit weird, was o.k., too. But Glowgower—that guy seemed to be a real schmuck.

CHAPTER THREE

February 23, 1943, Barksdale Field, Shreveport, Louisiana.

Sergeant Paul L. Milawski, U. S. Army Air Corps, sat on the foot-locker and surveyed his new surroundings. He noted that the almost new, wooden-framed building which served as the enlisted aircrew barracks was considerably more spartan than the dormitory type rooms he'd lived at the Martin plant in Baltimore, but he was nevertheless glad to be stationed somewhere with a warmer climate. Not that he was unused to cold weather, because he'd grown up in Toledo, Ohio on Lake Erie. The youngest of three sons of a Polish immigrant, he'd dropped out of high school after the tenth grade to take a job as an apprentice in a truck repair garage. He'd achieved the status of a regular mechanic by the time the war had broken out.

At age eighteen, he knew he'd be quickly drafted, so within days after war was declared, he'd volunteered for the Air Corps. The Air Corps was quick to recognize his mechanical abilities and sent him to airframe and mechanic's school in Boston. While there, he'd become fascinated with airplanes and volunteered for aircrew training and, as a consequence, two more service schools followed: aerial gunnery school where he'd taken his first plane ride in a North American AT-6 and the Martin school where he'd learned the specific systems of the B-26, including the operation of its power-assisted dorsal gun turret. Now, after over a year in the Air Corps, he was finally going to become part of an aircrew.

Milawski's new barracks mate, whom he'd yet to meet, Corporal Leroy (no middle initial) Rimbaud, U. S. Army Air Corps, thought it was funny that he'd joined the service to get out of Louisiana, given that they'd sent him back. He had no intention of ever visiting his hometown in Slidell, a place he associated with poverty and hopelessness. Fatherless since birth, the last he'd heard of his "maman," she was shacking-up with a half-caste shrimp fisherman.

As far as he was concerned, the war was the best thing that had ever happened to him; in peacetime, the military recruiters probably wouldn't have allowed a dirt-poor peckerwood like him through their front door.

He was downright amazed that the Air Corps had accepted an 18-year-old with a sixth grade education, even more amazed that they'd approved his application to become an aerial gunner. It took more than book learning to fire a machine gun at a moving target, he supposed. Firing machine guns with live ammunition had been the biggest thrill of his life. After he'd gotten over his initial fright, the flying part had been fun, too. The B-26 operational training here at Barksdale was something he looked foward to, but sure as hell hoped there wouldn't be any damn dagoes, wops, polacks, or Jews in the crew he joined, just regular American white boys like him.

Toward the conclusion of the briefing, Colonel Ridley informed the seated aircrews that most of them would pick up the balance of their crew assignments before today's mission, and that the names would be posted at the rear of the room. They were going out to the bomb range today, for the first time, and would be dropping 250 pound practice bombs. Navigators and bombardiers were specifically briefed with regard to the run-in times and initial points—IPs—on their bomb runs; the aircraft would bomb individually from 9,000 feet using variously assigned IPs.

When the briefing ended, Shaw saw a huddle of men at the rear of the room whom he guessed to be the new enlisted aircrews. Looking at the assignments listed under his name, he turned to the huddled group and inquired, "Are any of you Mi...uh, Milawski or Rim-bawd?"

One of the men, short and stocky, with blunt features and curly blond hair answered, "I'm Milawski, sir, flight engineer. You're Lieutenant Shaw?"

"Yep. You seen Rim-bawd?"

Before he could answer, a dark-haired youth with a pock-marked face, stepped up and said, "Suh, Ah'm Rimbaud"— he pronounced it 'Reembode'—"tail gunnah."

Shaw introduced the rest of the crew and asked Milawski and Rimbaud if they'd been issued their flight gear. He told them to return to their barracks to pick-up what they needed and meet him and the rest of the crew at the parachute loft.

After they left, Clementi turned to Shaw and quipped, "That tail gunner, what's his name, Rim-bow? Looks like a rodent with a bad complexion."

"Maybe," Shaw replied, minimizing the comment. "Doesn't matter what he looks like as long as he can shoot." He turned to Grattan and Glowgower. "You guys squared away, ready to make this bomb run?"

Grattan replied first, "The navigation problem doesn't look too hard...I'll give you plenty of notice before we turn onto our IPs."

Glowgower didn't offer a comment, so Shaw asked again, "What about it, Glow...got everything ready?"

The bombardier shrugged indifferently and murmured, "I quess."

Shaw was annoyed by the bombardier's attitude but let it pass.

A little later, Milawski and Rimbaud had collected their flight gear and were walking toward the parachute loft. Rimbaud turned to Milawski and asked in a confidential voice, "What you think of th' officers we got?"

"Dunno," the engineer replied.

"Look like upp'ty college types to me," the tail gunner drawled.

"What'd you expect 'em to look like, the Wright brothers?"

"Who?"

"Never mind."

Milawski continued to walk and asked after a few moments, "Where you from anyway? Ain't never heard anybody talk like you."

"Me? Ah'm straight outa' th' bayoh...they calls us Cajuns."

"Where's this 'buy-oh'?"

"You don' know? It's 'bout a'hunnert mile or so south a'heah."

"In Louisiana?"

"Yeh."

"You'll get to go home on the weekends, maybe?"

"No-suh-ree! No *way* ah'm goin' back there! N'orlans, mebee, but not back there."

As they walked on, Rimbaud inquired, "Where'bout you from, somewheres up in Yankee land?

"Yankee land? You mean up north?"

"Yeh."

"I'm from Toledo, in Ohio."

Rimbaud brooded over his discovery that the crew wasn't as all-American as he would have liked it to be: this flight engineer was probably a dumb polack and the co-pilot looked to be one hundred per cent wop.

Thirty-five minutes later Shaw leveled the B-26 at 9,000 feet and turned onto the run-in course Grattan had given him. After an interphone check, he asked Glowgower if he'd checked-out the bombsight for proper operation.

In front of the pilots, Glowgower peered into the Norden N-2 bombsight, a great masterpiece of American technology. The gyro-stabilized autopilot coupled to the sight would fly the plane from the IP to the aiming point, and as long as the bombardier inputted the correct data—groundspeed, altitude, wind drift, and time-to-release-point—the bombs could be preset to drop automatically when the crosshairs merged in the sight. When used properly, it was deadly accurate. Glowgower finally responded, "Bombardier to pilot, bombsight appears to be operational."

Grattan came on the interphone, "Navigator to pilot, we're five minutes from the IP, your new course will be one-three-zero." Just before the time had elapsed, he called, "Stanby for turn to IP," then seconds later, "MARK!"

Shaw turned the B-26 onto the new heading and announced, "Pilot to bombardier, you've got the airplane."

Glowgower flipped the bombsight engage lever and replied, "Ah...roger, bombardier has the airplane," then quickly added, "bomb bay doors coming open!"

"PDI is centered!" Shaw remembered to report. This made sure there wasn't any drift or crab on the airplane as it tracked to the target.

Back in the rear of the plane, Milawski and Rimbaud felt and heard the roar of the slipstream coming from the open bomb bay doors. The bombardier squinted into bombsight, hastily twisting the turn and drift knobs as he tried to keep the target centered. It was the first time he'd touched a bombsight in weeks, and he was overcorrecting —badly. Above him in the cockpit, it seemed to the pilot and co-pilot that the bomber was dancing back and forth across the target track. Shaw swore under his breath and wondered whether the problem was with the bombardier or in the bombsight system.

"Shit!" Came an exclamation over the intercom.

"Pilot to bombardier, what happened?"

"Uh...bombardier to pilot...the, uh, bomb didn't release." Glowgower's fumbling had caused them to miss the target, and the sight didn't drop the bomb. "Uh..there must be something wrong with auto release switch," he lied.

Shaw was aggravated now; if they didn't get their bombs dropped they'd lose their turn over target, and the group commander would chew his ass out. "Pilot to bombardier, on the next run, set the bomb selector to manual, and use the pickle switch, you got that?"

Five minutes later they turned onto a new IP and commenced the second bomb run. Glowgower opened the bomb bay doors and held the pickle switch in his left hand as he looked through the sight and frantically manipulated the correction knobs with his other hand. Up in the cockpit, the oscillations across the track to the target, if anything, seemed to have become worse. Shaw looked over at Clementi who just rolled his eyes and said nothing. Since the bomber was under autopilot control, there was little they could do except keep the airplane in level flight trim. Moments later the intercom came to life: "Bomb away!"

They repeated this process until all of the practice bombs were gone. When they pulled off the target for the last time, Grattan gave Shaw a course and time back to the airfield and the crew settled down, lit cigarettes, and munched the Hershey bars they carried in the pockets of their flight clothing. All except for the bombardier down in the nose: he was reasonably sure his bombs had missed the target and didn't look forward to the debriefing after they landed. As far as he was concerned, this job was just another in the series of insults the Air Corps had heaped on him. Everything was a damned test. He was sick of it! What could the bastards do—fire him?

The debriefing had not been pleasant.

The debriefer, a bombardier captain, had told them they'd done a good job of setting up the bomb runs from the IPs but that *none* of the bombs dropped had come anywhere near the target circle. In fact, the drops had been so wide of the target, the spotters weren't even sure where they hit. All in all, the performance had been unsatisfactory.

After the debriefing, Shaw told Glowgower he wanted to talk to him in private. Grattan and Clementi picked up their gear and left for the BOQ. There were no other people around, so the pilot asked the bombardier to sit at a table in the operations room. "You want a Coke?" he asked.

"No thanks."

Shaw looked at the bombardier's handsome face, trying to read it. He saw insolence and something else—fear?

Removing the cigarette pack from his shirt pocket, he studied it a second, then asked, softly, "What happened up there today, Glow?"

The bombardier stared at the tabletop and replied, uninterestedly, "We missed."

"We? You mean *you* missed, don't you?"

"Yeah, Shaw, I missed...so what of it?"

Shaw wanted to reach across the table and punch the bombardier's face. Instead, he allowed the anger to evaporate by calmly removing a

Lucky Strike from his cigarette pack and slowly lighting it. After a minute's silence, he asked, still composed, "Why did you miss?"

Glowgower looked down at the table and finally muttered, "You know what happened on the first run... something went wrong with the auto switch on the sight..."

"I don't believe you."

"What?"

"I think you lied, I think you were so far off the target on the first run that the bomb wouldn't release."

Glowgower felt like he was trapped in a nightmare. He wanted to run from the room—to escape. Finally he slumped in his chair and whispered, "Whatever you say, Shaw."

Shaw continued to press. "What about the other runs, when you dropped manually, what happened there?"

"What do you want me to say, Shaw? Admit I screwed up? Well, I screwed up! O.k.?"

The pilot forced the bombardier to meet his eyes and said, almost in a whisper, "I don't think you really give a rat's ass, Glowgower."

"What do you want from me, Shaw?"

"Simple. I want you to do whatever it takes to put the bombs on the target, do you understand that?"

Glowgower didn't respond. He just continued to stare sullenly at the pilot.

"If you don't show improvement when we go out to the range again, I'm going to ask group to replace you, to assign me another bombardier."

"On whose authority!" the bombardier challenged.

"On *my* authority, dammit! As aircraft commander, I can determine who on my crew is or isn't combat ready, and if you or anybody else doesn't make the grade, you're out of here!" Shaw wasn't sure whether he had the authority to get rid of his bombardier, but the threat sounded good to him.

"I don't care, Shaw, I'll just get a ground job."

"Hah!" Shaw continued his bluff. "An able-bodied young buck like you get a ground job! You're dreamin', Glowgower. Ground jobs are for old farts and 4-Fs. No...what they'll do is give you a rifle and send you to the in-fan-try...maybe make you a platoon leader!"

Glowgower shuddered at the implication. He didn't want to fight anyone face-to-face: he preferred the detachment of viewing his enemies through a bombsight. He really didn't want to fight at all, but now he had little choice, no options. What a stinking, blasted mess!

The pilot continued, talking softly again, "I expect you to get your act together now. Like it or not, the rest of us have to depend on you: we can get the plane to the IP, but you're the only one who can put the bombs on the target. It's an important job...*and you've got to do it right*. Half-ass won't get it!

The pilot got up and left the bombardier sitting alone at the table.

Later that evening, Shaw and Grattan were alone in the BOQ room. Grattan was sitting at the desk writing a letter.

Shaw threw down the magazine he was reading and turned to the burly navigator, "Any news from home, from your wife I mean?"

"Yeah, in fact, I got a letter from her today...says she's doing fine, the baby's due any day."

"Too bad you can't be there."

"Yeah, but I don't worry very much. Eleanor's as healthy as a horse, and her family's right there with her. Besides, I completely trust in divine providence."

"What?"

"Divine providence: God."

"Oh."

Grattan looked quizzically at the young pilot and reflected that he'd seen the record on his background. He smiled thoughtfully and said, "You looked at my file and are wondering why I left priesthood training, aren't you?"

Shaw was embarrassed by the correct assumption but admitted, "Well, yes, I was curious about it."

"It was because of a woman, somebody before Eleanor."

"Oh."

Grattan was on uncomfortable ground but decided to press the explanantion further. "You see, Ted, what happened...it didn't weaken my faith in God; it only changed the way I view myself. You don't serve God by simply being a priest or a minister; you serve God by seeking His will in *anything* you do, even preparing to fight in a war."

Shaw didn't say anything but gazed attentively at the big navigator.

"Do you believe in God, Ted?"

"Yes, of course."

"Do you ever pray?"

"Sometimes." In acutality, Shaw rarely prayed.

"I do, Ted...I pray every day...not just for Eleanor and our baby, but also for you and the rest of the crew."

Shaw was silent. He noticed a serene strength in the big navigator's eyes and a comforting quality in his voice. Grattan's declaration had given him an odd, undefinable sense of comfort. He fleetingly recalled the term, "bearing one another's burdens," but couldn't remember where he'd heard it. Changing the subject, he smiled at the burly man and asked, "You want to go to the club and get a beer? I'll buy."

Grattan grinned back, gave Shaw a friendly jab on the shoulder, and chuckled, "Sounds like a good idea, lead the way!"

Ten minutes later, Shaw and Grattan waded through the sea of uniforms toward the bar. The room was noisy and full of cigarette smoke, which hung in the room like a layer of low stratus clouds. The juke box in the corner thundered out a lively tune by Artie Shaw. A small dance floor improvised between the tables was filled with couples jitterbugging to the pulsating music. Since the wartime expansion of the base, the O-Club had become a favored hang-out among the local girls. The pilot and navigator had to shuffle sideways to reach the bar. Because there weren't any stools for them to sit on, they rested their elbows on the bar and waited for the bartender, a moonlighting corporal, to notice them. When the bartender finally acknowledged them, he bruskly asked, "What'll it be for you two gents?"

"Two beers," Shaw replied, "as cold as you got 'em." The bartender looked at the pilot as if he'd asked a stupid question then quickly spun around to reach in the cooler.

Shaw searched his hip pocket for a quarter, which would cover both beers plus a five cent tip. The bartender returned and slammed two sweating bottles down in front of them then took the quarter without comment. Shaw picked up the bottle, studied the label, and said, "I'm afraid to ask for a glass," then took a swig of the beer.

They both turned to watch the crowd and leaned back on the bar. Grattan had been in very few places like this, none, in fact, until he joined the service. Most of his experience in social affairs had been through the church and the school where he was employed. He and Eleanor occasionally met friends for a movie or dinner, but they never frequented places you would classify as drinking establishments. Drinking, dancing, and partying, however, were an integral part of service life, and though he had little desire to participate, he enjoyed observing it. Watching one of the jitterbugging officers on the dance floor suddenly fling his partner over his shoulder, he asked Shaw, "Can you dance like that?"

"Me? Not really," the pilot replied, "I can kinda' shuffle back and forth with my girl, Mary Beth. I like the music though...that Artie

Shaw's really hot."

"Your girl...Mary Beth. Are you serious about her?"

"We're engaged...gonna' get married, if that's what you mean."

"Have you set a date?"

"Nope. She wants to get married now, but I told her we have to wait, until...I haven't decided that yet."

"I understand."

Over Shaw's shoulder Grattan saw Glowgower moving toward the bar with a girl in tow. Though he was resplendent in a sharply creased gabardine uniform, the bombardier looked somewhat disheveled and was obviously drunk. Grattan was aware of the tension between the pilot and the bombardier and hoped the latter wouldn't notice them. He inwardly groaned when the bombardier started moving directly toward them, tugging the girl behind him.

Glowgower swayed in front of them and blurted with a mocking grin, "Well, well, well...here's my brave pilot and his trusty navigator." He stank of bourbon and cigarette smoke, and the girl behind him, whom he'd not introduced, seemed uncomfortable.

"Hello, Glow," Shaw finally replied.

Glowgower seemed unsure what to say next then turned to the girl and, with a sweeping gesture toward Shaw, said sarcastically, "Here in front of you, sweetie, is the perfect pilot...he never, I mean *never*, makes a mistake."

"That's not fair, Glow," Grattan interjected.

"Oh, isn't it...oh, isn't it? Well now...the trusty navigator is sticking up for the perfect pilot, isn't that quaint."

"Stow it, Glow," Shaw finally snapped, "you're way out of line!"

"Listen, Shaw, we're not in the plane...you can't order me around in here!"

Shaw bristled and leaned toward the bombardier. "Maybe not...but I'll wax your ass if you can't control your mouth," he hissed.

Grattan tried to move between the two men but Glowgower stepped around him, leaving the girl standing alone. The bombardier moved right into the pilot's face and bellowed, "You know what you are Shaw...a nitpicking son-of-bitch ...*that's what!*"

In a swift motion, Shaw threw a short, straight punch into Glowgower's face. The bombardier reeled backward and gaped at the pilot, dumbstruck.

Shaw looked at him, eyes hard as flint, and said, evenly, "You're wrong about the son-of-a-bitch part, but you're right about me being a nitpicker...and the way I see it, there are two kinds of pilots: nitpickers and dead ones. And, if you don't like being saddled with a nitpicker, you ask for a transfer, and I'll sign it."

Glowgower continued to stare stupidly at Shaw until the girl took his arm and moved him away from the bar. Shaw turned back toward the bar, slammed his fist on the counter and uttered, "Damn and blast it!" He was furious with himself; he'd completely lost his temper.

Grattan looked at him sympathetically. "That wasn't your fault, Ted. He asked for it."

"Thanks, Mick, but that's beside the point: you don't command people by beating the crap out of them. How're we going to fight the Germans or the Japs if we can't get along with each other?"

"You can't put it all on yourself, Ted."

He smiled at the navigator. "That's the same thing my girl told me."

At a table to one side of the bar, Clementi had watched the whole thing. He'd been about to get up and join the pilot and the navigator when he saw Glowgower and his broad go stumbling up to the bar toward the pair. He wasn't surprised at what had happened and decided that dumb-ass bombardier had had it coming to him. He admitted to himself that the pilot had treated him well enough so far, better than he'd expected—*but,* no doubt about it, that Shaw was one tough bastard, harder than granite. The idea of flying combat in B-26's still loosened his bowels, but he estimated that his chances were a hell of a lot better with Shaw than with some ham-fisted moron who'd probably auger them in *before* they got overseas. Keeping his seat, he watched the pilot and the big navigator leave the bar and walk out the door.

When Shaw and Grattan returned to the BOQ room, they were alone. Shaw opened his footlocker and got out his writing kit. He checked the ink level in the Esterbrook fountain pen his father had given him and wrote:

February 26, 1943

Dear Mary Beth,

I was going to write you tomorrow but want to tell you about this while it's still fresh in my head. I really fouled up tonight. I got in an argument with my bombardier at the O-Club and ended up slugging him. I don't know what got into me.

It started earlier today when I kind of chewed him out over our bomb scores. I know the guy was goofing off and told him he'd have to straighten up or I would get rid of him. I don't know if I can do that, but I felt I had to tell him. My navigator, Mick Grattan, told me just to let things cool down and blow over. I know he's right, but all of this really makes me wonder if I'm up to this job.

I think my co-pilot, Luce Clementi, has really made some progress. He's still not very friendly, but his flying has improved a lot. I thought we were all doing pretty good until this thing tonight came up with the bombardier. I think people must be harder to get along with when you're in charge of them. Mick seems to be an exception. He does a great job as navigator and is always a big help to me.

Please keep me filled in on Dad and Mom. Mom writes on a regular basis, but is careful never to tell me any bad news. I've worried about Dad ever since he got hurt. The cattle business is real good right now, but I know because of the war he doesn't have enough help.

I've given our getting married a lot of thought. I think you're probably right and I'm being too cautious like I always am. We'll make definite plans when I return from overseas. (I still don't have a clue about where we're going.)

Honey, when I think about you, I ache all over. I can't wait to get back home!

Your ever loving,
Ted

P.S. We're going back to the bomb range tomorrow. I guess I'll see what happens.

On ten trips to the bomb range over the next seven days, Glowgower's bombing scores underwent an extraordinary metamorphis— improvement was an understatement. Glowgower would arrive early at every briefing to go over the problem with the lead bombardier. During the briefings themselves, he sat on the first row taking copious notes and occasionaly asking questions about the target data. Leaving in advance of the rest of the crew, he invariably reached the assigned airplane first, where he would double-check the loading of the bombs and meticulously preflight the bombsight. They bombed the target circle from 8,000 to 12,000 feet, approaching from various wind directions, and practiced bombing at night using flares as their aiming points.

By the end of the week, Glowgower had amassed one of the best bombing scores in the group. The group staff officers had even suggested among themselves that this promising young fellow might one day turn into lead bombardier. During all this time, however, Glowgower had kept completely to himself and never spoke a word to Shaw or any other members of the crew unless it pertained directly to the flight or the mission. When they occasionally saw the bombardier at the O-Club, he acted as if they were invisible. Nor, oddly enough, did he ask for a transfer, and the issue simply never came up again.

Shaw was appreciative of Glowgower's improvement but was confused by the bombardier's icy attitude toward him and the others. He'd even tried to compliment Glowgower's performance with casual comments like, "nice goin'," "great job," and so forth, but had been met with a cold stare. There was a fundamental problem here that the young pilot didn't understand. Grattan, with a somewhat deeper insight, tried to explain it.

"I think what you're dealing with, Ted, is one of man's worst sins," the big navigator said one evening.

"Huh?"

"To some extent, all men struggle with the sin of pride." Grattan said this as if the statement were self-evident.

Shaw shrugged. "I don't follow you, Mick."

He gave the young pilot a thoughtful look. "Man, by his nature, doesn't like to admit he's wrong..."

"I know punching him was wrong," Shaw interrupted.

Grattan shook his head. "That isn't what I meant, Ted. I was about to say that, because of pride, men sometimes hate the person who proves them wrong...and I think that's where you are with Glow." He paused to consider his next remark, then continued, "Let me see if I can reconstruct the situation: I know you talked to him after that first trip to the bomb range, and I'm sure you probably criticized his performance. And later on...at the club...you drew a line in the sand, and he crossed it. So, you humbled him not only once but twice in the span of a day, and it was your job to discipline him. But, he doesn't see it that way. As far as he's concerned, you humiliated him and he hates you for it. And as for his performance on the range later this week, it is a very focused and determined rebellion: *He's doing everything he can to prove you wrong.*"

Shaw still wasn't sure he understood the navigator's explanation, but asked, "Then what can I do to patch things up between us?"

"Nothing...leave it alone, Ted. He'll have to see the truth himself."

CHAPTER FOUR

March 2, 1943, Barksdale Field, Shreveport, Louisiana.

At the next briefing, Lieutenant Colonel Ridley informed the assembled pilots and crews that their primary mission for the week, starting today, would be formation flying and gunnery. He stressed the importance of the information that had been gained from other units during recent overseas combat experience.

"Men, as you know, the 8TH Air Force has been operating B-17 heavy bomb groups out of southern England for almost six months. Their prime mission has been high altitude, daylight precision bombing. I won't kid you when I tell you that their losses have been high."

He waited for the murmuring in the room to stop.

"The Germans have had years now to prepare the anti-aircraft defenses around their cities and industrial sites. They have developed radar-guided, eighty-eight millimeter flak guns that can fire at our planes with deadly accuracy, even through the overcast. And their fighter defenses, ME-109's, FW-190's, and ME-110's, mainly, are at the highest level we've ever seen. They have widely dispersed bases that run all the way from the Channel Coast to the industrial cities. The long-range search radars they use can pick up our planes right after they take-off."

Most of the aircrew in the room wore grave expressions, some of them were visibly distressed, a few mouthed things like, "Oh, God." A couple of people bolted from the room to go outside and throw-up. Shaw and Grattan both held attentive expressions on their faces. Sitting next to Shaw, Clementi grimaced as he fought to control the fright-induced churning in his stomach and bowels. Glowgower, seated away from Shaw's little group, presented a stony mask, forcing himself not to display the panic he truly felt. Milawski, watching the faces of some of the others, was reassured by the seemingly calm expressions of Shaw and Grattan, even Glowgower. Rimbaud hadn't paid much attention to what the Colonel had been saying but thought the alarm he sensed in the room was both interesting and funny. These uppity college boys take things way too serious, he thought.

The Colonel waited again for the commotion to cease, and continued, "Men, I'm not telling you this to scare you but to give you a true picture of what you'll be up against. And the news is not all bad: we've learned a lot from recent combat operations and are already putting those ideas to work. Our intelligence on the location and composition of enemy flak gun locations has greatly improved. With this information, we can plot flak corridors to and from the targets which avoid the heaviest concentration of fire." He decided not to mention that this wasn't necessarily true when you reached your IP and started the run to the target. They'd get into that later.

"Let's talk about the fighters for a minute. One of the most valuable tactics we've learned is the importance of keeping our bombers in large, very tight formations. The large formations, we've found, create a zone of defense which is hard for the fighters to penetrate. We call them 'combat boxes,' and the primary element is the group. Within the group, each squadron will consist of three six-plane elements that will be arranged to provide both a horizontal and vertical dimension to the box." While he talked, he referred them to a diagram on the chalkboard behind him which illustrated the configuration of the formation from the front, side, and top. "These group boxes," he said, tapping the pointer, "are then assembled into wings that make the defensive zone even larger. The attacking fighters have found this formation to be so formidable that it has caused them to change their tactics: the field of defensive fire from our bombers was the strongest from the top, rear, and flanks of the formation."

Using his pointer, he indicated the shaded areas on the chalkboard diagram. "So the fighters began attacking the formations head-on where the fewest guns could be brought to bear, but we've effectively responded to that problem, too, by equipping our aircraft with more forward-firing guns." Pausing, he turned around and clipped a large three-view diagram of an airplane to the chalkboard. "The B-26B's which you will take overseas," he said as he pointed to the diagram, "will have a total of five foward-firing 50-caliber machine guns. When you add the two 50-caliber guns of the top turret, it gives you a total frontal protection of seven heavy machine guns."

The Colonel paused to light a cigarette and wipe his brow with a hankerchief. He wished there were a nicer way to put this, but there wasn't. "Men, the main reason I tell you all of this is to bring home the absolutely critical importance of maintaining formation. You can mark this down: aircraft that don't keep good formation probably won't survive...and just as important, when your formation is bad, you hurt everybody else by degrading the overall effectiveness of the box. Assembling and maintaining formation is something we will practice and re-practice in the coming weeks until we have it down cold." The Colonel paused, then asked, "Any questions?"

A young lieutenant in the middle of the room raised his hand and asked, "Colonel, does this mean we're going to England to be part of the 8TH Air Force?"

The Colonel allowed a smile and scanned the room. "Now, I didn't say anything about where we're going, did I?

Anything else? No...then I'll turn this over to Major Edrington who will give you the specifics on today's operation."

After the group briefing, Shaw and his crew met with Major Walter Chase, their new squadron leader, and Captain Roger Merrill, the leader of their six-plane flight. Though Shaw had met with both of them several times previously, he knew little of their backgrounds. Chase looked like a veteran pilot, but Merrill didn't appear to be much older than Shaw himself.

The plan for that day was to takeoff and work in individual six-plane flights. Merrill informed them he would use the call-sign "red leader" and they would be red two through six. He would take-off first and orbit the field in a wide arc to the west at 3,000 feet until they all formed up on him. This sounded easy but in practice was much harder. It took them a long time to form up, especially for the trailing planes that took-off last and after they did, the formation was unbelievably ragged. From the top, the formation was supposed to look like a capital "A" with straight legs, and from the sides, the aircraft were supposed to be evenly stepped-down from the leader. The aircraft were supposed to maintain a lateral separation of 50 feet from wingtip to wingtip and a longitudinal separation of 50 feet from nose to tail. None of them had ever done this—the results were predictably chaotic.

Merrill's voice constantly bellowed over the command radio with commands like: "Close it up, red five! Close it up NOW!" or "Break off, red two! You're too close! TOO CLOSE!" Maintaining the new type of formation was much trickier than Shaw had expected. The echelon and "V" formations they'd practiced in other training had been a lot easier. The restricted visibility from the B-26's cockpit presented an additional problem: from his place as number three on the right of Merrill, he had to look through the glazed framework above the cockpit to maintain position. After 30 minutes, he had a crick in his neck and his shoulders were aching. While he watched the lead plane above him and to his left, he had to make small control inputs on the yoke with his left hand and use his right hand to constantly make minute adjustments to the throttle settings. The combination required immense, unwavering concentration. Without shifting his gaze, he said, "Luce, you take it for a while." Grattan was crouching between the pilots watching. He didn't utter a word lest he interrupt their focus.

The co-pilot looked uncertain but replied, "I've got the airplane."

Immediately, the B-26 began to drift from the formation, and the radio clattered, "Close it up, red three! Close it up!"

Instead of retaking control, Shaw swiftly coached the laboring co-pilot: "Luce, stay on the controls! I'll handle the power for a while. Now...try to establish a reference point on his right wing and keep it right there in your window." The B-26 slowly crept back into position. "That's right, keep it right there...don't let that wing move." Shaw kept his right hand on the throttles and used his left hand to massage his neck and shoulders. He would remember to bring some aspirin next time. After another ten minutes had passed, while still watching the lead plane, he continued to coach his co-pilot: "The trick, Luce, is to make small, I mean *tiny*, adjustments to the power...so slight that you can't even tell the levers have moved. Now...I'll take the controls back ...you handle the power for a while."

For the first five minutes or so, Clementi's efforts to adjust the power caused the B-26 move in and out of the formation. Shaw patiently continued to tutor the sweating co-pilot: "You gotta' relax, Luce...barely use your fingertips...anticipate where you think the airplane's going and try to stay ahead of it." The in and out, back and forth movements of the B-26 gradually diminished to the point where they were maintaining a reasonably constant position relative to Merrill. They flew on this way a while longer until Shaw said, "Take a break, Luce, I've got the airplane."

Thirty minutes later, the formation turned around and headed back towards the airfield. They landed and broke for lunch, after which they took off again to resume their formation practice. During this session, Shaw had Clementi handle both the controls and the power. He told Clementi to ignore Merrill's constant radio clamoring and to listen only to him. With Shaw's verbal prompting, the co-pilot, after a time, was able to settle into a fairly unchanging position. Eventually, they developed a routine in which each of them took turns flying the plane. Shaw knew that many of the other aircraft commanders weren't allowing their co-pilots to even touch the controls during formation practice and, as a result, were wearing themselves thin. What they would do, he wondered, when they were required to fly hours on end in combat. If the aircraft commander were wounded, or even killed, what then? To him at least, such intransigence seemed like an accident waiting for a place to happen, and he felt better about what he was trying to accomplish with his little group, even Glowgower.

They continued formation practice for the next few days, and the more they practiced, the more second nature it became. Though not quite in Shaw's league, Clementi could now maintain formation as well as most of the others in the flight. Later that week, they practiced further by forming into squadrons and then into the overall group box. It pleased Shaw that his flight of six flew a tighter, smoother formation than many of the others. It was a majestic sight to be in an organized mass of so many planes, ninety-six in all, and watch them wheel around in the sparkling sunshine, framed by blue sky and puffs of cumulus cloud. At their place in the middle of the formation, they seemed to be encased on all sides by olive drab B-26's. While the planes in other flights seemed to be stationary, almost welded in place, in his nearby flight he could see the perceptible rising and falling of the big bombers in relation to each other as they rode through the currents of the air. It was a thrilling experience for all of them, evidence of their hard work. *This was real Air Power.* Even Glowgower up in the nose could not be indifferent to the sheer force of this spectacle.

When they parked the airplane and got out, a private from the group staff was waiting for them and told Grattan that he was wanted in the group commander's office as soon as possible. This caused Shaw a small shiver of apprehension because he feared that, perhaps, they were going to move Grattan out of his crew to one of the lead positions. Over the past weeks, he'd developed a strong friendship and a durable working relationship with the affable navigator. Losing him would be a blow.

A little while later, in the BOQ room, Clementi lay back on his bunk, casually flipping through a tattered copy of *Life* magazine, while Shaw retrieved his writing kit and sat down at the desk. Minutes later, Grattan suddenly burst into the room and slid to an abrupt halt in front of the pilot.

"I just got the news!" he cried, waving a small telegram in his hand. "It's a boy...IT'S A BOY!"

The big navigator was so excited, he grabbed the pilot's shoulders and bodily lifted him from the chair. "Can you believe it!" he exclaimed raucously. "Eight pounds, three ounces...WOW!"

Shaw, caught up in the excitement, embraced his big friend's shoulders, from which they moved around the room in a lurching jig that resembled a circus performer and a dancing bear.

When they stopped, Shaw, almost out of breath, asked, "How's Eleanor?"

"She's terrific!" Came through it without a hitch!"

Shaw dropped into his chair, asking, "Has he got a name yet?"

"Of course he does, boyo...he will be known as Michael Brian Grattan, *Junior*!

Clementi had watched the two men capering around the room with amusement. Getting up from his bunk, he offered his hand to the beaming Grattan, and said, "That's swell news, Mick, really swell... congratulations." While he was genuinely happy for Grattan, he couldn't imagine the resposibility of a wife and a child. Scary, he thought.

As usual Glowgower was nowhere to be seen. They went to the PX and helped Grattan select a box of cigars, then went to the O-Club where Shaw paid for two rounds of beer.

The navigator told them he was going over to the base switchboard to try to put a long-distance call to Pittsburgh. Shaw left Clementi at the club and returned to his room to write his letter:

March 5, 1943

Dear Mary Beth,

This is going to be shorter than I planned because it's late and we have a big day ahead of us tomorrow. Mick just gave us the greatest news! His wife, Eleanor, just had a baby boy that weighed over 8 pounds——I guess he's going to be a big fellow like his daddy. I am really happy for him but I have to tell you that I was a little bit jealous because I really look forward to the day we can start our own family!

We've made tons of progress in our training. Luce Clementi is really turning into a good co-pilot. He seems a little friendlier, too, but Mick has really become my rock, the guy I depend on most. He gives me real good advice, too. He's one of the smartest guys I've ever known. I worry that he's so good at his job that group will take him away from me and give me another navigator. Glowgower is the one who's really a puzzle. I told you in my last letter that he's become one of the best bombardiers in the group. Mick says he's doing it because he's trying to show me up somehow. Mick says that I have become some sort of father figure that he's rebelling against. Whatever it is, it's way over my head. I'm going to take Mick's advice and just try to let the whole thing blow over.

I'm getting too sleepy to keep this up.

Tell everyone at home I said Hi. Knowing you love me is one of the things that really keeps me going. You mean more to me than anything in the world!

Your ever loving,
Ted

A captain from the group staff talked to them that morning about gunnery. He said, "All of you, whether you've been to gunnery school or not, are going to have to learn gunnery. You pilots, too," he added. "Even if you're not in a position to fire yourself, you'll need to be able to identify incoming fighters and call them out to your gunners. Coordinated gunfire is the key to making these formations work. But before we go out and fly, all of us will spend some time on the ground practicing at the gun range. This may be old hat for some of you trained gunners, but you'll be the instructors for the other members of your crew who haven't had that kind of preparation."

Rimbaud wasn't happy about this. He didn't consider himself much of a teacher and, besides that, he had no desire to hob-nob with these college boys. He'd let that dumb polack, Milawski, handle it; he seemed like the suck-up type anyway.

The captain continued, "After you've spent some time on the range and have acquainted yourself with the M-2, 50-caliber machine gun, we'll go up in flight elements and practice against towed target sleeves. These sleeves will be sufficiently behind the tow planes so as to eliminate the danger of shooting down the tow planes themselves." He paused for a few seconds and said, "Now, remember this: you are never...*I mean never*...to open fire on a target sleeve until the tow plane has passed through your line of sight! You got that? Don't ever make a hasty shot...you should be tracking that target *before* you pull the trigger. Any questions so far?"

A hand went up. "Uh, Captain...what happens if one of us, I mean accidental like, hits the tow plane?"

The captain gave the questioner a stony look, then replied without a trace of humor, "You'll be kicked out of here so fast, boy, it will take your asshole two weeks to catch up with you!"

The trained gunners like Milawski and Rimbaud knew that aerial gunnery was not at all like shooting at a target from the ground, even one that was moving. They had learned that it involved shooting from one moving object at another moving object, like trying to shoot skeet from a moving car. To make it even more complicated, the shooters and targets were moving at hundreds of miles an hour in a three-dimensional environment.

Shaw in his youth had hunted wildfowl and other game, so had some notion of the concepts of lead and deflection. Clementi and Grattan, on the other hand, had never fired a real gun until they joined the service. Glowgower had done a little duck and dove hunting with his father but was far from being an experienced marksman. Milawski was better then most of them because of his previous gunnery training, but it was quickly apparent to all of them that Rimbaud, the swarthy little Cajun, was deadly with a gun. When the small man got behind a machine gun, he was suddenly transfigured: his face screwed into a macabre grin which exposed his yellowed teeth; his movements became noticeably smooth and graceful. He showed little enthusiasm, however, for sharing his talent with other members of the crew.

When Rimbaud turned in a nearly perfect score on the range the first day, Shaw asked him, "Hey...Leroy...why don't you show the rest of us how you did that?"

"Ain't nuthin' t'show, Lieutenant," he replied. "I jus' pointed this heah gun at that theyah targit...simple as that. You jus' gotta' practice some, that's all." Without further comment, he turned away from the pilot, walked over to a bench behind the firing line, and laid down with his hands behind his neck. Shaw was a little addled by the rebuff but turned around and said, "C'mon, Ski...let's get everybody together and try it again."

Before they flew again, they attended lectures on aerial gunnery where films and other training aids were used. They even watched the movie, *Aerial Gunner*, which starred Richard Arlen. Rimbaud slept through most of lectures and films, but the others were interested, knowing their lives may depend on it sometime. They were ready to fly again. Though he still maintained a frosty distance from the rest of the crew, even Glowgower looked forward to getting back into the air.

With the exception of Rimbaud, and possibly Milawsi, the first day of gunnery practice in the airplane had been a circus. The others, Shaw included, had not put a bullet hole anywhere near the target sleeves being towed by the Douglas A-24s. The A-24s, the Air Force version of the Navy SBDs, especially with the added drag of the target sleeves, weren't as fast as the B-26s carrying the gunners. The bombers were forced to stay throttled back in order to allow the target tugs to overtake them. The trick was to lead the tug with your sight bead and wait for the sleeve to enter the range bars. Milawski and Ribaud had been trained to anticipate the fast moving targets and be ready to fire at the sleeve, but the sleeve had usually come and gone before the others had even pressed the trigger.

They all took turns firing the guns. Rimbaud, with reluctance, gave up his tail gunner position to allow the others a try. In these older B-26's, the top turret was the only power-assisted gun. They didn't have a true waist position either, only a 30-caliber machine gun which fired through the belly of the fuselage just behind the top turret. The sole forward protection consisted of one 30-caliber flexible mount located in the nose dome. In the European theatre of the war, this airplane would have been a under-defended deathtrap.

Later in the morning, Clementi flew the airplane while Grattan sat in the righthand co-pilots's seat to call targets. The navigator observed that the tug would cross their position on their left side from above, but before he could say anything, Rimbaud screamed, "Bogey at eight a-clock high!" In the top turret, Shaw swiveled to meet the target, but saw Rimbaud's tracers already lancing toward the sleeve. God, but he cut that close, he thought. As the tug passed him, he opened fire, but because he'd miscalculated the deflection, his tracers fell wide of the target. The noise of the guns in the close confines of the fuselage was incredibly deafening, and the plane stank of burned cordite. The floorboard beneath Shaw's feet was littered with spent 50-caliber shell casings. He looked down momentarily at Milawski manning the belly gun, then continued his scan and waited for the next call, this time from Glowgower, who shouted, "Bogey at twelve o'clock high!" The tug had turned back in their direction to make an overheard pass. No deflection, Shaw noted, tensing himself to fire soon as he saw the tug pass through the sight bar. The recoil of the two heavy machine guns jolted the enitre airplane when he stabbed the trigger. As the guns traversed, he noticed his tracers walking their way through the target sleeve. From beginning to end, the process had lasted only seconds.

In the tail, Rimbaud reflected that this was more fun than sex, not that he'd had much experience with the latter. He figured it would be even more fun when they got overseas and shot at the real thing. The thought of it amused him. These college boys could drive him around over there so he, Leroy Rimbaud, could shoot them Nazi sonamabeeches out of the sky!

The B-26's were going back out to the bomb range, in formation this time, to learn how to bomb as a group element. One of the principal hazards of bombing from large formations, as combat experience had shown with a frightening reality, was aircraft dropping their bombs on other aircraft below them in the formation. Even if the bombs were still too high to explode, the sheer weight of metal was enough to tear off wings and other essential parts of the airplane. When they turned onto the IP, it was critical, therefore, that the squadron and flight elements of the group maintain proper station all the way to the aiming point. All of them would discover the difficulty of doing this in actual combat.

As Shaw and his crew converged on the IP as part of a large formation, their job was a little easier: they had only to listen in on the command channel and anticipate what the flight leader was going to do. The bombs would dropped only on command from the bombardier in the plane leading the group. Even so, Glowgower, in the nose, still studied the ground moving below him through his bombsight. When Grattan announced they'd turned onto the IP, he pulled back a lever to his left and called, "Bomb bay doors coming open!" He shifted his attention back to the sight and watched the bombing circle swim toward the crosshairs. He shot a quick glance at the bomb selector panel, while holding the bomb pickle switch in his right hand and listening for the drop command from the lead bombardier. *I will not screw this up*, he thought excitedly, for he had a larger mission than his Air Force job: to show Shaw and the others that he was as good as them. He would never give them the opportunity to humiliate him again. The results of the tireless work and effort he'd put into his bombardier training in the past few weeks had truly surprised him. It had given him a completely new type of self-assurance in his own abilities. In an odd way, he even enjoyed it! Too bad it was overlayed by a burning hatred.

Glowgower pickled the bombs within a second of hearing the command, "Bombs away!" from the lead plane. He watched the bombs descend on the target circle below. When they impacted, the bombs, filled with flour, made small, white circles on the ground. The bombardier imagined the destruction that would have been wrought if those bombs had been full of high explosive. He understood now what a well-disciplined bomber force could do to a target. God help our enemy, he thought.

As the large formation wheeled off the target and headed back to the base, Shaw asked Clementi to take over for a while, and sat back and rubbed the tension from his shoulders. He still had not remembered to bring any aspirin. He watched the co-pilot keeping formation with the B-26 to his right and extracted a Lucky Strike from the inside pocket of his flight jacket. He didn't offer the co-pilot a smoke because he knew he wouldn't want the distraction. He lit the cigarette and reflected it had been a good day's work.

When their B-26 began to unexpectedly yaw out of the formation, Clementi yelped, "What the hell...!" Shaw quickly scanned the instruments and saw the RPMs on number one engine climbing through the redline. "I've got it, Luce!" he shouted, grabbing the control yoke. "Shut down and feather one!" The co-pilot deftly shut down the engine and stabbed the feather button in well-practiced motions. While Shaw fought to bring the bomber under control, they drifted down and away from the formation. Clementi, thinking ahead, picked up the mike and called, "Red leader, this is red three...we've just lost number one!"

Shaw watched his airspeed stabilize and heaved a sigh, "Thanks, Luce...good work." Other planes in the formation had heard the call and had maneuvered out of Shaw's way. The suddenly radio blared back at them, "Red three, this is red leader, are you o.k.?"

"Ah, roger, red leader," Shaw responded, "but we can't maintain formation."

Merrill called back quickly, "Understood, red three...proceed back to base as a single ship," then added, "what are your intentions?"

"Red leader, I intend to ask for a straight-in approach to the active runway for a normal landing."

Merrill had detected no panic in the pilot's announcement, but asked, "Red three, what do mean...normal?"

"Ah, red leader, I mean a wheels-down landing using flaps."

"Understood, red three," came the reply, "but if you think the landing is unsafe, you have permission to bail-out." It occured to Merrill while making this remark that they had a hell of a lot more B-26s than they had aircrews trained to fly them.

"Negative, red leader...we'll give the landing a try."

"Good luck, red three."

"Ah, roger, thank you, red leader."

Grattan stuck into the flight deck with a alarmed expression and inquired, "What happened?"

Before anyone else could venture an answer, Milawski spoke up over Grattan's shoulder. "Musta' been an electrical glitch in the prop.

When the circuitry shorts-out, it causes the prop to go into full flat pitch, then the engine over-speeds." The young engineer looked at the pilot and added, gravely, "If you don't catch it in time, it can cause the prop and its casing to rip itself right off the engine!"

Shaw shuddered at the vision of a run-away propeller slicing through the fuselage, disemboweling whoever happened to be near it. "I've heard about this problem," he said, "but I've never seen it happen before."

The engineer continued, "It has to do with the servicing on the props and the electrical system on some of these older planes. We were told that the people from Curtiss had trained the Air Force people to fix it." He considered this statement for a moment then added, "But, I guess a few bad ones still get through..."

"Apparently," Shaw scoffed. This was the first *real* in-flight emergency he'd ever had to deal with. *It wouldn't be his last.*

Back in the tail, Rimbaud wondered how he was going to get out of the plane without the rest of the crew seeing him, for he had soiled himself. After the plane had fallen out of the formation, he had watched it slide narrowly between two other planes with only inches to spare, when fear seized him and his bowels exploded! Nothing like this had ever happened in gunnery school. It was *not* funny and he did not like it!

Shaw and Clementi landed the B-26 without mishap. The experience had sobered them in a positive way, underlining the seriousness of what they had been learning all these weeks. The Colonel had told Shaw and his crew that they'd "...done a real fine job." Shaw afterward wondered where Rimbaud had gotten off to.

CHAPTER FIVE

March 9, 1943, Barksdale Field, Shreveport, Louisiana.

Lieutenant Colonel Ridley looked out over the assembled mass of aircrews seated in the hall. The Colonel, a thirty-four-year-old, twelve-year veteran of the Air Corps, thought they're just boys really, sent to do a man's job. And where they're going, he considered, they'll have to grow up fast, real fast. He waited for the scuffling of chairs and feet to stop.

"Men, what I'm about to tell you is classified information and is not, I repeat, *is not* to leave this base! Is that understood?"

The seated aircrews chorused, "Yes sir!" and bobbed their heads in unison.

"We have received our movement orders," the Colonel continued. "We will depart this base in two days and travel in specified groups to Bolling Field in Washington, D.C. From there we will proceed to the Martin plant in Baltimore to pick up our new B-26s. You will stay organized in flight groups and will have one day—only one—to shake down your airplanes."

He could see the curiosity on most faces, trepidation in some. "Once you've checked out your plane, you will proceed—in flight elements again—to Gander, Newfoundland. You will land in Gander, rest and refuel, then take-off again, following a Great Circle route, for your final destination in Snetterton Heath, England!"

This caused a stir of hushed talking and a grating of chairs from the audience. He waited again for the noise to stop and continued, "As you may have already guessed, men...the 333RD is going to England to become part of the 8TH Air Force! Our group and others like us will form the medium bombardment arm of the 8TH's combat operations." He paused a moment. "Are there any questions so far?"

A hand came up in the back of the room, "Uh, Colonel, sir, where's this place Snet...uh, Snetton Heath?"

"You mean Snet-ter-ton Heath," the Colonel replied, pronouncing it in three distinct syllables. "It's in East Anglia but you'll see a map in a minute which will detail the location. Anything else...?"

In the time that followed, the crews received a more detailed briefing on the planned movement. They were advised that aircrews would proceed by C-47 transport to Bolling Field, and the ground crews would follow by train and troopship. This meant, of course, that the aircrews would arrive in England two or three weeks ahead of most of the ground personnel. A core group a mechanics and armorers would travel with the aircrews, and some spare parts and engines were already enroute to Snetterton Heath.

Shaw watched Grattan stuff his notes into his flight bag as he got ready to go to the navigator's briefing. "Well, I guess playtime's over," the pilot commented in a serious tone. "What do you fellas think of our orders?"

"Since you ask," the big navigator spoke first, in a acerbic tone, "I find it ironic and a little amusing that *my kind* is going over there to fight the King's battles again!"

Shaw quizzically raised his eyebrows. "Your kind?" He had no idea what the big man was referring to.

Grattan hooted, "The Irish, you dope!"

"I never thought of that," the pilot admitted. Shaw's knowledge of history was limited to the courses he'd been required to take in high school and college.

Grattan grinned at Shaw and the others. "If you didn't know it, the British, for centuries, subjugated and nearly starved the Irish people...that's the reason so many of us came to America in the first place. But, at the same time—this is the ironic part—Irishmen have made up over thirty per cent of the Crown's armies and navies. Without us, there would probably be no British Empire, and it's almost a certainty that they would have been deafeated by Napoleon. Now, having escaped on my grandpa's coat tails, I'm on my way back over there...is that ironic or what?" He looked at his watch, gasped, and abruptly stood up. "I've gotta' go...see you guys later!"

Glowgower had already departed. Shaw glanced amiably at Clementi, who'd yet to say anything. The co-pilot shrugged and said, "I'm not surprised about going to England because it's one of the last places I'd have picked."

"The last?" Shaw asked curiously. He had been told by Merrill and others that England was the best combat assignment. "What would you have picked first?"

"Well, somewhere like the Panama Canal Zone would have been my first choice," Clementi admitted with a sardonic grin. "But since they didn't give me that option, I'd have picked duty in the Mediterranean theater."

"Why?" He'd heard that the units Clementi mentioned lived in tents and were constantly on the move.

"Because they're operating out of Sicily and Southern Italy," the co-pilot explained. "I speak the lingo...even got relatives there...would've made out real well with the local senorenas."

Shaw laughed. "I don't know whether you've heard, Luce, but there are millions of women in England, too, and most of their men are gone...North Africa or someplace."

"You kiddin' me?" Clementi genuinely looked interested.

"That's what I hear." Like everthing else about the war, the stories he'd heard had been exaggerated.

In that incredibly short space of time, the impulsiveness of youth at work, Clementi's attitude about England completely turned around. *Millions*, he thought.

Shaw faced Milawski and Rimbaud and asked them, "What about you fellas?"

"England sounds good to me, Lieutenant," the young engineer replied first. "Better, I imagine, than a lot of other places they could've sent us." Rimbaud looked at the pilot impatiently and jibed, "They can send my dumb ass wherever they want ta'...you thew wid' us, Lieutenant?"

"O.k., you guys can take-off."

Two days later, Shaw and three other crews, with all their personal gear, boarded a C-47 for Bolling Field, District of Columbia. To Shaw's amazement, Glowgower brought one B-4 bag and only *one* footlocker. Though he hadn't confided his sentiments to the others, the bombardier honestly thought he probably wouldn't live long enough to have much further need of the tailor-made uniforms, and didn't give a damn about the personal belongings he left behind. He mused that some supply sergeant was probably trying the stuff on right now. The reality of the movement order had filled him with bowel-churning fear, the last of the unstoppable paths on which the Air Force had placed him. He tried to ignore it by staying focused on the details of his job and the preparations for the trip, but when he allowed his mind to wander, the fright would suddenly hit him like a bolt out of the blue. But even if he couldn't completely block it out, he would never allow the others to see it.

The flight to Bolling Field took over nine hours with an intermediate stop in Atlanta. This gave the four crews some time to discuss the impending journey across the Atlantic. Merrill informed Shaw that he would be leading the flight most of the way from Gander.

"Why me, Captain?" Shaw asked.

"Names's Roger," Merrill drawled. "The reason you're going to lead...is because Grattan's the only navigator in this bunch who's got his shit together on celestial navigation."

"I see." Shaw was mildly surprised.

Merrill cocked his eyebrows and dryly suggested, "Unless you want him to fly with me."

"No, that's o.k....we'll be glad to fly lead." The last thing Shaw wanted to do was embark on a trip like this with a strange navigator.

"I'll tell you now, Ted...I'm gonna' ask Chase to make you deputy lead for the flight from now on."

"Uh, thanks." The news was unexpected.

Merrill regarded the young pilot with a wry smile. "Ain't doin' you any favors...your outfit's just done a better job than the other crews in my flight, that's all. Means more work, you know."

Shaw smiled and nodded. He wasn't real sure that he wanted the extra responsibility.

Looking at him inquiringly, Merrill suddenly asked, "What's the story on your bombardier? Seems to be some kind of a loner. Look at him right now," he motioned with his eyes, "sitting in the back by himself, not sayin' a word to anybody. He got a personal problem or somethin'?"

"No. He's all right, just kinda' quiet, that's all." Shaw wasn't about to mention something he didn't understand himself.

"Well, whatever it is, the son-of-a-bitch knows how to put the bombs on the target."

"Right." Shaw was relieved to avoid any further conversation on the subject.

Shaw went up to the cockpit of the C-47 and noticed the approaching foothills of the Appalachians through the windscreen. The pilot looked over his right shoulder and asked, "You one of the B-26 drivers?"

"Yeah."

"How 'bout you spell me for a little bit so I can go back and visit the can? It's on autopilot...all you gotta do is watch it."

Shaw sat down in the left seat and scanned the instruments. Turning to the man wearing greasy work coveralls who occupied the right seat, he asked, "You the co-pilot?"

"Naw," the man grinned, and motioning rearward with his thumb, said, "the co-pilot's in the back catchin' some zees.

Besides," he patted the control column, "ol' Betsy here don't need no pilots most of the time, 'ceptin to land and take-off."

As the pilot watched the controls of the C-47 eerily move in response to the autopilot, he noted the contrast with the B-26, which had to be hand-flown every step of the way. Nice gadget.

March 31, 1943, Bolling Field, District of Columbia.

Most of the crew were dog-tired when they stepped off the C-47. Rimbaud asked if he could get a pass to go into town. Shaw considered the question and replied, "None of us are going anywhere until we check-in." In base operations, Merrill informed all four crews that they were leaving for Baltimore, 50 miles distant, at 0600 in the morning. They would keep everything but their flight gear loaded on the six-by-six truck assigned to them and travel by bus to the Martin plant to pick up the planes. The Martin people would brief them on the planes, and they would takeoff for Gander the following morning.

Rimbaud groaned, "I nevah been heah and was so hopin' t'see the Washintin' monument an' the white house."

"Sure, Leroy," sneered Clementi, "and the Smithsonian, too, I'll bet." The rest of them hooted with laughter.

Rimbaud didn't know what the Smithsonian was but wished that uppity college boy would shut his wop mouth.

"Sorry fellas', no passes," Shaw said with definiteness. "Let's get our quarters assignment, then find the chow hall."

The next morning, Shaw felt like he'd barely fallen asleep when the orderly came into room at 0430 and shook him awake. He dressed in his standard flying kit, which consisted of an issue wool shirt with a tie, wool pants, a service cap with frame removed—to accommodate the fit of the headphones—and his A-2 leather flight jacket. In his flight bag, he'd included a set of long underwear to wear on the trip from Gander, hoping it was enough. He despised freezing his ass off. Most of his military stations had been somewhere in the south and this was as far North as he'd ever been, causing him to wonder about the climate in England. Surely, he thought, it couldn't be any colder than this.

CHAPTER SIX

April 1, 1943, Martin Plant, Baltimore, Maryland.

She sat on the vast parking apron and waited. It was a cold, blustery day with a biting wind blowing in from the Chesapeake, but she didn't notice it; she was only two weeks old.

She had no name, just a serial number, 41-28334. She was not alone, for she was surrounded on all sides by her sisters. They were waiting, too. Though she had no name, they called her a B-26B-10-MA. The factory called her and her sisters "Marauders," but that wasn't a real name either.

She had been born in the large building located about one-half mile from where she stood. She was a vast improvement over her older sisters, who had given her such a bad reputation. Her wings, at seventy-one feet, were six feet longer, and her tail fin was almost two feet taller.

This caused her to be much better behaved. And these weren't her only improvements: her engines were more powerful and she now carried eleven 50-caliber M-2 machine guns, all but four of which could be fired forward. In her bomb bays, she carried ferry tanks for an additional 530 gallons of fuel in preparation for the long voyage she was about to take.

She waited for her young men to come and take her away, for they would finally give her substance. Without them, she was merely 37,000 pounds of aluminum, steel, rubber, glass, leather, and high-octane gasoline. Later she would carry up to 4,000 pounds of bombs and thousands of rounds of 50-caliber ammunition.

Some people thought she was pretty, a mass of compound curves, all very streamlined to give her great speed. What could not be seen within her shape was her strength—she had been born very, very strong. And later her young men would swear by her. Today, her dress was very plain: she wore only her olive drab and gray paint, decorated with white stars surrounded by blue circles on her wings and sides and *a six-digit serial number on her tail fin. Her boys would dress her up, though: they would paint large letters on her sides and stripes on her tail; they would paint little yellow bombs on her side to indicate the missions she'd flown; and they would paint her real name in large fancy letters on her nose for the whole world to see!*

She was ready.

They bypassed the Capitol on their bus trip to Baltimore, and poor Rimbaud never did get to see the Washington Monument. The heater in the bus had didn't work, so that the moderately-clad Shaw froze his ass off the entire way. Most of the others, more familier with northern tempratures, had had the presence of mind to bring their shearling-lined flight overalls and jackets.

Though all of them had been on a number of air fields, none could fail to be awed by the sight of the massive Martin plant in full wartime production. The parking ramp was crammed with B-26s awaiting delivery. It also contained a large number of Martin Mariner flying boats destined for the Navy. Shaw commented that they were the first seaplanes he'd ever seen.

"I've seen the Pan American Clippers taking-off from Long Island Sound," Clementi observed.

"Must be a sight." Since childhood Shaw had never tired of watching airplanes takeoff.

"Yeah, it's something," the co-pilot added. "They must run at least two miles before they become airborne, but that's not the surprising part."

"What's that?"

"You know I used to work downtown, in Manhattan I mean?"

"Yeah." Shaw had only seen photographs.

"Well, one day I just dropped into the Pan American office near Times Square, and I happened to see this rate schedule they had posted on the flights. You wanna' guess how much it costs to fly from New York to Southampton, England...*one way?*"

"I don't know...two hundred dollars maybe?"

Clementi snorted, "More like a thousand!"

"Are you serious?" The pilot thought he'd heard him wrong.

"No joke." the co-pilot smiled at his revelation.

The pilot gave him a perplexed look and asked, "Who could afford that kinda' money for a one way trip?"

Clementi realized that Shaw, despite his talents as a pilot and a commander, was considerably naive in the affairs of the real world. At the bank where he'd worked, the co-pilot had seen millionaires come and go on a daily basis, men with tremendous influence over business and industry. He laughed and said, "Hell, Ted, there are rich people in New York City who spend more than a thousand dollars having lunch!"

Shaw screwed his face into a facetious grin: he believed the part about the Pan American ticket, but that thing about lunch—Clementi must be trying to bullshit him. With a thousand bucks, you could buy lunch *and* dinner for the entire population of Big Spring!

In a room in one of the factory hangars, the pilots and crews were briefed on the characteristics of the the B-26B-10's—"block ten" aircraft the factory reps called them. Overall stall speed had been reduced, so they could expect them, at gross weight, to break ground at about 110 m.p.h. Rate-of-climb was improved, too, but cruising speed would be about 12 m.p.h. slower than earlier models. The reps went into great detail on other modifications and improvements to the airplane. They told them that future versions would have a Bell-manufactured, power-operated tail turret, but that these weren't ready for installation on the block tens; they could expect a field modification later on. They were informed that the planes they would fly had been towed into the hangar in front of the flight line to be pre-flighted and gassed for the trip tomorrow. The factory people instructed them to stow their gear in the planes as soon as possible so the weight and balance could be checked.

Shaw raised his hand. "How will we know which one is which?"

"Your name again?" the man asked.

"Shaw, Theodore J."

The man looked down at a piece of paper and looked back up at Shaw and said, "Your plane is tail number one-two-eight-three-three-four," then read off the rest of the list for the others.

Shaw could barely sit still. Grattan noticed the bright expectation on the young pilot's face and thought it was remarkably similar to his own expression when he'd been informed of the birth of his son. He said to the pilot, "Why don't you go have a quick look at the plane while we start bringing up the gear?" The pilot flashed him a huge grin and bolted for the door to the hangar.

"You're beautiful," the pilot whispered to her. He ran his hand down her flanks and noticed the sheen of her paint, not yet dulled by weather or time. "We're going to get along just fine, you and me," he intoned softly. "You're going on a long trip to do an important job, you know, and I'm going with you. I'll take good care of you...I promise." He was very, very proud of her.

Behind him, Shaw heard the shuffle of footsteps and the swishing of baggage. Turning, he saw his crew enter the hangar with the bags they would load aboard the plane. In order to save weight, they'd left their footlockers behind to follow them—they hoped—by other transport to England. The pilot stood before them with the delighted expression of a little boy on his birthday. As they halted in front of the nose, he raised an arm in presentation and said, dotingly, "She's a honey, isn't she?" While perhaps none of them shared the pilot's immediate zeal, they were, nevertheless, all of them, impressed by her pristine freshness—none of them had ever seen a brand new airplane up this close.

Grattan noticed his own smiling image reflected in the B-26's nose dome. Turning to Shaw, he declared, "She'll need a name, you know." The Air Force was encouraging all crews to personalize their aircraft. In fact, former sign painters and illustrators had been recruited from all over the enlisted ranks to paint very colorful and visible names and illustrations on the planes.

"Great idea, Mick!" the pilot enthisiastically agreed. "What should we name her?" The question was addressed to the group.

Milawski spoke up first, "You've got a girl, Lieutenant...what's her name?"

The question took him by surpise. "Ah, her name's Mary Beth," Shaw answered tentatively. The idea of naming a plane after her had never occured to him, seemed indecorous. It didn't seem to evoke much enthusiasm on the faces of his group either. "Why don't we come up with a something we all like?" he ventured with an expectant shrug.

"You know," Clementi suggested, tapping his chin, "I heard they're naming them after all kinds of stuff, like popular songs and movies." The co-pilot looked up while thinking about it.

"I heard a new song I really like the other day," Shaw remembered. "I think it's called *Take the A-Train* by..." He closed his eyes trying the recall the bandleader's name.

"Duke Ellington!" Clementi suddenly interjected. He hummed the melody and noisily snapped his fingers in accompaniment. "That's *it*! We'll call her *The A-Train*!"

"I like it!" followed Grattan. Milawski and Rimbaud both offered approving nods. Glowower expressionlessly stood to one side of the small group.

Her boys had given her a real name. It had yet to be painted on her side, but it was her very own name and she would keep it.

All of the crews met that evening to finalize the flight plan to England. It was to be the longest flight any of them had ever made, and none had ever crossed an ocean. Using the performance graphs in the back of their flight manuals and E-6 flight computers, they calculated the aircraft's range at various altitudes and power settings. They seriously discussed and reviewed the options and alternatives plans they would take in event of mechanical problems or unforecast bad weather. With Shaw's plane in the lead, they decided to fly in a loose trail formation, at intervals of 1,000 feet. If the weather clamped-down, forcing them to fly in or through cloud, they would close up into echelon formation and turn on their navigation lights. Under no circumstances would they allow themselves to become separated! When this had happened to other crews on trans-oceanic flights, some were never seen or heard of again— their young bodies, in all probability, claimed by the dark, frigid waters of the North Atlantic.

The leg from Baltimore to Gander, Newfoundland would be 1,290 miles; the over-water leg from Gander to Snetterton Heath, England would be 2,310 miles and would take about twelve hours, depending on the wind direction and velocity. Their route out of Gander would take them across the Labrador Sea over the ice dome of Greenland, and then into the open North Atlantic. If they ran into trouble, they could attempt a landing on the frozen wastes of Greenland and hope someone would rescue them, but once over the open ocean, their best chance lay in making it to Ireland.

If they left Gander at 0000 local time, it should enable them to make landfall—see the coast of Ireland—in daylight and be over England in the early/mid-afternoon, Greenwich Mean Time—they would lose 3.5 hours in Time Zone Changes. A daylight approach was important. Since all of them had had minimal training in night flying, finding Snetterton Heath in the dark would be a tricky, maybe even impossible. Once over England, they would continue to rely on their dead-reckoning plots until they could take fixes on landmarks they were certain of, because England, they had been told, was an incredibly easy place to get lost in an airplane. Unlike the United States with its identifiable north-south, east-west section lines, England was a mass of twisting roads and hedgerows that had been built up over a period of 2,000 years.

Grattan wracked his brain to see if there were any details he'd overlooked; he could think of nothing. They'd been provided a recommended flight plan by group, but it didn't take into consideration the many variables of weather and wind they were sure to encounter.

The perils of this journey brought to mind Lindberg who, sixteen years before, made nearly the same trip—alone—in an airplane with half their speed and found his destination in the dark. Compared to that, he imagined, my task ought to be a piece of cake.

They departed Baltimore the next morning and landed at Gander, Newfoundland at 1317 local time—they would take-off for England in less than nine hours. The ramp at Gander was covered with airplanes: C-47s and C-87s belonging to the U. S. Air Transport Command, and B-17s, B-24s and other B-26s on the way to England. When they dropped out of the nose hatch onto the pierced steel matting of the parking ramp, they were assailed by a freezing chill.

An Army six-by-six truck took them from their parking area to a quonset-type building which served as base operations, and after checking-in, they were directed to another quonset-type building where the mess hall was located. The mess hall was filled with lounging flight crews and reeked of cigarette smoke, burnt coffee, and sweaty clothing, an aroma they were all used to. They moved into the chow line at the end of the room.

Clementi frowned at the food in the large serving trays but asked for double-helping anyway. Shaw had never seen a human being eat as much as his skinny co-pilot. Clementi constantly complained about the food everywhere they went but always ate like a man condemned. Shaw looked with alarm at the growing mound of food on his co-pilot's tray and warned, "Don't overdo it, Luce...not today."

The co-pilot sneered at the contents of his tray and muttered, "Not a chance!"

They shared one side of a table with another aircrew.

Grattan finished his meal and pulled his navigational charts from his flight bag while sipping a tepid cup of coffee. "I think we ought to get a second opinion," he told them.

"A second opinion of what?" asked Shaw.

"You know, I'd like to get someone with some ocean crossing experience to review our flight plan."

Shaw shrugged. He had confidence in the work Grattan and the others had already done to plan the flight but said, "Whatever you think."

Grattan surveyed some of the people sitting at other tables. Nearby sat a group of Air Transport Service aircrews who looked like seasoned veterans. In their midst, a dark-haired man who looked to be about thirty seemed to be leading the conversation, using the typical extended palm gestures that pilot's use to explain flight maneuvers. Grattan picked up his flight bag and walked over to the man.

"Excuse me, sir?"

The dark-haired man looked up at the big navigator with a friendly smile and said, "What can I do for you, Lieutenant?"

"Well, sir, have you...have you flown across the Atlantic before?"

"About six times," he paused, then grinned as he said, "*this* month."

"Great!" Grattan beamed at him. "In that case, sir, you're just just the man I need to talk to. By the way, my name's Mick Grattan, navigator on one of the B-26s that just came in."

"I'm Ernie," the man said, "Ernie Gann." He looked at the others at his table and bawled, "Hey, you guys move over and give this man a place to sit!"

Grattan pulled out his charts and notes, spreading them out on the table. Gann ran his finger along the route the navigator had laid down and every few seconds or so grunted, "uh-huh" or "yep." After absorbing the picture, the man looked at the big navigator and said, "This is all right, but you'll make better time if you extend your route a little farther North to intersect Greenland here." He pointed at the chart.

"Won't that add distance to the leg?"

"Some, for sure, but it'll actually reduce your flight time en route...quite a bit. The big thing about the more northerly route is the hellacious tailwind you'll pick up on the second part of your leg when you start moving down the line of longitude. Can add as much as 100 m.p.h. to your ground speed!"

"Wow!" Grattan was amazed by the information, but added, "You're sure about this wind?"

Gann grinned at the big navigator and cracked, "Hell, this time of the year that wind's a lot more regular than old Slonie over there!" He pointed at an old, grizzled pilot sitting on the other side of the table who nodded in silent agreement.

Grattan jotted some figures in his notebook and ran a calculation on his E-6. He looked up at Gann and grinned.

"If you're right about this tailwind, it could shave at least an hour off our ETA...even with the added distance."

"Yep, you can count on that wind...but, one thing you need to watch out for along that route...*ice.*" The tone was ominous.

"Ice?"

"Yeah...is the B-26 a good ice carrier?"

"I'm not very sure about that, I'll need to ask my pilot."

"Is it equipped with de-icer boots?"

"No." Grattan's face became a mask of concern.

Gann frowned, but said, "Well, boots help but the main thing is taking quick action before the ice accumulation becomes dangerous."

The navigator looked at him questioningly.

"Listen close." Gann drew nearer as if confiding a secret. "Tell this to your pilot: *if* you run into ice, get your carb heat on pronto and *immediately* start descending and keep descending until you see the ice starting to flake off. And don't even think about trying to climb over it!" The older man smacked his palm with his fist for emphasis.

"Why?" All of this was new information to Grattan.

"At these latitudes you can always count on a positive lapse rate"— colder upper air—"so even if you get above the precipitation, you're likely to keep the ice you already have."

Grattan looked at him thoughtfully, then asked, "If we run into ice and need to descend, just how low should we go?"

The veteran pilot gave the navigator a kindly smile and replied, seriously, "Down to the wave tops if necessary. But," he added emphasis, "take it *real slow* on that last thousand feet...so you don't plow into the ocean! Your altimeter could be wrong by a hundred feet or more. Get everybody looking for the water, and one last thing: don't descend below two hundred feet indicated unless you're sure you see the water, all right?"

Grattan grinned and enthusiastically replied, "I'll remember! I can't tell you how much I appreciate your help, Mr. Gann! I'm going to pass on everything you told me on my pilot and the others in my flight." Grattan felt their chances of making a safe crossing had marginally increased and wondered why they hadn't been briefed on this information in the first place.

Gann patted the big navigator's shoulder. "Don't mention it, Lieutenant, I'm glad to help."

Armed with the new facts and figures, Grattan quickly returned the charts and notes to his flight bag and got up. But before making his way back over to where his crew sat, strongly pumped the older pilot's hand. As the navigator's back receded across the room, Gann smiled as he flexed his fingers and regarded the group of older pilots at his table. "You know, there's a real nice kid. If half of 'em are that bright, the Krauts are in for one helluva pounding!"

Grattan excitedly advised Shaw and Merrill of the navigational and other information he'd gleaned from the veteran pilot. They both agreed it was a better plan than the original. "Those ATS guys probably know more about ocean flying than anybody," Merrill said. "Most of 'em flew for the airlines before the war. And that stuff on icing ...Lord! I didn't even think about it!"

"Me neither," Shaw admitted. He surmised that the B-26, with its high wing-loading, would not be a very good ice carrier and wondered how many ice-laden planes had unaccountably spun into the ocean. Scary.

The three left the mess hall a few minutes later to go to base operations to check the latest weather forecast. The forecast wasn't ideal, but was flyable: broken to scattered cloud with a small chance of snow or sleet along the first half of the route; broken cloud to clear with no chance of precipitation along the second half.

When they returned to the mess hall, they found the rest of the crew lounging around drinking coffee and smoking cigarettes. Shaw told Clementi, "You ought to try to get your head down for a few hours, Luce. We're gonna' pre-flight at 2330 and try to have wheels in the well by 0000." Clementi nodded and began to collect his gear. The pilot looked at the rest of them. "Glow, you, Milawski, and Rimbaud will be able to get a lot of sack time on the flight over, but everybody will do some of the flying."

"That include me, Lieutenant?" Rimbaud asked with obvious excitement.

"Yeah, you too, Leroy...but," the pilot added with a mock grimace, "no farting in the cockpit, you got that?" He'd been told that the little Cajun was unbelievably flatulent.

Rimbaud, not sharing the joke, gave him a steely look and said, "Ah'll sho' keep that in mind, Lieutenant."

From one side, Glowgower said flatly, "I'd rather not."

"Rather not?" Shaw queried.

"Rather not fly the plane, o.k.?"

"Suit yourself, Glow." The pilot decided not to force the issue. The bombardier turned and left.

Shaw turned to Milawski and said, "Ski, I want you out there to supervise the fueling...make sure they don't overlook the ferry tanks."

The young sergeant smiled. "Right, skipper. I've got fuel flow charts ready to go, too."

Shaw stared at him for a moment with a silly grin on his face. It was the first time anybody had referred to him as "skipper." "Good work, Ski...thanks."

Rimbaud saw the exchange and definitely classified Milawski as a toadying suck-up.

The B-26, named *The A-Train,* lifted smoothly from the runway at

Gander at 0005 local time and climbed into the leaden northern sky. Her big engines throbbed resonantly as she punched through some of the low-lying layers of stratus clouds on her way up to her cruising altitude of 10,000 feet. She led the formation of three other planes, which trailed loosely behind her. The night was black as a coal sack, and the cockpit lights had been turned down so the glow of the dials was barely discernable. Occasional stars could be seen through the broken cloud cover above them.

Shaw watched the altimeter creep past 10,000 feet and allowed the bomber to climb up to another 500 feet, where he leveled-off. He moved the propeller controls back to 2,000 RPM and eased the throttles to 26 inches of manifold pressure. If the book was right, this should produce a fuel flow of ninety-three gallons per hour, leaving them a comfortable reserve of at least two hours. Nosing the bomber back down to 10,000 feet, he satisfyingly watched the airspeed indicator settle on 185 m.p.h indicated.

Grattan, standing behind him, glanced at the outside air temperature gauge, then spun the indices on his E-6 computer. "At this temperature and altitude," he announced, "our true airspeed is about two-oh-five."

Shaw minutely adjusted the propeller control until the throbbing noise settled into a steady hum. "I think that's got her...you take it a while, Luce." He pulled a Lucky out of his pack and vainly attempted to shield the flare of the Zippo with his palm. As the cockpit was suddenly bathed in light, he apologized, "Sorry, guys."

Milawski, squeezed in beside Grattan, suggested, "I could try to rig up some sort of electric lighter to the DC bus."

"Nice idea, Ski." The pilot smiled through a puff of smoke. "But I doubt if we'll need it."

"Why's that, skipper?"

"Our Air Force is not doing any of the night bombing," he answered. "They're leaving that to the Brits."

Clementi spoke up. "I heard that, too...but how do those RAF guys hit targets at night?"

"You remember when we bombed on those flares several times at Barksdale?"

"Yeah, I realize that...but how do they know the flares are in the right place?"

Shaw thought for a moment. "They have these pathfinders...I guess they're like our lead crews...who go out ahead of the main bomber force and try to pinpoint the target. When they find it, they drop marker flares."

"What if they drop 'em on the wrong place...they bomb it anyway?"

Shaw shrugged at the question. "I suppose. That's probably why we don't do it that way...not accurate enough."

"Well, I don't mind telling you," the co-pilot finally declared, "it would scare the holy crap out of me to take-off in the dark with a huge group of planes like that and be unable to see 'em all the way to the target and back."

"Yeah." Shaw shivered at the idea. "I'd rather take my chances in daylight in a big formation."

"What do you think they're gonna' do with us, Ted."

"I don't have a clue, Luce...not one."

The co-pilot tried not to ponder what lay ahead but the thought of it was irresistible. He was a lot more comfortable flying now and admitted that he'd learned a lot from Shaw. But combat! Other than minor schoolyard scrapes, he'd never been much of a fighter. Despite Brooklyn's tough reputation—much of it exaggerated by the movies—he'd managed to avoid situations that might have led to serious conflict; now he was on an inexorable path to a massive, dangerous conflict in Europe. What Colonel Ridley had said about German air defenses had scared him shitless. It couldn't be as bad as it sounded, he told himself. Don't think about it.

After they settled down to the cruising routine, Glowgower asked Clementi to move so he could go up in the nose. The co-pilot got up and allowed the bombardier to squeeze through the opening in front of the right seat. Once in the nose, the bombardier, unperturbed for the first time in hours, regarded the now familiar surroundings. This was the part of the plane that truly belonged to him, free from the inquiring faces of the others. It was temporarily roomier due to the absence of a bombsight, which would be installed later. He zipped his shearling jacket up to his chin to ward off the cold. Like Clementi, the idea of combat terrified him, but it was superimposed by a greater fear: that he would screw-up again on the job. It'll never happen, he resolved. He'd never forgive Shaw either. The thought caused him to allow a small smile. Making a crude bed from his parachute and B-4 bag, he lay down and closed his eyes.

Milawski had made himself a similar nest to lay on in the waist of the plane. He was far too excited to sleep. He wasn't thinking of combat but speculating on the wonders he would find in England: wondered what the cities and towns looked like, wondered if there were still castles and great palaces, wondered what the food would taste like, and wondered what the girls looked like. He'd heard his father and mother mention the old country—Poland—a place they usually associated with misery and strife. But England! Had to be a lot different, he thought. Well, different from Toledo anyway. His daydream was suddenly interrupted by Rimbaud's drawling voice.

"Hey, Milawski, what you thinkin' 'bout?" The gunner had been watching the far away expression in the young engineer's eyes.

"About England...why?"

"Ah don' know 'bout you, boy, but ah'm thinkin' 'bout them hot Anglish mamas!" He leered at his companion with a smile that revealed his yellowed teeth.

Milawski thought the tail gunner was a pig and avoided conversation with him whenever possible. He didn't have much choice right now and admitted, "Well, I've been thinking about that myself."

"Hah! Yo' kiddin' yo'self...them Anglish broads ain't gonna' take up wid no polack boy"!

Milawski sprang up and seized the tail gunner by the throat and screamed, "You filthy Cajun scum! You ever call me a polack again, I'll squeeze the life right outta' you!"

Rimbaud made gurgling noises and unsuccessfully tried to wrench himself free from Milawski's surpisingly powerful grasp. "Ah didn't mean nuthin'," he bleated, "let me go!"

Milawski scowled at the tail gunner and roughly pushed him away. Rimbaud had been temporarily stupefied by the young engineer's speed and aggression. He massaged the soreness in his neck and silently vowed to never let it happen again. Next time that polack came after him, he'd be ready.

Milawski lay back down and tried to relax. He knew he'd have to keep an eye on the Cajun from now on. Rimbaud was the type, he suspsected, who'd put a knife in your back when you weren't watching.

The commotion in back hadn't been heard in the cockpit over the roar of the engines. Both pilots were beginning to feel the monotony of the flight routine. There was an old saying that flying was largely a process of sheer boredom occasionally punctuated by moments of stark terror. This was especially true when flying over the sea during a moonless night. In the smooth air, the only evidence of motion was the reading on the airspeed indicator. The occupants of the B-26 floated in a netherworld, where sky, sea, and horizon had merged into a featureless void.

Behind the pilots at his navigation table, Grattan pondered whether the sky conditions would permit him to take some star shots in a few hours. They should be over the ice dome of Greenland in about three and a half hours, say 0430, but sunrise at these latitudes would be a lot later than usual, about 0900. When you figured the tailwind in, they should pick up Ireland sometime pretty soon after sunrise. He felt some small anxiety over making a landfall in the dark then chided himself when he remembered that they would have traveled far back down the line of longitude by that time and would be in full sunlight. Plus, he suddenly realized, they would have passed through two time zones by then. What on earth was he thinking about! Must be first ocean-crossing jitters, he decided. He'd studiously maintained a constant DR plot, but in the dark, it was virtually impossible to calculate drift. Stop worrying, he told himself! Poking his head and shoulders between the pilot's, he asked nobody in particular, "What do you think?"

Shaw looked at him quizzically then turned to Clementi with an ex-pression of mock alarm and declared, "When a navigator asks a stupid question like that, it means he's lost!"

The co-pilot, missing the joke, exclaimed, "What!"

"Well, it wouldn't be fair to say I'm completely lost," Grattan said, continuing the gag. "I'm absolutely sure we're somewhere between Europe and the North Pole!"

When the co-pilot's expression remained anxious, Shaw and Grat-tan laughed at him like a pair of hyenas.

"Where are we really?" he finally asked.

"My plot indicates we're about half way across the Labrador Sea." Grattan squinted up through the top of the canopy to see if the overcast was thinning. "But, I won't know our exact position until I take a star shot or see the coast of Greenland."

An hour later they entered solid cloud. Whatever grogginess Shaw or Clementi felt earlier was instantly gone. The navigation lights on the wings were surrounded by hazy coronas. Keeping the airplane level and on course required an unending instrument scan: altimeter, airspeed, needle-ball, rate-of-climb, artificial horizon, directional gyro—then start all over again. Because they were totally cut off from the world above and below, they could be miles off their track and not know it.

Shaw picked up his microphone. "Blue lead to blue one, you see us, over?"

The radio cracked, "Blue leader, blue one is closing in on your right wing and the rest of the flight is closing me, echelon right!"

Shaw was about to ask Merrill whether he thought they should de-scend below the cloud mass or try to climb over it, when he noticed an opaque sheen rapidly developing on the windscreen. "Luce!" he shouted. "Get on the carb heat for both engines, NOW!"

Looking out the side window and noticing the swift build-up of ice on the wings and nacelles, he called Merrill again, "Blue leader to blue one, we're in ice! Going down...follow me!"

Pulling the throttles back slightly to lose altitude, he and Clementi could only peer out of the side windows as they sank through the solid gray murk. At 7,500 feet some of the ice began to loosen and fritter off the windscreen. As they passed through 7,000 feet, they broached the bottom of cloud and saw the leaden sea below them. Noisy pellets of rain hit the windscreen, clearing the remaining fragments of ice. Like large olive drab insects flying below a ceiling, they scudded along the base of the cloud mass they'd been in. Fifteen minutes later they broke into the clear and could see the vast dome of the northern stars twinkling above them.

"Man alive!" Shaw exclaimed after a minute. "I'm glad that's behind us!" He picked up the microphone and called, "Blue leader to blue one, let's climb back up to ten thousand and go back to trail formation."

"Roger, blue leader...blue one is right behind you!"

He and Clementi flashed each other victorius mock salutes, both acknowledging that they had just experienced—and survived—one of those rare episodes of going from sheer boredom to stark terror. If they hadn't been so busy, they would have engaged in a fit of raucous laughter. Tension release, the experts called it.

Behind them, Grattan thought to himself, thank you Lord—and Ernie Gann—and started readying his sextant, chronometer and tables for a star shot. He crawled through the bomb bay back to the waist and shook Milawski awake. "I'm sorry, Ski, but I need your help for a couple of minutes, o.k.?."

"No problem," said Milawski as he rubbed the sleep from his eyes.

"I'm going to shoot some stars from the top turret," Grattan explained. "You write the numbers down exactly the way I call them out."

"O.k, I'm ready." The young engineer didn't know you could "shoot" stars but figured the big navigator knew what he was doing.

Grattan used the top turret to avoid rigging the retractable astrodome bubble in the nav compartment, which would have allowed in an unwanted stream of frigid air. He scanned the clear winter sky and, using a Brownell-Weems star finder, selected Procyon, Rigel, and Aldebaran. Each shot took a minute or two; he read the numbers off the sextant and gave them to Milawski. Ten minutes later, back at the nav table, he had computed three lines of position represented by three small pencil dots on the chart that were about thirty miles apart. Their position would be approximately in the center of the small triangle of the dots. A minute later, his smiling face appeared between the pilots and he proudly announced, "We should see the coast of Greenland any minute now. We'll need to turn to a new course of zero-one-seven in about a minute."

Shaw picked up his microphone, "Blue leader to blue flight, turn right to zero-one-seven on my signal."

Grattan, looking at his watch, gave him a sharp thumbs up signal. "Blue flight, turn now!" he called and rolled the bomber onto the new heading.

Turning back to Grattan, he asked, "Now, tell me where are we exactly?"

"We should pass about ten miles South of Godthab."

"Say that again."

"Godthab...it's on the Greenland coast. I don't know whether we'll see it or not, but my fix indicated we were only about fifteen miles South of our intended track, so our planned course change was reduced by a few degrees. But, we're a little ahead of schedule."

Shaw called Merrill on the radio and repeated the information. He turned back to the big navigator still standing beside him, knocked off his cap, and ruffled his sparse hair. "You know, Mick...you're a helluva lot smarter than you look!"

Before Grattan could think of a reply, Clementi, interrupted with the excited announcement, "Hey land! I think I see land!"

"Where!" demanded Grattan, squinting out the windscreen. Clementi pointed to the faint silvering that demarked the sea and the Greenland shore. The big navigator wasn't aware that the co-pilot possessed better vision than anyone else in the plane, 2015 in both eyes and excellent night sight. As they passed over the coast, the faint lights of Godthab hove into view, fifteen miles distant, from which the navigator was able to fix their position with geographical certainty. It took them only one and one-half hours to traverse the Greenland subcontinent, and Grattan took his last pilotage fix on Angmagssalik as they headed into the North Atlantic. Following the circle down, their course was now southeast, and their speed over the ground, with an estimated tailwind of 70 m.p.h., would be 275 m.p.h., which would put them in sight of land in a little over four hours.

When Grattan left the flight deck, Shaw motioned Clementi to lean over toward him. He cupped his hand over his mouth and whispered, in a conspiratorial voice, "Luce, if you see land again, keep a lid on it, o.k.?"

"Sure," the co-pilot nodded and whispered back.

They flew into sunlight about an hour later, and the sky became a vivid cobalt blue, punctuated occasionally by low-lying cumulus clouds. Over the next two hours, all of them, except Glowgower, took turns flying *The A-Train*. Shaw noticed that she flew better hands-off than the previous B-26s he'd flown. Must be the extra wing and tail area, he speculated.

He squatted between the pilot's seats and smoked as he watched Rimbaud fly the plane. Whereas Milawski's face had become a mask of worried concentration while he was on the controls, the swarthy tail gunner's eyes danced with the merriment of a kid on a playground. The little Cajun seemed to possess a high level of natural hand and eye co-ordination, and exhibited none of the stiffness that afflicts many people their first time on the controls.

Clementi, in the left seat now, reached forward to re-set the gyro-compass. Glancing at Rimbaud, he chuckled, "You think you could make a pilot, Leroy?"

"'Course not, suh," the gunner lowered his eyes and drawled with mock servility. "Ah ain't nearly edju-ma-cated 'nough t'do any kinna job like yos'."

Clementi ignored the implied insult and sat back in his seat to stare again at the unchanging seascape. Leaning forward in a sudden reflex, he thought he might have detected a smudge, some type of anomaly, on the horizon. He quietly nudged Shaw's shoulder and motioned to the windscreen with his eyes. The pilot furtively nodded.

Seconds later, Grattan appeared behind them and asked, jovially, "See anything yet? We ought to be getting close ...I make us about 30 miles out."

"Not yet," lied Clementi.

"Uh-uh," added Shaw.

Rimbaud cleared his throat as if to say something, when Shaw inclined his head in a sniffing motion and retorted, "What's that sickening smell! Leroy!"

The little gunner looked at him with bewilderment. "Ah din' do..."

"You get your smelly behind back to the waist right now!" The pilot hustled Rimbaud out of the right seat and pushed him through the doorway past Grattan. He'd explain it to the little man later and apologize.

With Clementi back in his seat, both pilots and the navigator were intently gazing through the windscreen in front of them, when Grattan suddenly gasped, "I think I see it!

"See what?" Shaw feigned confusion.

"Right there!" He pointed with his right index finger. "Yes...I'm sure! Woo-eeee!" Grattan hallooed, at the same time shaking both pilot's shoulders and causing the airplane to bob and weave. Glowgower even heard the comotion above him as he lay reclined in the nose on his improvised palate. The bombardier lifted himself to peer through the nose dome and observe the stain of land on the horizon.

Shaw called the flight on the radio and advised them they should be seeing Ireland, straight ahead. Replacing the microphone on its hook, he grabbed the big navigator's hand. "Well, Mick, that's twice now you've allowed us to cheat death!"

"Beginner's luck!" he joked. Thanks again, Lord, he said to himself.

The A-Train glided over Donegal Bay, Ireland at 10,000 feet. In the cockpit they all felt a surge of elation—and relief—which possessed every airman who ever completed an ocean crossing for the first time. It was an unforgettable experience.

"Hey, Mick!" shouted Shaw. "Make sure you've got the IFF turned on." The identification-friend or foe would transmit a radar return which identified them as a friendly aircraft. "I'd be real embarrassed if we flew all this way and got shot down by our own people!"

"Not to worry," Grattan replied, "I've had it on since right after we made the sighting."

"Isn't Ireland supposed to be neutral?" Clementi questioned.

"It is, technically," Grattan answered, "but it's still in the Anglo-British Zone of Defense."

"What's that?" The co-pilot's knowledge of international affairs could have been summarized on a match cover.

"A couple of years ago, even before we declared war, the United States and Britain made a treaty which forms a protectorate over most of the territory between America and Britain. It includes not only Ireland, but also Greenland and Iceland, which are Danish possessions."

"How 'bout that," Clementi said, half listening.

"Did you know that we are occupying Iceland?"

"Really? Helluva bad place to be stationed, I'd bet"

"There are worse places for sure," the navigator laughed. "Like a bunch of guys I went through navigator's school with who were sent to outfits in the Aleutian Islands. You know, in the Bering Sea."

The co-pilot looked at him blankly.

"You remember," Grattan went on, "the Japs invaded Attu and Kiska last year?"

"Uh, I think I heard about it..." Clementi paid more attention to baseball scores than war news.

Changing the conversation, Grattan declared, "We did all

right...getting assigned to England."

"Yeah," the co-pilot agreed. "I'm not crazy about going into combat, but better than living in some shithole like the place you mentioned a minute ago."

Shaw looked at them both. "You guys realize we've been damn"—he almost said *lucky*—"fortunate all the way around? A good assignment, a good group, and a good crew to boot...could have done a lot worse, you know, a lot worse." The pilot inwardly wondered if he was trivializing the danger that lay ahead of them.

"I think our crew's all right," Clementi added, "but I still can't figure out Glowgower. What's his problem, anyway?"

"Don't worry about him," Shaw said, optimistically, "he'll come around." Or maybe he won't, the pilot thought to himself.

In the span of their conversation—twenty-three minutes—they had crossed the northern part of Ireland and entered the Irish Sea. In less than forty minutes, they would cross the English coast at Liverpool.

Shaw looked over his shoulder. "Mick, try to start raising someone on the approach frequency they gave us. I'm sure they must be picking us up on their radars by now." Behind him he could hear the warble of the radio being tuned and Grattan repeating their radio call.

Grattan clicked the interphone, "Nav to pilot, I can't hear 'em yet, but I'll let you know as soon as I do."

Everyone in the plane was up and alert now, looking for the English coast to crawl over the horizon. Glowgower pulled himself to a sitting position and lit a cigarette. He was beginning to think of the things that lay ahead—the dangerous, creeping up things—when his thoughts were interrupted by a shout from Clementi. "Hey, Glowgower! You better come on up now...we're coming up on the coast pretty soon!"

Grattan continued the radio call. "Atlantic approach, this is Army B-26 three-three-four, over." When, a few moments later, an English-accented female voice replied to his call, he was so startled it left him speechless.

The voice inquired again, "Hallo B-26 three-three-four, this is Atlantic Approach, do you read me, over?"

"Ah...Roger, Atlantic Approach, this is B-26 three-three-four leading a flight of four, inbound to Snetterton Heath."

"Three-three-four, Approach, we have you on radar...please say your altitude, over."

"Approach, three-three-four, angels ten"—10,000 feet.

"Three-three-four, Approach, turn right to one-zero-five and descend to angels seven-point-five, over."

Grattan acknowledged the command and was advised to expect further instructions when they crossed the coast.

Hearing the radio call, Shaw pulled back the power to descend, and started the turn. They had seen the coast while Grattan was busy working the radios. The pilot keyed the intercom, "Hey, Mick...try to pick up the Armed Forces Radio...see if you can find us some music."

A few minutes later, the muted tone of Tommy Dorsey's trombone came wafting through his headset. Shaw wasn't a great fan of the modulated Dorsey sound, preferring the powerful rhythm of bands like Duke Ellington, Count Basie and Benny Goodman, but he'd listen to almost anything.

The music reminded him of home—Mary Beth and his parents. What they would think, he tried to imagine, if they could sit here with him and watch the coast of England spreading out before them. Few people from Big Spring had ever seen anything like this. His father, Henry Shaw, had seen England, Southampton in fact, twenty-five years ago as an infantry private in Major General Douglas MacArthur's Rainbow Division. Surviving the Battle of the Argonne Forest, Henry Shaw had returned to Texas to marry his sweetheart, who a year later, bore him a son, whom they named Theodore Jenkins Shaw, after his maternal grandfather. Shaw's father seldom spoke of the Great War and never mentioned his personal combat experiences, a mystery of his father's past that his son could only guess about. The elder Shaw did recently express some surprise that his old commanding general was still in the Army, and a theater commander to boot! While Shaw's father was wordlessly grateful that he would never be called upon again to climb over the firestep of a trench to charge into massed machinegun and artillery fire, he regretted with a profound sadness that his only son had been drawn into a the world's newest military vortex.

The English coast passed beneath *The A-Train's* nose just South of Birkenhead, a suburb of Liverpool. Flying through the brown-tinged haze, they all looked down upon the tangled mass of roads, rail yards, canals, factories, and houses which characterized the industrial heartland of England. The land bore a strangeness that was immediately apparent to all of them. Even the city dwellers like Clementi and Grattan had done all of their previous flying over America's sparsely populated southern and midwestern regions.

Looking down on the sprawling urban menagerie that connected Liverpool and Manchester, Clementi observed, wryly, "Gee whiz...doesn't look like the stuff in the story books." In truth, his mental picture of England had been shaped not by stories but by movies like *Robin Hood* and *Wuthering Heights.*

"Depends on what stories you read," Grattan answered. "Have you read Dickens?"

"Uh, I think so." Clementi had been required to read *David Copperfield* in high school but couldn't remember a thing about it.

"We're flying over the England that Charles Dickens desribed nearly a hundred years ago," the navigator explained.

"Right."

Below them on several occasions, they saw flights of airplanes, British and American. As they drew near to Leicester, they approached a formation of camouflage-painted twin-engined bombers in RAF markings. As the formation passed to their left, Shaw, pointing, asked, "Are those Wellingtons?"

Clementi shrugged but Grattan nodded.

Noticing how dated the fabric-covered Wellingtons looked in comparison to the sleekness of their B-26, Shaw asked, "They still fly those old crates in combat?"

"Not any more, I think," the big navigator replied. "They're probably from an operational training unit." Then added, incisively, "Like us, they're probably getting ready to see the elephant."

"See the elephant?" Shaw looked at him with puzzlement. Grattan can come up with the damndest things, he thought.

"It's an English figure of speech," he explained adroitly. "Means experiencing combat for the first time."

"Where'd they get that?"

"Kipling, I believe."

"Sure!" Clementi interjected. "Like *Gunga Den.*" He'd seen that movie, too.

Grattan gave the young co-pilot a kindly pat and said, "You kind of remind me of him, you know."

"Remind you of who?"

"Gunga Den, the Indian boy...you have the same dark, brooding eyes."

"I believe you're right, Mick," Shaw added with a smirk.

Clementi rolled his eyes and shook his head. "You guys are really full of it...you know that?"

"Enough of this inconsequential chatter, lads!" Grattan boomed. "We need to seriously start looking for landmarks. The city of Peterborough ought to be coming up over there,"he pointed, "and we should be able to see a body of water called the Wash about fifteen miles to the north. When we see those, the base'll be about another forty miles to our east, just southwest of the city of Norwich. When we get there, we'll overfly the base and watch for a green light."

"Can't we call 'em on the radio?" Clementi asked.

"This is not like the States, Luce." The big navigator regarded him seriously. "The Krauts listen to the radio traffic and probably can see us on their radar, too. If they could pinpoint where we're going to be, they could come over and shoot us down while we're landing."

"I hate it when that happens!" Shaw facetiously declared.

"No joke, Ted, the Germans monitor everything we say...they know every thing about us."

Shaw's expansive mood, however, could not be broken by the gravity of Grattan's comment. "Everything?" the pilot scoffed. "Do you suppose they even know Luce's middle name."

"Probably not." The navigator looked musingly at the co-pilot. "Just what is your middle name, Luce?"

"You guys never stop, do you? If you have to know, it's Eugene." He pronounced it Yew-jen-nay.

"Well, it's not as weird as Leroy's." Shaw mirthfully interjected.

Clementi and Grattan looked at him with curious smiles. "What's is it?" the navigator finally asked.

"No middle intital."

They all snorted in laughter.

Peterborough swam into the windscreen before them and they carefully got down to the task of finding Snetterton Heath. England had over a hundred airfields and more were being built; most of them, the bomber fields at least, looked the same. They were aware of the ignominious hazard of landing their flight at the wrong airfield, which was sure to incur the ridicule of the local aircrews. They had plenty of fuel, so they could slow down and take their time.

Shaw looked at his watch, which he'd re-set before they crossed the coast: it read 1347 GMT, for they were about thirty minutes ahead of the flight plan they'd filed in Gander. They had passed several airfields and were about thirty-five miles past Peterborough, but Grattan insisted they weren't there yet.

As a runway began to form in the distance over their nose, Grattan said, "I think that's it...Snetterton Heath."

Shaw keyed his microphone and said, "Blue leader to blue one, we have base in sight at ten miles on our twelve ...do you want to take the lead?"

"Negative, blue leader," came the reply. "Take us home!"

He keyed the microphone again and called, "Blue leader to blue flight, let's tighten this up and make it look good!"

The four B-26s drew into a neat echelon formation to the right. As they flew over the center of the field, Shaw keyed his microphone and yelled, "Blue flight, break!" One by one, the B-26s peeled off into a line astern formation, with about 1,000 feet separating each plane. Shaw drew a sigh of relief when he spotted other B-26's parked around the edge of the airfield below him. Completing his base leg and turning onto final, he watched the concrete runway grow in his windscreen. He glanced quickly at his co-pilot. "This one's mine, Luce, you can have the next one." The end of the runway slid beneath the wings of *The A-Train* and moments later, her tires kissed the pavement with scarcely a murmur.

As they turned off the runway, they were met by a jeep with a "Follow Me" sign on its back. It led them down a perimeter track to a hardstand where a ground crewman was waiting on them. Parked to one side of it was another jeep occupied by Lieutenant Colonel Ridley and an enlisted driver. Shaw braked to a stop, and he and Clementi began the process of shutting down.

They dropped out of the nose hatch and the Colonel met them with a resounding, "Welcome to England, boys!" Leaning against the side of the plane, Shaw hung back a moment while the others hefted their baggage toward the waiting jeep.

He caressed her side gently and whispered, "Thank you, ...thank you for carrying us on this long journey." He looked up at her, smiled, and whispered again, "You did a good job." He was immensely proud of her.

PART TWO:

CRUCIBLE

CHAPTER SEVEN

April 6, 1943, Snetterton Heath, England.

Though shrouded in the hanging mist typical of English mornings, the sun's rays cut through to cast irregular patterns of light on the pavement, buildings, and aircraft of the base. Except for the cement-block control tower and the arch-roofed maintenance hangars, the dominant architectural features of the field were the semi-cylindrical quonset huts in which the men slept, ate, and conducted the grim business of war. The dominant color was a sepia tone: brown-green grass, gray-brown concrete and olive drab buildings, aircraft, vehicles and clothing—the color of America at war. Parked around the perimeter of the field on hardstands, which were giant circles of concrete, were U. S. Army Air Force Martin B-26s, Consolidated B-24s and Douglas A-20s, all recently arrived. The base, in actuality, was nearly brand new. When you considered the fact that America, only fourteen months ago, had few planes, few trained aircrews, and no European bases, this airfield was nothing short of a miracle.

The only way the men could tell the base was located in England was the weather: it was damp and very chilly, the kind of climate that makes bones ache, an unwelcome surprise to the men who had recently arrived, even to the navigators who understood they were on nearly the same latitude as the Yukon Territory.

First Lieutenant Shaw stamped his feet and shoved his hands deep into the pockets of his flight jacket as he made his way along a gravel path to a quonset hut where the group commander's office was located. Accustomed as he was to the mild winters and warm springs of his native Texas, he didn't understand how a civilized society could thrive in such an uncommonly frigid climate.

The hut he entered a minute later was actually two buildings assembled end-on-end to produce a briefing room for the aircrews as well as a headquarters for the 333RD Bomb Group (Medium). The group commander, Lieutenant Colonel Ridley, had summoned him for a meeting in his office at 0700, immediately following breakfast. Rapping smartly on the doorframe, he was quickly greeted by the command, "Come!" Sitting in the office with the Colonel were Major Chase, his squadron commander, and Captain Merrill, his flight commander. Since he'd removed his cap, he didn't salute but snapped to attention and barked, "Lieutenant Shaw, reporting as ordered, SIR!"

"At ease," the Colonel said as he walked around from his desk and extended his hand to the young pilot. "You go by Ted, don't you?" he asked him.

"Yes, sir."

"Well, take a seat and relax...coffee?"

"No thank you, sir."

The Colonel smiled. "Feel free to smoke."

Shaw nodded and extracted a pack of Lucky Strikes from his inside pocket and stared a few seconds at the new white packages they came in. The Colonel produced his Zippo and lit the cigarette for him.

"We..." the Colonel motioned to the two other officers. "We are discussing the overseas organization of your squadron. Starting today, you will be the deputy leader of the number two flight under Captain Merrill." He paused a took a sip from his Coffee cup. "And Merrill, here, has been moved up to deputy squadron commander.

After you and Merrill both have flown a few missions, Merrill will move into the deputy squadron lead position, and you will take over number two flight."

Shaw's ears were ringing with this information. He'd anticipated the deputy flight commander's position, but to take over an entire flight so soon was a total surprise.

"You did a very good job with your crew in OTU. All of us," the Colonel nodded at Chase and Merrill, "feel you're ready to handle some new responsibility. "There's something else you need to know." The comment was made with a straight face. "You've been promoted to captain!"

Shaw was floored. He never, *never* had expected a promotion so soon. He'd only been in the Air Force a little over seventeen months; before the war, it could take a man five years or more to make captain!

The Colonel saw the shock on the young pilot's face.

He leaned back in his chair and said in a quiet voice, "In war things happen fast, Ted...too fast really. Only a year and a half ago...I was a captain." Grinning again, he extracted a pair of captain's bars from his shirt pocket and handed them to the young pilot. "These are an old pair of mine, *Captain*,...you'll have to buy the next pair yourself!"

"Thank you, sir." Shaw smiled at the older man with gratitude but wasn't sure he was prepared for the responsibility his new rank would bring.

The Colonel looked at young pilot's unlined face and clear eyes, wondering how many more like him they would need before this thing was over. He took a noisy slurp from his coffee mug and said, "Let's change the subject...there are some other things you need to know." The tone and expression became grave. "I've been here over two weeks now, and have attended several meetings at the 8TH Air Force head-quarters at High Wycombe. They are still working on an operations plan for the medium bombardment groups who are arriving in England now. Truth is that they are still undecided on the best method to employ us in this theater."

Shaw was a little puzzled why he was being included in a discussion about the group's operational plans but continued to listen with interest.

The Colonel answered his unasked question. "The reason I'm tell-ing you this is because it'll give you a better understanding of the information you're going to receive in future crew briefings." He paused and lit a cigarette. "The only combat experience we've had with the B-26 is with the 5TH Air Force in the Southwest Pacific Theater. The B-26 will commence combat operations with the 12TH Air Force pretty soon, but, as of now, they have no experience. The 5TH, on the other hand, has been using its B-26s for low-level bombing of tactical targets like harbor facilities, railroad yards, and supply dumps. They've done a pretty good job, but the 5TH wants to replace 'em with B-25s. You know why?" He answered his own question in an incredulous tone. "So they can convert 'em into gunships with up to eight fixed 50-caliber guns in the nose!" He clapped his hands and exclaimed, "Can you imagine that! Well anyway, they can't do that to a B-26."

The Colonel paused again to sip from the coffee mug. "Back to our problem." His face became grave again. "Fact is that the 8TH really doesn't have any kind of an op plan for using the B-26 in combat. The B-17s have hit some tactical targets on the coast of France and Bel-gium, but those were really just milk runs to get 'em started. The 8TH's prime mission with the 17s has really been strategic targets like facto-ries, refineries, and other centers of war production. The B-24 groups will be used the same way."

For the first time in his short military experience, Shaw had qualms about the wisdom of the people running the war. It amazed and alarmed him that they would send entire groups of airplanes overseas without knowing what to do with them. They'd been trained to drop bombs on targets. Surely, he thought, they couldn't have run out of targets.

"Anyway," the Colonel went on, "we expect to hear from headquarters soon. We can't put together a training program until they decide what to do with us."

As meeting ended and Shaw got up to leave, he was reminded of the old military adage, "hurry up and wait." The Colonel stopped him at the door and said, "By the way, you can also inform your navigator, Grattan, that he's been promoted to First Lieutenant, effective immediately."

The quonset huts the junior officers lived in were divided into four-man rooms; those occupied by the enlisted men, even the junior NCO's, were arranged in barracks-style, open bays. Shaw, Clementi, Grattan, and Glowgower shared a room while Milawski and Rimbaud lived in one of the enlisted huts. Unless you were a major or above, the concept of privacy was virtually nonexistent. Glowgower, however, was the only occupant bothered by the arrangement; he would have preferred a room to himself where he wouldn't be annoyed by the attempts at small talk by the others. He studiously avoided the conversation and light banter that took place among the rest of his crew. While he'd gotten to know a few of the other bombardiers in the group, they were really professional acquaintances who associated mainly with their own crews, not real friends. The Air Force had made a loner out of him. He tried to convince himself that he really didn't give a damn.

Shaw, Clementi, and Grattan returned to their room following a couple of beers at the hut, which served as the O-Club. Since it closed at 2000 on weeknights, they hadn't much choice. Grattan was usually content to lay on his bunk and read, while Shaw and Clementi were more hyperactive: they talked, listened to music, or played cribbage, a game Shaw had learned in the Air Force.

"Ted," Clementi asked, as he picked up a worn deck of cards, "where are all those English broads you were talkin' about? You know...the ones whose boyfriends are all overseas somewhere?"

"What'd you expect, Luce? A horde of females lining the fence as we came in to land, all screaming for your young body?"

"That would have been nice," the co-pilot replied.

"Well, boyo," Grattan looked up from his book. "In spite of your reputation as one of the world's great lovers, I recommend that you figure out a way to go out and find them...wherever they may be."

"We need to find a way to get into the town...into Norwich," suggested Shaw. "I'd like to see it myself."

"Why don't we check out the motor pool?" Grattan recommended. "Maybe they can fix us up with something."

"I'll check around..."

They had been told to expect mission-training exercises to begin as soon as the rest of the group arrived, but until then, they had a lot of free time on their hands. They were well rested from their trans-Atlantic flight and were bored with conversation, card games, and everything else they had been doing to occupy themselves. Two days later, Shaw was able to secure the use of one of the base jeeps for the afternoon. The motor pool sergeant was very emphatic in his instructions to Shaw: "Cap'n, you ain't gonna' see a lot a traffic on account of rationing, but you gotta' think *left* the whole time you're drivin'. We've had a mess of accidents...bad ones...'cause people don't think *left.*"

"Right, Sergeant."

"No, sir, *left.*"

Shaw drove the jeep down the gravel road which ran beside the hut where Clementi and Grattan were waiting. Glowgower had declined their invitation to go into town, saying that he had other business to take care of. The jeep Shaw was driving had a canvas top but no side curtains, and the pilot was already chilled by the short drive from the motor pool. He jumped from the jeep, shouted, "Wait a sec," and ran into the room to retrieve his shearling-lined jacket. When he returned to the group waiting on him, he asked, "Luce...you want to drive us in?"

"Uh...I." Clementi looked surpised.

"Do you want to drive?," the pilot repeated.

"Uh, no...I can't."

"You mean you've never driven a jeep?"

"I mean I've never driven anything," the co-pilot admitted.

"You don't know how to drive a car?"

"No."

The co-pilot's revelation completely astonished Shaw because everybody in west Texas had learned to drive by the age of twelve. In fact, he'd owned his first car, a beat-up Model T which his uncle had given him, at age fourteen.

"You tellin' me you can fly a 37,000 pound, twin-engined bomber...but you can't drive a car?"

"Honest to Pete, I never learned how to drive, never had the opportuniy. Besides, you don't need a car in New York ...it's a lot cheaper to ride the subway." The co-pilot, in fact, had never been outside of the New York City limits until he joined the Army Air Force.

"Well, Luce, when we get back from town, we'll try a little dual instruction on this jeep here...get you checked-out...piece of cake, huh?" Shaw climbed into the driver's seat, and turned to them with an odd grin on his face. "After we get outside the main gate on the main road, about every mile or so, one of you guys needs to remind me to 'think left.'"

"Think left?"

"Right."

The base was located near a major highway about fifteen miles southwest of Norwich in the Duchy of Norfolk. The city itself lay about thirty miles inland from the Channel Coast and about ninety miles north and slightly east of London. If you drew a straight line running east across the Channel, it would terminate at the city of Amsterdam, in occupied Holland. Norwich had been a quiet city surrounded by a province of small farms and villages—until it had been invaded. Not by Germans but by RAF and Army Air Force personnel who were establishing fighter and bomber bases all over the countryside. England, particularly the region called East Anglia, was fast becoming the world's largest aircraft carrier. It wasn't happening overnight, but the Allies were deadly earnest in their intent to take the war to Germany.

Shaw had no trouble keeping to the left side of the road but felt it was like flying a plane on instruments—you could never take you mind off of it for one minute.

The outskirts of the city displayed walled and fenced cottages, which turned into a series of two-story row houses as they neared the center of town. "Let's look for a bar, I could use some refreshment," Clementi suggested from the back seat.

"They don't have the kind of bars you're used to, Luce" Grattan observed. "What they have are places called public houses...pubs for short, where they serve beer mostly."

"I don't give a damn what they call it as long as I can get an ice cold brew."

Shaw slowed the jeep in front of a ancient-appearing two-story, Tudor-style building with a slate roof. A painted sign in front bore the legend, *Golden Sovereign*, and a few cars were parked near the entrance. "Does this look like one...a pub?" the pilot asked Grattan.

"Looks like it to me...let's go in and have a look."

Though he'd never seen one before, the inside of the pub was exactly what Grattan had imagined it would look like: a dark room with a low-beamed ceiling, chairs and tables of dark wood that looked hand-hewn, clean sawdust on the floor, a musty smell of tobacco smoke and old wood polish, and several middle-aged landsmen wearing slop hats quietly playing darts in one corner. They sat down at the small bar on wooden stools which had backs and armrests. The barman, an older man with gapped-teeth and ruddy features, stepped in front of them and asked, "May I get you gen'lmen summat'?"

"Three beers, please," Grattan replied with a smile.

"Roight you are, zur," said the barman, then wheeled away to snatch three large glasses from a shelf behind the bar and draw the beers from a immense wooden keg. He placed the foaming glasses in front of the three and said," There you are, zurs, that'll be one and a thruppence." Grattan laid a two-schilling piece on the counter and told the man to keep the change.

"Thankee, zur."

Clementi looked suspiciously at the dark, frothy liquid in his glass and asked, "You're positive this is beer?"

"They call it stout," Grattan explained. "It's really more of an ale than beer."

Clementi took a drink, coughed and almost spat it out onto the bar. "What the hell...it's hot!" he choked.

The barman overheard the commotion and spun around. "'Ot, zur?" he questioned, then touched the back of his hand to Clementi's glass and said benignly, "Oh, no, zur, it's not 'ot, 'tis nice and cool, so it is."

"I mean it's not cold," he told the man.

"Cold? Of course it's not, zur."

"Why not...why isn't it cold?"

"T'would ruin the taste, zur, so it would." The man smiled at the co-pilot in the kindly way that an adult smiles at a child who has asked an irrational question.

"Any thin' else, zur?"

"No thanks...this'll be fine."

Grattan advised Clementi that English beer was an acquired taste. Clementi glumly added warm beer to his long list of Air Force sufferings. Leaving the pub after finishing their drinks, the three drove into the center of the old city. They noticed a number of other Air Force servicemen walking down the stone-paved sidewalks, some with English girls on their arms. Other uniforms were in evidence, too, mostly the sky blue of the RAF, but occasionally the brown of the Royal Army or the dark blue of the Royal Navy. It seemed that most of the men in town, at least those younger than middle age, were wearing some kind of uniform. Britain had been at war for over four years and the austerity of many of the shops and stores showed it.

Grattan suggested they visit a small bookshop across the street. The only one of the three who was a studious reader, the amiable navigator enjoyed all types of books, including mysteries and western stories, and non-fiction works on scholarly subjects. While in England, he hoped he would have the opportunity to visit Stratford sometime, the home of the bard, William Shakespeare. Shakespeare had awakened his passion for great literature in his early teens. Clementi and Shaw, in contrast, rarely read anything as a form of entertainment.

Leaving Clementi outside to scout the sidewalks for any young, unaccompanied females who might happen to pass by, Grattan and Shaw entered the shop. After browsing a while, Grattan purchased a copy of author Nevil Shute's latest book, *Pastoral.* He showed the book to Shaw. "You might like this one, Ted, it's a story about an RAF bomber base." As they started to step out of the shop, Shaw, noticing a paper sign taped to the inside of the shop's front window, said, "Wait a minute...what's this?" The hand lettered sign announced a "NAAFI Tea Dance" scheduled the next day at a local meeting hall. "Hey, Luce, look at this...some kinda' dance." He pointed to the sign.

Clementi curiously examined the sign. "NAAFI? What's a NAAFI?"

"I've heard of it somewhere." Shaw looked up in thought. "Some kind of British USO outfit, I think."

"You want to go?" the co-pilot asked him with a hopeful expression.

"Uh...." Shaw really didn't want to go but heard himself saying, "Sure, ol' buddy...why not."

"How come you didn't ask me?" Grattan feigned a hurt expression.

Shaw chortled at the big navigator before Clementi could answer. "An old, bald-headed geezer like you would probably scare all the young women off."

"Geezer!" Grattan retorted in mock seriousness. "I'll have you know, Captain, most women, old and young, consider baldness to be a sign of virility!"

Clementi, embarrased by his ommission, apologetically said, "I didn't mean, Mick, you're welcome...."

Grattan held up his hand and smiled. "I'm just pulling your chain, boyo. I don't know how to dance and never developed a taste for tea. You guys can tell me what I missed when you get back." They drove back to the base in good spirits. It had refreshed them to be away from their military routine, if only for a few hours, and Shaw completely forgot about giving Clementi a driving lesson.

The next afternoon, dressed in pinks and greens, their Class A uniform, Shaw and Clementi caught a ride into Norwich on bus loaded with other officers and enlisted men from the base. As they settled in their seats, Clementi was overflowing with enthusiasm. He drummed his hands on the seat in front of him and declared, "Boy oh boy...can't wait! I haven't been in the same room with a women since we left Barksdale! What about you?"

"Lookie-lookie, but don't touch...that's my plan." In truth, Shaw didn't even plan to look. While his urges were just as healthy as the next man's, the sum of his romantic experience with women began— and ended—with Mary Beth Wainwright.

"Suit yourself, pal...I'm ready to touch some soft skin and smell some sweet perfume." Clementi wasn't surprised by Shaw's comment—the girl in Texas had a hold over the pilot he didn't understand.

The bus pulled up in front of the meeting hall where the dance was being held, and the servicemen began to file out and go inside. In addition to the girls congregated to one side of the large room, a large number of young men in RAF uniforms, stood around smoking and waiting on the band to set up. On the improvised stage, another group of RAF men were setting up the bandstand. A distinguished looking, middle-aged English woman stepped onto stage, and a very young, lank-haired RAF Leading Aircraftsman nodded to her that the microphone was ready.

"Good afternoon!" she boomed in a bright upper class accent. "I'm Mrs. Parkwood, your hostess for the dance, and on behalf of the Navy, Army, and Air Force Institutes, I welcome you all. We owe a special thanks," she said, pointing to the musicians, "to RAF Coltishall and the 78TH Fighter Wing band, who will provide the music today." She motioned again to the uniformed musicians standing behind her, and clapping her hands, caused the girls and the RAF personnel to erupt into a riotous round of applause, belatedly followed by the Air Force men.

"I welcome, too, our American friends from Snetterton Heath, who are recently arrived." The comment was met by audible groans and hoots from the RAF men. Noting that the men outnumbered the women by a margin of three to one, Shaw silently hoped both sides would keep their wits. He heard the hostess continue in a very firm voice. "For those of you who are new to NAAFI dances, you need to be aware of a few rules: one, no alcoholic drinks are allowed in the hall at any time. Anyone seen drinking will be asked to leave."

That'll help, Shaw thought. "Two, none of the girls may leave the hall while the dance is in progress. And three...*please* cooperate on this one...the girls are to change partners after each number. We want all of you boys to have a nice time, so we need to share the girls, agreed? There are refreshments and snacks at the rear of the room...please enjoy yourselves." She nodded to the band leader, a boyish trumpet player, who gave the band a one-two-three, and started a lively Kay Kyser tune.

The RAF men, veterans of these affairs, swiftly moved onto the dance floor and grabbed the available partners when the music started. The Air Force men were left in clustered groups next to the dance floor, looking a little dazed and disoriented. "Not exactly what I expected," Clementi grumbled, "not a bit. We may have to go head-to-head with these RAF jerks!" The comment was mainly bluster.

"You gotta' be patient, Luce," Shaw strongly warned him. "They knew what to expect."

The Air Force men were ready the next time. When the music stopped, they bolted onto the floor to claim their partners. A few of the RAF men protested but, to Shaw's relief, they reluctantly stepped aside to allow the Americans their turn. Clementi did not even get a good look at the girl he'd asked before the music started again. She was a short, pleasantly attractive girl with chestnut brown hair cut in a bob, who could not have been a day over seventeen. As they moved in time to the music, the co-pilot said, "Hi, my name's Luce."

"Luke?" she asked curiously.

"No, Luce...you know, like loose change!" He almost had to scream over the noise of the band.

She nodded prettily and shouted back, "Ay'm Sandra!" Which she pronouced as Sawndra. "Pleased t'meet ya."

"You from here...uh, Sandra?"

"Noo, actu'ly ay'm from Pakenham, noeth of 'ere." She had a soft, rounded country accent.

"Ay see you're a flyer...wot d'you fly?" she asked, pointing to the wings pinned to Clementi's chest.

"B-26 Marauders...you know the type?"

"Noo, can't say as ay do."

Clementi was about to explain further when the music stopped and a burly RAF Flight Sergeant appeared at his side with a stern expression. "Moi turn, mate," he ordered. Clementi was about to tell him to buzz off when the girl, an old hand at NAAFI dances, squeezed his arm and said, "Ay'll save one for you later."

Shaw stood at the back of the room, sipped a cup of strong, sweetened English tea and munched a small, tasteless cookie. The dance had settled into a reasonably civilized routine in which the RAF boys would monopolize the girls on one number and the Americans on the next. To Shaw's relief, only minor grumbling occured when the dance floor exchanges had been made. Since there was no place to sit, he leaned against a wall and watched the dancing couples gyrate around the floor. The British servicemen, he noted were far more conservative dancers than their more acrobatic American counterparts. The girls seemed adaptable to either style.

Clementi, he noticed, was a skilful dancer but not one of the gymnastic extroverts. The fast-working co-pilot had yet to dance with the same girl twice, each brief pairing following the same hurried pattern: "My names is____. I'm from____. I'm a pilot with____." Period. Clementi found it impossible to break the ice with someone during the brief numbers, trying to dance and nearly screaming to make himself heard over the clamoring music. Some of the girls, he hoped, would hang around after the dance and perhaps go somewhere for a drink. Standing on the rim of the dance floor, waiting for his next turn, he noticed directly in front of him the small pixyish girl who'd been his first partner. When he animatedly waved to her, she smiled brightly and, to the annoyance of her RAF companion, enthusiastically waved back. As soon as the song ended, he rushed onto the floor to claim her for the next dance number which, to his great relief, was a slow waltz.

"Would it be possible to see you after the dance?" he asked her quickly.

"Oh, noo, I canna' miss my ride back home." The question was answered with a friendly finality.

"Do you come here often, to Norwich I mean?"

"Noo, only t'dances, when we have transport."

Clementi was completedly stumped, knowing his time with her would run out in about one minute. Think quick, he told himself. "Do you have a phone...somewhere I can call you?"

She seemed hesitant, but said, "At work p'haps...you can try there and leave a message."

He groped for the pencil stub in his coat pocket and extracted a dollar bill from his wallet to write on. "O.k., I'm ready." Just then the music stopped and he was still scribbling down the number when an RAF Pilot Officer led her away in the opposite direction. A farewell glance and she was gone. Remembering he'd forgotten to ask her last name, he hoped there was only one Sandra employed at the place she worked. If he managed to get her on the phone, he gloomily wondered what his next move would be. Not much of a prospect, he concluded.

Soon after the last dance number ended, the girls obediently filed out of the hall, boarded an antiquated bus, and vanished in a cacophony of grinding gears. Shaw, at the back of the room, had not danced but had sipped the tepid tea and conversed with the other servicemen, one of them a schoolboyish, sandy-haired RAF Flying Officer based at nearby Coltishall. The British pilot, he learned, had been flying combat operations for over a year and had recently converted from Mk.V Spitfires to the newer ground attack version of the Hawker Typhoon. This airplane, he told Shaw, had been configured to carry bombs or rockets as well as the normal 20 millimeter cannon and .303 machine gun armament. The main targets assigned would be military fortifications on the French and Belgian coasts. "If we can knock-out some of the ack-ack guns," he explained, "we should make life a bit easier for you bomber boys."

"We've been briefed to expect pretty bad flak," Shaw said to the Britisher.

"Murderous, more like!" the RAF pilot warned in a tone that spoke of experience. "In the heavily defended sites, they can set up barrage fire that amounts to a wall of steel...anything that tries to fly through it is shredded!" He gave Shaw an appraising look. "You Yanks are bloody brave to have a go at it during daylight."

"What about the German fighters?" Shaw asked, soberly.

"Fighters!" The Flying Officer looked at Shaw with a grim expression. "They're even worse. At least you can fly around the stinking flak." He made weaving motions with his beer glass. "We've been bombing the Huns for almost two years, your lot for over six months, and it doesn't seemed to have caused them more than a bloody inconvenience." The RAF man emptied his glass and wiped his mouth with his sleeve. Staring vacantly into the empty glass, he murmured, "Our intelligence wogs tell us they're putting up fighters in record numbers. Makes one wonder, doesn't it?"

Though this information was not new to Shaw, it was sobering to hear it from the grim-faced combat pilot. He was thankful that his nervous co-pilot had not heard the conversation. When Shaw and Clementi met up again outside the hall, they decided to catch the bus headed back to the base rather than go pub-crawling.

Arriving at the base a half hour later, Clementi headed for the O-Club to make the last round, and Shaw returned to their hut. Glow-gower was gone, as usual, and he found Grattan sitting at their table writing a letter. The big navigator smiled up at the pilot and inquired, "How'd it go?"

"Nice...more like a church social, very up and up, no drinking and all, and the girls were mostly young, nice types. There were about three guys there for every girl, and a bunch of the guys were there from a local RAF base. You should have seen ol' Luce scampering back and forth to take his turn on the dance floor. Reminded me of a relay race. He and a lot of the other guys weren't too thrilled with the arrangement, but there was damn-all they could do about it."

"Any trouble?" Grattan asked.

"A few hot words now and then but no fighting. I can see how the RAF fellas' would be a little pissed with the Air Force showing up on their turf all of a sudden." Shaw sat on the bunk next to Grattan and lit a cigarette. "I talked to a couple of 'em...RAF guys...and they're not a bad bunch really. From what they told me, the stuff we've heard from group about the flak and fighters was no exaggeration, and it was a little scary to hear it from someone who's actually seen it first hand."

When Grattan got up and laid down on bunk, Shaw got out his writing kit and sat down to compose a letter.

April 11, 1943

Dear Mary Beth,

I just returned from a night on the town with Luce Clementi. Don't worry, I behaved myself!

Luce asked me to go to a dance in town, and I thought he'd be more comfortable if I tagged along. I played wallflower while Luce danced with the girls. I didn't see a girl there half as pretty as you!

I think I've made a lot of headway toward getting to know Luce better. When he comes out of his shell, he's kind of a fun guy. I hope he'll hold up when we get into combat. (Me too).

Glowgower still doesn't speak to me on a personal basis and I've pretty much given up trying to be friendly. I've never had any one stay mad at me like that. Mick says that things will change or not change, and there's not a whole lot I can do about it. Mick reports that Mick, jr. is growing like a weed, and he said that Eleanor really appreciated receiving a letter from you. I appreciate it, too. Mick has become my best friend in the Air Force. He understands people a lot better than I do and gives me good advice.

I'm getting more used to the English weather or maybe it's getting warmer here. Most of the group is here now, and I expect to be flying again as soon as tomorrow. I still don't know when we're going to start combat operations, soon I expect.

We have a big briefing in the morning, and I'm sure the brass will fill us in then.

I appreciate the extra information about Mom and Dad. I'm glad Dad's gotten some help on the ranch, even if they're wetbacks who may not stay too long. I've heard about prisoners of war being used as farm labor, but I don't know if any of them will make it down to cattle country.

Honey, I have to tell you that your decision to move to Dallas and work at the new North American plant makes me a little nervous. I know you can take care of yourself, but Dallas is such a big, wide-open place. I understand it's a real good opportunity, and that you're saving up for us.

You know I trust you always and will live with what ever you decide to do. As for us, as soon as I know when we're returning home, you can start planning a wedding date. Honey, it just sets me on fire to think about it. Every time I climb into the seat of that plane, I take part of you with me. It's the thing that really keeps me going. I must be the luckiest guy in the Air Force. Loving you means more to me than anything else in the world.

Your ever loving,

Ted

CHAPTER EIGHT

April 12, 1943, Snetterton Heath, England.

The aircrews stood to attention as Lieutenant Colonel Ridley briskly walked to the front of the briefing hut and ascended the low stage. "Good morning, men!" he resounded, facing the crowd. "Please take your seats. I want to welcome all of you who are newly arrived."

When the room became still, the Colonel's face was serious. "The big news today, men, is that the 333RD has received an operations plan from 8TH Air Force Headquarters. And as soon as this afternoon, we're going to start flying practice exercises." He waited for the chair-scraping to stop. "Like we did at Barksdale, we'll start the exercises in squadron elements and work up to flying as a group. I can't reveal to you yet what our exact mission plans are, but I can tell you that we're going to hit the Huns where it hurts...we're really going to nail the sons-of-bitches!" He was repeating a comment he'd heard from his superiors at headquarters. "You'll be led today by your squadron commanders, except for the 420TH, which I will lead. Later, when we practice as a group, Major Spinelli, Major Edrington, and I will take turns leading, and we'll do the same thing when we start flying combat. Please hold any questions you have until the briefing is concluded. Major Edrington is going to brief you on the exercize scheduled for this afternoon."

The tall, weathered-looking major stepped onto the platform and turned and smiled at the assembled crews.

"Gentleman, what I'm about to tell you today is classified ...for your ears only...cannot be discussed outside this room. As some of you already know, we've had some combat experience with the B-26 in the Pacific Theater, and 8TH has decided to use that experience here in Europe."

This caused some low murmuring among the men who had some understanding of what he was talking about. The Major continued, "We are not being assigned the same mission as the heavies...to go in deep and hit strategic targets; we are going after smaller targets which are harder to hit, something we can do with a level of precision that the heavies can't atch." The room became graveyard quiet: they waited for the boom to drop.

The Major leaned over the podium, his hands gripping the front of it, a neutral expression on his face. "The way we're going to do this, gentlemen, is to come in low...hit them at low level." Most of the seated men looked they'd been broad-sided—it wasn't something they'd expected to hear—*this wasn't what they'd been trained to do!* Shaw, not surprised by the news, remained rigidly pokerfaced. Clementi, taken aback completely, gripped the pilot's arm and hissed, "Low level! Where did they come up with that shit?"

"Get a grip on yourself, Luce." Shaw tried to sound reassuring. "You know they've got it all doped out." He silently suppressed his doubts about headquarter's lack of actual experience with low-level strikes in this theater. Only one way to find out, he thought.

The order in the room had degenerated to a babble of peevish whispering and shuffling feet.

"You men settle down and listen!" Edrington stamped his foot and suddenly barked. "Now..." he noisily cleared his throat. "The main anti-aircraft defenses the Germans have been building up are designed to knock down airplanes flying at anywhere between 15,000 and 25,000 feet ...you think about that for a minute." He paused to meet the gloomy stares coming from his audience. "We'll be going in *under* that to confuse their defenses, and we'll be under their long-range search radars, too...they won't see us coming. By the time they've scrambled their fighters, we'll be hauling ass out of there!" Sounds good, Shaw thought, but speculated whether the canny Germans were truly capable of being surprised. He hoped so.

"The British have had some experience with low-level ops," the Major continued the explanation. "Call 'em 'rhubarbs'...small formations that come in real low and hit tactical targets mainly. They normally do this when there's solid overcast or at least eight-tenths cloud cover...they come in under it." Listening to this, Shaw's thoughts flashed momentarily to the Typhoon pilot he'd talked to at the dance. "The RAF's been pretty successful at this," the Major went on, "but, unfortunately, it doesn't do much serious damage to the Germans, just mainly pisses them off." The comment brought a few smiles. "If we operate in a similar way in group strength, we can inflict a hell of a lot more damage! Any questions so far?"

A young frizzy-haired lieutenant raised his hand. "Are we gonna' have a fighter escort on these low-level missions, Major?"

Edrington knew the question would be asked and composed himself to answer. "No...we will not."

With this announcement, order dissolved again, causing the Major to slap his hand on the podium and bellow, "Listen up dammit! We're better off without an escort! If the fighters went along, they would have to be positioned above us, where they would be visible on radar...that would tip the Huns off bigtime and we'd lose the element of surprise!" The stony expressions on the faces of the men seated before him told Edrington they weren't convinced, not by a long shot. In truth, neither was he.

Edrington made a few more comments then turned the briefing over to Captain Burnside, the lead bombardier, a corpulent man in his mid-twenties with a mass of dark curly hair. "Mornin', gents!" he exclaimed with bustling humor as he leaped onto the raised platform like a perform-ing bear. "Since the Major told you what we're gonna' do...you might be interested in how we're gonna' do it. Are ya'?" The watching faces nod-ded, softened by the roly-poly bombardier's infectious liveliness. "First thing we've got to do..." he explained that the Norden bomb sights would be removed from the planes and replaced by a D-8 low-level sight. In the middle of the room, Glowgower sat bolt upright when he heard this. The annoucement of the low level missions had been a shock-ing blow, but he was completely incensed by the business of replacing the Norden with some Rube Goldberg gadget he'd never even practiced with. All of the proficiency he'd developed in medium altitude bombing was suddenly useless. Damn them all, he fumed. It would be like starting all over again—from scratch. It didn't occur to him that every other bombardier in the group was affected the same way.

The briefing broke into smaller groups, and Shaw and his crew sat in a huddle with Major Chase, their squadron commander. Chase was a short, muscular man in his mid-twenties who had recently been promoted to Ma-jor and given a squadron. "I know you boys are a kinda' spooked by this low-level stuff, but the experts up at 8TH figure it's the most defensible mission we can fly right now." He tried to sound confident.

One of the pilots, a sallow-faced Lieutenant, nervously asked, "What do, uh...the headquarters people expect our loss ratios to be on these missions, Major?"

"Loss ratios!" Chase retorted. "That's a dumb-ass question, Per-kins...why don't you ask me something I know the answer to?" Giving the shame-faced Lieutenant a shrug, he said, "We won't know that until we fly a mission ...o.k.?" He shook himself and cleared his throat. "Back to business ...today we're going form up into box formations and fly due west of here at 8,000 feet, cross the coast of Wales, just North of Aberystwyth, and run out into Cardigan Bay for about forty miles. Then we're going to do a one-eighty and drop down to the deck, say about 200 feet, and make a run-in back to the Welsh coast. We're going to use two IP's on this exercise: one to set up diverging headings for the flights and the second for the run-in to the target. Just before we reach the second IP, about six miles from the coast, we'll pop up to 2,000 feet to make our bomb runs. They'll have large markers set up as targets. As soon as we bomb the target, we'll dive back down on deck and haul-ass into the bay. After we've made our escape, we'll climb back up to our cruise altitude and return to base. We won't be dropping any practice bombs today; this is mainly low-level navigation and for-mation practice, got it?" Receiving an affirmative nod from the huddled group, he looked down at his wristwatch. "Let's hack our watches at 1006 in ten seconds ...three, two, one...hack! Engine start-up at 1030, taxi at 1035 and wheels in the well at 1040!"

Shaw had become bored by the six-day layoff and was glad to get back in the air again. When he and the crew walked to flight line to pre-flight *The A-Train,* he noticed an enlisted man standing on a short step-ladder painting something on the side of the group commander's B-26. He told Clementi to start the preflight with Milawski and walked over to the man on the ladder. The pilot smiled at the man and said, "Hi."

"Hullo....," the man squinted at the nametag on Shaw's jacket, "...*Captain*, what can I do for ya'?"

"You the group artist?"

"Kinda'...I lettered billboards before the war."

"Could you paint a name on the side of our plane?"

"Which one is it?"

Shaw pointed. "Three-three four over there...where those guys are standing...see it?"

"Uh." The man squinted again. "I think so. What do you want painted on it?"

"*THE A-TRAIN.*"

"After the song?"

"Right."

"How big you want the letters?

"About ten to twelve inches tall, that sound right?"

"That's on the big side."

"Well, she's a big airplane."

"O.k., what color you want?"

"Red...you got red?"

"No problem."

An hour and fifteen minutes later they crossed the coast of Wales at 8,000 feet and headed out into Cardigan Bay. Shaw was flying deputy flight lead right behind Merrill, about 25 feet lower, and there were B-26s stepped up on either side of him at 50 foot intervals. This position, like the transept in the letter "A," didn't allow him much leeway, but had the advantage of letting him to move directly into the lead slot if something happened to Merrill. Visibility was marginal because his view was substantially blocked by aircraft on three sides. Shaw discovered that his position wasn't very difficult to maintain in the smooth air over the bay.

The radio crackled to life. "Catfish leader to catfish flight, we are five minutes away from our turn-around and descent point, acknowledge, over."

"Catfish able."

"Catfish baker."

"Catfish charlie."

The A-Train was catfish baker-one. Shaw listened for the execute signal on the command channel and watched the movement of Merrill's tailplane in his windscreen. The radio came to life again, "Catfish leader to catfish flight, reverse course left to zero-eight-five, standard rate turn on my signal...MARK!" Eighteen B-26's began to wheel around to the opposite heading, some sliding in and out of formation, while Chase barked over the radio, "Watch your formation! Keep it tucked in! Close it up!"

Once the formation had steadied on the new course, they began their descent to the water. Except for a few who had engaged in illegal flat-hatting, most of them had not flown a B-26 this low before. They streaked in at about 220 m.p.h above the bay, turning the water below them into a continuous blur. Shaw was exhilarated by the wild sensation of speed, but grateful that he only had to watch Merrill's plane slightly above him, not the altimeter. If Merrill erringly flew them into the sea, he'd know it for only a second—at this speed, the water was like a brick wall. Without shifting his glance, he leaned over and tapped his co-pilot. "Luce....take it for a spell, o.k.?"

The co-pilot flexed his fingers, reached for the yoke, and said, "I've got it."

Shaw noticed Merrill's plane beginning to wander around in the windscreen. "Easy, Luce! he coached. "Take it easy, you're over-controlling...no different than flying at 8,000 feet...don't even think about the water down here...just watch Merrill up there, all right? That's better." The B-26 settled down as the co-pilot relaxed and found his groove. Shaw removed two APC tablets from the small tin in his pocket and washed them down with cold coffee and wondered how bad the shoulder aches might get on really long missions. While he was massaging the kinks from his shoulders, Grattan stuck his head between the pilots and told them, "We ought to be about six minutes from the IP if my calculations match the lead navigator's."

"Better tell, Glow," Shaw advised the big man. "I guess he's down there setting up that new bomb sight." The sight he was referring to, the D-8, worked similar to the adjustible sight on an infantry rifle: you set the range and elevation, then pickled the bombs when the target was interposed on the sight. Unlike the Norden, the bombardier didn't control the plane during the bomb run, but would guide the pilot by voice command. In this situation they would bomb visually, that is, all planes in the squadron would drop their bombs on command from the bombardier in the ship leading the flight. There really wasn't much for Glowgower to do as long as Merrill's plane stayed in front of them, and with no bombs to drop, he was little more than a spectator. It annoyed him to sit in the nose like a bump on a log waiting for the bogus drop command. When they'd practiced bomb runs back at Barksdale, he'd felt important—indispensable in fact, but now—any idiot could sit up here and press the pickle switch.

"Navigator to bombardier, expect to reach our first IP in about one minute." Each flight would turn onto a separate, pre-arranged course. If they converged on the target from four different angles, the theory went, they would prevent the anti-aircraft gunners from concentrating their fire.

"Roger," Glowgower answered from the nose.

"Navigator to pilot, standby for a left turn to a heading of zero-four-five on command."

The command channel came alive. "Catfish leader to catfish flight, turn to first IP...MARK!" The three six-plane flight elements wheeled onto four separate headings.

"Navigator to pilot, standby for new IP, turn right to a heading of one-three-five on command."

The radio crackled again, Merrill this time. "Catfish baker leader to catfish baker flight, turn to new IP..." several seconds elapsed, then "...MARK!"

Shaw rolled the B-26 into the turn, simultaneously moving the throttles forward as the flight climbed up to its bombing altitude of 2,000 feet. Leveling out and approaching the target, the flight maintained the higher power setting to give them an indicated airspeed of 240 m.p.h. There were now three separate elements of six bombers, each converging toward the same target from a different heading.

Glowgower spoke sharply into the interphone, "Bomb bay doors open! Intervalometer set!" The bombardier watched the rapidly approaching coast through the clear nose dome, the pickle switch tensed in left hand to toggle the imaginary bombs. They had told him to expect the target markers about a minute after they crossed the coast.

In the waist of the airplane, Milawski and Rimbaud sat huddled on the floorboard watching the sea swiftly recede behind them throught the small waist windows. "This low-level sheeit is fo' d'birds!" Rimbaud shouted over the roaring slipstream coming from the open bomb bay doors. The proximity to the white-capped sea made Milawski uneasy too, but he ignored the tail gunner's comment.

"Ain't gonna' shoot nuthin' down heah 'less some big ol' fish jump up after us!" the tail gunner jeered.

Scowling at him, Milawski barked, "In case you're too stupid to figure it out, them Kraut fighters can fly low, too...and I 'spect one of these days one's gonna' come right up our tail and drill your dumb ass good, Leroy!" The flight engineer grinned at the thought, and hooted, "Them Kraut fighters are armed with 20 millimeters that'll turn you into Cajun gumbo!" He laughed out loud.

Though the comment scared the crap out of Rimbaud, he just sneered back at the flight engineer and gave him the finger. That dumb polack bastard had been bad-mouthing him ever since the flight over. He'd wait until the right time in the right place, then he'd give the little wise-ass a taste of his Louisiana nigger-sticker.

The flight leader's radio crackled on again. "Bombs away!" Almost instantaneously, Shaw noticed the flash of the bomb release signal light on the top left side of his instrument panel, indicating that Glowgower had toggled the pickle switch. For whatever else he may think of the unsociable bombardier, he had to admit that the man had learned to perform his job with almost flawless precision.

Since there were no bombs, Glowgower waited about a minute then moved the bomb bay selector handle aft. He called on the intercom, "Bomb bay doors closed!" Shaw watched the doors close on Merrill's plane and followed him through the steep turn off target and descent back down to 200 feet. With the engines running at maximum continuous power, they dove toward the sea at over 300 m.p.h.

Flying low over the bay for five more minutes, they climbed back up to 8,000 feet and re-assembled the formation. Then, easing their speed back to 200 m.p.h, they reversed course toward Snetterton Heath. They were now sandwiched between a scattered cloud deck below them, and a broken layer of cloud several thousand feet above. Shaw hoped the base wasn't socked in. Weary from the stress of the exercize, the last thing he wanted to do was make a landing approach through cloud on instruments.

To his annoyance, however, the base reported a solid overcast with cloud bases at 2,000 feet above ground level—AGL—and visibility in haze and mist down to two and a half miles. Merrill advised them to separate at about one-mile intervals for the landing approach. They would overfly the base for about ten minutes to the East, do a one-eighty, and commence an instrument letdown using the radio compass. Right after they completed the turn-around point, Shaw abruptly announced to Clementi, "This one's yours, Luce...let's switch seats so you can see the gauges." He knew that his co-pilot hated flying on instruments and had had trouble with it in flight school. "This one's a piece of cake, Luce...you oughta' pop out a mile or so in front of the runway."

Clementi heaved a sigh, then reluctantly exchanged places, strapped-in, and took the controls. "I've got it," he said. Grattan came on the intercom, "Navigator to pilot, I'll follow you on the RC and give you a course for the runway in about a sec...start a 500 foot per minute letdown now." A minute later, the navigator called back, "Turn left to a heading of two-five-seven."

Clementi clicked his intercom button to acknowledge but kept his attention on the undercast toward which the aircraft was sinking. As the B-26 descended into tendrils of the gray murk, the co-pilot began the relentless tedium of his instrument scan. As he was still learning, flying an airplane on instruments was an unnatural act; the instructors in flight training told you to distrust your basic senses and instincts—the same ones you learned to fly with—and then they taught you to utterly and completely rely on the needles and pointers in the glass-faced gauges in front of you. The gauges are truth, they said, and if you failed to believe in them—you would die.

Clementi understood this, but he didn't like it. He held the course and watched the altimeter needle creep down through 3,000 feet. Ought to see something soon, he thought, pretty soon. He watched the RC needle waiver as they neared the station. Moments later the gray shrould parted and the airfield suddenly swam into view off to the left.

"Gear down! Full Flaps!" Clementi screamed. "We're high!" Jerking both throttles back to idle, he banked the big airplane in a swerving S-turn toward the runway. The end of the runway rapidly grew in the windscreen as the co-pilot jockeyed the throttles back and forth in an attempt to check the descent rate and slow the big bomber down. As the threshold of the runway slid under the nose, the co-pilot horsed back the yoke and jerked the throttles back to idle. *THUMP-SCREECH! THUMP-SCREECH!* The tires noisily protested as they contacted the unyielding pavement.

In the waist of the plane, Rimbaud rubbed his behind and exclaimed, "Skippah musta' let the wop land the plane again!" Milawski frowned at the comment, but he silently concurred it was easy to tell who was landing the airplane, no comparison really.

As Clementi steered the B-26 off the runway in the drizzling rain, he gave Shaw a scowl. "I'd give that landing about a two on a scale of ten."

Shaw mirthfully grinned at the frowning co-pilot. "Well, you know what they say about landings, don't you?"

Clementi derisivly rolled his eyes, then, laughing, they both recited the adage: "Any landing you can walk away from is a *good* landing!"

Later that day, the billboard painter who was probably one of the oldest PFC's in the Air Corps, stepped down from his ladder and admired his handiwork. The name on the side of the airplane in large, red, italic block letters read: *THE A-TRAIN.* Funny name for an airplane, he thought, but whatever makes these boys happy is all right by me. He gathered up his supplies, picked up the ladder, and left.

Her time of waiting was over. Her young men had claimed her and brought her on a long journey to a far place. Oh, how they had dressed her up: she now had large white letters on her sides; she had a broad white stripe on her tail; and she had her name...her real name...painted in large red letters on her side for the whole world to see! She was complete. Ready. Ready for war.

Over the next three weeks, the olive drab B-26s of the 333RD Bomb Group (M) became a common sight over Cardigan Bay and the Welsh coast, dropping hundreds of flour-filled, practice bombs until most of the pilots, navigators, and bombardiers in the group had developed passable proficiency in low level bombing. With *The A-Train* acting as flight lead, Glowgower flew as lead bombardier on several of the sorties, turning in some of the best bomb scores in the group. During this process, Clementi learned, to his consternation, that instrument approaches were a part of the standard bill of fare for flying in England.

In spite of improvement, he felt his efforts were was still amateurish—on the ragged edge of minimal competence. Shaw was pleased with their overall progress but frequently wondered if the training would ever end. He soon found out—their first mission had been scheduled for May 12, 1943.

CHAPTER NINE

May 12, 1943, Snetterton Heath, England.

The orderly awoke Shaw and announced, "Mission briefing, sir, at 0400." The pilot blearily looked at his wristwatch, which read 0315, and listened to the coughs and groans of the other men in the room as they got up. He hadn't slept well. Rolling up to a sitting position, a strange tightness gripped the pit of his stomach, caused bile to rise in his throat, accelerated his hearbeat. In his previous Air Force experience, he'd been nervous, excited, even a little scared, but this sensation was new. It was fear, he realized—old fashioned, gut-churning fear. If a man was going to see the elephant for the first time, as Grattan had cleverly put it, he would feel this way—unless he was nuts. In a way he was relieved that his fear had surfaced in tangible form; at least knowing it was lurking there, he could try to separate it from the process of rational thought. He would need his wits today, all of them. Maybe this is a good time to pray, he decided.

In the chow line that morning, the men seemed to move in slow, mechanical motions, as if thinking through each move, but, at the same time, they talked louder, the laughter exaggerated. There were several instances of sharp rebukes over trivial things. The tension in the atmosphere was palpable. Shaw curiously noticed that his normally ravenous co-pilot was eating little for breakfast—toast and coffee. The pilot wasn't real hungry himself but knew needed to get something on his stomach, would burn a lot of calories over the next five or six hours. "Luce, these flapjacks look good...how 'bout a couple?" he offered.

"All right," Clementi answered without enthusiasm. Shaw served himself then forked two large pancakes onto his co-pilot's tray.

Shaw noticed that even Grattan seemed have an expression of forced cheer. The pilot didn't worry—the big navigator was the strongest man in the crew. Behind Shaw and the others, Glowgower's handsome face wore the impassive, disinterested mask he always used as a veil over his emotions. The bombardier's struggle to maintain his outward demeanor and his inward focus was apparent to no one. Over and over, like a silent mantra, he superimposed one thought over the chaos of his mind: the mission and the target—after that, nothing mattered, didn't exist.

When the briefing started a little later, it included only aircrews from the 424TH squadron. The absence of the others was conspicuous, made the room seem cavernous. As he stepped up on the platform to get things started, the group commander's usual joviality was noticeably subdued—no question that they were getting down to serious business today. The large map board behind him was covered with a curtain, adding drama to the occasion. Facing them with a tight smile, Colonel Ridley said, "Because this mission is really a trial run, headquarters ordered us to use only one squadron. You men were selected today because the 424TH has consistently posted the best overall performance scores in the group...so we're giving you first shot."

Hearing the last comment, Glowgower could scarcely believe his ears; by turning in high bombing scores, he'd been partly responsible for the decision to use his squadron as the guinea pig! Well, he decided, this was just another shitty example of the way things worked in the Air Force: if you did a bad job, you got kicked out and sent to the infantry, where you would probably be killed; and if you did a good job, you were assigned a dangerous mission, where you would probably be killed. *Hobson's choice*, he cynically remembered.

When the Colonel reached behind him for the curtain covering the map, dead silence enveloped the room. Some of the men could hear their own heartbeats. The curtain parted to reveal a line of red chart tape, starting at Snetterton Heath and terminating on the coast of German-occupied Holland. The distance appeared to be less than 400 miles, round trip—a two and a half hour flight when you included the time to take-off and form up. Shaw fleetingly wondered if headquarters had deigned to give them a "milk run" for their first trip.

The Colonel lay the pointer on a place directly on the coast about fifteen miles east of Amsterdam and said, "Our target, gentlemen, is Ijmuiden, on the Dutch coast. The aiming point of the target is a large power plant, which not only powers the immediate vicinity of Amsterdam, but is also used by the Germans to supply electrical power to industrial cities in nearby Germany such as Essen, Dusseldorf, and Cologne. The power stations have become major strategic targets for the entire Allied bombing effort...if the Hun doesn't have power, he can't run his factories. The British have set up a special squadron to knock out the hydroelectric dams on the Rhine and Moselle rivers, and the heavies in the 8TH are going after oil and coal-fired plants in the Ruhr valley. This target...our B-17s have already tried to destroy it, but, so far, haven't inflicted any serious damage, for two reasons: one ...they can't get low enough to produce a bomb pattern that's tight enough to penetrate the reinforced concrete the plant's made of; and two...they got chewed up pretty bad because the target is heavily defended by a large number of well-sited 88 and 40 millimeter flak guns and is situated within twenty miles of the big German fighter base at Schipol." Scratch milk run, Shaw ruefully thought.

The last comment caused a paroxysm of coughing and chair-scraping from the seated men. Ridley waited for the commotion to cease and continued: "The people at headquarters believe, by coming in real low, we can get in and out before the Hun defenses are fully alerted. They also think, by dropping our bombs from minimum altitude, we can do some permanent damage to the target, maybe knock it out completely." He stopped, pulled a handkerchief from his pocket, and paused to swipe it across his face. "I'll be in the lead plane today with Major Chase, and Captain Burnside will ride as lead bombardier. O.k? Then that's the overview, men...Major Edrington will brief you on the specific op plan."

Edrington tiredly stepped onto the platform. He'd been up over thirty-six hours working on the details of the mission. Summoning his reserves, he informed them that the mission plan would involve the same ingress-egress pattern as their exercises over Cardigan Bay, except that they would climb only to 1,000 feet from the second IP to make their bomb run, which the lead bombardier would explain further in his briefing. They would maintain strict radio silence from the English coast until they reversed course off the target back over the North Sea. The only exception to this rule would be to call out enemy aircraft that were approaching the formation.

The intelligence officer, a moon-faced, paunchy first lieutenant who had been a corporate lawyer in civilian life, informed them in an unemotional tone there would be no Allied fighter escort on this mission. It was essential in order to maintain the element of surprise, he told them. "You goin' with us to make sure that happens, Lieutenant?" came an unidentified voice from the assemblage. Ignoring the question, he told them that the intelligence estimates provided by headquarters suggested that they should be able to get on and off the target before the big flak guns could depress enough to fix their range and elevation; however, the lighter AA, 40 millimeter and smaller, could be expected to react much faster. German fighters based at Schipol were a threat, he explained, but, deprived of advance warning from radar, it was questionable whether they could scramble the aircraft in time to catch up with the bombers as they headed back to England over the North Sea. Shaw remembered what Grattan had said about the Germans monitoring everything they did and wondered whether the defenses would really be caught napping. They would find out, he supposed.

Captain Burnside, seemingly unaffected by the gravity of their first combat briefing, jumped up on the platform and spouted, "Howdy, gents! You boys ready to go out and kick some Hun ass?" Some of the seated men managed weak smiles. "Yeah? Well, let me tell you about the little surprise package we're goin' to give 'em." Because of the relatively short distance to target and back, the rotund bombardier explained they would carry a 3,000 pound bomb load consisting of three 1,000 pound Mk.33 bombs with armor-piercing casings designed to penetrate concrete. The lower run-in altitude mentioned earlier would give them a tighter bomb pattern when they dropped. The detonators would be set to explode approximately ten seconds after impact, which would allow the bombs to penetrate into the areas where the vital machinery was located. They would bomb visually by flight off the lead plane.

The group meteorological officer was a nervous, bespectacled second lieutenant who looked too young to hold a commission in the Air Corps. The young man went into agonizing detail to describe the systemic variables that would affect their weather today. "Just give us the high points!" somebody yelled. What it boiled down to was that across the North Sea to the target, they could expect a broken cloud deck, seven- to eight-tenths coverage, down to about 3,000 feet but not low enough to interfere with their bomb run. The horizontal visibility over the target, he said, was forecast to be over fives miles with intermittent haze and smoke. There was a chance of solid cloud cover on the English coast when they returned with light rain or drizzle, in other words, a typical English spring day.

The last part of the overall briefing was conducted by Major Chase, who reiterated the procedures they'd followed in their practice exercises over Cardigan Bay. He reminded them of the critical importance of maintaining tight formation, especially without fighters to protect them, and emphasized the need for strict radio silence. "The longer we can preserve the element of surprise the better. But..if you see a bogie or what you think is a bogie, do your damndest to keep a clear head and call it off accurately...same way we practiced during gunnery training. I'll have anybody's ass who uses poor radio discipline...understand?"

Most of the one hundred seven men staring at him either nodded or mumbled their assent.

Chase paused and lit his seventh Camel of the day. Spitting out a flake of tobacco, he squinted and said, "Today, with the bomb load and fuel we're carrying, your plane's gonna' fly like a shithouse with wings! Take-off weights will be up to the limit. I want all you pilots to take this precaution: when you taxi into position for take-off, stand on your brakes and push your throttles all the way up to the stops...all the way! Don't release your brakes until you see the engines develop at least 60 inches of manifold pressure, got it?" Some of the faces showed surprise—this exceeded normal operating limits. "Once you're rolling," he continued, "wait for your airspeed to get to 120 before you try to unstick...and keep that power on until you're climb is established at 150." The seated pilots nodded their agreement. Chase was sure the group maintenance officer would scream bloody murder, but he didn't really give a damn—run-out engines were hell of a lot easier to replace than dead aircrews.

The navigators and bombardiers received a special briefing in which they were provided additional data on the navigation and bombing problem, which included recent reconnaissance photographs of the power plant and the areas near it. The photos, which had amazing resolution, had been taken two days before by a high-flying RAF photo-recon Spitfire. Glowgower could clearly discern the heavy flak sites situated around the perimeter of plant. If those sites opened up while they were over the target, he cheerlessly speculated, *they would be deader than hell.*

It was safe to say that Shaw's crew had never been at a higher level of readiness. Shaw, Clementi, and Milawski had pre-flighted *The A-Train* with extra caution, looking at everything twice. Glowgower had checked and double-checked the loading and fusing of the bombs. Grattan had committed the essential navigational information to memory, and could recite it like a play. Rimbaud checked every gun and every ammunition belt. And to complete the occasion, they had been issued flak vests and steel helmets to wear in the target area. Their training and equipment was about to receive the ultimate test.

They took off just before sunrise at one minute intervals, Major Chase's B-26 getting off first and orbiting the field at 5,000 feet in a wide circle until the gaggle of planes caught up and formed into the three elements of the squadron box, eighteen airplanes in all. *The A-Train,* eighth to take-off, tucked herself neatly into the deputy position behind

Merrill. The formation headed west through the leaden, early morning sky away from the coast so the German long-range radars would think they were on another practice mission. When they had flown far enough to be out of radar range, they turned back to the east and descended below the broken cloud cover to 200 feet. Because they were still in the semi-darkness of dawn, they skirted the cities and towns with their towers and tall church spires. Crossing the east coast of England a short while later, they dropped down so low that they skimmed the surface of the slate gray sea like a swarm of giant olive drab water bugs.

Shaw momentarily shifted his glance from Merrill's plane above him to Clementi. Despite the early morning chill in the cockpit, the co-pilot's face was pallid, and he was visibly sweating. "Take it for a while, Luce...o.k.?"

Clementi shifted position and reached for the yoke. "Got it."

The dim cockpit was momentarily illuminated by the glare of Shaw's cigarette lighter. He pointed the pack at his co-pilot. "Smoke?"

"Yeah...light it for me, willya?"

Noticing the slight tremor in Clementi's voice, he handed him the lit cigarette. "You all right, Luce?"

"Copasetic." The reply was strained.

Noticing, Shaw declared, "You know, Luce, the big difference between what we're doin' today and what we've practicing for three weeks is dropping live bombs on a real target."

Clementi thought Shaw was trivializing the danger. "C'mon, Ted...you really believe that? That the Krauts are gonna' be totally surprised?"

"Makes the most sense, doesn't it?"

Clementi shrugged, not shifting his glance from Merrill's plane.

In truth, Shaw wasn't completely convinced but felt he needed to brace up his shaky co-pilot. "Tell you what, Luce, I'll fly the plane from the first IP to the target and you can take over again after we're headed back home. That sound like a plan?"

"O.k."

The interphone crackled, "Navigator to crew, time to test guns." The drone of the engines was momentarily transcended by the staccato bark of 50-caliber machine guns. The spent casings clattered off the sides of the fuselage's interior, and the sharp tang of cordite entered the plane's atmosphere.

Shaw keyed the interphone, "Pilot to nav, what's our posit?" Grattan stood up and stuck his head though the bulkhead door, looking like he'd regained most of his cheerful composure. "I make us to be about ten minutes from the first IP.'"

The pilot nodded, reaching for the microphone again. "Pilot to crew, get your flak vests and helmets on ...everybody be on the lookout for incoming fighters!"

Time seemed to drag by. Grattan, back at his desk, recalculated the distance on his plot. "Nav to pilot, we're about a minute from the first IP."

"Rog," answered Shaw. "I'll take it now, Luce...keep your eyeballs peeled for Kraut fighters."

Using the turn of the lead plane as their cue, the other three flights each rolled onto their pre-planned headings. Each flight was now on their own until they reformed to return to base.

"Pilot to Bombardier, we have turned onto our first IP and should intercept our second IP in five minutes"

"Roger." Glowgower shifted his weight on the metal stool that functioned as the bombarider's seat and re-checked all the switches on his bombing panel. To minimize the spread, the bombs were set to "salvo" and would all drop at one time. Waiting for the Dutch coast to crawl over the horizon, he looked intently over the top of the reticle of the D-8 sight, which had been set for an altitude of 1,000 feet. The accuracy of the unsophistacted sight had surprised him during the practice exercizes on the Welsh coast. While there wasn't much more to do than hold the pickle switch and watch Merrill's plane, as deputy lead, he needed to be ready to take-over at a moment's notice. His fright had been held in check so far. Somehow, after they'd taken-off, the fear seemed recede into the background of his consciousness. In a curious way, the events surrounding him had taken on a sharp focus, heightening all his senses. He felt the airplane turn and heard the note of the engines increase.

"Pilot to bombardier, just tuned onto the second IP... climbing to bombing altitude!" The pilot's voice was clipped.

"Roger...bomb bay doors are coming open!" The Dutch Coast was now a distinct brown smear in front of him.

"Pilot to nav, position report!"

"On course...on course!" the navigator answered quickly.

"Target in sight!" cried Glowgower, ignoring interphone protocol. An enormous large structure with twin smoke stacks loomed before him. "Target is slightly to the left of our twelve o'clock position!" At nearly the same time, Merrill wheeled to reposition the formation on the center of the target. Watching their approach, Glowgower thought his heart was going come out of his chest—never in life had he experienced this level of excitement! The Dutch coast abruptly flashed beneath them, and he tensed his thumb over the pickle switch. Seeing the first bomb leave Merrill's airplane, he jabbed the pickle switch and screamed, "BOMBS AWAY!" As soon as the bombs thumped off their racks, he reached for the bomb bay door lever and felt himself crushed down into his seat by the massive G-forces of a steep diving turn. "Bomb bay doors closed!" He wrenched his body around to look at the target as it disappeared under the right side of the nose. *Where are the explosions?*

As the bombs left the plane, Shaw smartly moved the yoke forward to counteract the tendency of the airplane to balloon upwards, then wracked them into a steep left turn and pushed the throttles forward to keep up with Merrill. They were off the target and diving back down toward the coast at over 300 m.p.h. Some of the flak guns around the power plant had awakened with sporadic fire but not quickly enough to catch the fleeing B-26s.

"Pilot to crew, we're off the target! Watch out for fighters coming up on our six o'clock!" As the formation sped flat out over the sea, no fighters were scrambled to intercept them, and ten minutes after that, they were far enough away that nothing could catch them. The ruse had worked. Only Rimbaud was disappointed.

"Yee-haaaaaa!" Shaw whooped on the interphone, causing *The A-Train* to bobble slightly in the formation. "Pilot to crew...*we did it*...we nailed the bastards!" He turned to Clementi and gave him an exaggerated thumbs up. "What about it, ol' buddy! Piece of cake, huh?"

Clementi stared back at the pilot weakly. He'd been in a state of near catalepsy since they'd turned onto the second IP. Exhaling hugely, he wondered how long he'd been holding his breath.

"You o.k., Luce?" The pilot looked at him inquisitively.

"Uh-huh," he answered tentatively. He tried to shake himself alert. "Yeah...I'm all right."

"You ready to fly?"

"Yeah." The co-pilot reached for the controls.

"You got it."

The activity of flying the plane finally snapped Clementi out of his torpor. He tried to recreate the events of the previous ten minutes in his head, but nothing would come. What had happened to him? The fear had clamped onto him like a giant hand, shutting down his body and mind. It reminded him of being a small child just awakening from a frightening nightmare he couldn't remember.

Shaw could feel himself unwinding like a tightly coiled spring, experiencing the rapid onset of a post-adrenaline hangover. Noticing the dirty gray cloud base beneath which the B-26's were scudding, he was grateful there would not be an instrument letdown. The elation he'd felt earlier was being overtaken by a creeping lassitude. He closed his eyes for a moment but was startled by the interphone.

"Bombardier to pilot, did you see any bombs explode?"

Shaw sat bolt upright. The thought had never occurred to him! "Uh, I didn't notice," he answered and looked inquiringly at Clementi who merely shrugged.

"Pilot to crew, did *anybody* see any bombs explode?"

"Nav, negative."

"Top turret, negative."

"Tail, didn't see nuthin'."

Damn!

The debriefing indicated that *none* of the bombs had exploded. The fault had been traced to the device which armed the bombs. In order to arm the detonator, the small metal propeller on the nose of the bomb needed to spin through about eighty revolutions. When they had moved their bombing altitude down to 1,000 feet, the arming sequence apparently did not complete itself, and the bombs had fallen on the target unarmed—*duds*. They would have to do it over again.

CHAPTER TEN

May 15, 1943, Snetterton Heath, England.

After they had returned from the first mission unrequited, the brigadier general in charge of operations at 8TH Air Force headquarters informed Lieutenant Colonel Ridley that there was simply no reason why they couldn't saddle up and go after Ijmuiden again. It was an important target—had to be destroyed. Period.

The Colonel frowned at Major Edrington. "What do you think, Chet?"

The Major angrily stubbed out his cigarette and grimaced. "Think? I think it's a crock of shit! Those bastards send us bombs that don't work the first time and now they want to lay on the same mission five days later!"

Ridley looked at him with a dismal expression. "You think of anything we can do differently this time?"

"Not really. The details haven't changed."

"The mission order calls for a one-squadron strike...should we use the 424TH again?"

"Yeah," the Major said with quiet resignation. "I hate to stick it to Chase's outfit again, but they've already been there and have seen the target." Lighting another cigarette, he stared intently at the Colonel. "Why don't I lead this one, Bob?"

Ridley gave him a tired smile. "Thanks, but I'm leading it...going to leave Burnside behind, too."

"Whatever you say, Bob. I doubt this one's gonna' be a milk run."

"Probably not."

Across the base in their crew hut, Clementi rolled up on an elbow and watched Shaw sitting on his bunk. The pilot was leafing through a copy of *Stars and Stripes* and was tapping his foot in time to Benny Goodman's, *Sing-Sing-Sing,* playing on the Armed Forces Radio network. His face was seemingly relaxed and unperturbed.

"Ted?"

"Huh?" The pilot looked up and smiled.

"I...I've been wanting to tell you something."

"Shoot, ol' buddy."

"I froze up when we were over the target the other day." He sat up and looked at the pilot solemnly.

"You did?" The pilot's expression was quizzical. "You looked a little done-in when pulled off the target, but so did I."

"Uh-uh...I *really* froze up, almost paralyzed."

"Aw, Luce." The pilot grinned at him reassuringly. "You just got the first mission shakes...next one won't seem as bad, you'll see."

The co-pilot laid back down and stared at the ceiling. "Maybe so..." he murmured.

They heard the door open and Grattan came into the room, an unsmiling expression on his face. "We're on the loading order for a mission tomorrow," he announced, "briefing at 0400."

"The whole group?" Shaw asked.

"Nope, just us...the 424TH."

Clementi sprang to his feet and kicked the chair over next to his bed. "Damn them! I just knew it!" His tone was almost hysterical. "I just knew they'd send us back to bomb that son-of-a-bitchin power plant again!"

"You don't know that for a fact." The navigator tried to disagree.

"He's probably right, Mick," the pilot said evenly.

The co-pilot was trembling with rage. "And you think the friggin Germans'll be fooled this time? Hell no! Not one little bit!" He spat the remarks out.

Shaw put his hand on the excited co-pilot's shoulder. "Maybe so, but there's damn-all we can do about it... they're not gonna' ask us to vote on it."

"No." The co-pilot slumped, looking toward the floor.

"No use mopin' around," the pilot said. "Let's go get a cold one...I'm buyin'."

"I need something stronger than beer."

"All right."

While the others didn't notice, least of all the overwrought Clementi, Grattan's announcement had troubled Shaw. By nature, he wasn't a worrier, took most things in stride as they came. Ever since joining the Air Corps eighteen months before, he'd rarely questioned the wisdom of his superiors. After all, they had the big picture—the intelligence and data to make the big decisions. His job was but to follow orders. Simple as that. But this Ijmuiden thing, if his suspicions were true, didn't pass his test of sensible decision-making. Same target, same guns, same fighter base—same Germans. Was there something he missed that the higher-ups knew about? Unlikely, he thought—he'd been there, they hadn't.

When the three of them entered the O-Club, Major Chase was leaning on the bar nursing a drink. He turned, raised his glass, and motioned them his way, then ordered the bartender, a tech sergeant, to set them up with whatever they wanted. Noticing the glum expression on Clementi's face, he figured they'd already seen the loading order. Chase liked these boys—they were a first rate crew. After they greeted each other and sat down, Shaw and Grattan both ordered a beer, and Clementi asked for a double scotch and soda.

"Sorry Lieutenant, ain't got no scotch," the bartender apologized.

"You got any kind of whiskey?"

"Bourbon...Old Crow."

"Gimme a double on the rocks with soda." When the co-pilot's drink arrived, he picked it up and finished it in one draught. The pilot punched him on the shoulder and grinned. "You better slow down, boy...I heard that one hit bottom."

The co-pilot wiped his hand across his face and gave him a grim look. "No shit? I haven't even started yet."

"Guess you boys saw the loading order?" Chase asked matter-of-factly.

"Yep." Shaw spoke up first.

"Ridley told me about it a couple a hours ago...said the mission order came straight from headquarters."

They stared at him without comment.

"They think we can pull it off again, take that power plant by surprise." He snapped his fingers in a swift motion. "Just like that!" He looked down at his drink and frowned.

"What about you, Major?" Grattan asked candidly. "What do you think of it?"

"Me?" He looked the big navigator scornfully. "They don't pay me to think, friend...they pay me to climb into a B-26 and fly the son-of-a-bitch where they order me to go. Thinking is for staff pukes, not pilots."

"Why're they picking on us again?" Clementi asked in plaintive tone. "Why don't they send one of the other squadrons?"

Chase gave him a sharp look. "You know the answer to that already! We've been there, seen the target."

"They're crazy as hell to send us back so soon!" the co-pilot screeched. Turning away from Chase, he snatched up his glass and inhaled the rest of his drink.

Chase seemed unaffected by Clementi's outburst. "Maybe so," he said indifferently, "but the target's still there, ain't it? Still generatin' kilowatts for the ol' Thousand Year Reich? You got a better solution, Lieutenant?"

Clementi didn't respond. The others just stared.

Chase's features softened. Interrupting the lull, he said, "Let me give you boys a piece of advice: As long as you're over here in combat, don't think too much. Don't think about goin' home or goin' on your next leave...stuff like that. Just don't make plans. You follow me?"

They looked at him with puzzled expressions.

Chase coughed and continued the explanation. "Ever since you started your training, you've been workin' up to the point of goin' into combat. That's what your paid for, right?"

They nodded, staring but not understanding.

"Well, now you're there...your future and present have merged." He looked at them grimly. "Tomorrow...don't think about it. All you've got is today...nothing else." The last statement was a whisper.

"Oh sure!" Clementi's tone was disbelieving. "We're supposed to tuck it in like good little boys and not be scared, aren't we?"

"Scared!" Chase growled back at him. "Shit! I'm scared, you're scared, we're all scared...what's that got to do with it?"

The co-pilot gaped at him dumbly.

Chase gave Clementi a sad smile and placed his hand on his shoulder. "Look, being scared ain't the problem. Any man who ain't scared of combat is a damn fool. But here's the thing: you can't help being scared while you're up there on a mission but you can try to stop worryin' about being alive tomorrow." He threw a five dollar bill on the counter and said, "Hell, I probably don't know what I'm talkin' about...see you fellas' in the morning."

They returned to their hut in silence, each absorbed in his own thoughts. Clementi removed his clothes and flopped down on his bunk to a fitful slumber. Shaw and Grattan talked quietly about the advice Chase had given them earlier. The pilot believed that he really couldn't blank out the past, which contained people and things he loved like Mary Beth, his dad and mom, home; they still existed in his present, but he could *try* not to think of them in terms of his immediate future. Grattan told him that Chase had really spoken a fundamental truth, i.e., that God expects us to live only for the day and not to be anxious for the future, because, in God's view, present and "eternity" are the same, and that your "spirit" transcends both. Shaw thought about this, too.

No one was surprised the next morning when Colonel Ridley announced that Ijmuiden would be the target for the day. The only significant difference from the previous mission was that a squadron of the 322ND Bomb Group (Medium), another B-26 outfit, was taking off from Great Sailing, England an hour before them for an anti-shipping strike in the vicinity of the Frisian Islands. This move, it was felt, would provide a feint for their attack, which was about 100 miles farther South. He told them with certainty that their bombs would explode this time.

The aircrews sat there in a kind of stony silence until the intelligence officer's turn came. When the featureless Lieutenant unemotionally informed them that current intelligence estimates suggested they could surprise the defenses again, he was met with jeers and catcalls. No one, including Shaw's crew, believed him. Milawski elbowed Rimbaud in the side and whispered, "You're gonna' get your wish today, Leroy."

"What chu mean?" the tail gunner asked.

"The whole Kraut air force is gonna' be flying right up your smelly ass."

The tail gunner hissed back at him. "Ah'm ready...how 'bout you, Yankee boy?"

The meteorological briefing was different than the time before: the cloud cover expected over the target was less, a scattered layer at about 4,000 feet; horizontal visibility was expected to be unlimited with slight haze. Not CAVU but close—any patrolling fighters would see them coming for miles.

When the main briefing ended, there were few questions this time—they'd heard the answers before. Chase reaffirmed his cautions about take-off, radio silence, and tight formation. "Remember, if we get attacked by fighters, they'll be coming in high. Have your guns tested and manned about twenty minutes after we cross the English coast, then tell your gunners to keep their heads moving *all the time*, into the target and back out again. If the gunners see bogies, they should report 'em on the interphone, and navigators will report 'em to the rest of us on the command channel, is that clear?" Chase knew that some of these crews would probably not return from today's mission and tried to suppress the regret it caused him—it was out of his hands. "We really need to be on our toes, fellas', this one could get rough." There was nothing else to say.

At the navigator's and bombardier's briefing the information was essentially unchanged. From the new photos, Glowgower thought he noticed blemishes on the roof of the main building that could have been caused by the unexploded bombs, otherwise, it looked untouched, and the location of the flak emplacements hadn't changed either.

The bombardier left the briefing by himself, as usual. He had developed a personal philosophy similar to Chase's, but his version of it was more extreme, for he had blanked out both the future *and* the past. As far as he was concerned, he was already a dead man, one who existed minute by minute in the present. It worked until he went to sleep, then the nightmares would begin. They always followed the same pattern: he was trapped in the nose of a disintegrating B-26 that was spinning wildly into a smoky abyss, and when he screamed over the interphone, no one answered because he was alone...*utterly and finally alone*. He would awaken, saturated in sweat, disoriented, and then the fear would slowly recede back into the place where he kept it.

Shaw was flying *The A-Train* when the squadron crossed the Norfolk coast and dropped down to minimum altitude. This time they would fly to an IP further south of the target.

The A-Train was again flying deputy lead for baker flight, and would be second over the target behind Chase in able flight. Their second IP would be an approach from the sea on a heading of zero-four-zero. The sequencing had been set up so that the flights would be over the target about one minute apart. At their speed they covered almost three and one-half miles a minute, and the navigation needed to be dead on for the timing to work properly.

Twenty minutes later, Grattan came on the interphone, "Navigator to crew, test your guns." Shaw listened to the clatter of the fifties as Rimbaud, Milawski and Glowgower fired their guns. He switched the blister guns to "arm," depressed the nose of the plane slightly and pulled the trigger on the control yoke. The power of the heavy machine guns seemed to slow the plane momentarily. Relaxing his grip, he keyed the interphone. "Pilot to crew, get on your helmets and flak vests." The steel helmets—G.I. issue—and steel-lined vests were heavy and uncomfortable. The pilots took turns flying while each got into his gear. After fastening the chinstrap of his helmet, Shaw said, "Keep it till we reach the first IP, Luce."

"Got it." The co-pilot's face had taken on the waxen pallor that Shaw noticed on the first mission. The pilot couldn't think of any clever words of reassurance. No pep talk today.

Behind them, Grattan was frowning over his DR plot.

As soon as they crossed the coast, he had peered into his drift meter and thought he detected a strong wind from the north, but the drift meters were difficult to read this low. The navigator in the lead plane either hadn't discovered the error or planned to alter course sometime soon. Grattan's calculations of compass course, altitude, ground speed, and wind drift indicated that they were very possibly south of the track needed to intersect the first IP, and drawing further away every minute. He laid his instruments down on his metal table and moved to the door on the cockpit bulkhead.

"I think the wind is stronger than forecast and we could be ten or more miles south of where we should be," he told Shaw. "What do you think we should do?"

Shaw was undecided: if he called them on the command channel, it would be like firing a red flare for the Germans to see. "You're sure we're off that far?"

"No, not sure...more of an educated guess."

Shaw knew that Grattan was probably one of the best DR navigators in the group. "Damnation!" he hissed. "We can't break radio silence...that'd be worse than hitting the wrong IP. Let me think." They weren't in good position to give Merrill any kind of visual signal. He considered trying to send a flashing signal that would be noticed by Merrill's tail gunner.

Grattan looked at his wristwatch and said with a shrug, "We're nearly out of time anyway." A few seconds later the flight leaders rolled into separate headings for the second IP. They were committed now, error or no error.

"I've got the airplane, Luce. Just stick with me, o.k.?"

The co-pilot silently nodded.

"Nav to bombardier, we're possibly south of where we're supposed to be, which'll require us to dogleg to the North on the second IP."

"Roger, just how far off could we be?"

"Ten miles...maybe more."

Glowgower swore. "That'll add over two minutes to our bomb run," which was the only time they *must* fly straight and level, regardless of flak or fighters. Two minutes later, following Merrill's lead, Shaw rolled *The A-Train* into a left turn and increased power for the climb to 1,000 feet. Shaw called Glowgower to advise him they were at the second IP, but to keep the bomb bay doors closed until they crossed the coast. The interphone crackled, "Nav to bombardier, I think we'll cross the coast at Zandvort, about 12 miles south of the target, then we'll need to turn left to zero-one-two to intercept the aiming point."

When they leveled out at bombing altitude, an excited cry came from Milawski, "Top turret to crew, BOGIES! About twenty-five of 'em...high at our ten o'clock!" Shaw swiveled his head up to his left and, squinting, could detect a wedge of black dots speeding their way. At the same time, the command radio opened up, Ridley calling off the attacking fighters to the squadron. The pilot clicked the interphone, "Nav, call Merrill and tell him where we are." Shaw's stomach contracted as he watched the black dots resolve themselves into the deadly shapes of Focke-Wulf 190s. It appeared to him that the fighters were positioning themselves for a head-on attack on Chase's formation in front of them, stepped-up 100 feet above. Tracer fire erupted from the guns of the leading bombers and the cannons of the attacking fighters almost simultaneously. The tracer-filled gap between the adversaries swifty contracted, the fighters pushing down their noses and diving underneath the bombers. The attack had partially disassembled the formation, and Ridley came on the radio, "Close it up! Close it up!" Shaw watched with horror as a B-26 enveloped in flame in the left element of Chase's flight slowly rolled over onto its back and smashed into the sea with a massive splash. Then he shifted his attention to another crippled bomber which fell out of the lead formation, shedding pieces of its left wing.

Milawski called, "Top turret to crew, the fighters are above us, headed away to the right." The Dutch coast suddenly flashed below *The A-Train's* nose, and Shaw banked steeply to follow Merrill as the formation turned to the North. Grattan abruptly came on the interphone, "Nav to bombardier, target should be visible in about two minutes!"

"Roger! Bomb bays doors coming open now!"

Then the German guns opened up.

A curtain of oily black clouds suddenly enveloped them where the sky had been clear moments before. Directly to their front, Merrill's B-26 received a direct flak burst in the bomb bay and disintegrated in a single, massive explosion. *The A-Train* swerved through the turbulence left by the blast, small bits of flaming debris bouncing off the airplane.

Shaw increased power to move them up to the head of the flight, and shouted on the interphone, "Pilot to bombardier, we're lead! We've got the lead!"

Glowgower was momentarily dazed by the spectacle of Merrill's exploding plane but forced himself to pay attention to the problem at hand. "Roger, we're lead," he answered in a calm voice that seemed to come from someone else. Peering over the reticle on the D-8 sight, he saw the now familiar smokestacks of the target loom off the nose. "Bombardier to pilot," he called, "turn left five degrees. Target is about six miles away."

Creeping toward the target, *The A-Train* was relentlessly buffeted by the turbulence of the 88 and 40 millimeter flak bursts. The shells detonated in a *KA-RUMP!* that could be heard outside the airplane, producing a red fireball followed by a black cloud filled with steel splinters. The near misses were accompanied by a sound like gravel being flung against the side of the plane and a choking stench like rotten eggs. As they drew nearer, the B-26 to their immediate right took a direct hit that blew off its right wing, causing it to crazily cartwheel out of the formation. The German gunners now had had plenty of time to range the oncoming bombers and had set up a virtually solid barrage in front of the target.

Shaw fought to keep his mind on flying the plane as he watched the formation being systematically decimated like BB gun targets in a huge aerial arcade. A flak shell detonated close to the right side of *The A-Train,* revealing the incandescent red fireball in its center. The concussion from the blast flipped the big bomber on its side like a toy. As Shaw struggled to right the airplane, he heard and felt a shattering crash immediately followed by a high, howling noise in the cockpit. Looking to his right, he noticed a large, jagged hole in the fuselage next to Clementi. The co-pilot was howling, too. "Mick!" he screamed into the interphone, "get up here!"

Without replying, the navigator lunged onto the flight deck, looking first at the pilot then at the writhing form of the co-pilot. Before they could speak, Glowgower interrupted them with the cry, "Bombs away!" Shaw wrenched the bomber into a steep left turn and pushed the nose down, forcing Grattan the grab onto the co-pilot's seat as a handhold. After Shaw leveled the wings, Grattan kneeled down between the seats to examine the co-pilot's wound.

Shaw flashed him an inquiring look.

Grattan grunted as he held the struggling co-pilot back with his right arm. "His right leg's split open to the bone and he's losing a lot of blood!"

"Can you get him out of his seat by yourself?"

"I think so." The navigator tripped the latch on Clementi's seat harness, placed his hands under the co-pilot's arms and, splattering the pulsing blood all over the control pedestal, heaved the semiconscious form through the cockpit door.

"Tail gunnah t'crew, dos' bogie's comin' agin!"

"Where dammit?" Shaw demanded.

"'Bout seven a'clock high! 'Least twenty-five or mo'!"

Milawski interrupted. "Top turret to crew, the bogies are comin' from behind! They'll be in range in about ten seconds!" Shaw pushed up the throttles to increase speed in a vain effort to outrun the attacking fighters. As the fifties in the tail and top turret started thundering away, he dutch rolled the airplane to the right and left to throw off the aim of the fighters. Hearing and feeling the 20 millimeter slugs ripping into the skin of the airplane, he scanned the instruments for any sign of trouble. "Crew!" he cried, "report damage!"

"Bombardier, negative damage."

"Top turret, I see some holes in the wing outboard of the engines...don't see any fuel leaking out."

"Tail, sumptin' hit the right elevator."

The next alarm came from Glowgower. "Here they come again! Ten o'clock high!" The distance between the remains of the formation and the fighters closed at the frightening rate of 500 m.p.h., bringing the sleek forms of the Focke Wulf 190s almost immediately into gun range. The nose gun, top turret and blister guns opened up almost all together in a deafening cacophony. Shaw grunted with effort as he steered the bomber into the path of two oncoming fighters and fired the blister guns at the same time. They were so close that the pilot could distinguish the individual markings of the planes and see the helmeted heads of the pilots in the cockpits. Seeming to come straight at him, the tracer from the attacking fighter's 20 millimeter cannons leaped out and arced over the plane like incandescent snowballs. The bomber lurched; he heard the sound of tearing metal and felt the roar of the slipstream as the window beside him vanished into a thousand shards of exploding plexiglas. A sharp, burning sensation suddenly hammered his left arm like an electrical jolt. Looking down in a daze, he noticed a long, jagged rent in the sleeve of his flight jacket, from which blood was slowly pulsing onto the side console of the cockpit. He tried lifting it and gasped with pain. The plane bobbed and weaved as he flew it unsteadily with his right hand.

A whining, rasping noise came on the interphone, but because Shaw couldn't remove his hand from the yoke to use the microphone, he listened helplessly. Trying to keep his left arm stationary, he turned his head to the right and screamed, "MICK! COME UP HERE!"

The navigator, hands and sleeves covered with the co-pilot's blood, dashed to the cockpit door. "What's wrong!" He looked alarmingly at the pilot. "Oh, God...you're hit!"

"Get Glowgower up here now! Then go back in the waist and see what's wrong...somebody's hurt back there." Shaw could feel his strength ebbing and fought the torpor invading his consciousness. Grattan got on his hands and knees between the pilot seats, stuck his head into the opening to the nose and cried, "Glow! Come up! We need you up here...NOW!"

The nose section had been spared of damage so far. As the bombardier creeped through the opening next to the co-pilot's station, he was sickened by scene which met him on the flight deck. The area around the co-pilot's seat was spattered with blood, which trailed in a viscous stream all the way over the control pedestal through the door. The large hole on the right side of the cockpit and the missing window on the left created a shrieking din and a wind blast that ripped his cap off his head. He noticed with relief that the controls and the instruments on the pilot's side seemed to be intact. Crouching, he turned his attention to Shaw, who was huddled over the controls, his left arm bleeding and hanging limply.

The pilot grimaced at him with drawn features. "You've gotta' help me fly the plane, Glow. Mick's got to take care of the others."

The bombardier silently nodded, sat in the bloody right seat, and fastened the straps. He turned to the pilot and nodded again.

"Get on the yoke!" Shaw instructed hoarsely. "We're already climbing...I'll handle the power."

The bombardier tentatively placed both hands on the yoke.

Grattan reappeared. "Rimbaud got hit...took a cannon fragment in the butt. Milawski had already pulled him into the waist and was dressing the wound. He'll be o.k." He glanced at the bombardier then back at the pilot. "Let me see your arm."

"Wait till we level off. What about Luce?"

"He caught a big piece of shrapnel in his right thigh and has lost a lot of blood. I've got a tourniquet rigged that's stopped the worst of the bleeding. I gave him a morphine styrette and dressed the wound, but I think he's in shock. I laid him down in the nav compartment and covered him in blankets."

Shaw reached down and adjusted the elevator trim and pulled the power back as they leveled at 5,000 feet. "Hold it there, Glow...nice and easy." He took his right hand off the yoke and blinked painfully at the big navigator.

Grattan opened the first aid kit as Shaw struggled to turn sideways in his seat. Helping the pilot out of his flight jacket, he examined the bloody mess on his lower left arm. He ripped the sleeve off his shirt and peered closely at the wound. "Looks like something is wedged in your forearm. Yeah...a piece of plexiglass. Bleeding seems to have stopped...I'll leave the plexiglass alone and wrap a compress around it." The navigator doused sulfa powder on the wound, but when he applied the compress, the pilot shrieked, "Damnation!"

Grattan looked at him sympathetically. "I'm sorry."

"Never mind...finish it," the pilot croaked.

The navigator completed the bandaging of the pilot's arm, then helped him turn back around in his seat and re-fasten his straps.

Kneeling between the seats, Grattan scanned the horizon on both sides of the plane. "Have you seen any of the other planes in our squadron?" Grattan asked a moment later.

Shaw gave him a grim look. "Negative...not a one."

"Me neither," Glowgower added quickly.

"I'll try to raise someone on the command channel, then I better figure out where we are," Grattan said. "I'll give you a new course in a minute." He left the flight deck and checked Clementi in the floor of the nav compartment. The co-pilot's face looked like a white death mask but he still had a good pulse. The navigator sat down and keyed the command radio. "Catfish baker one to anybody in Catfish flight, do you read me, over?" He tried this several times. Nothing. Silence. "Nav to pilot, I can't seem to raise anybody." With a sigh he moved across to the nav table and set the plotter on his chart. By his estimate, they had flown about 60 miles away from the Dutch coast so far but were south of the course needed to get them to Snetterton Heath. Laying out a new course, he called Shaw. "Nav to pilot, turn right to a heading of two-niner-two. We are an estimated 30 minutes from the base at present speed."

In the cockpit, Shaw groaned. "O.k., Glow...I'll make the turn...you take over as soon as I get us steadied up." As he banked *The A-Train* onto the new course, he quickly scanned the instrument panel. Something didn't feel right—the airplane was sluggish. "Dammit all!" he hissed. "We're losin' oil pressure on number two...fast!" Shaw watched the gauge flicker, noticed a steady decline in the manifold pressure reading with a corresponding increase in the cylinder head temperature. "We're gonna have to shut the son-of-a-bitch down before it seizes and catches fire!" The new emergency lifted some of his wooziness. "Now listen to me, Glow...do *exactly* what I tell you to do!"

The bombardier looked his way and nodded.

"You on the rudders? Get ready to push the right rudder to the stop when I give the word!" Shaw reached down and pulled the mixture lever to idle cut-off and jabbed the feather button on number two engine. "NOW!" he screamed and grabbed the yoke to crank in opposite aileron and push down the nose. Taking his right hand off the yoke, he reached down and gasped with effort while he wound in full right rudder trim. "Keep that left wing down! That's right. Don't let the nose come up...keep the airspeed above one-fifty!" Feeling faint again, the pilot sagged in his seat. Watching the bombardier wrestle with the plane, he willed himself to reach over, close the fuel cock, and switch off the ignition to the dead engine.

In the waist, Rimbaud lay on his side curled into a ball. "Yous' right, Ski," he whimpered.

"What?"

"Sonamabeeches shot mah ass off!" The 20 millimeter slug that had glanced off the tail gunner's buttocks had removed a chunk of flesh the size of a baseball.

"Not all of it, Leroy...you still got some left."

"You taken' good care a'me, Ski...I ain' gonna' forget it." The tail gunner closed his eyes and groaned.

The A-Train limped toward the English coast alone. The wind whistled through the holes in her fuselage and wings. A strip of the fabric from her left elevator had ripped back and was flapping wildly in the slipstream. The right propeller lay still as the bomber wallowed and weaved through the air. A short while later, they crossed the Norfolk coast at Southwold and Grattan gave them a course correction to the base.

"Mick!" Shaw shouted over the noise. "We're gonna' try a straight in. You fire a red flare when we're about a mile out. Make sure everybody in the back is strapped-in." He turned to the bombardier. "Glow, we're both gonna' stay on the controls down final." He pointed to the control pedestal. "See the gear and flap levers there?" The bombardier nodded. "O.k....get the gear down when I say and give me 20 degrees of flaps."

Shaw could see the runway ahead and began to line the bomber up and reduce power for the descent. The airplane yawed back and forth as it dropped toward the runway. Shaw saw a red light arc over his head after Grattan fired the flare tube. Moments later, a green flare arose from the control tower, signaling the clear to land.

"Gear down! Flaps twenty!" the pilot shouted. Feeling the airplane become ponderous and shudder on the brink of a stall, he leaned foward on the yoke to force the nose down and regain airspeed. As the end of the runway rose to meet them with alarming speed, he cried, "Full flaps!" The big airplane wobbled uncertainly over the threshold. "Hold it there!" the pilot screamed at the bombardier, quickly moving his usable hand to yank the power off the good engine. Grabbing the controls again, he felt the strength fading from him as he fought to pull the yoke all the way back to his lap. "Help me!" he cried. The bomber hit the runway with a bone-shuddering shriek and bounced back into the air, then settled crabwise back down to the pavement in a tire-screeching jolt. The pilot frantically kicked the rudders back and forth to keep the careening airplane on the runway.

"Switches off!," Shaw groaned loudly. "Get on the brakes with me!" *The A-Train* began to slow and finally crept to a stop about 100 feet short of the runway's end.

After sitting numbly for a few moments, Glowgower got out of his seat and bent over Shaw, who was slouched across the control column, his head resting against the instrument panel. He gently pushed him back in his seat and unbuckled his straps. The pilot looked up listlessly and blinked.

"Can you make it through the nose hatch?" the bombardier asked him.

"Yeah..." he murmured.

A half a dozen vehicles were racing down the runway to converge on the stricken bomber. Doors flew open and seconds later, a young medic climbed through the nose opening into the cockpit, looked at Shaw, and asked, "Are you wounded, sir?"

Glowgower interrupted. "I'll take care of him." He pointed to the cockpit door. "You go back and take care of the co-pilot." He turned to Shaw. "I'll open the bomb doors so they can get him out...I'll be back in a minute." The pilot turned and leaned on the armrest so he could watch Grattan and the medic lift the co-pilot's recumbent form through the nav compartment door into the bomb bay. He felt someone grab his right arm to help him up and turned to see the bombardier facing him. Glowgower pushed the co-pilot's seat back and helped Shaw thread his way down into the nose. Other people reached up through the nose hatch to help lower the pilot to the ground. The medics lay him down on a stretcher, and the medical officer came to his side to examine the wound.

When the man's face came into view, Shaw feebly asked him, "Where's the rest of the squadron?"

His answer was almost inaudible. "As far as we know, you're the only ones who returned."

Glowgower leaned wearily against the plane as he watched the ambulance take the others away. A jeep waited to take him to the operations hut.

He whispered to her, "You saved our lives...you brought us back from a terrible place. I'll never forget you...never." He laid his head against her cool side and sobbed. He was one of her boys. He was the bombardier.

CHAPTER ELEVEN

May 19, 1943, 8TH A.F. Headquarters, High Wycombe, England.

The immaculately-attired Brigadier General motioned the two worn-looking Majors to sit in the chairs in front of his desk. He proffered a small wooden case containing cigarettes and asked, "Smoke?"

They shook their heads.

The General leaned back in his chair, made a steeple of his thumbs and asked pointedly, "Suppose you tell me what happened?"

Major Vincent Spinelli frowned. He hated overly-broad questions and took a minute to compose his answer. "Sir, since only one aircraft returned from the mission, we're not sure of the exact details; however, the debriefing of Captain Shaw and his crew indicated two primary factors: first and most important, the German defenses...both the flak emplacements and the fighters from Schipol...were ready for them." He stopped to clear his throat. "And second, when they crossed the enemy coast, they were about 12 miles south of their intended IP, which gave the Germans more time to set up their anti-aircraft barrage."

"What was the cause of the error on the IP?"

"Sir, according to Lieutenant Grattan, Shaw's navigator, the reason was a stronger wind from the north than what was forecast in the met report."

"Couldn't they have compensated for the wind?"

"Well, sir, as you know, they were at minimum altitude ...the drift meters aren't too reliable that low."

"Do you know how many planes actually made it to the target?"

"No, sir, the lead plane with Colonel Ridley and Major Chase was apparently shot down by flak before they reached the target, so we have no record from the lead element, but Lieutenant Glowgower, Shaw's bombardier, thought he saw two planes ahead of him before he reached the target, and Captain Shaw was sure one other plane from his flight made it over the target. We don't know if any of the planes from charlie flight ever made it to the target."

"Have you seen the bomb damage photos?"

"Yes, sir."

"You agree the damage was negligible?"

"Yes, sir, it looks like the two planes in Shaw's flight were the only ones who actually hit the target."

"Overall...a pretty sorry performance, wouldn't you say, Major?"

"Sir?"

"I mean, they missed their IP, then made what appears to be a very disorganized approach to the target."

Major Chester Edringtron, who had quietly listened to the exchange between Spinelli and the General, exploded.

"That's a load of crap, General!"

"What?"

"The reason the mission failed is because *you* ordered them back too soon and the Huns were waitin' on 'em!"

"You're out of order, Major!"

"No, sir, I'm not. This low-level stuff was ill-conceived in first place...a bad mission that was badly timed!"

"I'll have you relieved, Major, if you don't watch your step!"

Edrington stared at the General with contempt. "I don't give a rat's ass what you do with me, but I won't stand still and let you blame the aircrews who died on this fiasco...one you planned yourself!"

"You better get yourself under control, Major, because your group's going back to Ijmuiden again!"

"NO!" Spinelli jumped to his feet—his answer was a hoarse bellow.

"What do you mean...*no?*" the General hissed through his teeth.

Spinelli defiantly leaned toward the general and spoke in slow, measured tones. "What I mean, sir, is that I will fly a single ship mission back to that target, but I will not...*under any circumstances...*take any other squadron or element of the group with me.*"

The General was momentarily speechless—he was used to subordinates following his orders, whether they liked them or not. "You want me to find somebody else to lead it?" he eventually said, his voice threatening.

"No...I told you I would lead one plane."

The general noisily swiveled his chair around, turning his back on the two majors. "Both of you are dismissed! Get out of my office!"

The repercussions from the disastrous attack on Ijmuiden managed to reach all the way across the Atlantic Ocean to the desk of General Henry H. Arnold in the new Pentagon Building. The politicians in

Washington, specifically the Senators on the Truman Committee, renewed their attacks on the B-26 program, blaming it for the failure of the mission. The General wondered out of frustration if the damn airplane was somehow jinxed, but quickly suppressed the notion. He deliberated the back-channel message he'd just received from Major General James H. Doolittle in Tunisia. Doolittle, who had read the confidential after-action report on the raid, informed him, in explicit terms, that the first mission had been short-sighted and the second mission had been *sheer lunacy*. If the planners at 8TH Air Force had taken the time and trouble to look, he had consisely argued, they would have discovered that the B-26 wasn't currently being employed in low-level strikes in any other theater of the war. This was a sure case of a bad workman blaming his tools, he had said. The General made up his mind. He ordered Major General Ira Eaker, commander of the 8TH Air Force, to stand-down all of his B-26 groups from combat operations until further notice. The imbecile of a brigadier general who planned the missions ought to be court-martialed—he would like to shoot the son-of-a-bitch himself—but, to minimize the growing controversy, he'd order him relieved of command and sent to a supply depot where he would never be heard from again. Thinking ahead, he considered his opinion about who might relieve Eaker as commander of the 8TH at some point. He wondered whether Doolittle and Eisenhower would get along.

May 25, 1943, Snetterton Heath, England.

Newly promoted Lieutenant Colonel Vincent Spinelli, recently appointed to command the 333RD Bomb Group (Medium), glanced up from his desk to observe the young pilot entering his office. Noticing that the pilot was carrying his left arm in a sling and seemed, in a matter of weeks, to have lost much of his boyish appearance, the Colonel cheerlessly wondered what this kid would look like six months from now—*if he lived that long.* Helluva way to grow up.

"Hello, Ted...have a seat there next to Chet. How's it goin'? Everybody treating you o.k.?"

"Fine, uh, Colonel. Everybody's been swell."

"How's the arm?"

"Lots better, sir...I'll be back on flight status in a week."

"By the way, I dropped by to see Luce Clementi on my way back from headquarters. That piece of shrapnel really tore into his leg, but the doctors told me he'll be as good as new...be up walking in two weeks or so." Clementi had been moved to a large military hospital near London. "They also told me it'll be about a month before he's cleared to fly again. He told me to send you his regards."

Shaw fought the emotion welling up in his throat. "That's..." his voice cracked "...thank you for telling me, sir."

Changing the subject, Spinelli gave him a humorous look. "Paid a visit to your tail gunner yesterday, at the dispensary...what's his name?"

"Rimbaud."

"Yeah, Rimbaud...quite a character, isn't he?"

"I suppose that's one way of describing him, sir."

"Told me I ought to put your flight engineer up for some kind of medal for taking care of his wound. Said it would look good for the Air Force if somebody besides a college boy got one!" The memory of Rimbaud making the comment caused Spinelli to slap his leg and hoot with laughter. Composing himself, he regarded the pilot seriously again.

"On the subject of medals: you, Clementi, and Rimbaud will all receive Purple Hearts for your wounds."

Shaw looked at him with a steady gaze. That was one decoration you didn't have to thank anybody for.

"The officers in your crew will also receive the Distinguished Flying Cross and the Air Medal...your enlisted men will receive the Air Medal, too."

"Thank you, sir." Hesitating a moment, he gave Spinelli a thoughtful look. "Sir? Uh...I've got two personal recommendations for medals."

"Go ahead."

"I want to recommend both Lieutenants Glowgower and Grattan for the Bronze Star with a 'V' for valor. Lieutenant Glowgower took over as lead bombardier after Merrill's plane was hit...made a perfect bomb run on the target through all that flak. Then after we came off the target, when Luce and I got hit, he helped me fly the plane back on one engine. We'd have been goners without him." The memory of the experience caused him to grimace. "And Mick...Lieutenant Grattan...he figured out where we were and was able to plot a course to the target after we hit the coast. Then after we got hit, his quick thinking saved Clementi's life, kept him from bleeding to death." Shaw inwardly shuddered at the recollection of Grattan's blood-splattered flight clothing. "What those guys did, sir, is the bravest thing I've ever seen."

"Ted, I want you to repeat everything you just told me to Corporal McIlroy, my clerk, so he can put it in writing. I'll endorse your recommendation and do everything in my power to see that it gets approved."

"Thank you, Colonel."

"Now, Ted, I want to talk to you about something else." Spinelli got up and sat on the corner of the desk near the pilot. "Except for your crew, the 424TH squadron has, for all practical purposes, ceased to exist. But, I intend to rebuild it...your crew and three crews from other squadrons will form the nucleus." Pausing to light a cigarette, he blew the smoke sideways, away from Shaw. "I'm going to appoint you as the new deputy squadron commander...the other three will be your new flight leaders."

Shaw's face went blank. "I don't know, Colonel...." The idea of more resposibility for more people didn't appeal to him.

Spinelli stood up and put a hand on the pilot's shoulder. "You and your crew have had a tough time, Ted, but you've got to move on...there's still a job to do." He looked at the young pilot sympathetically. "I need your help."

Without expression, Shaw quietly said, "O.k., Colonel."

Spinelli sat back down on the desk. "You'll be glad to hear that they're sending us a new squadron commander up from 12TH who's flown the B-26 in combat. He'll also help Chet, who'll be deputy group lead and ops officer from now on. You have any questions so far?"

Shaw was secretly glad to hear that someone with previous combat experience was coming into the group. Maybe it would help. "Sir, I hear the group's been placed on stand-down, is that true?."

"Yes." Spinelli didn't mention that the order had come all the way from Washington, D.C.

"You know how long it might last?"

"Hard to say, Ted. For one thing, I've been told we're going to be moved...they want to use this base strictly for heavy bombardment." He moved closer to the pilot and almost whispered. "Keep this under your hat: it's my hunch... *strong hunch*...they're going to take us off this low-level stuff and let us re-train for medium altitude ops."

Shaw smiled at the Colonel, visibly brightening with relief. The last statement had come like a reprieve from a death sentence. Though he'd never said so, not even to Grattan, he shared the opinion of other aircrews in the group who felt that the second Ijmuiden mission had been a suicide run. This was good news. They needed it.

"Room! Atten-HUT!" Major General Ira Eaker strode purposefully to the front of the briefing hall and stepped onto the low platform. As he viewed the faces staring at him, he saw undisguised hostility and suspicion. Looks like a lynch mob, he thought. Well, can't blame them—he would probably feel the same way if he were sitting out there.

"As you were, men...please be seated." He waited for the scuffling of the chairs to settle down. The General tried to compose his grizzled features into something that looked unperturbed. "Men," he continued, "I haven't got a lot to say, but there are a few things I wanted to tell you in person." Pausing, he looked around the room, meeting the grim stares. "As your theater commander, the first and most important thing I want you to know is that you will not...*I repeat*...will not be sent on any more indefensible missions.*"

The faces in the room were still disbelieving, hard as granite.

"By 'indefensible' I mean that you will not be sent on combat missions where you are at a foreseeable tactical disadvantage." He stopped—it wasn't registering—then slowly said, "I'll try to spell it out for you:

"Item one! On future missions, you will have a fighter escort both to and from the target."

A low murmur of approval could be heard.

"Item two! You will not be placed into known flak corridors where there is a significant chance of barrage fire being set up between you and your target."

The harsh expressions of the crowd mellowed slightly. Listening from the second row of seats, Shaw had expected to hear these developments but was a little surprised that General Eaker had come all the way up from High Wycombe to deliver them in person. He was impressed.

"Finally, item three!" The General stepped from behind the podium and leaned toward them. "You can mark this down, men: no more low level operations...none! Neither the 333RD nor any other B-26 group will be employed again in this theater on any type of low-level mission..." This was the closest thing to an apology they would ever get.

The room came to attention again as the General stepped off the platform. Watching him leave, Lieutenant Colonel Spinelli arose from his seat and turned around to face the room. He could have told them the same thing, but hearing it from the top man was a real shot in the arm. The faces of the young aircrews staring at him showed visible relief. Well, I'm pretty relieved myself, he thought.

"Seats, men!" Spinelli barked. "Smoking lamp is lit." He waited for them to light their cigarettes and quiet down, then said, with genuine enthusiasm, "Gentlemen, the good news...the good news is that we are going back to the mission we were trained for in the first place: targets at medium range, bombing from medium altitudes." This brought on an appreciative murmur—they all knew it meant they would not be sent against heavily defended strategic targets. "You all know what that means," he continued: "good formation, good navigation, and good bombing. That's something I know we can do...and do it well!" When Spinelli had received the appointment to command the group, he resolved to do everything in his power to prevent the 333RD from becoming just another hard-luck outfit. Today, they had been given something important: hope.

Later that day, Spinelli sat in his office with the newly-arrived commander of the 424TH Squadron. He looked at the lanky, fair-haired officer and said, "We're real glad to have you join this group, Bobby. You're combat experience in the 12TH is going to help us out a lot. I won't kid you when I tell you this Ijmuiden thing threw a wet blanket on the morale of our aircrews."

"Not surprisin', Vince, not surprisin' a'tall," the man drawled.

"Your deputy's on his way over here. I know you didn't pick him, but I think you're gonna' like him. He's a top notch crew commander and is one of the best B-26 drivers in the outfit. Name's Shaw, Captain Theodore Shaw...he goes by Ted."

"Hmmm...seems like ah heard a'him somewhere."

They both turned to see Shaw standing in the doorway with his cap under his arm.

"Well, dog my cats!" whooped Major Robert M. Armistead, the new commander of the 424TH squadron. "Ah know this boy! He's the one who re-wrote the B-26 flight manual on his conversion check ride!" He jumped up and pumped Shaw's hand. He beamed at Spinelli and pointed at Shaw. "Why this boy's the most natchel B-26 pilot I ever saw!"

Shaw grinned at Armistead and said, "Good to see you again, Major."

Armistead cuffed him on the shoulder and chortled, "Hey, boy, this heah's the Air Force...you jus' call me Bobby from now on." He turned to Spinelli. "Right, Vince?"

Spinelli smiled weakly. "O.k., Bobby." He'd known Arimstead back at MacDill and had always been appalled by his informality toward senior officers and subordinates alike, but he was nevertheless his top pick of B-26 pilots from the 12TH Air Force. The troops would love him.

"Hell, jus' two years ago," Armistead drawled, "I was a first looie and ol' Vince there was a passed-over captain. War has an amazin' effect on military careers, don't it?"

The next morning Armistead met with the four aircrews that comprised the total complement of the 424TH squadron. Sitting down with them, cap cocked on the back of his head, he said, "We might still be in stand-down but that don't mean we ain't gonna' fly." He looked at Shaw. "Ted, ah'm gonna' fly with your crew till the M.O. clears you, o.k.?"

Shaw's brow puckered. He wasn't thrilled with the idea of his crew flying with someone else.

Armistead looked at him and scoffed, "I seen the look you gave me, boy...don't worry, ah ain't gonna take 'em away from you!" Lighting a Camel, he expressively blew out a gout of smoke. "We're expectin' replacement crews from the States this week. They'll be bringin' in some new planes, too, block twenties with the new tail turret. You can have one of the new planes, Ted."

"No thanks."

"What?"

"I like the one I've got."

"Yeah," Glowgower quickly added.

"Right." Grattan interjected conclusively.

"Well, you boys suit y'self...don't matter to me none." Armistead liked Shaw's crew. He doubted if there was one better in the whole European Theater. Funny, he thought, the way fate puts certain people together. "One thing I want you boys to understand right quick...ah ain't no expert whose gonna' tell you how to do everythin'...no suh! The tactical situation heah ain't a'tall like North Africa, so we gonna' have to learn it step-by-step, you folla' my drift?"

Shaw liked what he was hearing. Armistead, despite being very laid-back, radiated confidence, a quality that Chase had lacked. Maybe, he thought, the deputy commander job won't be too bad after all.

"Ah don't have no crystal ball," Armistead continued in his characteristic drawl, "but ah 'spect we gonna' be given tactical targets when we get back into combat. That's jus' about all we did in the 12TH. We tried bombin' ships, too, but all we did was make lots of hellacious waterspouts and probably concussed a few million fish." The lanky major snorted as he thought of it. "But we found out after a while...we found out we could do a lotta' damage to targets like roads, bridges, rail yards, supply dumps, and the like. Airfields, too. I tell ya'...a B-26 group can make some kinda' mess outa' an airfield. An' you know what else?" His face became serious. "We flew all a'these missions 'tween 9,000 and 12,000 feet and hardly...I mean hardly ever lost an airplane." Armistead paused to light a cigarette.

A tow-headed, baby-faced captain who'd been a deputy flight commander in one of the other squadrons spoke up.

"Major..."

"I tol' you mah names's Bobby...how many times ah'm gonna'

have to tell you?"

"Uh, Bobby...did you, I mean your B-26 group in the 12TH...was it always escorted by fighters?"

The lanky officer shook his head. "Not always. But that's 'cause there were times we didn't need 'em. Down there, you see, the Eye-ties had just about folded up and the Germans didn't have near the fighter coverage they got here, and they didn't have radar vectorin' neither. Ah kin tell you it's a whole different ballgame here, ah mean, a lot more dangerous. Cunnel Spinelli tol' me he wouldn't order no missions 'less we get fighter coverage all the way to the target and back. And our fighters...the P-47s they're usin' over here got plenty 'nough range to escort us, not like them heavies. Ah ain't lyin' when ah tell ya' ah'd rather take a whippin' than fly B-17s in this theater." He shook himself in an exaggerated shudder. "Can't 'magine goin' all the way into Nazi land an' back without a fighter escort!"

Three days later, Shaw's persistence finally wore the M.O. down, and he was released to full flight status. They had removed a shard of plexiglas the size of a spearhead from his left forearm plus a few smaller pieces the size of arrowheads. The largest wound left a puckered red scar that ran from his wrist half way to his elbow. The arm still smarted when he tried to lift anything heavy, but he—as opposed to the M.O.—felt it was sufficiently healed to permit him to fly. Despite Armistead assurance, he had chafed and fretted when his squadron and crew flew a number of practice missions without him. He didn't even mind the fact that he was going to have to break in a new co-pilot, at least temporarily. Clementi, he'd been told, would not make it back from the Air Force hospital in St. Albans until sometime after they moved the group.

Tech Sergeant Buster Ripley, the maintenance crew chief, sat in the shade with Milawski under the wing of *The A-Train*. He spat a viscous stream of tobacco juice on the turf next to the hardstand and grunted, "I reckon you can tell Cap'n Shaw this bird's ready for a test hop."

The flight engineer smiled. "I checked everything out, and it looks like you guys done a real fine job, Buster."

"Weren't nothin' real bad wrong with 'er 'cept that right engine, and we done bolted on a brand new 'un. All them flak and bullet hole's been patched. Man alive! You boys was powerful lucky...if several a'those hits had been an inch or so different, she'd caught a'fire and blew!"

Milawski involuntarily shivered. The day after they landed, he'd gone down to inspect the damage to the plane and had been horror-struck by the close proximity of some of the flak and shell strikes to fuel and hydraulic lines. A piece of shrapnel the size of a dinner plate had penetrated the fuselage just inches aft of his seat in the top turret and had exited the other side. Had it hit a few inches farther forward, he'd be dead. Ripley's remark about "luck" was a gross understatement.

Miles away, at the St. Albans hospital, Clementi winced as he struggled to shift to a more comfortable position in his bed. While the flak fragment had severely lacerated his femur muscle and cut the femoral artery, the bone had only been creased. The doctor told him it had taken over 300 sutures to put the whole thing back together. The tourniquet had saved his life. The pain wasn't as bad now, but it hurt like hell when they got him up to walk. Shaw had called and left a message saying that he and the other members of the crew were trying to wrangle transportation to come down and visit him. Clementi wasn't entirely sure that he wanted to see them; they were a tangible reminder of the stark horror he'd just been delivered from. Over and over, he'd relived the spectacle of the death-laden wall of flak around the target, Merrill's plane instantly disintegrating in a fireball, the incessant fighters diving on them like insane sharks. He speculated whether anyone else in the crew had experienced a level of fright like his; no, he decided, none of them are that weak. It made him remember what Chase had said about thinking too much. Poor old Chase, he thought, now just an unidentifiable lump of human offal somewhere on the Dutch coast. He wondered what Chase had thought about at that last moment. How in the hell can you stop thinking?

And what could he do about it? He could resign his commission and turn in his wings. Then what would they do with him? Send him to the infantry as a private? Because he'd been wounded in combat, he doubted it. Given his civilian work background, they'd probably send him to some rear area post and turn him into a clerk. He'd share an office with people who were losers and cowards—like him.

The thought made him sad and ashamed. In contrast, he'd been proud of his accomplishments since OTU—the discovery that he wasn't a half bad pilot. Shaw seemed unreservedly proud of him, too. And the crew—they gave him sense a belonging, a feeling of being an important part of a team, something he'd never experienced with other men. Slowly shutting his eyes, he put off thinking about his plans again until tomorrow.

The 333RD Bomb Group (M) was packing up and getting ready to move the following day. All of their personal gear and some of the group's equipment was being loaded into the planes. Shaw decided he better get a letter off while had a few minutes:

June 2, 1943

Dear Mary Beth,

My arm is healing up real well and I've returned to flight status. We haven't talked to Luce, but the group commander visited him the other day and told us that he's coming along fine and could be up and walking in a week or so. I told you about Leroy Rimbaud—Ha-Ha. He's got a real conversation piece on the right cheek of his behind.

I wanted to tell you about Joe Glowgower, our bombardier. You know we've had a pretty rocky relationship since OTU. Well, since that last mission, we've pretty much buried the hatchet if you know what I mean. We haven't become running buddies or anything like that yet, but we're getting along pretty well and have had a few nice conversations. Mick says that combat has been a learning experience for all of us but especially for Glow. He says Glow has a new identity, a better one, than he had before. It's all above my head, and I just have to take Mick's word for it.

On the subject of Mick, I'm real concerned that they are going to make him a lead navigator and take him from my crew. I would really hate to see that happen. It could happen with Glow, too. There's not much I can do about it. I flew this week with a pickup co-pilot I've never even met before. He was a decent pilot but it was really strange having somebody other than that skinny Italian in the right seat.

Guess what! The guy who gave me my B-26 check ride at MacDill is my new squadron commander. Small world, huh? He's a real good guy and one heck of a B-26 pilot. He's already flown more than 20 combat missions and is teaching us a lot of useful stuff.

I'm glad you're all settled in Dallas. I've heard about the P-51s your plant is building but none of them have made it over here yet. I've been told they will have the range to escort the heavy bombers all the way into deep targets and back. I can tell you that will save 1,000s of lives. Thank the Lord we don't have to go that far!

We're going to move to a new base tomorrow, and I'll write

again as soon as I get settled. Honey, I love you more than anything in the world and miss you more than words can express.

Your ever loving,
Ted

When Mary Beth Wainwright, over 6,000 miles away in Dallas, Texas, received this letter and the past few Shaw had written to her, she was puzzled and troubled by his omission of anything about their marriage plans or coming home. She wasn't worried about him changing his mind, for they were inextricably close to each other in a way that many people never achieve. He'd never been one for mushy love letters, and his correspondence had always been generally informational and terse, but he usually mentioned something about coming home to her. Had he simply blanked it out for some reason, she wondered? Whatever it was, she decided it would do no good to press the matter. Before he left the last time, he'd bravely told her not to worry about him—that it would make things harder for both of them, but how could she not? How could she not?

CHAPTER TWELVE

June 6, 1943, Boxsted, England.

The move to the new base had gone off with a minimum of fuss, and the group was now located in the Duchy of Essex about seventy-five miles south of Norwich and about fifty miles northeast of London. The airfield, which had been English farmland before the war, wasn't exactly "new," having been one of the many small aerodromes used by the RAF during the Battle of Britain, in the summer of 1940. Since the American contractors and constructors had worked their magic, however, the base bore little resemblance to its humble RAF origins. Like most U.S.A.A.F. bases in England, it was dominated by a concrete runway—somewhat shorter than Snettereton's—sided by a tarmac, green-painted control tower and maintenance hangars, a perimeter track dotted with hardstands and revetments, and the inevitable collection of quonset huts of various sizes. Most Air Force personnel serving in other theaters, like the South Pacific or North Africa would have have considered these accomodations and facilities to be opulent, which was why, in other war zones, the 8TH was euphemistically referred to as the "Hollywood Air Force."

In addition to the 333RD Bomb Group (Medium), the base was home to several fighter groups flying P-47 Thunderbolts. When missions were scheduled for the heavy bombardment groups, Boxsted's P-47s could be seen roaring down the runways to accompany the heavy bombers to the Dutch or Belgian coast, the limit of the fighters' range, after which they would return to base, re-arm and re-fuel, then take-off again to meet the bombers on their return home. In the beginning, the heavy bombers' losses on daylight, deep-penetration missions had been grievous, with sometimes over twenty-five percent of the formations being decimated by flak and enemy fighters. With the improvement in tactics and armament, however, losses had been reduced to less than ten percent, an "acceptable" rate of attrition according to the Air Force planners. In plain mathematical terms, this meant that if one hundred American heavy bombers participated in a mission to industrial targets in Germany, between seventy-five and one hundred young airmen would be killed, wounded or captured. In 1943, if an American airmen were assigned to fly a twenty-five mission tour on B-17s or B-24s in the ETO, there was a good chance—better than even probably—that he would never finish it. The greatest danger lay in the first few missions—green crews frequently made mistakes that cost them their lives. But against this backdrop of danger, U.S.A.A.F. doctine—daylight precision bombing—was having its designed effect: the means of the Third Reich to equip its Nazi war machine was slowly but inexorably being reduced. As Winston Churchill had aptly stated in another context: It wasn't the beginning and it wasn't the end, but it was the beginning of the end.

In addition to the unremitting day and night bombardment of German strategic targets, the Allies in England were planning the largest, most ambitious operation yet to take place in the war. The code name assigned to it was "Operation Overlord," but it would always be known as "D-Day," the invasion of Normandy. The Allies weren't ready yet; military planners felt it would take nearly another year. But attacking the industrial centers which supported the Nazi war machine wasn't enough, the Allies needed to attack the machine itself, and the 8TH Air Force had recently acquired the perfect weapon to do this: the Martin B-26 Marauder.

At medium ranges, 600 to 900 miles, a B-26 could carry nearly the same bomb load—4,000 pounds—a B-17 carried on a mission to Germany. At medium altitudes, 9,000 to 12,000 feet, a B-26 could hit smaller targets with far greater accuracy than the high altitude heavy bombers. They could be employed against targets like major roads, bridges, rail lines and the marshalling yards where trains were assembled, canals and dock facilities, fuel and ammunition storage facilities, supply dumps, and overland convoys—all essential to the German war machine. Moreover, they could assault the German defenses themselves: airfields, troop garrisons, artillery and armor parks, and fortified gun positions. The Allied planners knew the German's ability to fight back had to be substantially weakened before the massed American and British troops could cross the Channel and gain a foothold on the European continent.

"You coming with us, Glow?" In the three weeks since the Ijmuiden mission, the bombardier's relationship with the crew of *The A-Train* had undergone a rapid transformation.

Glowgower—and many others—had discovered that combat can be

a curious leveler of human relationships: men who would never associate with one another under ordinary circumstances due to differences in upbringing, religion, social position, or personality, often experience a unique kinship when they have been thrust together under fire. Glowgower's deep-seated enmity toward Shaw and the other members of the crew had vanished somewhere in the tumult of the last mission. Although it had not been an occasion of apologies or tearful embraces, Shaw and the others treated him as if the previous disunion had never existed. The nightmares unaccountably disappeared.

"Uh, I wonder if it's really a good idea?" Glowgower looked at Shaw with an worried expression. He genuinely wanted to go with them but didn't want to cast a pall over the planned visit with Clementi.

Shaw face creased in a grin. "I think it's a great idea," he said without any hesitation. "All of us want you to come."

"Well, you know, Ted, seeing me might not..."

Shaw interrupted, gently squeezing the bombardier's bicep. "He'll want to see you, Glow...I know he will."

Glowgower's handsome features brightened. "O.k., sign me up."

Later that morning, Shaw, Grattan, Glowgower, and Milawski rode the train from Colchester, near the base, to the King's Cross station in London, then changed to another train bound for St. Albans. The wartime train was unbelievably packed with traveling American and British servicemen, many of whom were required to stand or sit in the aisles for most of the trip. The interior of the passenger car they occupied stank of cigarette smoke, dirty canvas web gear, wool uniforms saturated with body odor, and gun oil—the all-pervading smell of an army in passage. Outside the train windows, on the roadways that wound through the English countryside, they observed seemingly endless convoys of six-by-six trucks and other military vehicles hauling troops and the materials of war to various locations. And whenever or wherever they looked up, they saw airplanes—always airplanes—coming from or en route to the airfields which had sprouted all over East Anglia. But noticeably mixed into the backdrop of this martial presence, were the indomitable Essex and Hertfordshire farmers and drovers, working their fields or tending their flocks as their forebears had done generations before them through countless other wars.

When the train finally stopped at the station siding in St. Albans, Shaw and his small group, finding no buses or taxis, were forced to hike the final two miles to the hospital, dragging their baggage with them. It was a muggy June day, and perspiration began to trickle down the sides of their khaki-clad bodies. When they were still half a mile away, Milawski, puffing with exertion, removed his cap and used it as a fan. "Whew! Good thing Leroy couldn't come... we'd all be carryin' that rascal by now." The tail gunner was on the mend, but had yet to be returned to full duties or allowed to travel. "Hey," the engineer asked in a mirthful tone, "has he shown any of you officers where he got hit?"

"No," all of them replied curiously.

"No? Well, that's kind of funny 'cause I'll bet he's shown it to just everybody else on the base. Every time someone asks him how he's doin', he always says, 'Lookee heah! Ah'll sho' yous!' then drops his pants!"

Milawski's accurate imitation of the swarthy little Cajun's accent together with the vision of his bared buttocks caused them all to fall down in a convulsion of laughter.

"Well, that's certainly something I can look forward to," quipped Grattan as he wiped a tear from his eye.

They walked up a stone staircase into the foyer of the old hospital building, and Shaw asked the orderly stationed at front desk for the location of Lieutenant Clementi's ward. They tried hard not to stare at the patients as they wordlessly made their way down the hall. Seated in wheelchairs were men minus a leg or a foot, and some who had lost both; other men were walking with bandaged stumps where arms or hands had been or were encumbered by plaster casts of varying sizes; and some men were being led down the hall with bandages over blind eyes. These were the ones who were fit enough to be up and about.

Watching the door, Clementi saw Shaw and the others step into the ward, caps under their arms, carefully looking around like lost little boys. Throwing a tattered copy of of *The Saturday Evening Post* on the metal bed stand beside him, he pulled himself up in the bed. As he watched the grinning faces approach, he fought against the constriction in his throat and the tears welling at the backs of his eyes. He'd never been more glad to see anybody.

"Hey, Luce! How's it goin', ol' buddy?" Shaw boomed as he bounded the last few steps to Clementi's bed. All of them, except Glowgower, encircled his bed, grabbing his hand and jostling his shoulders. The bombardier hung back a few moments, then stepped forward and offered his hand. "Hello, Luce, nice to see you."

"I'm glad you came, Glow...really." Clementi looked at the bombardier intently for a moment, continuing to grip his hand. "I know what you did...Colonel Spinelli told me when he came by."

The co-pilot looked around quickly. "Where's that no-account Leroy?" he demanded.

Milawski, poker-faced, answered, "You heard...you heard he got wounded, didn't you?"

"Yeah, Spinelli told me he took one right in the ass." Clementi gave the engineer a worried look. "He's gonna' be all right, isn't he?"

"The M.O. said he couldn't travel just yet, but he's absolutely tip top!" Trying with difficulty to suppress a laugh, Milawski said, "When you do see him, Lieutenant, you be real sure to ask him about his wound."

They all laughed so loud the other occupants of the ward curiously looked their way.

"I don't get it," Clementi said in puzzlement.

"Oh, you will, Luce, take my word for it," Grattan explained.

"How's the food here?" Shaw asked.

"Dogshit," the co-pilot replied disapprovingly.

"Doesn't look to me like you've missed any meals...you may even have gained a few pounds, huh?"

"Well what do you expect me to do, starve?"

"We chipped in and brought you a present." Shaw reached down into his valv-pack and brought out a bottle which he handed to Clementi.

The co-pilot looked at it appreciatively. "Gee, thanks, fellas', Black & White, my brand...how'd you know?"

Grattan laughed, "Well, boyo, you haven't exactly made your drinking habits a secret."

"You guys want a nip right now?" the co-pilot gleefully suggested. "There are some paper cups over there by the water cooler."

"Why not," said Shaw, who had never tasted anything stronger than bourbon mixed with Coca-Cola.

When all the cups were filled, Glowgower stepped foward and said, "I propose a toast to...*The A-Train* and her merry crew!"

"HERE, HERE!" All of them shouted, throwing their back drinks in one vast gulp. Shaw, oblivious to the power of undiluted scotch, erupted in a spasm of violent coughing, causing Grattan to grab his arm and pound his back. After a minute, the pilot took a deep breath and weakly smiled at them with tears streaming down his face.

All of them hooted loudly at their discomfited aircraft commander, and Clementi laughed with mirth he'd not felt since the mission. He pointed to the cabinet beside his bed and said, "Hide the booze down there so the nurses and orderlies won't find it."

"Will they confiscate it?" Grattan cautiously asked.

"Good stuff like this?" the co-pilot winked confidentially. "Hell no, they'll drink it!" Pointing to the baggage beside them, he asked, "Where you guys headed to when you leave here?"

"We're going into London for a couple of days and then back to Boxsted," Shaw told him. "By the way, we got all your stuff moved to the new base."

"You get my pinups, the Vargas girls?" Clementi had decorated one side of the hut's wall with them.

Shaw slapped his forehead in an open palm gesture. "Damnation Luce! You wanted to keep those things?" The co-pilot stiffened and looked at him in alarm, but before he could say anything, Shaw reassuringly conceded, "Just kiddin' ol' buddy...got 'em all. Hey, before we go, you need anything, smokes, reading material?"

"Uh-uh, they got us covered. Red Cross brings us cigarettes, newspapers and magazines...everything we need."

After saying their goodbyes, Clementi watched his four friends file out the door then stop momentarily to turn around and wave at him with silly grins on their faces. The visit had left him with a warm glow of inclusion. Making the decision he'd been struggling with since the mission, he put the notion of quitting completely out of his mind. It wasn't simply a question of quitting flying, he realized, but quitting *them*. Somehow, he would just have to learn to deal with the fear. Perhaps Chase had been right after all.

Leaving St. Albans, Shaw and the others took the train back to King's Cross and rode the Underground to the Tower station, where, at Grattan's suggestion, they disembarked. As they passed through a number of Underground stations, they noticed people, whole families, bringing bedrolls in preparation to spend the night. On the streets above, they saw entire blocks of buildings—obviously not military targets—reduced to rubble as a result of three years of the German Blitz. If you discounted the fleeting images of the bomb strikes they had seen during the Ijmuiden mission, this was the first time any of them had been confronted with the indiscriminate destruction wrought by war. It was a sobering realization—they were here to bring the same sort of thing back to the enemy.

They walked toward the river and found a small pub near the entrance to the Tower Bridge. Inside, as they were drinking pints of the dark, bitter beer, Shaw suggested they should look for a place to spend the night.

"Let's go to the Air Force club...it's near Piccadilly, I think...and ask around," Grattan suggested.

"Good idea, but let's take a taxi this time...we get back on that subway, there's no telling where we'll end up."

"We can stay at the USO if we have to," Milawski said.

Shaw lit a cigarette and said, "I don't know about you, but I'd like a little more privacy and a hot bath."

"I like the sound of that!" Glowgower interjected.

Half an hour later, Grattan, Glowgower, and Milawski stood outside the entrance to Air Force Club while Shaw went inside to get information about a place to stay. Milawski, an NCO, was self-consciously aware he was not welcome at the officer's club.

"Uh...you guys can go on without me," Milawski said uneasily. "I'll be o.k."

"Nothing doing, Ski...we'll stick together," Glowgower said flatly, playfully slapping the young engineer in the shoulder.

A few minutes later, Shaw was back. "Well, Fellas', there are some places with rooms, but none of 'em are here in the downtown area." In other words, he failed to say, not close to the night spots frequented by servicemen.

"Doesn't matter to me," Grattan said.

"Me neither," added Glowgower.

They took another taxi out to the Kensington area and found an old, turn-of-the century tourist hotel with two vacancies. Filled with a vague, moldy smell, the place had seen better times. The halls were covered in threadbare carpets and the rooms, each containing two old-fashioned steel beds, were floored in peeling linoleum. A small, grimy sink occupied the corner of each room, with a communal toilet and bath at the end of the hall. Compared to their recent military accommodations, it was the lap of luxury.

As soon as the elderly bellman unloaded their valv-packs and musette bags, Shaw announced semi-seriously, "You men agree that the senior officer present ought to have first shot at the bath?"

As he reclined in the large, footed cast iron tub a short while later, the steaming hot water seemed to melt away all of the accumulated tension and fatigue of the past month. It was great to get away from the base and its interminable routines. Shaw liked Air Force life and loved the flying—most of it—but the endless briefings and meetings, the planning and the paperwork, the red tape, all drove him to distraction. And now, being Armistead's deputy in the squadron, meant more of the same. He sat up and reached for his cigarette pack and lighter laying on the stool beside the tub. Lighting the cigarette, he blew the smoke upward toward the old cracked and discolored plaster ceiling. It reminded him of the way the land sometimes looked from the air, with its vari-colored landscape and intertwining rivers, streams and roads. The world always looked good from up there, clean and unblemished. Sliding down in the tub until the water reached his chin, he closed his eyes. Unaccountably, images of the Ijmuiden mission flickered into his mind, the flak buffeting them like angry thunderclaps, the tracer fire from the attacking fighters lancing toward them like incandescent baseballs, aircraft on either side of them disintegrating in a flash of burning fragments. Suddenly sitting bolt upright in the tub, he rubbed his eyes and dunked his head in the water several times, as if to drown out the frightful vision. Emerging from the tub, he dried himself vigorously with a rough towel.

"It's all yours, Mick," he informed his roommate several minutes later.

"I'll wait a while." The big navigator stiffled a yawn. "I'm going to take a little nap...haven't been in a place this quiet since my last leave."

Shaw closed the shades and lay down, too, with the towel still wrapped around his middle; and after a few minutes of listening to Grattan's quiet snoring, he too dropped into a deep, dreamless sleep.

The four of them, visibly rested, scrubbed and refreshed, reassembled later in the small lounge located off the hotel lobby, which was occupied by small groups of servicemen. Unlike service clubs, it was quiet and dark, the conversation held to a low murmuring. Seated at one of the tables was a small group of British Army officers, identified as 8TH Army veterans of the Western Desert by the regimental flashes on their tunics. They regarded the group of Americans for a moment, then looked away. Over to one side, several Air Corps officers wearing the shoulder patch of the 8TH Air Force looked up and motioned them to have a seat around their table.

As they sat down, a smiling young lieutenant wearing pilot's wings asked, "What outfit you guys from?"

"The 333RD Bomb Group out of Boxsted," Grattan answered first.

The lieutenant looked puzzled. "That a new B-17 or B-24 group?" he asked.

"No, we fly B-26s."

"B-26s...cripes almighty! I heard about the mission against that Dutch powerplant. Did you know any of those guys?

"Yeah, all of 'em...they were from our group."

"Man! You guys are lucky you didn't go on that one!"

Shaw looked at the lieutenant solemnly. "We did...we were the only ones who made it back."

The others stared at them in shock for a moment. "Gee, I mean that musta' been tough...really tough."

"Yeah." Shaw changed the subject. "What do you fellas' fly?"

The lieutenant smiled like someone who had just been invited to talk about his favorite subject. "Thunderbolts, P-47s," he said, proudly. "We're based up at Biggin Hill.

"How you like 'em?" Shaw asked. "The '47s, I mean."

"Great airplane! A real pussycat to fly, very stable gun platform, and *fast*, with loads of firepower...eight fifties! Not much of a dog-fighter, but if you get a one-oh-nine or one-ninety on your tail, all you have to do is head for the deck and they can't catch you. The only bad thing about 'em is the range, can't escort the bombers far enough. They tell us we're getting drop tanks pretty soon that'll give us another 160 gallons, extending our range at least another two hours."

Grattan made a quick calculation in his head. "That still won't allow you to make it to deep targets."

"Nope." The lieutenant looked at him gravely. "That won't happen until we get P-51s, the B Models equipped with the Merlin engine, and I hear that'll be another six months or longer."

"You fellas' will probably be escortin' us sometime soon," Shaw said.

"Yeah?"

"We'll probably be flying combat ops again in a month or so."

"Where to?"

"They haven't told us anything yet, but I'm bettin' it'll be tactical targets in France, Belgium, and maybe Holland."

"If that's the case," the lieutenant made a broad sweeping gesture with his arms. "We'll be able to cover you all the way in and back out!"

Glowgower, who had been silently listening, spoke up. "What kind of combat ops have you guys flown over here so far?" For the next thirty minutes, the fighter pilots regaled them with tales of air-to-air combat between their P-47s and ME-109s and FW-190s, illustrated by rapid hand movements and sputtering sound effects. The B-26 crew was simultaneously mesmerized and encouraged by the unbridled enthusiasm of these young Thunderbolt pilots, for they were deadly serious about the business of killing German fighters. "You guys going downtown to find some action?" the lieutenant finally asked.

"Not me." Shaw and Grattan answered almost at the same time.

"How 'bout you two?" He grinned brightly at Glowgower and Milawski."

Milawski looked warily at the all-officer group. "Uh...I don't know."

The lieutenant smirked, leaning foward to give him a playful punch on the shoulder. "Don't you worry, Sarge," he said offhandedly, "most all of the joints down there are open to everybody."

Glowgower looked at the engineer. "Sounds good to me me, Ski...let's go."

Shaw and Grattan watched the mixed group leave. "I don't blame those fighters boys for wanting to take Glow with them," the pilot quipped. "He'll attract every woman within ten miles. You notice the way women stare at him?"

The big navigator smiled at the suggestion. "Yeah, but he doesn't seem to flaunt it."

"Hellfire, man, when you already look like a movie star, why do you need to flaunt anything?"

"I suppose. You hungry?"

"Yeah, starved."

"I saw a place a couple of blocks from here, looked nice."

"Lead the way."

A short while later they sat in a corner at a small candlelit table. Grattan looked around and said, "Eleanor would love this place."

Shaw tilted his head and wrinkled his nose. "What's that smell...kinda' stinks in here."

"I think its curry and garlic...they use to season the food."

Shaw looked with confusion at the menu. "What kinda' food is this anyway?"

"I believe it's Indian."

"Indians! In England?"

"Asian Indians, you dope...they're part of the British Empire."

"Oh, right. You've eaten this kind of stuff before?"

"No, but I've heard it's good."

"Well, I certainly hope it tastes better than it smells."

"Don't worry, you'll like it."

A very small, dark woman dressed in a traditional sari took their order. Shaw ordered the same thing as Grattan, a lamb curry served on rice. Shaw idly picked up a few of the bottles from the condiment tray on the table and sniffed their contents. "Hey, this smells sorta' like chili pepper sauce," he said.

When the woman set their plates in front of them, Shaw liberally doused his food with the dark red sauce from one of the bottles.

"I'd go easy on that stuff," the navigator warned.

"Why?"

"It's probably very spicy."

Shaw smirked at him and scoffed, "I grew up in Texas, friend...been eatin' hot sauce on my food all my life." He forked a giant bite of the sauce-laden food into his mouth and began to slowly chew.

The smile on his face suddenly transformed to alarm. Swallowing the food, he croaked, "Hot damn!" and downed the tumbler of water at his side in one gulp, then reached across the table, seized Grattan's water glass and drank it down, too. "Woo-ee!" he exclaimed as he wiped his mouth and loosened his tie. "I like it!"

After the table had been cleared, Shaw, long accustomed to generous American mess hall portions, observed, "These folks must not be big eaters...I'm still kinda' hungry."

"Haven't seen many fat people around here, have you?" Grattan commented dryly.

Shaw gave him a puzzled look. "Guess I haven't paid much attention."

"Did you know the people here have been under strict food rationing since 1940?" Before Shaw could answer the question, Grattan continued, "Things like beef and dairy products are virtually impossible to obtain...all of it is earmarked for the military."

"You wouldn't know it from the local people you run into," Shaw ventured. "I mean they seem cheerful enough."

"I've noticed the same thing...you can't help but admire their backbone." Grattan looked at him thoughtfully. "That's kind of funny...I'm not exactly an anglophile..."

"Anglo-what?" Shaw looked at him questioningly.

"Means being an admirer of English culture. But you have to understand this: my Irish ancestors hated the English for good reasons. In fact, I was brought up to believe that all Englishmen were merciless tyrants. But being over here and seeing these everyday common folk in a wartime situation compels me to re-examine my opinion of them. As a nation, these people, it seems to me, have an inexhaustible quantity of courage and endurance. You understand?"

"I think so," Shaw answered out of politeness. The big navigator frequently talked over his head.

"Makes you wonder, though," Grattan said in a contemplative tone.

"About what?" The pilot asked.

"Makes you wonder whether Americans would hold up as well in the same situation."

Shaw gave him an astonished look. "Americans? Are you serious? We're the toughest people in the world! Why, when these same people invaded us, we kicked their limey butts all the way back across the Atlantic Ocean, didn't we?"

"Right." The big navigator smiled benignly at the pilot's simple approach to complicated questions, then queried, "Makes you wonder if the Germans are made of the same stuff."

"Boy, I hope not," Shaw replied. "But they're gettin' it a lot worse, aren't they?"

"Much worse, or will be. Our Air Force has started bombing them by day and the RAF already bombs them at night. All of their big cities will be systematically gutted before its over."

Shaw gave Grattan a sober look and asked, candidly, "You think bombing the populated areas is wrong, Mick?"

"Wrong?" The big navigator looked up in thought. "I'm not sure I can answer that one, Ted. I suppose I would call it a necessary evil...necessary because the Germans have really given us no choice. If we don't smash their industry, the war could go on indefinitely, and killing civilians who live and work in the industrial areas is an unavoidable consequence, I guess."

"How long do you think it's gonna' take, Mick?"

"You mean to win the war here...just in Europe?"

Shaw understood the war was global in scope but had a very limited understanding of the military campaigns being conducted in other parts of the world. "Just here," he eventually replied.

Grattan gave the pilot an earnest look, then sighed, "We've hardy begun really. This year we got a foothold in southern Italy, but the Italians caved-in almost all at once. You can be sure that the Germans won't give in as easily. We'll have to invade the north coast of France, sometime next year probably, then we'll have fight them all the way across the European continent until we meet up with the Russians, on the Eastern Front. A lot of it depends on how much progress the Russians make on their front." He paused to gaze at Shaw. "To answer your original question, I think it will take two years or more."

Shaw was impressed by the navigator's grasp of the situation. "Where do you get all the information on this stuff, Mick?" he asked.

Grattan's ruddy face creased in a wry grin. "Newpapers and magazines, boyo...same ones everybody else reads."

Two days later, when Shaw and the others returned from London, the training for medium missions went into full swing. It was mostly a re-hash of the things they'd practiced during OTU: box formation, precision bombing with the Norden sight, navigation and radio procedures, and gunnery against towed sleeves. Shaw sometimes wondered if any unit in the entire Air Force had ever received more training. Somewhere in this process, however, Shaw and the rest of his crew had ceased being the trainees and had become the trainers. In the course of it, Shaw flew with most of the squadron's flight leaders and with the new pilots who'd recently come in from replacement pools. Occupying the co-pilot's station usually, he worked with them to refine their flying technique from the form-up to the bomb run. On the days he led practice missions, he became the one screaming over the radio: "Watch your formation! Close it up! Keep it tight, dammit! You're too close, TOO CLOSE!" The new pilots found him to be relentlessly meticulous and demanding, always pushing them to the limits of their abilities, but at the same time, even-tempered and fair. All who flew with him were duly impressed by the seemingly effortless precision with which he flew a B-26, and after a time, began to comprehend the soft-spoken Texan's constant admonition: "Think *with* the airplane, don't react to it...will it to do what you want it to do."

In early July, Clementi returned, still limping a little, but otherwise none the worse for wear. His flying was rusty, but after several days with Shaw, who made him fly *The A-Train* from take-off to landing, much of it from the left seat, he regained his groove. After a week, the co-pilot felt like he'd never been gone.

There were briefings every day on a variety of topics.

The group's navigators and bombardiers became more familiar with the cities, towns, rivers and general terrain of northern France, Belgium, and Holland than they were with own backyards. The engineers were taught how to troubleshoot and repair every conceivable type of battle damage. The gunners learned how to clear guns and change magazines with rapid efficiency. They were almost ready to go back to war.

The second week of July, pilots, navigators and bombardiers were ordered to attend a special briefing. As the room came to attention that day, Colonel Spinelli walked to the platform accompanied by a limping RAF officer.

"Seats!" the Colonel barked, allowing the attendees a few moments to get settled. Owlishly smiling at them, he began, "Gentlemen, in today's briefing you'll get a general overview of railway targets from the vicinity of Cherbourg, here in France," he tapped the map behind him with the snooker stick he used as a pointer, "over to Aachen, just across the Belgian-German border. With us today is Squadron Leader Harry Tompkins of British Air Intelligence," he motioned to the RAF officer standing beside him, "who is an expert on the subject." He stood aside and said, "Squadron Leader?"

The slight, sandy-haired RAF officer limped over to the podium and smiled through slightly gapped teeth. Those sitting on the first few rows noticed he was wearing the embroidered wings of an RAF pilot and had the distinctive British DFC ribbon pinned to his tunic.

"Good morning, Chaps!" he piped in a high nasal voice.

"Some of you may have noticed that I am a pilot...or was, until I got this..." He rapped his right leg with the pointer and was rewarded with a hollow wooden *thunk*. "But before I was a pilot, I was a railroad man and have seen most of the rail installations on which you will be briefed." Pausing, he lit a briar pipe, which looked like a permanent fixture of his pale face. When the smoke cloud dissipated, he continued, "Now...if you gentlemen will oblige me, I shall direct your attention to the rail system maps that have been specially prepared for this briefing. You can see that these lines are color coded according to their role in the scheme of the rail system." Using the pointer and talking at the same time, he methodically explained the function of the various lines and how they interconnected with marshalling yards, switching stations and cities along their route. By the time this part of the briefing was finished, most of the assembled pilots, navigators, and bombardiers had reached a practical understanding of the rail transportation system running from Western Normandy to the German border.

Tompkins stopped to use a penknife to clear the tobacco ash from his pipe, then rapped it noisily several times on the side of the podium. "This, chaps," he drew a circle around the entire map with his pointer, "is the primary circulatory system which carries the life blood of the Nazi Reich to its West European occupied territories. Without it, Jerry cannot maintain sufficient logistical support to hold or defend these territories for any extended period of time. A panzer division, for example, requires massive quantities of fuel and ammunition just to fight in place for one day. Because of the virtually impenetrable naval blockade put up by our combined forces, their only alternative to rail transport is to try to move material in trucks over roadways at night. As you might imagine, this would reduce the re-supply of their army and air force to a mere fraction of that which they are presently moving by rail.

"One of the fastest means of denying Jerry the use of this system is the coordinated destruction of its key rail bridges. If we can remove a bridge...here or here, for example," he indicated the positions with the pointer, "it would interdict the flow of material along that route for days, and in some instances, perhaps weeks. The RAF has been attacking these targets for over two years in operations we call 'circuses,' but has been unable to inflict major damage because of the small numbers of aircraft used, which usually consists of three or four Blenheim light bombers with a Spitfire escort. As for the heavy bombers, yours and ours, the targets are simply too small for them to achieve any level of precision. But we," he pointed to himself, "and your Air Force," pointing to Spinelli, "believe the B-26s, dropping their bombs from 9,000 to 12,000 feet in tight, group formations, can destroy these bridges...completely."

The last statement caused a stir of enthusiastic murmuring among the seated aircrews. They could do this job.

"O.k., chaps, let's get down to cases and talk about Jerry's defenses." The murmuring abruptly ceased.

"As you probably know, the Luftwaffe has fighter stations that run from the Channel Coast all the way across the Low Countries." Using the pointer again, he swept across the map from west to east. "And these bases are directed and controlled by Wurzburg radar stations spaced at intervals here and here." Turning, he stabbed the map in several locations with the pointer. "You can expect fighter opposition to be quite intense, as they will see you assembling before you cross the English coast."

The comment led to a round of low muttering and chair-scraping from the audience.

Tompkins paused a moment to regain their attention. "To protect you against this threat, you will be screened by fighter escort long before you reach the enemy coast. One or more Thunderbolt groups, I am told, will be used to escort your group on these targets, and RAF Spitfires can be made available as well. This will neutralize most of the danger, and those who should happen to get through, will be subjected to the massed firepower of your group."

He stopped to refill and light his pipe. "Now flak...your missions will be planned in such a way as to route you around the major concentrations of 88 millimeter, radar-guided batteries, but the important bridges are protected by their own flak sites as well, mostly the 40 millimeter Bofors stuff, which are optically sighted and effective up to 15,000 feet. When the flak defenses around a particular bridge are deemed to be a significant threat, however, a fighter-bomber sortie will be mounted to precede you to remove or minimize them."

A hand went up. "Sir, what fighter-bombers are you talking about?"

"RAF Typhoons, I expect. They are armed with two 20 millimeter cannons and use 3.75 inch rockets...and those chaps are specialists at this sort of thing."

The comment caused Shaw to remember his conversation with the RAF pilot at the NAAFI dance in Norwich and speculate whether he would be involved.

When the briefing concluded a short while later, the room buzzed with lively conversation. Glowgower turned to Shaw and the others and said, bluntly, "Sounds like somebody finally got their shit together."

"What about those bridge targets, Glow?" Grattan seriously asked. "You think they can be hit from a medium bombing altitude?"

The bombardier's face screwed into a facetious grin. "If *you*," sticking his index finger into the navigator's chest, "can get us to the right IP, I can put the bombs smack in the middle of the friggin bridges."

Shaw was encouraged, not doubting for a moment that Glowgower and Grattan could do their jobs. Spinelli had told him that on future missions only the lead and deputy lead elements would continue to carry navigators. He'd been advised of other crew changes, too: they would start carrying an extra gunner who was also a trained radio operator. The new radio/gunner would man the top turret while the flight engineer would operate the two 50-caliber machine guns in newly-improved waist gun positions, thereby enhancing the defenses on the flanks of the formation.

For the 333RD Bomb Group (M), the refining process was finally over—*now the real fight would begin.*

CHAPTER THIRTEEN

July 17, 1943, Boxsted, England.

The first rail bridge target assigned to the group was located on a canal near the city of Lens, in the province of Artois, about twenty miles west of the Belgian border and over sixty miles inside the French coast. Reconnaissance photographs showed that it was an older iron truss structure supported by two stone pilings. The bridge contained two of the main tracks running between Paris and Brussels, and its destruction would disrupt the major northeastern supply route to the enemy-occupied French capital.

The intelligence briefing indicated medium flak defenses, 40 millimeter on both sides of the bridge, augmented by 12.7 millimeter machine guns that would be out of range at the bombing altitude assigned. An hour in advance of their ETA over the target, a flight of Typhoons from RAF Tangmere would be dispatched to deal with the guns. The main threat to the group, the intelligence officer warned, would come from the fighter aircraft scrambled from bases, which lay within fifty miles of the target. P-47s out of Duxford would meet them off the English coast, accompany them all the way to the target, orbit the target area during the bomb run, then escort them back to the English coast.

The weather to and over the target was forecast to be clear, seven to ten miles visibility in light haze and smoke, with a widely scattered deck of cumulus between 6,000 and 7,000 feet that wasn't expected to obscure the target.

When they returned to base, the briefer said, there was a chance of broken overcast—six to seven-tenths coverage— together with a thirty per cent chance of light rain.

The navigation route to the target would take the group almost due south across England to Folkstone, where they would cross the coast, turn southeast until they reached Montreuil on the Artois coast, then turn again almost due east to Lens, their IP. The planned route would skirt them between the German fighters based at Abbeville and St. Omer and keep them away from the heavy flak. The heading from the IP would be zero-one-zero, slightly east of north, and the distance to the aiming point twelve miles, a three and one-half minute run to the target. The timing was tight, they explained, but the navigators should be able to pick up the landmarks easily. Without ceremony, the assembled pilots, navigators and bombardiers hacked their watches at 0427 GMT.

Navigators and bombardiers attended a separate briefing and were shown high-resolution photos of the area from the IP to the target. Maintaining an altitude of 10,000 feet from the English coast to the target, they would bomb visually by squadron with intervalometers—the device that sequenced the bombs—set at 100 milliseconds.

The 424TH Squadron received a final briefing from Armistead, whose manner was noticeably more businesslike this morning. The call sign for group lead was "shortstop" he said and the squadrons would be identified by color code. Armistead's B-26, named *Friend or Enema?*, would be "white leader," and *The A-Train,* deputy lead for the squadron, would be "white able two." They would be positioned on the left wing of the group 100 feet below the lead squadron, *The A-Train* taking station directly behind and slightly below *Friend or Enema?*.

"You boys done a damn good job so far," Armistead said with none of the usual rashness in his voice, "but we ain't practicin' no more and there ain't room for any margin of error...*any*. We gonna' bomb by squadrons since this is a small target, and you pilots gotta' keep your formation tight...ah mean tight!...so we can keep our bomb spread small enough t'hit this bridge. If we don't destroy it, we or somebody else'll have to go back and hit it again...and going back to the same target a second time can be a real sumbitch...." Pausing to look at Shaw, he queried, "Am ah right, Ted?"

"That's a fact," Shaw asnwered gravely.

"Radio discipline," the lanky major went on, "we done talked that one to death, ain't we?"

They nodded.

"Well...ah'm gonna' tell you agin...stay off it!... unless you see bogies that ain't already been called out or else you got some problem with your plane which won't let you keep up with the formation, got it? O.k., Ted you got anythin' to add?"

Shaw stubbed out his cigarette and tried to cover his pre-mission jitters with an expansive smile. "As you fellas' know, we're gonna' take-off in sections of two to cut down on the form-up time. But remember...this time you're carryin' 4,000 pounds of bombs, so you pilots need to allow your engines to develop full emergency power before you release your brakes. If everybody does this, the section take-offs oughta' go real smooth. Next thing...as soon as you break ground, get your gear up *pronto* and hold the nose down until you see your airspeed reach 150 m.p.h." Meeting the gaze of each pilot, he said, slowly and firmly, "You pilots have heard this a million times...but let's go over it again one more time: if you lose an engine, salvo your bombs, *if you have time,* and belly-land straight ahead, but, do not...I repeat, *do not* attempt to turn back toward the field! I don't care what obstacles or terrain you've got in front of you, understand me?" They understood—losing an engine on take-off with a full bomb load was a B-26 pilot's worst nightmare. Shaw's litany continued: "When you start your climb toward the form-up area, use as much power as you need to get into position...*don't* fall behind the rest of the squadron, because you've got plenty of fuel." He looked over at Armistead. "That's all I have to say, Bobby."

Armistead quickly glanced at his wristwatch then looked at the crews with the laid-back, crooked grin they were used to. "You peckerwoods ready to go out and kick the shit outa Herr Hitler's railroad system?" he sneered. Most of them responded to the comment with a taut laugh—Shaw's crew just smiled. "All right then! We're gonna' start engines at 0615, taxi at 0620 and take-off at 0630, got it?" A collective nod. "Then, load 'em up and head 'em out!"

A hour later the group's B-26s were climbing into a sparkling blue sky over the Thames Estuary. Because the sun had not yet heated the ground enough to cause any perceptible thermal activity, the morning air they rode up on was as smooth as velvet. Their throttles had been moved back to an economic climb power setting that would enable them to reach a cruising altitude of 10,000 feet at the same time they left the Channel coast behind at Folkstone.

Shaw glanced over at his co-pilot who was concentrating on *Friend or Enema?,* framed in the upper half of his windscreen. Clementi held the yoke loosely with his fingertips, gazing up with his mouth held slightly ajar, and periodically adjusted the throttle levers so fractionally you couldn't tell they'd moved. Their relative position hadn't changed ten feet in any direction from the squadron leader's B-26 since they formed up. Shaw looked over his shoulder to watch the rearward flights in the squadron and occasionally used the radio to tell them to tighten up their formation. It was easy now, in the smooth air, but would be

harder in the light to moderate turbulence they were likely to encounter as they neared the target.

Grattan poked his head between the pilot seats and announced, "We
should be over Folkstone in about ten minutes, then we'll turn left to a
new heading of one-four-two. Ought to see the fighter escort about the
time we make the turn."

Shaw smiled at the big man. "Stay on top of things, Mick...." His
face became thoughtful. "You know, in case the nav in the lead ship
misses something." He was thinking of the botched approach to IP on
the last mission. "I'll call 'em this time," he added.

"You bet." Grattan gave him a knowing look.

Shaw thumbed the interphone, "Hey, bombardier, you awake up there?"

"Just barely," came the response. "You need something?"

"Negative, just checkin'."

Shaw pressed the button again. "Top turret, que pasa, amigo?"

"Top turret to pilot, uh...did you call me?" The new radio/gunner,
Staff Sergeant Francisco Vega, was a Mexican-American from Laredo,
Texas who had only joined the crew a week before. Vega had gone
through OTU on B-17s and had never flown in a B-26 until he joined
the 333RD. Like everybody else in the 8TH Air Force, he'd heard about
the Ijmuiden fiasco and wasn't exactly overjoyed with his new assignment.

Shaw grinned and picked up the microphone. "I said what's happening, friend...habla Espanol?

"Uh...top turret to pilot, si, si, Senor."

Back in the tail, Rimbaud shifted his weight to the uninjured side of
his rear end while listening to the interchange between the pilot and the
radio/gunner. While he'd decided that polacks weren't so bad, especially Milawski, he determined to keep an eye on the new spic. They
knew all about Mexicans in the bayou—they'd cut your throat and steal
your wallet if you weren't careful.

Like a ninety-six piece precision instrument, the group majestically
wheeled to a new course over Folkstone and began their approach to
the enemy coast. Grattan nodded and tapped his watch. "Right on
schedule," he told the pilots. "I'm going keep a backup DR plot...I'll
keep you posted."

The interphone crackled, "Tail gunnah t'pilot, ah see lil' friends at
eight a'clock high!" He was referring to the fighter escort coming from
Duxford.

"Roger, tail." Shaw looked up to his left and could see a mass of
tiny dark specks approaching. A moment later the command channel

erupted, "Hold your fire! I repeat, hold your fire! Friendly fighters coming our way."

Grattan keyed the interphone, "Navigator to crew, time to test your guns!" Moments later, *The A-Train* rattled to the concussion of eleven 50-caliber machine guns discharging at once. As soon as the noise abated, Glowgower called, "Bombardier to pilot, I need to come up and arm the bombs."

"Roger, come on up," Shaw answered, then turned to Clementi and said, "take a break, Luce...stretch your legs a minute." Clementi moved out of his seat to allow Glowgower into the flight deck. The bombardier nimbly made his way through the flight deck and nav compartment and stepped into the bomb bay where he removed the fuse wires from each of the ten 500 pound bombs hanging in two vertical racks. After fusing the bombs, he checked the alignment of the shackles on the track down which the bombs would travel when released. He looked around for any other irregularity in the bomb bay area and, satisfied, started making his way back to the nose. Stopping beside the nav table, he peered over Grattan's shoulder at the neat notations on the navigational chart.

"How're we doing, Mick?" he inquired.

The navigator looked up and flexed his shoulders. "Looks good...like we're right on the money. Spaulding," he said, referring to the lead navigator, "seems to know where he's going. Ought to hit our IP without any problems. Shouldn't be hard to find a city the size of Lens in this weather. You ready?"

"Yep...just hope like hell I don't have to take the lead at the last minute." They gave each other telling glances. "Besides," Glowgower said, "Armistead's bombardier knows his stuff...came over to us as a deputy squadron lead from a B-17 group and already has ten missions under his belt. Talked him at the club the other night...thinks he got the shit end of the stick because of being sent to a B-26 outfit. I told him the Ijmuiden thing was just a fluke, a foul-up...that he's better off with us."

"Maybe you're right, Glow." Grattan hoped so.

Giving the big navigator's shoulder a squeeze, he hastily said, "Gotta' go...good luck!"

Grattan glanced up at him. "You too, my friend."

They were only minutes now from the French coast, which was visible in front of them. The fighter escort, stationed at intervals 2,000 feet above them, made zigzagging sweeps back and forth across the bomber formation. While the sight of the P-47s was reassuring, the gunners in the B-26s nevertheless maintained a constant vigil, scanning the backdrop of the sky for anything that shouldn't be there.

A moment later the command channel came alive. "This is short-stop to all flights, enemy fighters are approaching at nine o'clock high! Escort is turning to engage!" Hundreds of heads in the cockpits and turrets turned to watch part of the P-47s peel off onto an interception route to the North. The radios in the fighters were on a different frequency, so they could not listen to the cryptic chatter between the fighter pilots.

Shaw keyed the interphone, "Pilot to crew, be ready for incoming bogies...call them out when you see them!"

"Tail, rogah."

"Turret, roger."

"Waist, roger."

"Nose, rog."

While the fighters above them were seconds away from the approaching enemy, the group crossed the coast and swung to the east toward the city of Lens, sixty miles distant.

"Turret to crew, bogies!" screamed Vega. "I count thirty-plus ME-109s at our four o'clock high and climbing." This meant the formation was being converged upon from two directions. No sooner had the gunner said this, than another section of the P-47 top cover banked away to meet the new threat. As the escorts wheeled into position on each side of the formation, the gunners warily scanned for any breakthroughs.

"Turret to crew, I see four 109s passing directly overhead...looks like they're pulling ahead of us." The eyes of the gunners tracked the enemy fighters as they passed over and drew ahead of the formation, then suddenly and violently split-essed back toward them.

The command channel erupted, "Shortstop to flight, prepare for head-on attack!"

"Pilot to crew, here they come! Waist and tail, they'll be passing your way!" At 1,000 yards, the 109s opened fire at the lead element. For a few seconds, the enemy fighters and B-26s exchanged tracer fire across a swiftly diminishing interval, then, missing them by what seemed to be scant feet, the fighters pushed down their noses and dove steeply beneath the formation to escape most of the massed machine gun fire. Milawski and Rimbaud were only able to squeeze off a few rounds as the evading 109s passed underneath to their left.

The command channel crackled. "Red able two to shortstop! We've been hit...losing oil pressure on number two engine...returning to base!"

"Roger, red able two...good luck!" As the stricken B-26 turned back to the West, a P-47 detached itself from the fighter group and moved into a protective position above the bomber.

"Pilot to crew, anything else comin' our way?"

"Nose, negative."

"Turret, negative."

"Waist, negative."

"Tail, nuthin'"

"Navigator to pilot, looks like we're about fifteen minutes from our turn to IP."

"Roger."

"Heah dey come agin!" Rimbaud cried. "Five o'clock low...looks like 'bout ten 109s after the straggler!"

An equal number of P-47s above dove down to meet the attackers, trying to cut them off before they could close the range to the crippled bomber. The 109s turned into the P-47s and began to trade fire. One of the 109s suddenly shed a wing and, trailing smoke, began to crazily spin toward the ground below. The remaining 109s broke away from the Thunderbolts then pulled up to the west to reestablish their attack position. The sky to the north seemed to be a maze of criss-crossing fighters maneuvering to gain firing position on one another. Within minutes, however, the enemy fighters had disappeared from view and the P-47s were re-forming over the group. This was the first time most of the bomber crews had seen the enemy. The air-to-air duel with the German fighters had lasted a little less than three minutes—an eternity in aerial combat.

The command radio came on again. "Shortstop to flight, keep your eyes open...those fighters will be back!"

The air had gotten bumpier, and B-26s were bobbing and weaving to maintain formation. The shimmering ribbon of the Lys River passed beneath them and, through the slight haze, they could see the city of Lens about twelve miles off their nose, with Arras barely discernible to the southeast.

"Navigator to bombardier, expect a turn onto the IP in three and a half minutes...your heading will be zero-one-zero."

"Roger, nav...can you give me a wind drift reading?"

"Estimated wind is three-zero-zero at twenty-five."

"Rog." Glowgower tweaked the wind correction into his bombsight and waited for the turn. He wouldn't be using the sight, however, unless Armistead's plane got knocked out of the formation between the IP and the target. Being the backup was in some ways harder than leading, because he had to divide himself between being ready to take-over instantly and bomb from the sight, while at the same time never taking his eyes from the lead bombardier's plane. Having an extra set of eyes in the top of his head would have helped. The formation turned left onto the IP. Grattan keyed the interphone, "Nav to bombardier, we'll be coming up on the target in about one minute."

"Rog...bomb bay doors coming open!" Glowgower looked foward and could see only a few scattered puffs of smoke from anti-aircraft fire. The Typhoons must have done their job, he thought fleetingly. The city was receding below them, and he could barely distinguish the bridge to their front.

"PDI is centered!" cried Shaw.

"Rog...intervalometer set!" Glowgower glued his eyes to the open bomb bay doors of Armistead's plane, holding the pickle switch in his right hand. Seeing the first bomb leave the bomb bay, he thumbed the switch at the exact moment the order, "Bombs away!" was shouted over the squadron channel.

Shaw instinctively pushed *The A-Train's* nose down to counteract the ballooning tendency of the lightened bomber and heard Glowgower cry, "Bomb bay doors closing!", then rolled the airplane into a steep left bank to follow *Friend or Enema?* off the target.

Glowgower craned his head against the G-forces of the turn to peer down toward the target and, though the bridge itself was obscured by the huge cloud of smoke and dust kicked up by the detonating bombs, he noticed a series of explosions flashing from one side of the canal to the other at the site of the bridge. Over 237 tons of TNT had just been rained on an object about 25 feet wide and 150 feet long!

"Shortstop to flight, enemy fighters incoming at nine o'clock! Escorts are engaging!" The Focke Wulf 190s were approaching on an interception course that would place them almost directly in front of the bomber formation.

"Turret to crew, Bogies! I count thirty plus FW-190s at our ten o'clock passing to the front." The covering P-47s turned into them on a converging course. This time, the 190s had the height advantage, and the Thunderbolts would be forced to pull up sharply and make snap-shots before the attackers passed over them. The Focke Wulfs zoomed through the tracer fire that arced up toward them, intent on the bombers below. Looking up from *The A-Train*, the crew watched in fascination as one of the attackers suddenly erupted into a mass of flaming smoke, followed by a jettisoned canopy and a tiny human figure tumbling end over end. The gyrating form was jerked to an abrupt stop by the blossoming of a brown-colored parachute which began to lazily float down toward the bomber formation. While at least half of the Focke Wulfs had been destroyed or driven from the pursuit, the survivors relentlessly bored into the bombers.

"Pilot to crew, here they come! Twelve O'clock, almost level!" A section of four fighters was heading directly for their squadron. Shaw watched the distance close with his finger poised on the trigger to the four blister guns. The Germans opened fire first because of the greater range of their cannon armament. Seconds later, all of *The A-Train's* front firing fifties opened up nearly at once and poured tracer fire into the approaching attackers. Every member of the crew could hear the sickening *thunk-thunk-thunk* of cannon shells slamming into their plane, when, suddenly, the lead 190 disintegrated before their eyes. Flying through the debris left by the fighter, the torso of a human body slammed into their left wing and went twirling into the slipstream, trailing a red mist.

"Pilot to crew, report damage!"

"Tail t'pilot," Rimbaud answered in an amused tone, "they done shot up our tail agin!"

"Report the exact damage, dammit!"

"Tail t'pilot, there's a hole in the tail fin 'bout halfway up and the fabric been shredded on the rudder in 'bout the same place. Look like there's a small rip in the left elevator, too."

"Bombardier to pilot, negative damage."

"Nav, negative damage."

"Turret, negative."

"Waist, negative"

Shaw tested the rudder. It seemed a little mushy; he'd have to watch it when they slowed down for landing. The rudder trim was completely jammed, but he sighed with relief as the elevator responded to the trim wheel. Shifting his glance to the other side of the cockpit, Shaw noticed, other than wearing a grim expression, his co-pilot appeared to have things under control. "Take it a while, Luce."

"Rog...I've got it."

Above him, Shaw noticed a thin line of black smoke streaming from the right engine of *Friend or Enema?*. He called Armistead, "White able one to white leader, you've got smoke coming from your number two...also see some holes in your right wing around the engine nacelle."

"Roger, white able two, we know about it...be ready to take the lead if we have to shut it down."

"Roger, understand." From his experience, Shaw knew you could never be sure about the extent of damage to an engine unless it caught on fire or seized. You could carefully watch oil pressure and temperatures, but a problem could turn from minor to major in an instant. The

R-2800s in the B-26, fortunately, were noteworthy for their ability to sustain an incredible amount of damage before they quit running.

Shaw looked out of the cockpit side windows to scrutinize the squadron's formation. They weren't out of the woods yet—there was a good chance enemy fighters would hit them again before they crossed the coast. Noticing several planes out of position, he called out on the squadron frequency, "Charlie flight! Dog flight! Get those stragglers in position...NOW! You gunners wake up and keep those turrets and guns moving!" The formation slowly welded itself back into place, the gunners renewing their vigilance...just in time.

"Shortstop to flight, enemy fighters incoming at your ten o'clock high and climbing, escort is turning to engage!"

Shaw keyed the interphone. "Pilot to crew, anyone see 'em yet?"

"Turret to pilot, wait...got 'em! See what looks like twenty-plus ah, ME-109s, turnin' left to get in front."

"Nose to pilot, I see 'em now! Eleven o'clock high!"

Above them the P-47s had pushed their throttles to the stops, causing their 2,000 h.p. engines to emit a thin stream of smoke. They climbed directly in front of the bombers so they could turn and meet the attacking 109s head-on. This time the enemy was outnumbered two-to-one. The bomber crews craned their necks to watch, engrossed, as the two opposing lines of battle converged.

Shaw, also caught up in the spectacle, shook himself back to reality and grabbed the microphone. "Pilot to crew, don't watch the P-47s...keep a lookout, I repeat, look for incoming bogies!"

The air-to-air battle between the fighters was joined 10,000 feet above them in a twisting and twirling melee of aircraft. The P-47s had managed to gain a height advantage and were able to dive en mass into the formation of 109s. The enemy fighters, in spite of opening fire first, were not equal to the accumulated firepower of the defenders. Several of the 109s dramatically came apart in the face of the P-47's massed 50-caliber guns while others spun away trailing smoke and flames. Pieces of wings, fuselages, and tail-planes came fluttering down toward the bombers like metal confetti from a grotesque parade. Several parachutes were seen to open, to be carried southeasterly by the prevailing wind. To the left of the formation, the bomber crews observed one P-47 on fire, spiraling down toward the serrated pattern of the ground below.

Vega spotted movement on his right side. "Turret to crew," he called, "I see a pair of 109s coming around on our right, about nine o'clock, level...but hold your fire, hold your fire! There's a bunch of P-47s comin' right up their asses!"

The flight of six P-47s drilled in behind the 109s for a no deflection shot at less than 500 yards. The tracers reached out from the Thunderbolts and tore into the enemy fighters like an invisible buzz saw. The 109s started shedding pieces and seemed to stagger, almost stop, in mid-air. One Messerschmitt's canopy flew off and a figure came tumbling out only to smash violently into the tail, the mangled body of the enemy pilot twirling away grotesquely, the parachute never opening.

For the westward-moving bomber formation, the coast—and safety—were only now minutes away. Their egress route would be the same: cross the coast at Montreil and turn northwest toward Folkstone. Clementi sagged with relief as he looked down and saw the glinting water of the Channel pass beneath their wing. The fighter attacks had been terrifying, and he'd almost crapped his pants when he heard the cannon shells striking the plane, but it had not been nearly as bad as the stark, naked fear which had all but immobilized him on the first two missions. Except for a few brief spells en route and the run-in from the IP to the target, he'd flown the entire mission, listening to Shaw's constant stream of instructions to him and everybody else. Now that they were out of immediate danger, his body was wracked by lassitude, an overpowering desire to shut his eyes and allow himself to go limp. He reached over and nudged the pilot, who was looking out the left window at the formation. "Hey...you take it. I need a break, o.k.?"

"I've got it!" Shaw grinned at him and took the controls. "You've did good up there today, Luce...real good." Clementi wearily smiled back, too tired to share the pilot's elation. "Luce, hop out of your seat and take a stretch, o.k.?." The co-pilot unfastened his straps and heavily pushed himself up on the armrests, then slid sideways out of his seat.

Without averting his eyes from the lead plane, Shaw keyed the interphone. "Hey, bombardier...come on up to the flight deck!"

"Rog...on my way!" Moments later, Glowgower squeezed through the opening on the right of the flight deck and eased into the right seat. Clementi and Grattan leaned on the door opening of the flight deck and gave the bombardier grinning mock salutes.

Shaw glanced at the bombardier and asked off-handedly, "You wanna' fly it for a while?"

Glowgower looked at him quizzically. "In formation? You've got to be shitting me. You guys want to hear about the target or what?"

"O.k, bombardier," the pilot laughed, "give us the scoop."

Glowgower coughed once and tried hard to keep a nonchalant expression on his face, but his face slowly dissolved into a clownish grin, and he exulted, "It was absolutely shit-hot, fellas...I mean *hot!*" He pounded the top of the instrument combing for emphasis. "Of course we won't know for sure until we see the post-strike photos, but I'd bet money that over ten percent of the bomb sticks hit the bridge itself. I'll be surprised if there's *anything* left of it! Looked like the lead squadron dropped their bombs a little long, but I think our squadron and the blue squadron on our right put the bombs smack on top the target. I saw our bombs hit, and the explosions walked from the south side of the canal all the way across the bridge to the other side! I couldn't see tail-end squadron very well because of all the smoke, but I think they dropped a little early ...won't matter though."

Shaw, Clementi, and Grattan smiled with genuine amusement at the gesticulating Bombardier—they'd never seen him act so animated about anything.

The rest of the trip was uneventful. Armistead was able to nurse the sick engine on *Friend or Enema?* all the way back to Boxsted. When they began their letdown back over the Thames Estuary, *The A-Train*, without any rudder trim had a tendency to yaw to the right as power was reduced. Clementi had resumed his seat but did none of the flying. Shaw looked at him and said, "Luce, put your foot on that left rudder and lean into it." The pilot watched the ball-bank indicator as the co-pilot applied his weight. "O.k....that's good...keep it there." The pilot massaged his left thigh which had gotten cramped while he was holding the abnormal pressure on the pedal. The B-26 was a heavy airplane with completely manual controls, and it took brute strength to hold a control surface against the slipstream without the compensation of a trim tab.

There were breaks in the overcast hanging above the base, which enabled them to make a visual approach to the runway. *The A-Train* softly touched down in the type of landing so characteristic of Shaw, and queued up behind the other B-26s making their way down the perimeter track to their hardstands. As they pulled into their slot, Shaw waved to Ripley, the smiling crew chief, who could see that airplane was in much better shape today than when it had returned from the last mission.

When they dropped from the nose and waist hatches, Ripley handed each of them an ice-cold bottle of beer.

Shaw grinned and slapped him on the back. "You must be some kinda' mind reader, Buster!" He held the dripping bottle to his forehead. "I've been thinking about a cold beer since we crossed the English coast."

Armistead came ambling over, his khakis stained with sweat. "WOO-EE!" he hollered. "Hey chief, you got another one of those?" Ripley handed the beer he was holding to the lanky major, who tipped it up and finished it off. Armistead wiped his face, smacked his lips, and said, "You boys know why beer is better than women?"

They shook their heads.

"'Cause beer never cares when you have another beer!"

They all laughed noisily except Rimbaud, who didn't get it.

Forty-five minutes later, the debriefing finished, they were on their way to the mess hall for noon chow. The post-strike reconnaissance photographs arrived at Boxsted by courier plane later that afternoon. The photos revealed with utter certainty that bridge had disappeared; the only thing remaining was the jagged stone stub of one of the pilings. Even the stone parapets which had supported either side of the bridge had been demolished. The railroad tracks for hundreds of feet on both sides of the canal were a mass of tangled wreckage. This bridge could not be repaired—*it was gone.* Fifteen of the B-26s had sustained varying degrees of damage from the fighter attacks, but none serious enough to permanently ground any of the airplanes. The B-26 which had lost an engine during the first attack made a successful emergency landing at huge airfield at Hawkinge and would be returned to service. The most serous injury had been a radio gunner who had his left index finger blown off by a 20 millimeter shell. There were several other flesh wounds caused by flying splinters of metal, but no other injuries. Three of the escorting P-47s, however, failed to return. Bomber crewmen thought they saw several parachutes, but at the distance they were watching from, couldn't be sure whether they were American or German. The Red Cross, when the information was available, would inform American authorities of captured P.O.W.s.

Several days later in his office in Tunis, Tunisia, Major General James H. Doolittle smiled as he examined the aerial photo that had been delivered to him in a diplomatic pouch. It showed an area of total destruction around a French canal where an important rail bridge had once stood.

CHAPTER FOURTEEN

September 1, 1943, Boxtsed, England.

The 333RD Bomb Group (M) was assembled in parade formation by squadron on the tarmac on front of the main hangar. The local weather that day was mild and dry except for a blustery wind from the east that caused the ranks to sporadically wave when the men had to suddenly clap their hands on top of their heads to keep caps from blowing off. In complete contrast to their usual lack of formality, all of the group's personnel were splendidly decked-out in Class A uniforms with decorations, caps at regulation angles, fresh haircuts, and polished shoes. To serve as a backdrop for the ceremony, several B-26s had been parked on the tarmac opposite the formation. Colonel Spinelli and the group staff, assembled in a loose rank in front of the parked planes, chatted quietly with several dignitaries who had arrived from 8TH Air Force headquarters.

The group adjutant called the formation to attention and ordered all units to report. After the reports were made, he executed a smart left face, saluted, and barked, "Group all present and accounted for, SIR!"

Spinelli conversed briefly with the general officer at his side, who nodded, then both of them walked briskly to the end of the first column of ranks. He and the general came to a halt before the commander whose squadron was assembled on right of the formation and exchanged salutes. Spinelli read off a list of the names of officers and men who were to report, "Front and center." After the named individuals came forward and snapped to attention, the general stepped in front of the first one and began to read a citation from a sheet of paper his aid handed him. The general intoned, "Lieutenant...for conspicuous gallantry in the defense of your country...during the dates...in aerial bombardment operations against...it gives me great pleasure to award you the...." Then he pinned the medal on the left breast pocket of the recipients blouse, shook his hand, and said, "Thank you, son, your country's proud of you." The process was continued until each medal was awarded.

Spinelli and the general moved on to the next squadron and repeated the process, and then to the next. The last squadron to be recognized was the 424TH, commanded by Major Robert M. Armistead. As they approached, Armistead bellowed, "Squadron! Atten-HUT!" and performed a crisp regulation salute. Spinelli called the names of the officers and men to be decorated. As soon as those called advanced forward and stood to attention, Major General Ira Eaker, commander of the 8TH Air Force, stepped directly in front of Armistead, who was one of the officers named. The lanky squadron commander remained ramrod still and in keeping with military custom, fixed his eyes at a position slightly above the brim of the General's cap.

The General's weathered visage creased in a smile. "Are you the one they call Bobby?" he asked.

Armistead's eyebrows rose in surprise. Uh-oh, he thought, and stammered, "Y...yes, suh."

"Well, Bobby, I've heard of you." The General gave him a shrewd look. *Trapped*, thought Armistead...it's all finally catching up with me.

"From what I've heard, son," the General continued, "you're doing a damn fine job."

Armistead forced himself not to sag with relief. "Thank you, Gen'ral," he said after a moment's hesitation.

General Eaker read the citation awarding Armistead the Distinguished Flying Cross and Air Medal, shook his hand with a warm smile, and said, "I'll be following your career...Bobby." Armistead wasn't sure whether that was good or bad.

Captain Theodore J. Shaw was next in line. The General looked into the pilot's clear blue eyes and youthful face and wondered at the process that turned boys like this into such formidable warriors. "Your name is Ted, isn't it?" Shaw was taken aback by the General's familiarity.

"Yes, sir," he answered, his voice almost cracking.

"Your reputation precedes you, Ted," the General said in a kindly way. "I've been told you're one of the best B-26 aircraft commanders in the theater."

This was the closest Shaw had ever been to a general officer, let alone talk to one. The compliment only added to his awkwardness. "Thank you, General," he said in a voice about half an octave higher than usual.

The General read the citations Shaw received for the Purple Heart, Distinguished Flying Cross and Air Medal, pinning each decoration on the pilot's tunic. Then he paused, addressing his attention to the entire group, and said, "Once and a while it is my great privilege to recognize men for personal bravery and valor far beyond the normal call of duty..." He paused and read the citation in his hands, for the Silver Star Medal, which made specific reference to the Ijmuiden mission: that despite the deadly defenses around the target, Captain Shaw had continued to lead the mission after his commander had been shot down, and that, despite wounds suffered by himself, he was able to fly his severely damaged aircraft and its crew back to safety.

Shaw was floored this time, his ears ringing with the words of the citation. He even wondered if they'd made a mistake. But the General smiled at him again as he pinned the medal above the other three and said, in a fatherly way, while squeezing the young pilot's arm, "I'm proud to know you, son...proud you're part of my Air Force."

First Lieutenants Michael B. Grattan and Joseph H. Glowgower—who had received his promotion in late-July—were both awarded DFCs, Air Medals, and Bronze Stars with a "V" for valor. First Lieutenant Luciano E. Clementi—also recently promoted—received the DFC, Air Medal, and the Purple Heart. Sergeant Paul L. Milawski, Staff Sergeant Francisco X. Vega, and Sergeant Leroy (NMI) Rimbaud—also promoted—all received Air Medals, and Rimbaud, with undisguised glee, received his Purple Heart! At this point, they were the most highly decorated crew of the 333RD, and they were the only ones who seemed surprised about it.

As they fell out and walked back to their huts, Shaw pointed to the medal with the purple and white ribbon pinned to Rimbaud's pocket. "You know what that means, Leroy?"

"Uh...," Rimbaud grunted and waited for the answer.

"What it means is you saw the elephant and lived to talk about it."

The swarthy little gunner looked at him questioningly. "Elephant? What kinda' sheeit you talkin' 'bout, skippah? Sometime you officers say things that don't make no sense t'nobody...none a'tall."

In the six weeks after the first mission against the rail bridge on the canal near Lens, the 333RD flew twelve more missions against railway targets in northern France, and *The A-Train* and her crew participated in nine of them. A combat routine had been developed in which the loading orders would specify about sixty aircraft for a given mission, thus allowing the group to train newcomers before sending them into combat and "down" various aircraft for needed maintenance and overhaul. *The A-Train* had just completed her second engine replacement and had been retrofitted with a new Bell M-6 power-operated tail turret, which now positioned the guns below the gunner and afforded a wider field of fire. An additional 50-caliber fixed machine gun, fired from the cockpit, had been installed in the lower right quadrant of her clear nose dome, and the flexible gun in the apex of the nose had been retained, now giving her a total of twelve guns.

On the twelve missions flown, eight B-26s had been shot down or destroyed by flak or enemy fighters, and two more had been lost in operational accidents. In this total, forty-nine men were known or presumed dead, and another twenty-one were unaccounted for. This computed to a loss ratio of a little over one and one-half percent, which was at least three or four times better than what the heavy bomber groups were experiencing, better, in fact, than the training accident ratio at MacDill the previous year; indeed, B-26 aircrews had a somewhat above-average chance of finishing a thirty-five mission tour.

Another twenty aircraft had sustained varying levels of battle damage during the missions, sixteen of which were repairable enough to be returned to service. In relation to the aircraft damaged in combat, six crewmembers were seen to bail out over enemy territory—POW confirmation from the Red Cross had been received on two, five were killed or died from wounds sustained in combat, seven received wounds that resulted in permanent disabilities, and another twelve received injuries from which they fully recovered.

The A-Train had been hit on several occasions by cannon fire from attacking fighters and by fragments of flak from guns sited around the rail installations they'd attacked, but none of her crew had been hurt. On their seventh mission, a cannon shell had severed one of the main hydraulic lines in the bomb bay, forcing them to crank down the gear and land at 130 m.p.h., without flaps. In order to stop the racing bomber before it reached the overrun, both Shaw and Clementi had stood on the brakes, blowing both main tires in the process. But Ripley and his mechanical magicians had gotten the airplane back in service within twenty-four hours. On more than one occasion, they had been given the opportunity to get a brand new B-26B, a Block Twenty-Five aircraft, but this had been unanimously vetoed by the crew every time, and even Vega, the newcomer, had become attached to the now aging and tattered bomber.

Shaw and his crew had led the squadron on three of the missions and had been group lead on one. Glowgower's bombing scores had been near perfect and Grattan's navigation, as usual, had been impeccable. This was precisely what Spinelli and Edrington had planned: that on any given mission, a number of qualified crews could be called upon to lead squadrons or even the group. This was what the military experts call "planned redundance," and why, by the war's end, there were Air Corps lieutenant colonels who were only twenty-five years old.

Later that evening Shaw and Grattan were in the room of their hut alone while Clementi and Glowgower were taking their nightly sojourn at the O-Club. The base was very near Colchester, and a considerable number of local girls could be found at the O-Club after working hours. A stiff but friendly competition developed between the fighter pilots and the bomber boys for the attention of the ladies. Clementi had discovered that women were drawn to Glowgower like moths to a flame, and made a point a stationing himself next to the bombardier at the bar. Clementi was nice looking in a dark, Latin way, and girls enjoyed his company once they got to know him, but he wasn't someone you would pick out in a crowd.

Noticing several girls staring at the bombardier, Clementi commented in an offhand way, "What is it about you, Glow, that causes these babes to look at you with their tongues practically hanging out?"

"It's a curse," the bombardier replied seriously.

"What?" Clementi looked at him questioningly.

"I said it's a curse...a millstone around my neck."

"I don't understand."

"You would if you were me." He looked at the co-pilot with dead frankness. "All of my life, people...people who don't even know me...have formed an opinion of me based upon the way I look. They're not interested in me, the real Joe Glowgower...the person inside." He pointed to himself. "No...they only notice what they see. And it's been that way since I was a little kid. Everybody around me: relatives, teachers, friends, girls...*especially girls*." Glowgower looked at Clementi with a tragic smile. "You know how I lost my virginity? When I was thirteen, a girl four years older than me who, at the time, was supposed to be my babysitter, seduced me!"

Clementi almost knocked over his drink. "Wow!" he coughed, "I've never had a problem like that!"

"Then count yourself lucky...I'd trade places with you in a minute."

"You would?" The co-pilot reacted with authentic surprise.

The bombardier regarded his friend intently. "Well, what I mean is that people don't judge you because of the way you look."

"Oh, thanks."

"No, listen...you're not a bad looking guy, you can hold your own with the ladies, but, at the same time, people judge you *by what you do*, and that's what is really important, you follow?"

"Yeah, I think I'm beginning to see your point."

Glowgower continued, mildly surprised at himself for spilling his guts this way. "But you know something? This war had been a good thing for me...because here..." he made a sweeping gesture around the room with his arm "...it doesn't matter one damn bit what you look like. The only thing that seriously matters is how well you measure up in combat...everything else is, you know, secondary."

The two regarded each other in silence for a moment. Clementi finished his drink, then turned to the bombardier. "How about you and me, Glow...have we measured up?"

Glowgower gave a half smile. "We got off to a rough start, me especially, but I think we're over the hump."

"You seem to be, but...combat flying still scares me shitless," the co-pilot replied confidentially.

Glowgower leaned back against the bar and looked over his shoulder at the co-pilot. "Me, too, pal...every time we fly."

"Really?" Clementi seemed surpised by the admission.

"Man, you always seem so...uh, steely-eyed, like Ted."

Glowgower's handsome features turned to a glare. "That's pure bullshit! We're all scared, man, even Ted and the others! You'd have to be crazy to fly into flak and fighters time after time like we do and not be scared. It's just that we all have different ways of controlling it. Like me, I think about this box...I put it in this box." He mimicked having a box in his hands and snapping the lid shut.

Clementi looked at him uncertainly. "I've got a box, too, but it...the fear...gets out of my box a lot of the time." He heaved a sigh. "You know, that Ijmuiden thing almost did me in...I almost quit..."

"Don't sell yourself short, man!" Glowgower broke in suddenly. "If I'd been wounded on that trip, I would have felt the same way. Probably would be in some psycho ward right now on a Section Eight!"

"Really?"

"Sure...took plenty of guts for you to get back in that right seat."

The co-pilot merely nodded but was cheered by the bombardier's statement.

Glowgower gave him a mischievous grin and nudged him in the side with his elbow. "C,mon, pal, let's cut out all this serious crap and concentrate on the real reason we're here!"

In the hut, Shaw got out his writing kit and began to compose a letter. Since they'd started flying combat, he had not written as often, really didn't have as much to say, but felt guilty about it. He lit a Lucky Strike and began:

September 1, 1943

Dear Mary Beth,

The group was put on stand-down today (that means no missions were scheduled) so all of us could attend a big formation. I had to make sure everybody in my crew was squared-away. Leroy Rimbaud needed a little help, but they all looked pretty sharp. The reason for the formation was to award medals to air crew members who have earned them since we started combat. Just about everybody whose flown over five missions got an Air medal and about fifteen officers received the DFC (me included). But I have to tell you I got the biggest surprise of my life-—they awarded me a Silver Star for that mission we flew against [CENSORED]. They took a bunch of pictures, and the group PIO said you and the folks would probably see something about it in the Dallas and Big Spring papers. I still don't understand why they gave it to me. I only did what any pilot would have done in the same situation. Mick and Glow each got the Bronze Star, and I think they did more to deserve it than me. Well, sometimes the military works in strange ways.

We have flown [CENSORED] missions now, and I feel like we're getting the hang of it. Even Luce Clementi seems to have settled down after that [CENSORED] thing and is flying even better.

I think Mick and Glow have turned into the best navigator-bombardier team in the group. Since I'm flying lead or deputy lead all the time, I guess I'll get to keep them for the time being. Mick tells me that Mick, Jr. is crawling around now and ought to be walking in a couple of more months. Eleanor recently mailed us a box of chocolate chip cookies, but they were pretty beat up by the time they arrived here. They were still delicious, and we watched Luce empty the box of crumbs into his mouth. Makes me think of your home cooking, honey—the best I've ever had!

Thanks for going by to see Dad and Mom last time you were home. I can't believe the amount of cattle Dad's running with the extra range he's renting. I wonder if all those Mexican hands will stay on after the war's over. I hear they work cheap. Might be a problem when all the servicemen return home. I wonder, too, if the new business will hold up after all this is over.

I'm sorry I haven't been writing more often but they're really keeping me busy around here. Bobby Armistead is not too good with all the squadron paperwork and I help him out nearly every day. Just routine stuff mostly but it wears me out. On top of that we're on the loading order for tomorrow morning and will have to get up in the wee hours.

I sure miss you, honey. Thinking of you is one of the main things that keeps me going. You are the most important thing in my life. I love you so much that words can't express it.

Your ever loving,
Ted

Shaw purposefully didn't mention the Purple Hearts that he, Clementi, and Rimbaud had received. He didn't want to remind her of the constant risk he was taking every time he flew, and she was thoughtful never to inquire in any of her letters. When she read this letter, however, the first she had received in over a week, she detected an undefined weariness. They asked him to do so much; she could almost feel the weight of his responsibility. She realized the danger he was in, too. So many people she knew at home had lost sons or brothers or other loved ones in parts of the world she'd never even heard of before. A girl she worked closely with at the plant had recently lost her fiancée, a B-24 crewmember, on a mission against some unpronounceable place in Rumania. Every day huge lists of servicemen killed or missing in action were published in the newspapers. She laid the letter on her bedside table, turned out the light, and softly cried herself to sleep.

CHAPTER FIFTEEN

September 27, 1943, Boxsted, England.

When the mission map was unveiled the next morning, the plastic overlay showed a red line running from East Sussex to Rouen, one of the largest cities in the French province of Normandy. The target was not a bridge this time but warehouses near the railroad marshalling yards along the line that connected the city to Paris, 75 miles to the southeast. These warehouses, the Colonel explained, were one of the major supply depots the Germans used to support their military installations in Normandy. Two other B-26 groups would join in the mission to hit the marshalling yards and other rail installations near the target; they would approach the target from different directions to confuse the defenses, particularly the fighters. But timing was critical, he said, so the individual bomb groups wouldn't run into one another over the target area.

The intelligence officer stepped onto the platform and overlaid another transparency which indicated the location of the heaviest concentrations of flak. Each navigator, he said, would be provided with a similarly marked map in the navigator's briefing. While the route they would take into the target and back out would avoid the worst flak, they should expect heavy concentrations of 88 millimeter in the immediate vicinity of the target. The nearby fighter bases at Dieppe, La Havre, and Caen could be expected to scramble fighters to attack them before they reached the target. To counter this, he said, three P-47 groups would be used to escort them in and out, plus two squadrons of RAF Spitfires would meet them near the target. Because of the Spitfire's shorter range, he explained, they would be forced to take a more direct route. He asked for questions.

A hand went up. A youthful lieutenant asked, "Captain, are the Krauts starting to run low on fighters? I mean we've seen bunches of them knocked down on our missions."

"Not that we can tell," the briefer informed him in an impassive tone. "The information we get from reconnaissance photos and the resistance network suggests that enemy fighter defenses are maintaining a constant level of strength, that is, they've been about the same for the past month."

This produced a babble of grumbling and whispering in the audience. It was incomprehensible to them how the German Luftwaffe could suffer such loses day after day, and still fight back with such ferocity.

The weather should be clear all the way to the target and over it, the meteorological officer said, with some smoke and haze around the aiming point. They would be racing against the movement of a front on the way back, however, and there was a slight chance that Boxsted could get closed in. He assured them if that happened, they would be diverted to land at bases farther south until the front moved through.

Their route would take them over the English coast at Hove, then southeast for 80 miles to intersect the French coast at Saint-Valery-en-Caux. They would fly a further 27 miles southeast to their IP, a town called Pavilly, which lay on a major junction of the railway, then make their bomb run another 12 miles to the warehouses. This was another tight run-in, less than four minutes, but would minimize their exposure to the heaviest flak concentrations.

At the navigator's and bombardier's briefing, Grattan and Glowgower carefully examined photographs which were less than twenty-four hours old. They were going to have to thread the needle in order to end up over the target at the right time. Rouen was a congested target with many other industrial buildings near the warehouses. If they missed the target and had to go around a second time, they would be murdered by the flak. They would bomb visually as a group from 10,000 feet with intervalometers set at 200 milliseconds. Grattan and Glowgower glanced at each other knowingly—this was going to be the toughest one since Ijmuiden. At least they had some altitude and fighter cover this time.

The A-Train would be leading the 424TH on this one, positioned on the left wing of the group, 100 feet below the lead element. The group leader's call sign would be "pitchfork," and *The A- Train* would be "black leader." The seated members of the 424TH listened to Shaw as he intoned the usual cautions: they had heard it all before—take-off, formation, radio discipline, emergency procedures, etc.—but it didn't hurt to be reminded.

"Some of you fellas' are new," Shaw said as he looked at the faces of those he was referring to. "This'll be your second or third mission." He paused to light a cigarette. "You heard in the briefing that there'll be a lot of flak today, especially when we get close to the IP. You pilots have to remember to hold your airplanes *rock steady* all the way down the bomb run." Pausing, he gave them a hard stare. "If I see *anybody* taking evasive action on the bomb run, I'll have your ass when we get back, you got that?" A few solemn nods. "And another thing...I don't care how bad things get, *don't drop your bombs until you hear the order from lead*, understand?" Terrified aircrews were known to sometimes drop their bombs before they reached the target and turn away from the flak. "Any questions?"

A sallow young pilot named Jeffries, one of the new ones, asked, uncertainly, "What you said, Captain, about keeping rock steady on the bomb run...uh, what do we do if fighters are diving right into us?"

Shaw regarded his questioner with a small smile. "You won't have to worry about fighters on your bomb run. The Krauts aren't crazy enough to fly through their own flak. Anything else?" He looked around and stubbed out his cigarette. "O.k., troops, let's go out and win one for the gipper!"

Later, when they were nearing the coast at Hove, Shaw craned his head to the left then leaned up to look around Clementi to his right. Some of the newer pilots were slipping in and out of formation. He frowned and picked up the microphone. "Black leader to black charlie one, is your flight havin' problems?"

"Negative, black leader."

"Then why isn't your flight keeping formation, black charlie one?"

"We're working on it black leader."

"Get it squared away...NOW!"

"Ah...Roger, black leader."

Clementi looked at the furrowed brow of his pilot as his head swiveled back and forth to watch the squadron. Since Shaw was leading today, the co-pilot knew he would do most of the flying until they left the target; but he would rather be occupied with flying as opposed to sitting there and waiting for the fighters to attack or the flak to open up, and flying the squadron lead position wasn't as exhausting as keeping close formation in the deputy slot. Shaw's job was harder, he supposed, like spinning plates: once you got them all going on one side, the ones on the other side would begin to wobble, and so on. He had gotten so used to hearing the pilot bark orders over the radio that it had just become part of the overall background noise with the engines and the slipstream; but the guns—no one could ever get used to that.

"Nav to pilot, expect a left turn to a new heading of one-three-nine in one minute."

"Rog," Clementi answered for the already preoccupied Shaw. He tensed himself to notice any movement from the group leader's plane. As soon as he saw Spinelli's B-26 enter a left bank, he followed the turn and slightly reduced power to allow for the smaller radius of the path his squadron would take to maintain position. As they completed the turn, Shaw slapped his hand on the top of the instrument panel and picked up his microphone to chastise the flights with stragglers. The pilot didn't do this because he was a mean-spirited hard ass, but because stragglers were sitting ducks for attacking fighters, *dead meat*. All through the bomb groups, heavy and medium, it was an established fact that those who maintained tight formations experienced higher rates of survival.

"Navigator to crew, test your guns." The easy part of the trip was over. From this point on, the gunners would remain at their positions, continually moving their guns and scanning the sky from horizon to horizon. The gunners were reassured by the sight of the P-47s overhead, weaving back and forth diagonally across the formation. The so-called "weave" technique had been invented by a U. S. Navy fighter pilot in the Pacific theater as a method of protecting dive bombers and torpedo planes from attack by Japanese fighters.

The interphone crackled. "Bombardier to pilot, I need to come up and arm the bombs."

"Come on up," Shaw responded and turned to his co-pilot. "Take five, Luce." As soon as Clementi moved out of the way, Glowgower scrambled through the opening and made his way back to the bomb bay to fuse the six 500 pound bombs they were carrying. This was the normal bomb load for longer missions, especially when there was s chance of weather-related delays on the trip back. He was back on the flight deck a few minutes later.

"How's it goin'," Shaw inquired.

"Copasetic," the bombardier replied tersely. "I'd better get back up front before things get hot...see ya'," and disapppeared into the nose.

Shaw knew that Glowgower was worried about this target, had shown it in the grim set of his face. The pilot was worried, too. Over his shoulder, he saw Grattan approach. As usual, the big, ruddy-faced man seemed unaffected by the danger they were entering. It wasn't that the navigator was unafraid—during missions the bile crawled up his throat like everyone else, but he accepted that God had appointed him to this time and place for greater purposes than he could comprehend. Whether his life lasted another minute or another hundred years was God's decision, he believed, not his, and whenever God chose to end it,

He would take him home—to his real home. Shaw and others in the crew held similar beliefs, but unlike the navigator, it did not enter their conscious thinking.

"Where are we, Mick?" Shaw asked.

"About five minutes from the coast, I'd say...the lead nav seems to be bang on."

Shaw smirked at him. "Bang on? Are you goin' native or something?"

"Rioght, Guv'na, yew 'av summat' agin' it?" he mimicked.

They were interrupted by the command radio. "...Enemy fighters approaching! Eleven o'clock high! Escorts are turning to engage!"

Vega keyed the interphone. "Turret to crew, I see 'em! Thirty plus FW-190s climbing up to our twelve..."

"Pitchfork to all flights, prepare for head-on attack!"

The P-47 group nearest the attackers, dropped their tanks, fire-walled their throttles, and turned to meet the threat head-on at a combined speed of over 600 m.p.h. The bomber crews watched the discarded tanks tumble down through the air like acrobatic minnows as the gap closed between the fighters. The Thunderbolts, opening fire at 1,000 yards, scythed directly into the enemy formation. Several of the opposing Focke Wulfs flew to pieces in the face of the massed machine gun fire and two more dropped away trailing smoke. The rest had turned away from the pursuing Thunderbolts in a diving turn well below the bomber formation.

"Tail t'crew, the bogies is behin' us now, low."

"Nav to pilot, expect a turn to a new heading of one-five-seven in one minute." Clementi was flying again and simply nodded at Shaw, who was looking over his shoulder trying to keep the enemy fighters in sight. Several sections of P-47s had reversed course to chase the 190s out of sight. The ribbon of the French coast flashed beneath them as the interphone came to life. "Nav to bombarider, IP coming up in eight minutes...expect a left turn to a new heading of one-seven-three."

"Rog, give me a wind reading when we're a little closer."

"Will do."

"Pilot to tail, any sign of those fighters?"

"Tail t'pilot, they still behind us some ways, six a'clock, low, but look like they catchin' up. Uh-oh! They comin' right toward us now...from unnerneath!"

"Pilot to waist, be ready...they might come on either side."

"Roger, I can't see 'em yet."

"Tail t'crew, P-47s done caught some of 'em, but look out! Heah they come!" Rimbaud tracked a Focke Wulf with the new M-6 guns as it pulled up on an interception course with the formation. With the new set-up, he could depress his guns almost 20 degrees lower than allowed by the older version. As he watched the enemy plane swim into the range bars on his sight, he mentally calulated the lead, but waited another moment for the distance to close. Counting to himself, one, two...he depressed the trigger on the gun control grip. The twin guns hammered with a staccato bark as the Focke Wulf swiftly merged with the crosshairs of his sight, its nearness enabling him to clearly discern the black-helmeted head of the pilot through the windscreen. With morbid fascination he watched his tracers converge on the Focke Wulf's cowling, rooting up bits of metal, until the entire front end of the attacking plane suddenly vanished in a shower of debris.

"Got 'im! Got that sonomabeech!" He craned his neck to watch the hulk of the dismembered 190 roll over and spiral down to the earth below. No parachute was seen.

"Pilot to tail, nice goin'...you see anything else?"

"Tail t'pilot, they gone...don't see nuthin'."

"Nav to bombardier, estimate wind out of one-seven-five at thirty...almost dead on our nose. Expect turn to IP in one minute."

"Rog." Glowgower set the correction into his bombsight and turned to re-check the position of the switches on the bombing panel. Looking through the clear nose dome, he could see a carpet of dirty black puffs of smoke laying ahead of them. The Kraut gunners must be checking their range before we get there, he reflected. Then his attention turned to a large group of planes emerging from an immense bank of smoke like a school of dun-colored fish. Watching them turn away to the west, he squinted and shielded his eyes from the mid-morning sun to see them better. They were B-26s! One of the other groups coming off their target! He recoiled in horror as one of them, less than a mile away, exploded from a direct flak hit and fluttered down to the earth like a fractured toy. No chutes.

"Pitchfork to all flights, turn to IP...*now!*"

"Bomb bay doors coming open!" Glowgower cried.

"PDI is centered!" came from the cockpit.

The bombardier peered through the eyepiece of the sight. All he could see was smoke, probably coming downwind from the target bombed by the other group. He waited. They had about two more minutes for the target to become visible or be forced to abort the run. After a few more moments, he keyed the interphone, "Bombardier to pilot, target obscured by smoke...be ready to go around!

"Shit!" Clementi exclaimed.

Shaw glanced over at him. "I'll take over, Luce!"

"No!" The co-pilot waved him away. "I'm o.k...I'll fly it!"

"Pitchfork to all flights, turn left and follow me! I repeat, turn left and follow me...NOW!" The formation wheeled around on two dog-leg courses to re-intercept the IP at Pavilly. This would add another seven or eight very deadly minutes to their time around the flak-infested target area. The only consolation was that the enemy fighters were keeping their distance until the bombers emerged from the target.

"Pitchfork to all flights, climb to 12,000 feet and re-set your invertalometers for 225 milliseconds...ACKNOWLEDGE!" This move would throw off the gunner's range and deflection but would probably degrade the bombing accuracy.

Shaw watched Clementi lean down and, without shifting his gaze from the lead element, move the throttles up to increase power for the climb. The co-pilot was maintaining position despite the confusion of the turn and the constant buffeting from the concussion of flak bursts exploding near them. Shaw swiveled his head right and left to watch the rest of the squadron, intermittently shouting commands over the radio to the flight leaders to close up their stragglers.

"Nav to pilot and bombardier, expect turn to IP heading of one-seven-three in one minute...It'll be a ninety degree left turn."

Shaw nodded to Clementi and picked up his mike and announced, "Black charlie flight, prepare to reduce power and slow down for a sharp left turn...maintain position on me!" This maneuver was precarious because the left-hand flight would have to slow almost to stall speed to keep position while the right-hand flight would have to firewall their throttles to keep up.

"Pitchfork to all flights, turn to IP...*now!*" The formation began to disassemble as they started the acute turn back to the south. The radio was full of excited chatter from squadron and flight leaders trying to bring order back to their formations.

Glowgower ignored the confusion and tried to block out the distraction of the billowing flak bursts which scattered fragments of deadly metal hail against the sides of the B-26. The bomb bay doors were still open and the shrieking noise of the slipstream filled the plane, the air smelling of carbon smoke and burnt cordite. Since much of the smoke had drifted away from the target, he was able to view the twisted wreckage of the marshalling yards below him through the bombsight and could see the distinct, black rectangles of the warehouses just ahead. "Bombardier to crew," he called, "target's in front of us...lead's headed right for it."

The command channel screamed to life. "Bombs away!"

Glowgower jabbed the pickle button and listened to the bombs clatter from their racks. "Bomb bay doors closing!" he cried, immediately followed by the sensation of being pushed into his seat by the G-forces of a steep right turn. Straining to see over his left shoulder, he observed a massive column of white smoke arising from where the bombs had struck. "Man! Look at those secondaries!" he shouted. "That's got to be ammunition going up!"

As they sped away from the target, the entire crew of *The A-Train* felt the unmistakable *KA-RUMP* of a flak shell exploding off on their rear quarter, accompanied by the sickening sound of rending metal as the shrapnel tore into the plane.

"Pilot to crew, report damage!" Shaw screamed.

It was a near miss but a large fragment of the shell had entered the belly of the fuselage just forward of the waist window and carved into the crouching Milawski. Vega jumped down out of the turret seat to see a large pool of blood spreading underneath the supine engineer. Rolling him over, the gunner's stomach involuntarily convulsed. "Oh my God!" he screeched over the interphone. "Ski's hit...he's hit bad!"

"Pilot to nav, get the first aid kit and go back there!

Vega, get back in the turret! Rimbaud, stay where you are!

Those fighters will be back in a minute!"

A minute later, Grattan, kneeling over Milawski's still form, wept with frustration as he fought to keep himself under control. The wound had disemboweled the engineer, causing his intestines to spill out onto the floorboard beside him. The navigator picked-up the bluish sticky mass with his hands and began stuffing it back into the red cavity of Milawski's abdomen. Dousing sulfa all over the wound, he packed it with several cotton compresses, then jabbed a morphine styrette into the unconscious engineer's right leg. Trembling, he tried to think of what to do next. Blankets, he thought, to control shock. Ignoring the persistent chatter over the interphone, the shouts calling out the position of attacking fighters, he raced to the locker containing the blankets. After returning to the waist and covering Milawksi in layers, he noticed that the wounded engineer's pallor had gone deathly white. Grattan reached under the blankets for the engineer's wrist to see of he could detect a pulse. Barely a flicker. Leaning close to the engineer's face, he tried to determine if he could feel any breath from his nostrils. Nothing. He heard the hammering of the guns around him and was pelted by the spent shell casings raining down from the top turret. In the corner of his vision he saw a dark shape flash by the waist window. On his knees, he wracked his brain—what else can I do? Oxygen? Yes! The B-26s usually didn't fly high enough to require the crew to go on oxygen, but each crewmember carried a mask just in case. Grattan fumbled for Milawski's mask and found it hanging on a hook on the side of the fuselage. He twisted the valve on the regulator and clamped the mask onto the engineer's face. The air bladder didn't move. He felt for a pulse again. Nothing. The hand felt cold and clammy. Gently, he placed the lifeless hand on the engineer's chest, covered his face with the blanket, and intoned a short prayer. There was nothing else to do.

Grattan made his way to the flight deck and slumped against the door opening. The pilots didn't notice him for a moment until Shaw turned his head and looked at him questioningly. "How's Ski?" he asked.

"He's had it." The navigator grimaced and looked down.

A look of disbelief crossed the pilot's face. "You mean he's dead?"

"Yes, took a fragment in the gut that almost tore him in half."

Shaw noticed for the first time the blood on the navigator's hands and sleeves. "Where...what did you...?"

"In the waist...I covered him up."

"I guess that's all you can do."

A nod.

"You'd better get back to your station and figure out where we are."

"Right."

Vega didn't have time to notice the engineer's inert body covered up beneath his feet. He was watching a section of Focke Wulfs in a climbing turn to his left. "Turret to crew, bogies at eight o'clock level! Ten plus FW-190s climbing!"

"Pilot to crew...looks like they're pulling ahead for a head-on attack...get ready!" Shaw noticed a gaggle of P-47s 4,000 feet above them diving and turning toward the 190s but didn't think they'd get there in time to cut them off. When the 190s were about a mile ahead, they rolled inverted and split-essed back toward the bombers. Glancing at the co-pilot, he said, "You fly...I'll shoot." Clementi grunted without looking at him. Poising his finger on the trigger which controlled five of the six forward firing guns, he cried, "Get ready! Get ready!"

Glowgower hated frontal attacks from fighters more than any other aspect of combat flying. Bad as flak was, he reasoned, you couldn't actually see the shells coming. If they got you, they got you, and you'd probably never know what hit you. But the fighters! They were a horrific sight as they grew in size, spouting glowing baseballs of lethal cannon fire toward you, leaving you with no place to hide within the thin aluminum skin of the airplane. He squinted at the oncoming pair of

Focke Wulfs over the metal sight of his flexible 50-caliber mount. Gunnery was not his forte. He felt like he was wasting ammunition most of the time, but it was better then sitting there doing nothing. Watching the fighters come into range, he tracked the leader in his sight and tightened his right index finger on the trigger of the gun. An instant before he could depress the trigger, the five fixed guns opened up, one of which was located next to his right knee. The incredible noise and vibration momentarily stunned him before he added his gun to the general melee. The enemy tracers arced toward him for what seemed like an interval of minutes but was in fact less than two seconds. An instant before the fighters disappeared below the formation, his ears were assaulted by a shattering *CRASH!* and the bombing panel next to his left knee disappeared in a shower of fragments. A 200 m.p.h. wind was howling through a jagged hole in the lower left quadrant of the nose dome. Feeling a sharp, stinging sensation, he looked down and was amazed to notice a piece of the bombing panel impaled in his left calf. Blood was pulsing out around the wound. "Bombardier to pilot," he called, "I need some help up here!"

"What wrong?" Shaw asked.

"I'm hit...in the leg."

Shaw took the controls and turned to Clementi. "Luce, go down there and help him. See if you can get him up to the flight deck." Clementi unstrapped, moved the seat back and slipped through the opening under his side of the panel. Glowgower was still seated on his stool with a tangle of wreckage to his left. "Where is it?" The co-pilot had to scream to make himself heard above the din in the nose. The bombardier grimaced in pain as he weakly pointed down to his calf. "Can you turn around to the left so I can get to it?"

The bombardier's face contorted in a mask of agony as he struggled to move himself around. Clementi opened the nose compartment first aid kit and removed a morphine styrette. The bombardier grunted when the co-pilot plunged it into his left thigh. The narcotic kicked-in suddenly, causing the bombardier to spasmodically vomit all over the crouching co-pilot. Clementi ignored the mess covering him and sprinkled sulfa powder on the wound. He looked up at the bombardier, face dripping, and said, "I'm gonna' have to wrap something around the wound until the medics can take that thing out of your leg, o.k.?" Cutting away the tattered material of Glowgower's pants leg, he deftly wound a cotton bandage around the calf, careful to avoid putting any pressure on the protruding metal fragment. "You think you can move up to the flight deck?"

The bombrdier blinked uncertainly. "I'll try."

Clementi moved to the bombardier's right side and looped his arm around his shoulder. "O.k....here we go...just try not to put any weight on your left leg." He began dragging Glowgower backward through the opening. Halfway through, Grattan reached down and pulled the bombardier the rest of the way into the flight deck. Glowgower groaned with pain as the navigator bodily carried him through the cockpit door into the nav compartment, then lay him down on the floor. Grattan inspected the wound. Blood was seeping around the bandages but the arterial bleeding had stopped.

Glowgower blinked up at him.

Grattan smiled. "You're going to be fine."

"How's Ski?" the bombardier asked weakly. "I didn't hear..."

The smile vanished. "He didn't make it."

The bombardier's eyes closed, tears streaking down the sides of his face, his shoulders trembling.

The group took an exit route to the West of Rouen, then north back up to the French coast so they would be out of the way of the next group coming in to bomb. When they were back over the Channel and out of danger, Shaw looked at Clementi and said, "I'll fly the rest of the way to base...you've done more than your fair share today." The co-pilot was truly drained and slumped in his seat. The pilot lit a cigarette and said, tiredly, "Tough mission, huh?"

"That's the understatement of the day," the co-pilot snorted. "A few more like this and all of us will..."

"Shut your mouth!" Shaw snapped at him. "Don't say it...even if you think it!" The pilot was frustrated and angry, not at anyone in particular, but in general, maybe a little bit at himself. Flight emergencies, flying damaged airplanes under stressful circumstances were part of his stock and trade, something he could handle. But people being torn to pieces by flak and cannon—death was beyond his expertise. Intellectually, he understood there was nothing he could do about it, but he despised the gut feeling of helplessness he was left with. Leaning over, he nudged the co-pilot's shoulder. "I'm sorry, Luce, I shouldn't have..."

"No...it's o.k.," the co-pilot interrupted, a bleak smile on his face. "You're right anyway...some things ought to be left unsaid."

"Well, we sure as hell clobbered the target."

"Yeah...that's something."

They proceeded the rest of the way in silence. Shaw was anxious to land so the M.O. could attend to Glowgower's wound, but, due to the cloud cover and low visibility surrounding the base on their return, was forced to fly east out to the Naze then turn back west again to fly the RC for an instrument letdown. As they pierced the murk and saw the runway, Grattan fired a red flare indicating wounded aboard. When the tires finally kissed the pavement, the fuel gauges were reading empty. After the engines were shut down and the propellers spooled to a halt, the pilots could hear a high keening wail coming from the rear of the plane.

Clementi arched his eyebrows and looked quizzically at Shaw. "What the hell is that?" he asked.

"I think it's Rimbaud."

The pilot slapped her, then he slapped her again. "Damn you! Why did it have to happen to him?" he asked her. "He was only a kid...barely twenty." He leaned against her, his forehead resting on her cool flank, while small rivulets of tears ran down her side and dripped to the ground below. "I'm sorry," he exhaled hoarsely, "so sorry...." It had finally happened: the crucible had consumed one of her boys.

CHAPTER SIXTEEN

October 14, 1943, Boxsted, England.

The Group had been placed on temporary stand-down and a special briefing had been announced. It was common knowledge that the other B-26 groups in England had been placed on stand-down, too. The reason for this was unknown to most, but the most persistent rumor suggested that they were going to be packed-up and sent to join the 12TH Air Force in Sicily. Some even speculated that they were going to China to join up with General Chennault in the 14TH! Whatever it was, the officers and men of the 333RD Bomb Group (M) knew something was up.

Colonel Spinelli had known about the change for over a month, ever since Lieutenant General James H. Doolittle had taken over command of the 8TH Air Force, but had been sworn to secrecy on threat of court marital. It was all part of a huge operation being planned, the one the planners at High Wycombe referred as "Overlord." Spinelli, because he viewed himself primarily as a line combat pilot—one of the people in war who have to go out and do the dirty job of killing— hated his periodic dealings with the tedious, rear-echelon staff officers at headquarters. Their obsessive preoccupation with secrecy, which he felt mostly unecessary, greatly annoyed him. After all, what did the Germans think the Americans were doing in England anyway: Boosting British GNP? Impregnating widows to make up for population losses? They *know* why we're here. What he detested in particular was the inability imposed on him by headquarters to keep the troops informed, when everyone from the squadron commanders down to the mess boys in the chow hall repeatedly inquired, "Hey, Colonel, when are you gonna' fill us in?" Today, finally, they would find out.

The briefing hall was packed. All of the aircrews, officer and enlisted, were there plus the senior NCOs among the ground personnel. Buster Ripley, recently promoted to techinical sergeant, was shoe-horned in next to Vega, Rimbaud and Sergeant Elmo Tilden, *The A-*

Train's new flight engineer/gunner. Tilden, a stocky, unprepossessing, nineteen-year-old from Muskogee, Oklahoma, had flown ten missions with another B-26 crew before being moved to *The A- Train.* Shaw considered himself fortunate to have him because many of the new crews were no longer carrying men trained as engineers. Tilden had been readily accepted and liked by everyone in the crew except Rimbaud, who regularly reminded him that he wasn't half the engineer his predecessor, Milawski, had been. Rimbaud also speculated that the black-haired, black-eyed Tilden was possibly part Indian, a heathen savage by all accounts!

After the room was called to attention by the adjutant, Spinelli strode to the front of the hall accompanied by a dark-haired, bespectacled man with three stars adorning the epaulets of his Class A blouse and a "crushed" fifty-mission cap atop his head. The man, who had recently been promoted to the rank of lieutenant general, looked more like a banker than a combat commander, but, in fact, had flown combat with the AEF in World War I and most recently commanded the 10TH Air Force in India.

"Get ready to bend over and spread your cheeks," Clementi whispered sotto voce to no one in particular. Glowgower snorted and had to cover his mouth to keep from laughing out loud. Shaw frowned and gave both of them dark looks.

Spinelli stood to one side of the platform, looking at the bespectacled General, who gave him a quick nod and strode briskly up to the podium. The General took a moment to survey the expectant faces of the men standing at attention before him. So young, he thought—even the officers were hardly more than boys. "Take your seats, men!" he said in a vigorous tone. "Feel free to smoke."

When the commotion stopped, leaning forward on the podium, he said, "I know most of you are wondering who I am and why I'm here." The room became utterly silent. "I'm Lewis H. Brereton, commander of the 9TH Tactical Air Force. As of today, your unit, the 333RD Bomb Group (Medium), has been transferred under my command. I'm here today to welcome you to the 9TH. Your group has a fine combat record so far, and I'm delighted to have you in my organization!"

"Why this is happening? You deserve to know." He paused to withdraw a corona cigar from his shirt pocket and light it with a flourish. Blowing a cloud of smoke toward the ceiling, the General continued, "The war has reached the point where the strategic and tactical missions of the Army Air Forces in the European Theater need to be divided. The 8TH Air Force, which your group has been a part of since February, will continue to take its strategic mission into the German heartland. The 9TH, on the other hand, will be charged with prosecuting the tactical mission in this theater. To do this, we are assembling the largest operational unit in the Air Force." Larger than the entire pre-war Air Corps, he thought, but did not mention. "Included in this move are all other B-26 and A-20 groups which are now in England, plus a number of fighter groups and all of the transport groups previously assigned to he 8TH. The Air Defense, Engineer, and Service commands will be joining us, too.

"What effect can you expect to have on your group?" He leaned back from the lectern as the room fell deadly silent. "Well, for the time being, it won't change much at all; you'll continue to fly the same kinds of missions you've been flying since July. And you can rest assurred that whatever targets you're assigned, you'll be flying *from medium altitudes and with a fighter escort!.*"

The last comment generated a noisy murmur of approval.

The General paused to make his next point. "But, when we cross the Channel, gentlemen, the 9TH Air Force will become part of an 'army in movement'...chasing the Kraut war machine back to where it came from...and the 333RD will be moving along with it!" Pointing to the audience, he exclaimed, "You'll be the Blitzkrieg in reverse!"

The announcement was followed by a round of enthusiastic hooting and foot stamping.

Smiling, the General held up his hands and shouted, "Thank you, men! I like your spirit!" As the noise settled, he regarded them seriously, leaning forward. "Now men, I've got to tell you something you're not going to like..." The room grew utterly quiet again. "Your mission requirement has been raised from thirty-five to fifty."

The momentary silence began to build up into a low buzzing noise like a hive of angry bees. Spinelli had been informed about the new requirement and was privately relieved he wasn't the one annoucing it. There were justifiable reasons for the change, he knew, but he didn't expect the men to be happy about it, especially the guys who were over the mid-tour mark. The bastards at headquarters should have made the change back in July, when the group was taken off stand-down. It was a fact that the crews would have to fly more missions to get the job done before the invasion of Europe, like working overtime to meet a deadline. The B-25, B-26, and A-20 groups in other combat theaters were all required to fly fifty missions or an equivalent number of combat hours.

Facing the hard looks being given to him by the seated men, the General dryly asked, "Any of you..." he pointed around the room. "Any of you want a transfer to a heavy group that's only required to fly twenty-five missions?"

After a moment of silence, an unidentified high voice in the back of room shouted, "Not no, General! BUT HELL NO!"

They might not like it, but the point was taken.

Shaw, Grattan and Glowgower had been stoic about the mission requirement change, not really surprised, but Clementi had been incensed, gone ballistic.

"I'm not gonna' stand still for this crap," he railed as they walked from the briefing hall. "I'm gonna take it up with my Congressman!"

"Who is...?" Grattan asked.

"Umm..." The co-pilot looked sheepish. "I'll have to look it up...my pop has met him."

"What do you think your Congressman will do about it?"

"Uh...I don't know." Clementi was unsure of himself.

"Listen, Luce," Shaw said pointedly. "I suggest you just tuck it in and tough it out. We're military officers ...we're just supposed to follow orders."

The co-pilot shrugged. "Even if it's unfair?"

"Yeah...even then."

After considering the idea for a moment, Clementi's brooding expression transformed into a curious look. "Hey, since we're not flying today, you think the bar is open already?"

They laughed and pounded the skinny co-pilot's back.

In the interval since the raid on the warehouses in Rouen, *The A-Train* had flown seventeen more missions, primarily against railway bridges and other rail targets in Northern France. The airplane had been hit a number of times by shrapnel from flak and 20 millimeter cannon strikes from fighters, but no serious damage had been inflicted. Ripley claimed that if all the patches were removed, their airplane would look like a flying cheese grater. The only crew injury had been to Tilden, the engineer/gunner, who, in the process of clearing a jam in one of the 50-caliber waist guns, smashed his right thumb when the bolt suddenly retracted. The wound required five stitches and caused Tilden's thumb to swell up like a small eggplant, but didn't merit a Purple Heart. The first two weeks of this period, they had flown five trips with pick-up bombardiers until Glowgower returned to flight status after recovering from the leg wound he'd received on the Rouen mission. The wound, affecting only the muscle, healed quickly after being cleaned and sutured. The bombardier had been awarded a Purple Heart at a ceremony in early October in which all members of the 333rd had received a Distinguished Unit Commendation. As to the rest of *The A-Train's* crew, Shaw, Clementi, Grattan, and Rimbaud now had credit for twenty-seven missions; Vega had credit for twenty-five; Glowgower had twenty-two; and Tilden had twenty. No question that they were veterans now, salty.

After three months of combat operations, the loss ratio in the group had gradually continued to improve, hovering somewhere around the one per cent mark. Not because the Germans were giving ground, on the contrary: they had added the more heavily armed ME-109G and rocket-firing ME-110s to their bag of defensive tricks; but, the Americans, at the same time, were getting more experienced at the trade of combat flying. Tactics improved for fighters and bombers, leaders got better at leading, and aircrews got better at flying, a far cry from the first tentative steps taken over a year ago.

On the other side, the Nazi propaganda-makers were telling the German population that the Allies would be stopped on the beaches, that their aerial armada would be defeated by "wonder weapons", that the Thousand Year Reich was still forthcoming. But the American aircrews knew differently; *they knew they were winning*. They didn't doubt it for a moment.

CHAPTER SEVENTEEN

October 21, 1943, Boxsted, England.

Shaw, dressed in the class A officer's uniform, known in the service as "pinks and greens," walked into the tiny cubicle Major Robert Armistead used as the squadron office for the 424TH. Parking himself in the chair next to the regulation metal desk, he removed his cap and said cheerfully, "'Mornin' Bobby, you got the three-day passes ready for me and my boys?"

Armistead critically viewed the well turned-out young officer seated before him, noticing the sharp creases in his uniform and the neat knot in his tie. The only decoration above his left breast pocket was a tarnished pair of pilot's wings. Although Armistead was often contemptuous of military formality and frequently led the drink-induced horse-play at the O-Club, he was nevertheless a stickler for a proper military appearance. Pointing to Shaw's left blouse pocket, he drawled, sarcastically, "Why ain't you wearin' your ribbons...Cap'n?"

"I..." Shaw was taken aback by the question.

"You just bein' modest, ain't you?"

"Ah, uh-huh..." Shaw mumbled, continuing to stare perplexedly at the frowning major.

"You just don' want to put on the dog...and make out like you're some kinda' hero, right!"

"Yeah, I guess that's it." Shaw smiled weakly.

"Baloney!" Armistead abruptly retorted and sat up in his chair. "Why you think they give 'em to you if you ain't supposed to wear 'em, huh? Answer me that!"

"I don't..."

"Well, Cap'n," he interrupted, "if you ain't proud your nation's honored you, *ah am...*" the lanky major scowled and pointed to himself "...and so's the rest of the group!"

"O.k., Bobby." Shaw surrendered.

"That goes for the rest of those peckerwoods in your outfit, too. Got it?"

"Got it."

"By the way," Armistead said listlessly, leaning back with his eyed half closed, "you can have this..." he waved the pass in front of the pilot's face "...as soon as you and the rest of the white trash that follows you around are in proper uniform."

Two hours later, the crew of *The A-Train* stood waiting at the Colchester station for the train to London—they and over a hundred other uniformed men were headed in the same direction. Most of the uniforms were O.D. green--American—but scattered here and there was the brown of the British Army, the blue-gray of the RAF—which included Canadians, Australians and New Zealanders—plus a few dark blue jumpers of Royal Navy jack tars. The officers stood around in small, indifferent groups and smoked, taking care not to soil their uniforms, while the enlisted men lounged on B-4 bags, musette bags, or sea bags and slept, gambled, or sang ditties. A train pulling a line of flatcars containing artillery pieces and M4 Sherman tanks rumbled through the station without stopping. The aircrews didn't even seem to notice the train but quickly craned their necks and shaded their eyes to watch a group of RAF Spitfires forming up 2,000 feet over their heads, and continued to follow them as they headed southeast toward the Channel coast.

"I wonder where they're going?" Clementi, gazing up at the departing Spitfires, said to no one in particular.

Looking up at the same time, Grattan answered, "Probably to one of the German fighter bases, maybe Abbeville or St. Omer.".

Squinting back up at the departing aircraft, Clementi said, "They're not carrying bombs. What'll they do when they get there?"

"They dare the Krauts to come up and fight...they call them 'sweeps.'"

The co-pilot looked questioningly at the navigator. "Does it work...do they come up and fight?"

"Not usually." Grattan had learned this from an RAF fitter—mechanic—he'd visited with in a tea room in town.

"Then do they just turn around and come back?"

"Nope, if the Krauts don't take the bait, they dive down and shoot up the field with their guns."

"With their guns?" Clementi looked at him with disbelief. "That's crazy! They would be putting themselves into the range of every German flak battery and machine gun on the field."

"Right."

"I don't see the point of it, Mick."

"Well, the Brits believe if they strafe the field often enough, they'll eventually force the Germans to come up and defend it."

Clementi gave the burly navigator an amazed expression.

Grattan pondered an explanation. "The sweeps, I think, are not used to encourage air-to-air combat *per se*, but are part of a larger strategy designed to reduce the overall effectiveness of German air defenses."

Clementi looked totally blank.

Unperturbed, Grattan continued, "If the Allies can destroy the German fighters at rate faster than they can be replaced, you reduce the military threat to Allied bombers in the same proportion. It's kind of like a game of aerial chess in which the fighters...who probably think of themselves as knights...are really the pawns." Pleased by his explanation, he gave the co-pilot a bright grin. "Does that make sense?"

"Oh, you bet," Clementi commented with a note of sarcasm. Cocking his thumb in Grattan's direction, he looked at the others and asked, "Where does he come up with all that high-powered bullshit?"

"Must be what they teach 'em in navigator's school," Shaw responded indifferently.

"Sounds like something a staff puke would say," Glowgower offered.

Grattan smiled hopelessly and shrugged. "That's what I would expect to hear from a group of people whose reading tastes don't go beyond Captain Marvel or The Green Hornet." Boys at play, the navigator thought with amusement—and, in my own way, I'm one of them. The easy fellowship warmed him.

The locomotive with its old, beat-up coach cars pulled slowly into the station. The train, which had originated at Harwich, was already half-full, and would stop again at Chelmsford and Brentwood before reaching the station at King's Cross. It was every man for himself. The crew of *The A-Train*, veterans of this mode of travel, yanked the door open on one of the coaches even before it stopped and jumped in like paratroopers, dragging their bags behind them. Six of them compressed themselves into two bench seats, facing each other three abreast with Tilden sitting on the baggage in the middle.

Looking around at the cramped surroundings, Glowgower curiously asked, "Any of you guys ever make a trip in a Pullman car with a sleeper and a diner?"

They shook their heads...no one had.

"I did once," he continued, "in '39, with my old man. Rode from Louisville to New York City to see the World's Fair."

"Hey, I was there, too, at the fair!" Clementi said with excitement.

"We might have passed each other without even knowing it."

"Maybe we did." Glowgower looked at the co-pilot. "You remember the big Air Corps display in the main exhibit hall?"

"You mean the one where they had all these big models on tables and real planes hanging from the ceiling?" Clementi's face took on a preoccupied expression as he recalled the vision.

"Yeah, that's the one. I must have come back to it ten times," the bombardier confided. "Anyway...it made such an impression...made me think about joining the Air Corps some day to become a pilot."

"Well, I was impressed, for sure...but not like that," Clementi quipped. "Back then, I was what...eighteen? The only thing I was interested in was the Dodgers and broads."

"Then what did, Luce? Why did you decide to volunteer for pilot training?" Since Shaw had never dreamed of being anything else, he was curious.

The co-pilot looked at him with a sheepish smile. "You remember the movie with Ray Milland, *I Wanted Wings*?"

Shaw nodded at him with an even gaze. He wasn't about to tell them that he'd sat through it twice the first time it showed in Big Spring, and saw it again the following night without Mary Beth, who flatly refused to see it three times in a row.

"Well I had a date with this absolutely stunning number with bazooms out to here." Clementi motioned with cupped hands. "And she went on and on about how perfectly marvelous and heroic the Air Corps pilots were, and had I ever thought of becoming one? 'Of course,' I told her. 'Already looking into it, in fact.'"

Glowgower's brow creased in a huge grin. "You mean you volunteered to impress a dame?"

Clementi gave him a helpless shrug.

"Our intrepid Luce is certainly not the first," Grattan interjected in a matter of fact tone. "You might be interested to know that entire wars have been caused by a pretty face. You remember the story in *The Iliad*, when the Homeric Greeks invaded the city of Troy because of a woman named Helen. And don't forget Delilah, Bathsheeba, and Cleopatra."

"Of course not," chimed Shaw.

"If you really thought about it, Luce," Grattan said, tongue in cheek, "you were in all probalility motivated by a desire to protect this young woman from the evil clutches of facsist world domination, weren't you?"

"Sounds good to me," Clementi replied with a chuckle.

The co-pilot reached over and poked the slouching Rimbaud, who had said nothing since entering the train. "What about it, Leroy?" he asked in mock seriousnes. "What made a fine Cajun boy like you want to become an air gunner?"

"Me?" Rimbaud yawned listlessly, then leered at the co-pilot. "Ah jus' wanted t'be somewheres close to college boys like you...so's all that ed-ju-ma-cation and good manners would rub off on me." The tail gunner leaned over slightly, let a blattering fart, then fanned it in the co-pilot's direction. "Oh, 'scuse me, Lieutenant, ah forget ah ain't spose t'do that no more."

Shaw and the rest of them erupted into a fit of raucous laughter that caused the other occupants of the coach to turn around and stare.

A Royal Army "brown job," sitting across the aisle from them, looked up from the newspaper he was reading and remarked disgustedly to his companion, "Bleeding Yanks ...over-paid, over-sexed and *over here!*"

When the train halted at the Chelmsford station, another wave of men in uniforms surged aboard. There were no seats left, so the aisles were crammed with a pulsing human cargo, which nearly toppled like dominoes when the train lurched into motion. "Reminds me of the up-town subways at rush hour," Clementi commented. "Except half the passengers there were women," he added with a wink, "not soldiers with b.o. and bad breath."

Shaw, sitting on the aisle, felt a jar to his shoulder, and looked up at a pale, youthful RAF flying officer who was being pressed against his seat.

"Sorry," the young RAF man said, trying vainly to brace himself against the motion of the coach.

Shaw smiled at him, then turned to Tilden. "Elmo, scoot over and give this guy a place to sit." He motioned him to sit on one of the B-4 bags and, removing a pack of Luckies from his pocket, asked, "Smoke?"

"Thanks, awfully," the young man said with a large smile that revealed overlapping front teeth. Accepting a light from Shaw's Zippo, he turned his head sideways to blow the smoke toward the aisle. "Where are you chaps based?" he inquired, squinting from the smoke.

"Boxsted," Shaw told him.

"Ah, near Colchester...fighters or bombers?"

"Bombers...B-26s," Shaw answered.

"Why yes, Marauders!" the young man said with keen enthusiasm. The RAF usually identified aircraft by their factory names rather than numeric designators. "I've seen you chaps come over our 'drome in battle formation, en route to the French coast, I imagine."

Shaw noticed an embroidered winged insignia above the young man's pocket with the diagonally stripped DFC ribbon pinned below it. He also saw that he had a young-old face: youthful at a glance, but old and weary around the eyes. "You're a bombardier?" Shaw asked, pointing to the insignia.

"We're called bomb-aimers in our service, but we do the same sort of thing."

Grattan leaned forward and asked, "What type of plane do you fly in?"

"Lancs...at Saxonby."

"Flown many missions?"

"Well, I'm on second tour, actually, flew twenty-five on Wimpys"—referring to the twin-engined Vickers Wellington —"and have done fifteen trips so far on Lancs"—referring to the four-engined Avro Lancaster.

"Forty missions! I guess you're used to it," Clementi commented.

"Bloody hell!" he exclaimed with a huge grin. "I practically shat myself on every trip!"

All of them smiled at the young RAF officer's unashamed revelation—they knew exactly how he felt.

Glowgower was intrigued by the fellow bombardier and asked seriously, "Fill us in a little on what night operations are like, that is, if you don't mind."

The young RAF Officer regarded the group sitting around him. Never had he casually shared his experiences with anyone other than fellow RAF aircrew. Though not familiar with all the decorations these Army Air Force men were wearing, he did recognize the purple and white ribbon worn by four of the group, the one Americans awarded for being wounded in action. These chaps had seen the elephant, he decided. They were bomber boys, too, not the "Brylcreem" types who flew fighters. Brothers-in-arms.

"Don't mind a bit," he eventually said in a melancholy tone. After accepting another Lucky Strike from Shaw, he began. For most of the next half hour, the crew of *The A-Train* listened with fascination and horror to the young man's chronicle of being on "ops" with RAF Bomber Command: taking-offs in the semi-darkness toward Germany; often never seeing another airplane, although there were hundreds in the "bomb stream"; being "coned" near the target by probing searchlights; shrill calling over the interphone to "corkscrew port" or "starboard" away from attacking night fighters; flying over targets bathed in a maelstrom of fire; returning with shot-out engines, with wounded and dead aboard; and ditching in the Channel, nearly freezing to death before being picked-up. "Funny," he said softly, "practically every chap I knew on the bomb-aimers course and in my first squadron has gone for a burton."

"What?"

"I believe you Yanks call it 'bought the farm.'"

They sat in silence for a moment, the young-old flying officer, quietly staring out the window of the coach with a far away look. Suddenly, he sat up and smiled, revealing again the overlapping teeth. "What I find bloody mystifying," he declared, looking at each of them, "is how your lot does it in broad daylight."

Shaw responded by giving the young flying officer a brief explanation of their formation tactics and how the fighter screen worked.

The young flying officer gave him a perceptive smile. "You make it sound as safe as houses...don't the Jerry fighters occasionally break through your escort?"

Before Shaw could answer, Vega interjected, "You bet your sweet ass...when the 'Bolts can't cut 'em off, the sons-of-bitches are all over us."

"What about your gunnery...are you able to fend them off?"

"Most of the time." Vega still talking. "Depends on how many and what direction they come from. Low attacks on our beam are the worst 'cause we can't bring anything to bear but the waist guns." The gunner imitated the relative motion with his hands. "But head-on attacks are always the scariest...like playing chicken."

"Chicken?" The flying officer looked puzzled.

"Yeah," Vega continued. "You know, like when two cars come at each other head-on, the first one to turn away is the 'chicken.' Get it?"

Comprehension dawned on the flying officer's face. "They do this in the U.S....play this chicken game?"

Vega grinned. "All the time."

"Bloody amazing."

"Are you from London?" Grattan interrupted, changing the subject.

"No, I'm a Cornishman, from Falmouth, actually, but I'm quite familiar with London...on my way there now, in fact, to join some of my mates."

"We've been there several times," the big navigator explained, "but, you know...still don't know our way around very well."

"Oh, right...let me put you chaps in the picture..."

Grattan produced a notepad and scribbled down the names of recommended hotels, restaurants, pubs, and clubs. As the young man explained the "tube," the navigator drew a neat sketch of the major subway lines and how they interconnected with each other. "You'd almost have to live here to understand the buses...stick to the tube and take a taxi if you're too sloshed to find an underground station, happens to me all the time," he winked.

Grattan folded the notepad and returned it to his pocket. "You've been a great help, uh...I don't think you told us your name."

"Jeremy Lytton...but my mates all call me Jerry."

Grattan extended his hand. "I'm Mick Grattan." Then pointing to each one in turn, he said, "These unrefined cretins are Ted Shaw, Luce Clementi, Joe Glowgower...we call him Glow, Leroy Rimbaud, Frank Vega, and Elmo Tilden." Handshakes were exchanged all around.

Looking at them with a grin, the young flying officer said, "You chaps must be an example of what the social scientists call the American 'melting pot.'"

Rimbaud decided that RAF officers were just as full of shit as their American counterparts.

The train slowed as the outskirts of London began to slide by the windows, the change seeming to invigorate the torpid servicemen occupying the coach. Shaw's little group had agreed in advance that the officers and sergeants would split up on this trip. Vega, who'd been stationed near London while he was in the B-17 group, had told Shaw, "No offense, skipper, but me and the guys," referring to Rimbaud and Tilden, "will have a lot more fun without you officers taggin' along." Shaw had unenthusiastically consented but told them to meet back at the station in two day's time.

"Where to?" Shaw directed the question at Grattan.

The navigator studied his notepad. "Green Park," he announced. "We can go downstairs and catch a subway." Thirty minutes later, they were outside on the street, clutching their valv-packs, walking with overcoat collars raised to ward off the chill autumn wind. After a short walk from the subway station, they stopped in front of an ornate Victorian hotel with a marble entrance and a awning-covered walkway, framed on either side by gardens containing trimmed boxwoods and flowers. Grattan pointed toward the brass double doors and said, "This is one of the hotels recommended by Jerry."

"Looks expensive," Shaw said cautiously.

"Jerry said it was reasonable, and besides, we can pool our money and share a room." The hotel was in truth above the means of the young RAF officer, but he knew the higher-paid Americans could probably afford it.

The lobby and reception were marbled, too, with beveled mirror walls set with flickering gas-lit sconces. Shaw looked up with awe at the enormous crystal chandelier hanging above his head. The place had a mild aroma of cigar smoke and lilac scent. Glowgower quickly stepped up to the registration desk and booked the room, a suite over-looking the park, then motioned the bellman to take their bags to their room. "Your bag, sir?" the liveried bellman asked Shaw, who was star-ing, open-mouthed, at the vaulted ceiling above him.

"What?" Shaw looked at the man.

"Your bag, sir...may I take it?"

"Oh, sure." Handing the valv-pack to the man, he turned to Glow-gower and asked, "What's this place costing us, Glow?"

"Fifteen a night," the bombardier replied calmly.

"Fifteen what?"

"Pounds."

"Pounds! Are you serious!" Shaw retorted. "That's almost forty bucks a day..."

Glowgower made a shushing motion with his index finger. "It's o.k., Ted, we can handle it," he said quietly. The bombardier had al-ready paid the clerk for both nights with his own money. In addition to his first lieutenant's pay—$267 per month, which included flight pay and overseas pay—his father regularly sent him a $100 money order every month. Having accumulated over five hundred dollars in savings, with little to spend it on, he planned to blow as much of it as possible over the next two days.

The bellman preceded them into the room and pulled back the blackout curtains on the large French window facing the park, allowing the late afternoon light to flood in. He placed the bags in the adjoining bedroom and returned to ask, "Will there be anything else, sir?"

Glowgower handed the man a pound note and said, "Have some-one bring up two bottles of your best scotch, some soda, and a bucket of ice, please. Oh, and please send up some beer, too, a case ought to be enough."

"Right away, sir." The man bowed and left.

Shaw stood in the middle of the richly-paneled sitting room, gazing from one side to the other. "Look at that," he said, pointing to the other side of the room. "A hotel room with a fireplace."

Clementi, slouching in one of the deep arm chairs, waved his arm at the pilot and sighed, "Hey, Ted, quit acting like a tourist and sit down!"

Shaw walked to the silk-covered settee, slowly lowering himself to a sitting position as if he might muss the fabric. Leaning back to look up at the chandelier, a miniature of the one in the lobby, he said, "This place is really somethin' else..."

"You mean uptown, top drawer...the Ritz!" Clementi interrupted. "I could spend the rest of my life in a joint like this, no joke." The co-pilot leaned back and smiled with his eyes closed.

A discreet knock came on the door and Glowgower got up to open it for a white-jacketed waiter pushing a cart covered by a white linen tablecloth, on top of which sat the liquor, mixers, beer, and the ice he'd ordered. The man wheeled the cart to one side of the settee and asked if they needed anything else. Glowgower shook his head and handed the man a pound note.

"Thank you, sir, thank you, sir...just call me if you need anything," the man, obviously pleased with the generous tip, said as he bowed out backwards.

The bombardier clasped his hands together and asked, "Who's having what?"

"On the rocks for me," Clementi answered first.

"I'll take ice and soda with mine," Grattan responded.

Glowgower suggestively held up the pinch bottle of 12-year-old double malt scotch to the pilot and queried, "You having one, Ted?"

"Well, yeah, but real heavy on the soda, o.k.?"

"Comin' up."

Glowgower poured and mixed the drinks with a flourish.

When he had handed each man his drink, he raised his glass and asked, "What shall we toast to?"

"How about Jerry...the RAF guy who recommended this place," Clementi suggested.

"Hear, hear...to Jerry!" they intoned loudly and clinked their glasses.

Clementi sipped his drink and appreciatively sighed, "Uhmmm...this is what I call extra smooth."

"Definitely, most definitely," Grattan seconded. Though a moderate drinker, the big navigator appreciated the flavor of fine whiskey.

Shaw frowned slightly, looking at his glass. "Tastes kinda' metallic, don't you think?"

The other three smiled kindly at him. "Just goes to show," Grattan said with mirth in his voice, "that you can take a boy out of the country, but you can't take..."

"The country out of the boy," Shaw answered for him.

"Not to worry, boyo." The big man affectionately squeezed his shoulder. "At least you're still teachable." They had several more drinks—Shaw switching to beer on the second round—and shared the easy fellowship of a close-knit combat crew.

"You guys ready to go get something to eat?" Glowgower asked after a while.

"I'm weak from hunger!" Clementi cried, falling limply to the side of his chair.

"What's on the top of your list, Mick?" the bombardier inquired.

"Let's see." Grattan flipped open his notepad. "The Claridge," he announced. "It's in a hotel not too far from here."

"Is it another Injun place?" Shaw asked expectantly.

"Not hardly, it's a four-star restaurant, boyo."

"That's that mean?"

"It serves good food."

"Probably means it's expensive, too." Shaw was not really cheap, but for most of his life, had been forced to save money for flying, college, or anything thing else he wanted to do. Economy had become an ingrained habit.

"Don't worry about it."

"I won't."

While Clementi, Grattan, and Glowglower all considered Ted Shaw to be the best B-26 aircraft commander in the entire ETO, and a great guy to boot, they had privately organized a friendly mutiny to the effect that their Captain would not be in charge of entertainment on this outing.

When they reached the front door of their hotel, it was drizzling outside, so Glowgower instructed the doorman to call them a taxi. After a short ride, they pulled up in front of the Claridge, and a liveried doorman wearing a top hat snapped the cab door open for them. Shaw gaped at the man for a few moments until Clementi poked him from behind and ordered, "Bail out, Ted."

Glowgower led the way as they walked through the palatial lobby toward the restaurant. Walking purposefully up to the formally attired maitre'd standing behind a podium just inside the door, he nodded and cleared his throat.

"Have you a reservation, sir?" the man abruptly looked up and inquired, immediately noticing the lieutenant's bars.

"No, I don't" the bombardier replied, smiling.

"Oh, then I'm afraid it will be quite impossible to seat you, sir," the maitre'd said, starting to turn away.

"Is that so?" Glowgower calmly challenged, at the same time withdrawing a five pound note from his inside pocket and laying it on the podium in front of the man.

The man's cold expression instantly transformed into a pleasant smile. Pocketing the bill without comment, he quickly consulted the journal-sized book in front of him. "Let me see...why yes! We've had a cancellation and will be able to seat you gentlemen immediately." The maitre'd snapped his fingers and cried, "Albert! Show these gentlemen to table twenty-three." Behind Glowgower, none of others had witnessed the swift transaction.

When they were seated a few minutes later, Clementi surveyed the elegant surroundings and commented, "I'm surprised we could get into in a swank place like this without a reservation."

"The war must be hard on business," Glowgower offered in surmise.

The co-pilot sniffed appreciatively when a waiter passed by carrying a covered tray. "Bet the food's good, too...not like that dog slop the Air Force feeds us three times a day!"

"Dog slop?" Grattan snorted. "If that's what it is, we ought to rename you Fido!"

"Or Rover, maybe," Glowgower said with a laugh.

"Bow-wow," Shaw added.

Clementi smirked and gave them an Italian salute.

A white-jacketed elderly waiter handed them menus and apologized for the limited selection caused by wartime shortages.

"What do you recommend?" Glowgower asked after briefly glancing at the menu.

"The rack of lamb is very good, sir," the waiter replied.

Glowgower handed the menu back and said, "That'll be fine, make it four...that sound o.k. to you guys?" They nodded.

"Would you gentlemen care for a drink before dinner?" the waiter inquired.

"Do have champagne?" Glowgower asked him.

"Yes, sir, but in limited quantities I'm afraid." Very expensive, in other words.

"Then bring a bottle and four glasses, please."

"Right away, sir."

The waiter returned minutes later with an iced silver bucket containing a magnum bottle of champagne. Rotating the bottle in the ice until he adjudged the temperature to be correct, the waiter popped the cork with a loud "bang" that caused Shaw to flinch and, with a practiced flourish, poured a dollop into Glowgower's crystal stemmed glass.

Glowgower picked up the glass, giving it an appreciative sniff, drank the dollop then nodded to the waiter. When all four glasses had been filled, Glowgower raised his to the others and solemnly said, "To Ski."

"Ski," the others chorused and tipped their glasses.

Setting down his glass, Shaw smacked his lips and announced, "This stuff's not too bad...I think I like it!"

Grattan refilled the glasses, raised his and toasted, "To Roger Merrill."

"Roger Merrill," they intoned, and drank again.

The toasts continued several times for Ridley, Chase and others until the bottle was drained. Like warriors for countless generations before them, the four men celebrated, rather than mourned, their comrades departed.

Glowgower placed the empty bottle upside down in the bucket and nodded to the others. "Another?"

"Might as well," Grattan agreed, a little more color in his face than usual.

"I could go for a little more of the stuff myself," Shaw said with enthusiasm, draining the last few drops.

Glowgower slightly raised his hand and the waiter suddenly appeared as if by magic and took the order for another bottle. When the second bottle was half-finished, the bombardier peered over his glass at the pilot and advised with friendly caution, "I'd go easy on the champagne, Ted."

"Why?" Shaw replied, his Texas accent becoming more pronounced. "It's like drinkin' beer, idn't it?

"No, it's a lot more potent than beer and might make you sick, too."

"Sick? Ah've never been sick on booze!" Shaw challenged.

The waiter appeared at the table with two other white-jacketed men carrying linen covered trays. Shaw colored with embarrassment when the waiter unfolded the linen napkin and placed it on his lap. The waiter ceremoniously whipped the cover from one of the trays and began serving the food. When he'd finished, he asked Glowgower first, "Mint sauce, sir?" The bombardier said, "Please," and Grattan and Clementi followed suit. When the waiter got to Shaw, the pilot peered suspiciouly at the contents of the silver bowl. "I'll pass," he said with a grimace. "You got any fifty-seven sauce?"

"No, sir, I've not heard of it."

"How 'bout ketchup...you got that?" The others glanced at each other with barely controlled amusement.

The waiter gawked open-mouthed at the pilot for a moment, but composing himself, said, "I'll see what I can find, sir," then spun on his heel and left. He returned minutes later bearing a small silver bowl and ladle containing ketchup.

"I'd rather have a filet, but this is really good," Clementi said between mouthfuls.

"Delicious," Grattan agreed a moment later.

"Yes." Shaw lied. Given the choice, he would have preferred a cheeseburger with everything and fries on the side. The ketchup did little to help; it really needed Bar-B-Q sauce, he thought; and the vegetables, whatever they were, were hardly cooked. He smiled at the others while he ate, determined not to be a wet blanket.

Later, after desert, they all smoked large Havana cigars with a desert liqueur in lieu of the traditional English brandy. Glowgower, during a trip to the men's room, had settled the bill and the tip. When Shaw wanted to argue about it, the bombardier had calmly smiled at him and lied, "You can get the next one, pal."

As they sipped the last of their after-dinner drinks, Glowgower asked, "Where to next, gents?"

Before Grattan could retrieve his notepad, Shaw blurted, "Why not the Air Force Club?" From the moment they'd been seated at the Claridge, he'd been self-consciously aware of the fact that they were the most junior officers present, in fact, the *only* junior officers present. Smiling imploringly, he asked, "Do you mind?"

After a brief ride from the Claridge in a cab, Shaw, swaying slightly from the effects of the alcohol, entered the jam-packed Air Force club near Piccadilly in the company of Clementi, Grattan, and Glogower. While the building and furnishings of the club were unmistakably British in origin, the atmosphere inside was unquestionably American. The high noise level, together with the hanging clouds of cigarette smoke, the odor of spilled beer, and the gyrating dancers was an acute contrast to the sophisticated environment from which they'd just come. The familiarity made Shaw feel at home.

The four officers squeezed around a cocktail table that would have normally accommodated only two people. Clementi, as soon as they were seated, began to search the crowded room for unattached females.

"First round's on me," Shaw announced with a lop-sided grin. "What you fellas' havin'?" Taking their orders, he got up, weaving slightly, and waded through the sea of bodies to the bar, returning a minutes later with half-spilled drinks.

Clementi took a sip of the scotch he'd ordered and coughed, "This stuff tastes like bilge compared to what we drank in the room!" Returning the glass to the table, the co-pilot's attention was drawn suddenly to a pretty blonde in a WAAF uniform—the women's branch of the RAF—who had just stepped up to the bar. The tailored cut of her blue-gray tunic, he noticed admiringly, only seemed to accentuate the trim curves of her figure. Abruptly standing up, he declared, "Make way guys! Target at two o'clock level!" The WAAF, noticing him walk toward her, quickly averted her gaze. Stopping a couple of feet in front of her, Clementi bowed slightly and asked in his most polished New York banker tone, "Pardon me, miss, would you care to join my friends and I for a libation?" He pointed to the crowded table six feet in front of them.

The WAAF looked uncertainly at the dark-haired co-pilot with the engaging smile, then glanced over at the table he was pointing to. They look reasonably civilized, she thought. Her date, a P-47 pilot who was supposed to have taken her to dinner an hour ago, had apparently stood her up. She'd only intended to have one drink and leave, but heard herself say, "I'd be delighted, Lieutenant...lead the way."

Clementi guided her elbow toward their table, grabbing a chair from another table along the way. When they arrived, the others hastily stood up, grinning like out-sized boys. "I'm Luce Clementi," the co-pilot said to her.

Taking his hand then looking in turn at each of the others, the blonde WAAF said, in an educated accent, "I'm Anne Seton." After making the remaining introductions, Clementi squeezed her into a chair between himself and Shaw.

"May I get you a drink, miss?" Grattan offered after a moment of silence.

"Yes, please...a pink gin, and do please call me Anne." Her voice had a charming musical quality.

Clementi tried not to stare at her. While Anne Seton was not stunning in the show-girl sense of the word, she was unmistakably a classic English beauty: delicate features, regal neck, flawless complexion, and large, piercing blue-gray eyes. Everything about her appearance suggested a neat trimness, including the simple coif of her slightly less than shoulder-length, amber-blonde hair. Clementi was enthralled. This was a stylish woman, nothing like the mostly late-teenage girls the co-pilot had briefly encountered around Norwich and Colchester.

"You're an RA, uh...I mean, WAAF officer?" The co-pilot stammered, trying with difficulty not to be tongue-tied.

"Yes, a section officer," she answered with a pleasant smile, revealing even teeth.

"Would you like cigarette?" he asked.

"Yes, thanks very much." Clementi handed her a cigarette from his pack and lit it. Her eyes were large and luminous in the sudden flare of light.

"What kind of work do you do...as a WAAF, I mean?" he asked, looking at her with an intent gaze.

She exhaled the cigarette smoke away from him. "Radar intercept at the chain home station near Chelmsford."

"Really?" Clementi recalled the train stop on the way to London. "That's not too far from us, I think."

"Where are you based?"

"Boxsted, we're down here on a pass."

"Oh, yes...used to be an RAF station." Pointing to the wings pinned above Clementi's pocket, she commented, "You're a pilot...what do you fly?"

"B-26s...we're the officer crew." He pointed to Shaw. "Ted there is our aircraft commander, I'm the co-pilot, Glow's our bombardier and Mick...oh, there he is." Grattan was standing beside them with the girl's drink. "Mick's our navigator."

"Then you must be with the 333RD Bomb Group," she stated matter-of factly. Her knowledge of this surprised them all.

"That's right!" Grattan said with a grin. "How did you know that?"

"We see you at our station on radar all the time, your IFF, especially when you're returning from missions."

"Would you like to dance?" Clementi interrupted, indicating the crowded dance floor with his eyes.

Listening to the boogie-woogie staccato of the music, she smiled and suggested, "Let's wait for something a bit slower, if you don't mind."

"No problem."

A few minutes later, the small band began a rendition of Glenn Miller's *Moonlight Serenade*, and Clementi led the girl to the dance floor.

As they moved out of earshot, Grattan commented, "Pretty."

"Very," Glowgower chimed, then suggested, "why don't we haul ass to give Luce a little breathing space?"

Shaw blinked at him from the other side of the table. The pilot had been unusually quiet since returning with the first round of drinks and, in truth, wasn't feeling too great, the combination of food and champagne apparently beginning to have an effect. "Listen," he said hoarsely, eyes somewhat unfocused, "you guys can stay, but I wanna' go back to the hotel."

"I'll go with you," Grattan answered, then turned to the bombardier. "That o.k. with you, Glow?"

"Well...I've had it, too. Let's all go together."

Out of the corner of his eyes, Clementi noticed Grattan and Glow-gower leaving the room with the unsteady pilot tucked between them. Then turning his attention back to the girl in his arms, he marveled at the almost weightless sensation he was feeling.

When Clementi and Anne Seton returned to the table, she evinced mock surprise that the others were gone. "It seems your friends have abandoned you, Lieutenant."

"Uh, yes...please call me Luce." He looked at her awkwardly. "Can I get you another drink, another pink gin?"

"Yes, that would be nice." Her tone was cool.

When Clementi returned with the drinks several minutes later and sat down beside her, she regarded him with a serious gaze. "Luce, I hope you're not getting any ideas about me...I'm no Piccadilly commando."

He gave her a puzzled smile. "Piccadilly commando? I'm not sure what you mean by that, Anne."

She smiled back at him knowingly "I believe Americans call it a one-night stand."

"Oh." Clementi met her gaze. "That was never my intention."

Seeing the sincere expression in his dark eyes, she relaxed. In her experience, many men, looking for something more than friendly conversation, would be ready to ditch her at this point. This one, she decided, might be different. "Would you like to go someplace quieter for a drink?" she asked. "I know of a place not far from here."

Clementi's face creased into a grin. "That would be swell." Leaving the stuffiness of the Air Force Club, the two of them walked out into the cool air of the street, covered by a dome of stars.

"I hope you don't mind," Anne Seton said as they strolled together, arm-in-arm, "but the noise and activity of your club wears on me after a while. The RAF club's just as bad," she added.

"I get tired of it myself." While Clementi had grown accustomed to the boisterous atmosphere of Air Force clubs, he missed the sedate cocktail bars of mid-town Manhattan.

They arrived shortly at a small bar that was populated by a mixture of British uniforms, young women and older civilians. Several men in RAF tunics sat around an old, upright piano, softly crooning a melancholy tune. A red-faced waiter in a white apron took their order after they were seated in a booth off to one side of the bar.

"How do you like England so far?" she suddenly asked.

"To be honest, I really haven't seen much of it, from the ground, I mean, but I'm glad to be here rather than the Med or the Pacific."

"Why is that...because your name's Italian?"

"No. Before the group got its orders, I thought I'd like to go to Italy...what with speaking the language and all. Anyway, the Italian people are pretty much out of it, as far as I know. But since we were ordered to England, I've come to like it here."

"You said you're from New York...tell me about it."

The suggestion caused Clementi's face to light up. Speaking with undisguised fervor, he told her about the towering sky scrapers, Dodger Stadium—he gave Yankee Stadium and the Polo Grounds a brief mention—Madison Square Garden, the Shows, his job at the bank, his studies at C.C.N.Y., and his family in Brooklyn. When the conversation drifted closer to the present, he told her that he'd never seriously considered becoming a pilot or joining the military until just before the war broke out.

"Neither did my brother," she said.

"Your brother?"

"Yes, he was about to become a school teacher when the war started, then he joined the RAF and became a pilot."

"Where is he now?"

"Dead," she said quickly. "Didn't return from a raid on Hanover about six months ago."

"I'm sorry."

She put her hand on his and nodded.

"Do you have other family?"

She told him about her widowed mother in Surrey—her father had died from respiratory problems connected with being gassed in WW I—and a sister whose husband had been taken prisoner in the Western Desert over a year ago. Stopping the conversation suddenly, she said, "I'm sorry...this all sounds so sordid, doesn't it?"

"Not at all." Clementi had gained a meaningful insight on the personal impact of the war.

"Let's change the subject anyway," she said. "Tell me about your crew."

Starting with Shaw, then moving on to the others, Clementi described their backgrounds, hometowns, and what he knew of their family origins. He related some of their trials together in OTU, plus the trans-Atlantic flight over, but purposefully skipped over most of their combat experiences.

"What a marvelous collection of different people," she said after he finished.

"Yeah, but the amazing thing is how well we work together. You know, *click*." He intertwined his fingers as an illustration.

"Tell me," she asked. "what makes it work?"

"Mainly it's Ted, the aircraft commander...you met him."

"Really? He seemed awfully quiet and reserved...I don't remember him saying anything."

"Oh, he's pretty reserved all right, and tonight he was maybe even a little drunk." Clementi smiled at the thought of Shaw being drunk. "Besides, you'd have to see how he handles the plane to really know what I'm talking about."

At the same time in fact, Clementi's aircraft commander was stumbling into his hotel room supported on each side by Grattan and

Glowgower. "I think I'm gonna' be sick," Shaw groaned as they walked through the door. In swift motions, Grattan removed the green-faced pilot's uniform blouse and necktie and hustled him into the bathroom. Bending the pilot's suffering form over the commode stool, the big navigator said, "Let 'er rip, boyo." With an opening retch, Shaw powerfully vomited the expensive scotch, expensive champagne, roast lamb, and everything else he'd eaten or drank that day into the toilet bowl. After a diminishing series of dry heaves, the pilot sank to the tile floor and rested his forehead on the cool rim of the commode. The year 1943 had heralded a number firsts for Ted Shaw: crossing an ocean, visiting a foreign land, flying in combat, getting wounded in action, receiving a medal for valor, and getting falling-down drunk and puking his guts out.

When Clementi took Anne Seton back to her billet in London later the same night, she agreed without hesitation to go out with him for dinner the next night. To Clementi's pleasant surprise the following evening, Anne Seton had steered them to a small Neopolitan-style Italian cafe she was familiar with. After sharing a four-course dinner accompanied by a splendid Chianti and an apertif—Clementi had, to Anne Seton's amusement, unashamedly finished the food remaining on her plate—the couple had spent the balance of the evening talking at a quiet pub near the WAAF billet. By the time the evening was finished, both of them had learned a great deal about the other.

Standing with her later at the entrance to her billet, Luce Clementi was almost certain that he was in love. Never in his previous experience—having avoided serious relationships for the most part—had he been with a women to whom he felt so utterly emotionally and intellectually attracted. Simply being near her right now imparted a tingling sensation that was too much for words.

Anne Seton looked into the co-pilot's dark eyes, which displayed a mischievous quality when he talked. She had decided she enjoyed this man's company, more than anyone she had seen in a long, long time. In their conversations, she had intentionally not mentioned her previous fiancée, an RAF pilot killed during the Battle of Britain in the summer of 1940—an experience that had left her in an emotional abyss for over three years. The death of her brother the past May had had the effect of compounding the depressing reality of this seemingly never-ending war. But something about this American—a year younger than her, she had learned—caused her to feel alive again, vibrant. He was nice looking: sharp features dominated by large brown eyes and dark eyebrows; but more importantly, he was intelligent and considerate, even if in the brash way of the Americans.

They stood silently on the stone stoop in front of the billet, his arms encircling her waist, her face nuzzled into the hollow of his shoulder, both of them savoring the nearness. Clementi had kissed her several times, briefly and tenderly.

"I've had a marvelous time, Luce...can't remember when I've enjoyed myself so much," she finally whispered.

"Me, too," he said, meeting her steady gaze. "I really want to see you again, Anne."

"I'd very much like that, too."

In the cab the next morning on the way back to King's Cross station, Glowgower reviewed the contents of his billfold and counted sixty dollars remaining. He smiled to himself, thinking he would try to do better next time. Shaw, sitting next to him and noticing this, asked the bombardier, "You runnin' a little short, Glow?"

"Nah, I'm in good shape."

"Well, let me know if you need a few bucks because I bet you've spent over a hundred."

CHAPTER EIGHTEEN

November 29, 1943, Boxsted, England.

The target for the day was one of 333RD's old nemeses: the large German fighter base at Schipol. Fighters from this base had ravaged the 424TH Squadron on the low-level raid to Ijmuiden last May. Of course the circumstances would be vastly different this time. They would go in escorted at group strength and bomb the field from 12,000 feet. Piece of cake, they said. Even so, nemesis targets were part of the bomber business: for the heavies in the 8TH, it would always be Schweinfurt; for the heavies in the 15TH, it would always be Ploesti; and for RAF Bomber Command, it would forever be the night raid on Nuremburg. Spooky. Bowel-loosening.

The mission briefers told them that the attack would achieve two important objectives: it would impair the future effectiveness of the field as a defensive position against the planned Allied invasion of the continent, but the immediate impact would create a diversion for B-17s and B-24s en route to strategic targets in the Ruhr Valley the same day. The B-26 group would be escorted by P-47s and P-38s, although the '47s would have minimal loiter time around the target, even with drop tanks. The longer-range P-38s would probably bear the major burden of defending the B-26s as they came off the target and headed toward the North Sea. The twin-engined P-38, a very successful fighter adversary in other theaters, particularly in the southwest Pacific, had not been as effective against the more-maneuverable ME-109s and FW-190s in the high altitude air battles over Western Europe. But until the P-51s arrived, it was the longest-range escort available. The bombers still needed all the protection they could get because the Germans, if anything, seemed to become more aggressive as the air war moved deeper into their homeland. The B-26 crews had yet to see the new Kraut plane mentioned in recent intelligence reports—the Messerschmitt 410, a twin-engined, designed-for-purpose bomber-killer armed with four forward-firing 20 millimeter cannons—and unashamedly hoped they wouldn't see one today either.

The main threat, according to intelligence reports, would be the flak defenses surrounding the enemy base. RAF rocket-armed Typhoons and 9TH Air Force bomb-armed P-47s were scheduled to hit the field to suppress the defenses before the B-26s reached the target. The B-26s were not after the German planes, however: their chief target would be the large steel reinforced, concrete runways. If the enemy was deprived the use of its runways, the mission planners asserted, of what use are its planes? To accomplish this, the bombers would carry four 1,000 pound bombs with casings specifically designed to penetrate reinforced concrete. The fuses would be delayed slightly to allow the big bombs time to drive deeply into the runways before exploding. Another group of B-26s and a group of A-20s would be coming in behind the 333RD for a mop-up mission to bomb hangars, supply and maintenance buildings, and fuel stores.

The group was briefed to take-off from Boxsted starting at 0630, so they would be up-sun on their approach to the target. After forming up in the group box to the west of the base, they would fly an east-north-east heading to Gravenhage—also known as the Hague—on the Dutch coast and continue on this heading until they intersected the major rail lines just South of Voorschoten, where they would turn to a more northeasterly heading. Voorschoten would be the IP, giving them an 18-mile—five point four minute run—to the target. The bombers would fly straight up the railway lines to Schipol, which lay just Southwest of a major intersection. The airfield was big, couldn't miss it in a shit storm, they were told.

This would be *The A-Train's* thirty-seventh mission, probably the most dangerous since the one she'd flown to Rouen back in September. Because they possessed the highest mission total for a single airplane, it was no surprise that Shaw and his crew were regarded as the old hands of the group. They even looked older, some would say. Not that they had physically aged very much—though their mothers would have noticed the deeper lines that had been etched in their faces—but mainly because of their demeanor, a business-like approach to combat flying that was neither nervous nor blasé. A sailor would refer to it as keeping an even strain, which, in 1943 Air Force parlance, was known as staying "copasetic." Although their progress toward the fifty-mission goal was common knowledge in the group, Shaw's crew studiously avoided discussion of the subject both among themselves and others outside the crew. If an outsider, usually a new arrival, happened to bring it up in casual conversation, he was was politely asked—the first time—to change the subject.

Armistead in *Friend or Enema?* would be leading the group with *The A-Train* behind him in the deputy slot. In a bomber formation, being in the lead element had both advantages and disadvantages. It was an advantage on the run-in to the target, in the areas heavily defended by flak, because you had a good chance getting away before the gunners could fix their range, but it was a decided disadvantage during fighter attacks, either coming in or going out, because the fighters always tried to kill the leaders first. Talking to them just before take-off, Armistead emphasized the importance of quickly getting to the "rally point" after they turned off the target. They expected to be attacked by fighters, not only en route to the target, but also coming off, and the rally would enable them to reform and egress in a tight defensive box.

An hour later, *The A-Train* had crossed the English coast at Felixstowe and was climbing through a solid cloud deck at 9,000 feet. At 10,000 feet and still climbing, the formation of bombers broke through the uppermost layer into dazzling sunlight, punching through the peaks and pinnacles of the cottony cloud tops like flying dolphins. Miles ahead along their course, true to the prediction of the meteorology briefing, they could see the deck breaking up.

As they cruised over the top of the diminishing undercast, Clementi flew the plane while Shaw scrutinized the integrity of the formations on either side of the lead element. Their concentration was interrupted when the interphone crackled and Grattan's voice announced, "Time to test your guns!" No matter how many times air crewmen experienced it, the deafening sound of the 50-caliber guns and the reeking smell of the cordite never ceased to stimulate their adrenal glands. After this point, all of their senses—sight, sound, feel, and smell—were elevated to a heightened state, and would carry them until they were on their way back to England and safety.

In the tail of *The A-Train*, Leroy Rimbaud looked out over the sights of his twin gun mount and wondered whether he would score his fifth confirmed kill today. The title of "ace" was not an officially recognized distinction for enlisted air gunners—"Sumthin' them college-boy fighter hot shots keep fo' themselves," Rimbaud had been heard to grumble—but it was nevertheless an article of pride. The little Cajun's score thus far was four confirmed destroyed and five confirmed damaged, the latter category of which did not count as a "kill." Giving specific gunners credit was problematic because, during the confusion of an aerial melee, with hundreds of guns being fired all over the group, it was exceedingly difficult to determine who shot what in a given space of time.

In the waist of the airplane, a short distance forward of the tail gun mount, Elmo Tilden, who was generally more concerned with staying alive than counting kills, bawled loudly over the noise, "Hey Bayou Boy! You gonna' make ace today!"

"Shut yo' big injun mouf!" the tailgunner retorted, turning toward Tilden.

The dark-eyed engineer hooted back at him, "If you do ...you think they gonna' promote you to master sergeant or maybe warrant officer...huh?" Tilden guffawed at the scowling tail gunner. "I can see it now! Leroy Rimbaud ...highest rankin' peckerwood in the Air Force!"

Rimbaud slid off his seat, facing the young engineer, and hissed, "Ah tell you what, boy...if'n ah wanted any shit outa you, ah'd jus' unscrew the top of yo' head and dip it out!" These exchanges had become a regular part of the mission routine. After a moment of mutual smirking, Tilden and Rimbaud flipped one another obscene gestures and returned to their positions.

"You got the heat turned up all the way?" Shaw asked Clementi as he gave the zipper on his shearling jacket another tug. On this day, at 12,000 feet, the outside air temperature gauge was indicating 17 degrees Fahrenheit.

"Yep," the co-pilot relied flatly.

"I thought I asked Ripley to check it after the last mission we flew."

"You did."

"Well," the pilot scoffed, "the son-of-a-bitch ain't puttin' out like it's supposed to." The heater was in fact working perfectly, but the B-26, like most other bombers of the day, wasn't pressurized, and leaked air like a sieve.

The co-pilot, focused on the task of keeping *Friend or Enema?* in the right position relative to the upper part of the windscreen, responded with a monosyllabic grunt. Leaning slightly on the left armrest with his head tilted against the seatback, he'd just attained the most comfortable position in his seat vis-a-vis holding the yoke with his right hand and moving the throttles with his left. He hoped Shaw wouldn't ask any more questions about the damned heater.

Shaw keyed the interphone, "Pilot to tail, how's the low squadron look back there?"

"Wait one." Rimbaud squinted down and visually calculated the distance between the low squadron, the tail-end charlie, and the two middle squadron elements. Shaw had shown him how to do this in practice exercises. "Tail t'pilot, ah believe they's lower and furthah back than they spose t'be."

"Rog." Tuning the command channel, using Armistead's call-sign, Shaw snapped, "Haystack to green leader, move up and tuck it in!" Armistead expected Shaw to be an extra set of eyes and issue orders accordingly when the 424TH was leading the group.

"Roger, haystack...we're movin.'"

A minute later. "Tail t'pilot, they movin' in... lookin' better."

Above them, the fighters were pulling contrails in the freezing, humid air. The criss-crossing patterns of the brilliant white wakes were a beautiful sight to the watching bomber crews but at the same time a conspicuous signpost to any enemy fighters that might be approaching. Contrails or no, the Wurzburg radars on the Dutch coast had by now picked them up, plotted their probable track, and scrambled fighters from Schipol and Rotterdam. The two formations, still unseen to each other, were converging at a combined velocity of over 500 m.p.h., at which speed, it takes only six minutes to close an interval of 50 miles.

Two minutes later, the command channel came alive. "Haystack to all flights! Escort reports enemy fighters approaching at one o'clock, high...a mix of thirty plus single engine and twin engine fighters...escorts turning to engage!" The aircrews of the 424TH noted that Armistead's habitual Mississippi drawl all but disappeared.

"Turret to crew, got 'em! Looks like twenty-five 109s and 110s climbing around to our twelve o'clock high!" Vega tracked the approaching antagonists through the pipper on his gun sight. "Turret to crew, they're splitting up now!" The gunner's voice had raised to an excited pitch. "The 109s are coming straight-on...the 110s are turning past our twelve, coming around on our left!" The Germans obviously intended employ the tactic of attacking from two directions at once.

"Haystack to all flights, prepare for head-on attack! I repeat, prepare for head-on attack!" The P-47s, their drop tanks now tumbling away, were maneuvering to cut-off the 109s to their front while the larger P-38s were turning hard in an effort to intercept the 110s. The gunners and pilots tensely scanned the airspace ahead of them and on either side as the opposing formations rushed to meet each other. A known tactic of the 109s was to simply bore straight through the oncoming Thunderbolts—irrespective of losses—in pursuit of their real quarry, the bombers. When attackers and defenders met, to the bomber crews observing them, they appeared to merge, then disconnect, in a micro-second. Emerging from the melee, two of 109s spectacularly disintegrated in mid-air and several others staggered away trailing smoke, while most of the enemy formation had been diverted away from the path of the bombers. However, like stalwart hounds in pursuit of their prey, a few of the 109s had managed to forge on through the screen toward the B-26s, to be met seconds later, by the awesome fusillade of the massed bombers' four hundred eighty 50-caliber machine guns opening fire almost all at once. Inside the bombers, amid screeching calls on interphones, the guns created a deafening racket, raining spent shell casings and expelling the pungent odor of cordite. The incendiary rounds from the 109's cannons and machine guns erupted toward the B-26s like streams of incandescent balls, then, in a the blink of an eye, the attackers were diving through the bombers like barracuda through a school of tuna, causing the bomber formation to waver and expand. The fight was over almost as soon as it had happened.

A frenetic call crackled on the radio. "Red leader to haystack, we're hit...losing fuel! Request permission to return to base!"

"Roger, red leader...return to base...and good luck!"

"Haystack, this is red able one...I've got the lead!

Other calls were heard from the squadrons reporting damage, but none serious enough to require any more aircraft to turn back.

Then the 110s struck.

"ROCKETS!" Someone screamed over the radio.

"This is haystack, who said that!"

"Ah, this is red baker one...rockets incoming at nine o'clock, level!

Seconds later, the fence post-sized rockets whooshed through the formation like huge Fourth of July fireworks. Unguided, most of them swept harmlessly past, but one impacted the tail of a B-26 in the left element of the lead squadron, blowing off all of the rudder and most of the vertical fin. Maintaining its position for a few moments, the stricken bomber gradually yawed out of formation and began an uncontrolled roll onto its back. In the midst of this death spiral, several small shapes were seen to eject themselves from its waist doors.

"Haystack to all flights, report chutes!"

"Red baker two to haystack...I saw three!"

"This is green leader...I thought I counted four!

The pilot, co-pilot, and bombardier didn't make it out before the plane entered an inverted flat spin, trapping them inside with centrifugal force. Shaw, watching the mortally wounded B-26 disappear below him, was acutely reminded of the fact that, for crewmembers in the forward compartment, the B-26 was a difficult aircraft from which to escape. The pilot's manual, he remembered, suggested lowering the nose gear and exiting the aircraft through the nose hatch or, better yet, jettisoning the bombs and escaping through the bomb bay. Fat chance!

he reflected grimly, when your airplane is on fire or out of control or both. The pilot considered for a moment the plight of the crew members who did make it out: they would have to take their chances on the ground and hope like hell they met up with the Dutch Resistance before being discovered by the patrolling German Army. If captured, they would be turned over to the Luftwaffe—the German Air Force—and ultimately sent to Germany to wait out the rest of the war as a P.O.W. in a Stalag Luft Camp. Better than dying.

As the B-26 group crossed the Dutch coast at Gravenhage, they began to encounter multiple flak bursts from the radar-directed 88 millimeter guns. A moment later, Armistead's plane, *Friend or Enema?,* sustained a hit that sheered the propeller from the number one engine right off the shaft, causing it to spin away like a berserk pinwheel. As his airplane sharply veered from the formation, Armistead frantically called to Shaw. "Black able one...take the lead! Take the lead! Can't maintain formation!" While Armistead and his co-pilot wrestled the crippled B-26 away from the group, barely under control, a covering P-38 peeled-off and took a protective position behind them.

"Black able one to haystack, we've got the lead! Good luck Bobby!" Seeing Armistead leave the formation, Clementi had already advanced the throttles to move *The A-Train* into position. Shaw keyed the interphone, "Pilot to bombardier, you hear that? We're lead!"

"Rog, we're lead," came the calm reply.

"Nav to pilot and bombardier, IP coming up in one minute. Standby for a left turn to zero-four-two."

"Roger, nav...can you give me a drift reading?"

"Rog, estimate wind over the target to be one-seven-five at twenty."

"Got it."

"Haystack to all flights," Grattan called, as lead navigator, "turn to an IP heading of zero-four-two...MARK!"

At the same time Clementi smoothly banked *The A-Train* onto the new course, Glowgower announced, "Bombardier to pilot, bomb sight engaged!"

Shaw keyed the interphone. "PDI is centered...you have the airplane!"

"I have the airplane!" Glowgower repeated. "Bomb bay doors coming open! Intervalometer set!"

From this point, the autopilot coupled to the Norden bombsight would fly *The A-Train* to the target. The pilots needed only to keep the airplane "in rig" so the bombsight could do its work in an accurate fashion. The sight, a sophisticated but nerveless mechanical contrivance, unlike the human occupants of the plane, was not afraid of the flak and *never flinched.* Glowgower, in preparation for the run, had preset the sight to "automatic," so when it "saw" the correct position of the aircraft relative to the target, it would automatically release the bombs.

"Bombardier to pilot, target coming up! Clear and unobstructed!" As he watched the huge runways resolve themselves in the optics of the sight, Glowgower mused, just like they said—impossible to miss. Holding the microphone tuned to the command channel in his left hand, he waited for the red light to flash on the bombing panel, indicating the sight had released the bombs. The light winked on and he instantaneously screamed, "Bombs away!" Listening for the reassuring *clack-clack* made by the bombs as the shackles released, he continued to peer into the sight as the iron monsters made their swift journey toward the target.

As soon as the bombs were gone, Clementi, without any prompting from Shaw, fire-walled the throttles and wracked *The A-Train* into a brutal, diving turn to the right. Pulling almost three Gs through a nearly vertical bank, the crewmembers of the bomber felt their faces sag as the invisible hand of gravity pressed them down in their seats. While Clementi flew the airplane, Shaw watched the formation as they came off the target and handled the command radio. "Haystack to all flights!" Shaw bellowed into his microphone. "Turn to rally point...I repeat, turn to rally point!" The rally point was a large lake about five miles South of Schipol.

In the middle of the turn, a B-26 to the right and slightly behind *The A-Train* took a direct flak hit where the number two engine joined the wing, neatly separating the engine and cowling from the wing with the still spinning propeller lifting the whole thing away like some kind of bizarre helicopter. An instant later, the gas tank in the plane's right wing ignited, spewing a sheet of flame. Two small figures miraculously detached themselves from the conflagration only moments before the plane disappeared in a thunderous fireball.

"Two chutes...saw two chutes!" came an excited voice over the radio.

"This is haystack, identify yourself!"

"Ah...this is white charlie four, I saw two chutes before she blew up!"

"This is white leader...confirm two chutes!"

As Shaw struggled to watch the flaming mass disappear behind and below him, he snapped up his microphone. "Haystack to all flights, reform! I repeat, REFORM!" The formation had scattered over the target, and the pilots were paying more attention to evading the flak bursts than assuming proper position on their leaders. The fighters, Shaw fully knew, could return at any moment, and if formation discipline were not maintained, the group could be decimated. Gradually, the departing B-26s, their numbers reduced by flak and fighters, closed the gaps in the box and regained the integrity of their formation.

Shaw sighed then keyed the interphone. "Pilot to turret, you see anything out there?"

"Negative, but I'm lookin.'"

When they crossed the Dutch coast again, Grattan came on the interphone, "Nav to pilot, alter course to two-five-one...that ought to get us home."

"Rog." Shaw rested his eyes a moment then glanced over at Clementi. "I'll take it, Luce."

The co-pilot nodded tiredly, raising his hands from the controls. Stretching and flexing his arms back and forth, he tried to relieve the cramps caused by hours of continuous formation flying.

Looking out over their nose, Shaw examined the mass of cumulous clouds building up along their course over the North Sea. The cloud base, which he calculated to be below their present altitude, seemed to reach up into infinity. If they could reach it quickly, it would shield them from further fighter attacks—a fair trade-off against the prospect of having to fly on instruments. Shaw's thoughts on the matter were interrupted by a radio call from the P-38 fighter leader.

"Keystone to haystack," in the typically crisp, matter-of-fact tone of the fighter pilots, "we have identified multiple bogies at your nine o'clock, about level, distance about five miles...we'll try to cut 'em off."

"Roger, keystone...we're tryin' to make it to that cloud bank in front of us." Shaw watched the P-38s flying overhead peel-off and go "buster," trailing twin plumes of exhaust smoke as they accelerated under full military power.

The sharp-eyed Vega saw the bogies first. "Turret to crew, bogies incoming! I count twenty-five plus 109s at ten o'clock...looks like they're climin' to come in on our high side!" Rotating the turret slowly, the gunner tracked them through his gun sight. "They're turnin' toward us now... attacking! Comin' in on our left...say ten o'clock high!" Vega quickly calulated that if any of the attackers got through, the B-26s would be able to bring to bear only three guns apiece—the top turret and the flexible nose mount—and due the attack angle, many of the planes in right element of the box wouldn't be able to fire at all.

Vega watched pursuing P-38s dive toward the attackers, estimating that the big fighters would be required to open fire at about forty-five degrees of deflection. As the range closed, the Lightnings began firing short bursts at 1,000 yards in an effort to split the German formation. The 109s doggedly held their course despite the cannon and machine gun tracer rippling in their midst. As the distance contracted, however, the five-gun armament of the P-38s reached optimal range and began to tear into the 109s with telling effect, causing many of the attackers to roll over on their backs and dive to safety.

Vega watched a 109 break left to avoid a pursuing P-38, then abruptly snap into a right vertical bank that caused it to pull vapor streamers from its wingtips. "Turret to crew, a single 109 coming our way at nine o'clock, almost level!" Watching the enemy fighter resolve itself in the range bars of his sight, the gunner made a quick correction for lead, trying desperately not to flinch as the fighter's lethal cannon tracer arced toward him. Vega depressed the trigger on his handgrip and stared at the path of his tracers as they climbed toward the onrushing plane. Holding his breath and fighting to remain calm, he made minute corrections to the lead angle until he saw his tracers stitching across the fuselage and wing root of the 109. When the approach of the attacking fighter was so close that Vega could distinguish the individual rivets on its engine cowling, the 109 seemed to explode at the seams, the wings and fuselage sections crazily flipping away in different directions.

"ARIBA! Got that gringo son-of-a-bitch!" Vega exulted over the interphone.

"Ah saw'im!" cried Rimbaud. "Good shootin, Cisco!""Nice goin', amigo!" Shaw enthusiastically added. A minute later, *The A-Train* and the rest of the formation were enveloped by the protective womb of the cloud, and Shaw called, "Haystack to all flights, turn on navigation lights ...I repeat, turn on navigation lights!" In cloud, the bombers would only be able to see the planes nearest them, then just barely. The pilot keyed the interphone, "Cisco, come down and try raise the base on radio."

"Rog...on my way."

Behind, the pilots, Grattan ticked off the distance on his chart. "Nav to pilot, estimate English coast in twenty-eight minutes."

"Roger, nav...go ahead and inform the other flights."

"Bombardier to pilot, comin' up." Clementi got out of his seat to give Glowgower room to enter the flight deck. Shaw, glancing at the bombardier momentarily, motioned him to sit down in the right seat while Clementi moved back and squatted between them. "How'd it look?" the pilot asked.

"I'm sure we clobbered the target." Glowgower slumped back in the seat and yawned hugely, the two-hour adrenaline surge beginning to wear off. "I positioned our plane so our bombs would hit the far end of the runway and the rest of the group's bombs would walk down it from one end to the other."

Vega interrupted. "Radio to pilot, I've got the base on button two, but there's so much static, you can't understand 'em."

"O.k., try again in ten minutes."

"Rog."

The group continued to fly on instruments into the deepening cloud mass. Pellets of sleet and gusts of turbulence began to lash at the planes. Frowning at the darkening scene appearing through the windscreen, Shaw turned to his co-pilot. "Luce, take-over till I figure something out...let me know if we start pickin' up any ice." Formation-keeping was becoming increasingly hazardous with the combination of diminishing visibility and unstable air. After a minute, Shaw called on the command channel, "Haystack to all flight leaders, descend to five thousand feet and stand by, I repeat standby, to break off and proceed to base independently, ACKNOWLEDGE!" After the other three squadron leaders responded, Shaw advised them to await a navigational fix. "Pilot to nav," he told Grattan, "give the other flights our latest position as soon as you've got it plotted." When Grattan had completed the position report, Shaw called, "Haystack to all flights, break off...EXECUTE!" As he watched through his side window, the departing B-26s faded into the murk. He considered their next problem. "Pilot to engineer...Elmo, calculate out our fuel state and find how much time we've got left at present speed."

"Rog...will do."

"Cisco, try to raise the base again."

"Rog." Minutes later, Vega reported back, "I've got the base, weak but readable."

"Thanks...put 'em through up here."

"Go ahead...you're patched in."

"Haystack to home plate, over."

"This is home plate...go ahead," came the garbled reply, punctuated by the crash of static.

"Haystack is inbound with a flight of fifty-two B-26s...request advisory on local weather, over."

"Wilco, haystack, stand by..." Another voice came on the radio. "Haystack, this is home plate...be advised that a line of thunderstorms is approaching the base on a heading two-niner-five moving at twenty-five miles an hour...expect ceilings of less than five hundred feet with visibility of less than one-half mile in blowing snow. Current altimeter is twenty-eight point five with surface winds out of two-seven-five at thirty miles an hour, gusting to thirty-five. Recommend you divert south, I repeat, divert south."

"Shit!" Shaw exclaimed. It was a bad situation getting worse. Pausing a few seconds, he answered, "Received and understood, haystack, out." He sighed and thumbed the interphone switch. "You heard 'em, nav...what're our best alternates?"

Grattan stuck his head between the pilots a minute later. "I recommend Uxbridge...that'll get us far enough South out of the bad stuff, and we'll go right over the north edge of London to find it." Which meant, to Shaw's relief, that nobody ought to get lost.

Shaw nodded to the big navigator then ordered Vega to put the radio back on command channel. "Haystack to all flights, be advised that base is below landing minimums, I repeat, base is below minimums! Prepare to divert south to Uxbridge...that's Uncle-X-Ray-Baker-Roger-Item-Dog–George-Easy...stand by for further instructions...ACKNOWLEDGE!" The unseen aircraft called back one by one. He turned to Grattan. "Lay a track to the alternate and call 'em up and give 'em the new course."

Grattan's voice came on the radio a minute later. "Haystack to all flights...turn left to two-two-zero...MARK!" Another minute later, "Haystack to all flights, estimate one hundred forty-two miles to alternate. Landmarks enroute are..."

Shaw finally slouched in his seat, lighting a Lucky Strike. He yawned expressively, rubbed his eyes and flashed a grin toward Clementi. "You think we earned our flight pay today?"

"We ain't out of the woods yet." The co-pilot grimaced then squinted at the wing in the gloom to see if he could detect any of the telltale signs of ice building up.

Tilden poked his head into the cockpit doorway, holding a piece of paper in his hand. He looked quizzically at the solid gray mass outside the windows and quipped, "Like pea soup, huh?"

"Yep," the pilot answered, then asked, "What's the story on our fuel, Elmo?"

"We're not fat, skipper...down to two hundred ninety gallons close as I can figure, and at this power setting, that'll give us 'bout one hour, ten...give or take a few minutes."

"Thanks, Elmo." Shaw eased the power back to 30 inches of manifold pressure, moved the prop controls to 2,100 RPM, and made a quick calculation on his E-6. "That ought to give us another fifteen minutes at least," he announced to Clementi and Tilden. "Mick," he used the interphone, "what's our ETA to Uxbridge at the new airspeed?"

"Wait one." Grattan noted the reading on his airspeed indicator, computed a new groundspeed, and measured the distance on the chart.

"I estimate forty-four minutes if my plot's any where near correct. You know, I haven't had a visual fix since we crossed the Dutch coast and can't determine drift in these clouds, so I could be off twenty miles either way."

"Haystack to all flights, go to max conserve on power ...I repeat, go to max conserve...ACKNOWLEDGE!"

A series of replies, some garbled, came back over the command radio. Shaw hoped they all got the message. "Mick, what's radar station is closest to us?"

"Looks like Chelmsford."

"O.k., look up the their call sign and frequency, get 'em on the radio, and ask if they see any of us."

"I've got 'em," the navigator replied a minute later. "You want me to switch you to this channel so you can listen?"

"Rog, do it."

"Jupiter this is haystack, how do you read, over?"

"Haystack this is Jupiter, I read you five-by-five," a modulated female voice answered.

The A-Train wobbled as Clementi sat up straight in his seat while holding onto the yoke. He was sure he had just heard the unmistakable voice of Anne Seton in his earphones. Turning suddenly to Shaw, he cried, "Why, that's her... Anne!"

"Jupiter, we are a dispersed flight of B-26s, approximately thirty miles East, at angels five, en route to uh...," he looked at the symbol for Uxbridge, "King two-one-one. Do you see us on IFF, over?"

"Roger, haystack, we count fifty plus aircraft on your identifier."

"Thank you, Jupiter, can you give us a radar vector to King two-one-one?"

"Roger, haystack, stand by...turn right to two-three-one. You are three-three miles from station and eight-one miles from King two-one-one."

"Roger, Jupiter, thank you again."

"Glad to be of service, haystack."

Shaw keyed the interphone. "Hey, Mick, before you sign off, tell 'er 'Luce says 'hello.'"

"Jupiter, this is haystack, Luce Clementi says to send his fond regards," the navigator said in a humorous tone.

"Oh, Luce...hello!" the female voice cried in contravention of prescribed radio procedure, then excitedly added, "Hope to see you soon!"

Shaw punched the blushing co-pilot on the shoulder and chuckled, "You've got friends in high places, ol' buddy!"

"Yep," Clementi sighed then turned his attention back to the airplane. When they crossed the English coast ten minutes later, shafts of light began to appear in the cloud mass, and by the time they had intersected the Thames River on the outskirts on London, the overcast was broken to scattered, revealing patches of earth below them.

"Guess you won't get to make an instrument let-down into Uxbridge today," Shaw commented indifferently.

The co-pilot snorted, sarcastically, "You know I hate it when that happens!"

"You want me to land?" the pilot asked with a grin.

"You still know how?" the co-pilot sneered.

"Maybe you can sorta' talk me through it, huh?" They guffawed at each other. Shaw took the controls and thought about how far they had come, all of them. Unbelievable, almost.

CHAPTER NINETEEN

January 23, 1944, Great Dunmow, England.

The bomb group had been moved again as part of the burgeoning expansion of the 9TH Tactical Air Force. The new station was only thirty-five miles west of Boxsted, but was more isolated from the main rail and highway thoroughfares, in the boondocks, in other words. As a result of the sparse female population in their new locality and a decided absence of social amenities in the nearby villages, the troops grumbled and sputtered about the move until they were reminded that, next time, they would probably be living in tents, like real soldiers! Clementi, however, was thrilled to death, for Great Dunmow was only 20 miles from Anne Seton's WAAF billet near Chelmsford. With help from Shaw and Ripley, the co-pilot had mastered the art of operating a jeep in England. In fact, he'd become one of the most frequent visitors to the base motor pool and was unaffected by the motor pool sergeant's constant reminder that "Them jeeps ain't personal transportation for lieutenants." Since he'd learned how to drive on the left, the others were mirthfully concerned that he would be a potential hazard to himself and the rest of the motoring public when he returned to the United States.

Through the month of December and into the New Year, when weather permitted, the 333RD Bomb Group (M) continued to fly missions against a variety of tactical and military targets in Northern France and Belgium, with particular emphasis on targets in the areas around Cherbourg, Caen, and Le Havre. The aircrews couldn't understand how a train or truck could still move in this area, but they did. In fact, the Germans and their conscripted work crews seemed to be able to repair facilities as fast as the bombers could tear them up. Don't worry about the enemy, the Air Force target planners had said: it's a race, and *we're winning.*

The group's combat loss ratio had leveled out at about one per cent. If a "sortie" equaled one aircraft flying one mission, then the ratio computed to a loss of one aircraft for every hundred sorties flown. But the losses never occurred with mathematical evenness: they might fly five or six missions without a scratch, then lose four or five planes on a bad one.

The A-Train had completed her forty-ninth combat mission the previous day, an attack on an important rail bridge on the Touques River north of Lisieux, halfway between Caen and Le Havre. They had turned the recently rebuilt bridge and much of the track on either side of it into a lot of disassembled metal and wood rubbish. The German supply route into Caen and Cherbourg would be disrupted for a couple of days at least, maybe three.

For Shaw, Clementi, Grattan, and Rimbaud, one more trip would complete their tour; but, Vega needed three more, Glowgower needed five, and Tilden, seven. The disparity bothered Shaw, but there wasn't anything he could do about it, even if he was one of the old salts around the group.

The next morning, in the group operations office, Colonel Spinelli looked over at the Robert Armistead slouching in one of his chairs. "Hell, Bobby," he said in a resigned voice, "I'd give 'em a milk run for this last trip if it was up to me. I know they'll be the first in the group to finish, but you know this isn't some big deal like the *Memphis Belle* with the brass all swarming around with movie big-shots like Frank Capra taking pictures of of the whole thing."

"Dammit, Vince!" Armistead sat up and angrily retorted. "They're entitled to special treatment...they're the only survivors of that suicide run on Ijmuiden."

"It wasn't a suicide run, Bobby," Spinelli said harshly. "And besides, it's got nothing to do with our mission assignments. You got that?"

"Ah know, Vince...ah know." Armistead's voice became quiet. "Shit, it's just not fair."

Spinelli was used to the mercurial outbursts of his operations officer. "I haven't seen the mission order," he said calmly, "but the next one might be an easy one. Let's wait and see...o.k.?" He pointed toward the frost-encrusted window and said with finality, "This piss-poor weather's gonna' keep us grounded for a while anyway."

Across the base in their hut, Shaw was sitting at the desk reading a letter while Grattan was lying on his bunk reading one of the pocket-sized books provided free of charge to servicemen. Clementi and Glowgower were sitting on the latter's bunk playing gin rummy with a well-worn deck of playing cards. Shaw suddenly sat up and barked with laughter, causing the others to look his way.

"What's so funny?" Clementi asked.

The pilot held up the letter he was reading. "It's a letter from Mary Beth about her brother, Julius. She says he was home on leave from the Marine Corps a few weeks ago. Just came back from that invasion at Tar..." He looked at the letter. "Tar-ruh..."

"You mean Tarawa?" Grattan suggested, pronouncing it with an accent on the middle syllable.

"Yeah, that one. Anyway, while he was on leave, he tore up about every beer joint and honkytonk around Big Spring and spent most of his leave in jail."

"Is something the matter with him?" Clementi asked.

"Not really." Shaw gave the co-pilot an amused look. "You'd just have to know Julius. Not much up here," he pointed to his head, "but a real bad-ass, if you know what I mean. The day after Pearl Harbor, Julius went on a rampage and said he was gonna' join the Marines so 'I can kill those slant-eyed son-of-a-bitches with my bare hands.' He really said that." Shaw's expression became grim. "And that battle, you know, Tar-whatever, he got a citation for overrunning a Jap machine gun position...they said he killed fifteen or sixteen of 'em by himself!"

The others gazed at him in amazed silence.

"I'd rather take my chances in the Air Force...any day," Glowgower finally said in a thoughtful tone.

"I don't mind killing the enemy," Clementi added sarcastically, "but I don't want to be close enough to smell his breath!"

In a theater of war, servicemen seldom had the opportunity to compare the casualty statistics among various types of combat operations. In the case of England-based bomber crewmen like Glowgower and Clementi, they had heard news reports about thousands of soldiers being killed in places like Guadalcanal or Anzio beach, or read about ships in a particular convoy being sunk with a loss of all hands, or learned through the grapevine about a nearby bomb group that was experiencing above-average losses, a "hard luck outfit" they would say, but that was as far as their information usually went. It probably would have surprised them to find out that on a day-to-day basis American bomber crews actually suffered a comparably higher casualty rate than infantry soldiers or sailors. The bomber crews didn't think of it in such terms, but it was a fact: *they invaded enemy territory every time they flew a mission.*

Three days later the weather cleared and 9TH Air Force headquarters ordered the group to fly a mission against the rail bridges at Namur in the southern region of Belgium only 65 miles from the German border. The 333RD would be one of three B-26 groups that would bomb three different bridges on the junction between the Sambres and Lesse Rivers. These bridges, the planners said, connected the major railways running between Belgium and the German industrial cities of Cologne, Dusseldorf, and Duisberg. The mission would be the first American strike against these bridges and would be one of the deepest raids yet flown by any of the B-26 groups. Reading the order, Spinelli solemnly concluded that it was no milk run, *not even close.*

When the briefing began at 0400 and the curtain was removed from the wall map to reveal the target deep into Belgium, the briefing room was filled with a chorus of jeers and boos. "Son-of-a-bitch!" Clementi blurted loudly enough for others around him to hear. "I knew this was gonna' happen. "I knew it! *I just knew it!*"

"Put a lid on it, Luce!" Shaw hissed. "What'd you expect 'em to do...send us on an air show over Piccadilly?"

"You'd think the brass-hatted bastards would give us an easy one!" the co-pilot whispered harshly.

Shaw turned to his co-pilot, an enigmatic smile on his face. "Well...you know what they say..."

Clementi looked at him contemptuously, smirked, then they both chanted in unison, "If you can't take a joke, you shouldn't have volunteered!" Shaw punched the obstreperous co-pilot on the shoulder and whispered, seriously, "Listen up ol' buddy...you might learn something useful."

Armistead, who conducted the operations briefing, used a pointer to trace the route to the target: they would cross the English coast at Southend on Sea and fly an east-southeast heading to De Panne, a coastal town near the French-Belgian border, then proceed inland 102 miles to their first turning point, a small lake to the north of a place called Certfontaine. This comment generated a string of *sotto voce* expletives and guttural grunts from the audience, causing Armistead to slap the pointer on the table and yell, "Button it up!" Returning the pointer to the map, he continued: from Certofontaine, they would fly east another 26 miles to Dinant, the IP. The northerly IP course would take them 18 miles straight up the Lesse River to the target, a bomb run of four and one-half minutes. When you took into consideration the time for take-off and form-up, he explained, the expected duration of the mission was a little over three hours. This was going to be a full group effort: ninety-two planes would be participating with another six in stand-by to cover any aborts.

The intelligence officer, the same one who had been a corporate lawyer before the war, now a captain, informed them in a very dry, laconic manner that flak defenses on this trip were expected to be light to nonexistent, which produced a murmur of approval from the seated aircrews. Their route, he said, would take them well south of the populated areas of Gent, Brussels, and Charleroi, and they shouldn't expect any 88 millimeter stuff until they were right over the target. Their bridge, located three miles south of Namur on the Lesse River, was a turn of the century three-span, iron truss structure containing two tracks. Since the middle span had to be raised and lowered for river barge traffic, its destruction would have the added benefit of disrupting supplies being moved on the waterway, too. They could expect enemy fighter opposition after they crossed the Belgian coast, he explained, with the principal German fighter fields along their route being located at St. Omer and Ostend. The P-47s would be with them as far as Mons, about 50 miles inside Belgium, but the P-38s would escort them all the way.

One of the pilots, a flight leader in the 420TH Squadron, raised his hand and asked, "We gonna' see any of the new German stuff, like the ME-410s or the rocket planes?"

"Rocket planes!" the intelligence officer cried in surprise. The data on the German jets and rocket planes was classified "Top Secret" and known by very few people outside of intelligence circles. "*Where* did you hear about that?" he demanded.

"At the O-Club," the pilot replied poker-faced.

"*Who* told you?" the briefer insisted.

"Why *you* did, Captain," the pilot answered with a stoney expression, then added, "I think you were shit-faced at the time." The room convulsed in a fit of laughter.

When the clamor died down, the intelligence officer, used to being lampooned by the aircrews, said, seriously, "Back to the question about the 410s: there aren't any at St. Omer or Ostend that we know about. I think you'll see the usual mix of 109Gs, 190s, and rocket armed 110s." *As if that weren't bad enough.* Continuing the explanation, he said, "The German apparently haven't got many operational 410s yet and are holding them back to defend big targets inside Germany." Because it was sheer speculation, he did not mention the remote possibility that enemy fighters could be scrambled to intercept them from bases inside Germany. But it was a fact that the fighter bases at Koblenz and Cologne were only a hundred miles, as the crow flies, from their target, a distance that could be covered in a mere 20 minutes at 300 m.p.h.

The lead bombardier, the unflappable Burnside, bounced onto the platform for his part of the briefing. With forty-eight trips under his belt, he was next to Shaw's group in mission seniority. "'Mornin', gents!" he boomed, waving his arms like a cheerleader, then cried, "who are we...WHO-ARE-WE!"

"THE BEST AND BRAVEST BRIDGE BASHING B-TWENTY-SIX BOMBER BASTARDS IN BRITAIN!" the audience roared in a crashing chorus.

"You bet your ass you are!" the animated bombardier yelled. Composing himself, he went on to explain that half of the planes would carry a load of three 1,000 pound armor-piercing bombs, which they hoped would reduce the pilings and parapets, and the others would carry six 500 pound high-explosive bombs, which should take care of the metal structures and the track beds. Given the number of conspicuous landmarks leading from the IP to the aiming point, he drolly informed them that even a dumb-ass like him should be able to find the target today. In truth, Burnside was one of the best in the business, and they all knew it. They would bomb visually off the lead plane at 9,000 feet, he said, with intervalometers set at 200 milliseconds. When the stocky bombardier finished, he raised his arms and, in a mock British accent, cried, "Well then, chaps, let's go out there and..."

"Press on! PRESS ON, REGARDLESS!" the seated aircrews chorused loudly in a parody of the RAF Bomber Command motto. Burnside wasn't aware of it, but he was a *bona fide* expert at stress release.

Weather would be a question, the meteorology officer said. If a cold low pressure system moving west across central Germany reached the target before they did, the target might get socked-in by a solid overcast all the way down to 2,000 feet. In such event, they would get an abort signal for Namur and try to bomb the secondary, the marshalling yards southwest of Brugge. Either way, he said, the weather at the base on their return was forecast to be clear.

When the navigator's/bombardier's briefing concluded, Glowgower winked at Grattan and said, wistfully, "I guess this is the last time we'll do this together, Mick."

The burly navigator smiled wearily and sighed, "Yep...kind of hard to believe." Looking at the bombardier thoughtfully, he said, "You know I'm really going to miss you guys, but I don't mind telling you

I'm relieved to get this behind me...really tired of it."

Glowgower gave him an earnest smile. "I understand how you feel. If I had a wife and a kid I'd probably feel the same way." He paused and tipped his cap to the back of his head, revealing his dark, lustrous hair. "But, Mick, I'd be lying if I told you I wasn't going to miss it." His expressive eyes took on a meditative quality. "For me, flying combat over here has been...well, it's really hard to explain."

"I understand, boyo," Grattan said, placing his hand on the bombardier's shoulder. *You've discovered who you really are*, the navigator thought to himself, *and you like what you've found*. Giving Glowgower's shoulder a squeeze, Grattan smiled, "I heard some rumor that when Burnside finishes, you're going to take over as lead bombarider for the group."

"It might happen," the bombardier replied with unconcealed pride. It wasn't official yet—Burnside had told him informally—but when it happened, it would entail an immediate promotion to captain. "Who would have believed it?" Glowgower beamed.

"I would...I'm proud of you, Glow." He was.

Two hours later, the Belgian coast hove into view as a brown smear on their windscreens. Spinelli was leading the group under the call sign "pitchfork," and the 424TH was flying the tail-end charlie position 200 feet below the lead element. Since flak was not a major threat today, the low slot was probably the safest place in the group. Shaw wondered if they'd been put there on purpose. Clementi was keeping *The A-Train* in formation behind Armistead's *Friend or Enema?* in the deputy slot. The co-pilot was so accustomed to flying this position that he had memorized virtually every dent and blemish on the bottom of Armistead's battle-worn plane.

Now that the guns had been tested and the bombs were armed, the bomber crews tautly marked time until someone announced the approach of enemy fighters. They had been informed in the briefing that the heavy bombers were also flying a mission today, one which would take them across the middle of Holland, 100 miles to the north of the B-26 groups, but no one thought for a minute that it would draw the fighters away from them. No, the Krauts were imminently clever bastards: they would attack them first, then land to refuel and rearm, and take-off after the slower B-17s and B-24s who had further to go.

At the very moment they crossed the Belgian coast over the small town of De Panne, the command radio cracked to life, "Pitchfork to all flights, escort leader reports a large formation of bogies approaching our three o'clock position." The top screen of P-47s were over 10,000 feet above them and could see much farther over the horizon; the vision of some of the fighter pilots was legendary.

"Pitchfork to all flights, escort reports bogies as a mixed flight of forty-plus 109s and 190s at about fifteen thousand feet on our ten o'clock...they're on a parallel course, pulling ahead. Escorts are now turning to intercept."

"Pilot to turret, see anything, amigo?" Shaw asked.

"Negative," Vega answered, "still too far away."

They didn't expect a head-on attack today. The Germans had wised-up and favored attacking B-26s low on the front quarter where most of the guns couldn't bear. But the bombers had a trick up their sleeve, too: if time permitted, the group would turn *en mass* into the attackers in order to present more of their frontal aspect, a maneuver they had practiced successfully in mock battles with P-47s.

Vega was back on the interphone a half a minute later. "Turret to crew, I see the bogies! Forty or more! They're high, say six thousand feet above us and are still on our ten." He mentally calculated the angle of intercept, then added, "The '47s will get to 'em first."

Veteran crews like those of *The A-Train* had seen this aerial drama unfold many times, but it never ceased to frighten and fascinate them. The fight, when it came, would take place high above their heads; the men in the bombers would be forced to crane their necks and strain their eyes to see it. The P-47s had retained their height advantage, and in air-to-air combat, height could be rapidly exchanged into maneuvering advantage and speed. From experience learned in combat, the Thunderbolt groups were constantly revising and refining their tactics to deal more effectively with their German adversaries. At the same time it was a game of numbers, too, for every day the Americans were putting more fighters in the air to protect the bombers. In the battle developing today, the attackers were outnumbered two to one. The combination of speed, maneuverability, firepower, tactics, and numbers was what the experts referred to as "air superiority," the ability to dominate and control the airspace over the battleground at a given time. As the range rapidly closed, the leaders of the two-plane P-47 elements armed their guns and identified their targets.

"They broke!" Vega shouted. "The bogies have scattered all over the place!" The 109s and 190s had veered away in different directions in an effort to end-run the P-47s and hit the bomber formation from a different angle, but the Thunderbolts, expecting the move and diving at a speed in excess of 400 m.p.h., were able to turn and overtake the fleeing Germans. The sky above and to the right of the bomber formation was filled with twisting and turning fighters, some of them on fire and spiraling toward the checkered pattern of the Belgian fields below them. Floating down and away from the bombers, several of the brown-colored German parachutes canopies could be seen. For the present time, the P-47s and P-38s owned the piece of sky through which the B-26s were traveling.

As they moved deeper into enemy territory, the call of "Bogies!" became persistent and nearly continuous, but their aggressive escorts were able to fend the attackers off at every turn.

"Nav to pilot, we'll cross Mons in about a minute." Their heading would take them several miles south to avoid the known concentrations of flak, but of much deeper concern to them was the fact that they had reached the place where the P-47s were at the limits of their range.

Vega involuntarily shuddered as he watched the receding Thunderbolts wheel around to the west, away from the formation. The P-38s still holding position above them gave him some assurance, but he knew the picnic was over.

"We'll be making our first turn in about seven minutes," Grattan said, squatting between the two pilots. "From there, it'll take us another eight and a half minutes to reach the IP."

"Thanks, Mick," Shaw said. He motioned at Clementi. "Luce, I'll take it when we reach the IP, but I'll switch the guns over to your side...I'll fly, you shoot, o.k.?"

"O.k.," the co-pilot grunted without shifting his attention.

"Pilot to bombardier, you got everything ready?"

"Rog," came the unhurried reply. In the nose of *The A-Train*, Glowgower was experiencing the mild euphoria that was fueled by the combination of fright and adrenaline. He was used to it...didn't even think about it any more.

"Pitchfork to all flights, escort reports thirty plus bogies comin' our way at nine o'clock high!"

"Pilot to crew, you heard that...keep your eyes peeled!"

The approaching enemy were still outnumbered but had a better chance of getting to the bombers through the less-maneuverable P-38s. "I see 'em!" cried Vega. "I count twenty-plus 109s and ten 110s above us, comin' around on our ten o'clock position."

"Pitchfork to all flights, stand by for a left turn on my command...NOW!" The formation banked into the turn for about 15 seconds followed by the abrupt command, "ROll-OUT!" But at nearly the same instant the turn was completed, the twin-engined ME-110s on their left loosed their rockets into the formation at range of 2,000 yards. One of the lethal missiles scored a direct hit just behind the cockpit section of a B-26 in the left element, blowing the airplane neatly in half, the wings wildly fluttering off in different directions. No chutes. In front of them, almost directly now, the deadly cannon fire began to wink at them from the noses the ME-109s that had penetrated the screen of P-38s. The Lightnings were swinging around hard at maximum power to make chase but would not be in a position to intercept before most of the attackers made contact with the bombers. When the range was down to 1,000 yards, the frontally firing guns of the bombers opened-up almost as a unit, adding their tracer fire to the swiftly closing gap.

"Left side, left side!" screamed Shaw, alerting Tilden to be ready in the waist position.

The 109s zoomed through the tightly packed B-26s like minnows through a shoal of larger fish, departing in a wake of tracer fire from the waist and tail gunners aboard the bombers.

The command radio boomed to life with reports of planes that had been hit. One B-26 in the lead element, feathered its number two engine and dropped away from the formation, turning back toward the west. To his right, Shaw noticed another damaged bomber sink away trailing a massive sheet of flame from its left wing. As he watched the mortally-wounded airplane founder toward the patchwork of ground below, its bomb bay doors flew open and the bombs it was carrying tumbled out, followed almost immediately by three small figures tumbling end over end. Three more popped out of the waist doors. Seconds later, the plane came apart in a billowing explosion. Six chutes were reported—the pilot didn't make it out.

With two planes destroyed so far and one of them too heavily damaged to remain with the formation, the mission was already taking an ominous turn—and they hadn't even reached the IP.

The command radio crackled to life. "Pitchfork to all flights, stand by for a forty degree right turn on my command...NOW!

Grattan, studying the group's progress on the chart laying in from of him, called, "Nav to pilot, with the two turns we've made, we're a little east of where we should be." He looked again at his notations. "We'll have only a minute or so between the next turn and the turn onto the IP."

The radio iterrupted them. "Pitchfork to all flights, turn left to a new heading of zero-eight-two...NOW!

One minute later. "Pitchfork to all flights, standby for the turn to IP course..." then five seconds later "NOW!"

"Bomb bay doors coming open!" Glowgower shouted over the

interphone. "Intervalometer set!" he quickly added.

"P.D.I. is centered!" called Shaw.

Glowgower could see isolated puffs of flaks around the target ahead of him. Not as bad as some of the targets they had bombed, he fleetingly thought. Through the optics of the bomb sight, he watched the silver ribbon of the Lesse River wind below him, then glanced out the clear nose dome and keyed his mike. "Can see the target coming up...looks like we'll get a good drop." Holding the pickle switch in his right hand, he fixed his gaze on the open bomb bays of the planes above him in the lead element. The seconds slowly ticked off until he heard Burnside scream "Bombs away!" in his headset, causing him to thumb the switch in his hand almost out of reflex. When the panel indicated that all bombs were gone, he pulled the lever to his left all the way aft and cried, "Bomb bay doors closed!" *The A-Train* bobbled due to sudden loss of 3,000 pounds, and the bombardier felt himself wrenched into a sagging turn to the left. The target was embroiled in so much dust and smoke that he couldn't see where their bombs had landed.

"Pitchfork to all flights, form up! I repeat, form up!"

Because of the relatively light flak encountered around the target, the group had not become widely scattered, and the integrity of the box was quickly regained. The escorting P-38s were still watching over them from their perch 10,000 feet above. Unseen by the departing B-26 group, the invisible beams of the Luftwaffe radar stations between Ostend and Cologne were tracking the probable route of their departure and had scrambled fighters from Troisdorf, just south of Cologne inside Germany. The attackers were due to arrive any minute.

Minutes later, the command channel came alive. "Pitchfork to all flights, escort leader reports large formation of bogies coming our way, six o'clock high!" As the big P-38s turned onto a one hundred and eighty degree intercept course, the approaching enemy fighters separated into two elements flying parallel to either side of the bomber formation. Near the tail-end of the box, Vega, shading his eyes against the glare of the plexiglas, was one of the first gunners to spot the two distinct wedges of dots coming their way.

"Turret to crew, I see 'em! Can't identify the types yet, but I see two groups of 'em comin' up...one of 'em on our eight o'clock...another on our four o'clock. They're comin' in high." Squinting, he tried identify the types of aircraft. "Looks like twenty 190s on each side followed by some twin-engined jobs...can't make 'em out yet."

The converging P-38s were on a good intercept heading to cut the attackers off, but once they met the formation, they would forced to reverse course and a play a game of catch-up. The P-38s were marginally faster than the 190s, but would burn up a lot of time and airspeed during the turn-around. When the Germans were nearly abreast of the bombers, the Lightnings curved into them and opened-up at 1,200 yards, the effective range of their 20 millimeters cannons. Most the 109s broke to avoid the massed fire, while the twin-engined attackers attempted to outdistance the P-38s by diving straight ahead out of range.

Vega intently studied the blunt-nosed, ugly outlines of the steeply descending twin-engined Germans, remembering the identification silhouettes he'd been shown. He grimaced and keyed the interphone, "Turret to crew, I think those twin-engined bogies on our ten o'clock, low are ME-410s!"

Shit! Shaw thought in fear and disgust, it'll be like dueling with flying tanks! He snatched up his microphone. "Green able one to Pitchfork, those bogies at ten o-clock, low are ME-410s! I repeat, 410s!"

"We see 'em...thanks."

"Pitchfork to all flights, prepare for attack on your ten or eleven o'clock...they're comin' in low!

Glowgower watched the 410s perform reversing turns that would head them back toward the formation. He had seen this maneuver before and knew they would execute a sharp pull-up to bring the B-26s into their sights. His flexible 50-caliber nose gun could be brought to bear on them, but most of the bomber's guns would be useless until the attackers were almost on them. As the inelegant snouts of the fighters resolved themselves into recognizable shapes through the clear nose dome, he involuntarily shivered. Exhaling deeply, he tracked the nearest one with his gun, thinking he would never—*not ever*—get used to this no matter how many missions he flew.

The black-helmeted leader of the section of 410s going after the low squadron, pulled up and tried to draw a bead on *Friend or Enema?*, but the angle was too steep and he quickly decided to fire instead at the plane below it. As the distance shrank, he could see the outline of a man in the nose pointing a machine gun at him. He squeezed the trigger on his control yoke.

Glowgower watched the balls of fire from the 20 millimeter cannons leap toward *The A-Train* as he attempted to track the oncoming fighter in the sights of his gun. At first, the cannon bursts all seemed to be curving below the nose, but as the German pilot pulled up slightly to correct his lead, one of the massive shells entered the nose dome at its base, taking off the top of the bombardier's once handsome head in a crimson splash and blowing away most of the roof of *The A-Train's* nose compartment. Right behind the ravaged nose compartment, the 200 m.p.h. wind unpredictably pouring into the flight deck would have blown Clementi from the co-pilot's seat had he not been strapped-in.

"What the hell!" was all that Shaw could exclaim while he fought to control the crippled bomber as it tried to career against the aerodynamic drag created by the shattered nose. "Luce!" the pilot screamed. "Are you o.k.?"

The co-pilot had been temporarily stunned by the sudden blast of wind, which had blown off his cap and earphones. "Yeah!" he shouted over the noise, "I'm all right!"

"Get on the rudders with me! She keeps trying to turn left." Shaw wound in full right rudder trim to compensate for the pressure on the rudder pedal. Shifting his attention to the interphone, he called, "Pilot to bombardier!" No answer. "Glow!" he screamed, "Answer me! Are you o.k.?" Nothing. Next to him, Grattan was leaning through the door to the flight deck. The wind was blowing through the cockpit with such force that it flattened the big navigator's thin hair against his scalp. "Mick!" the pilot had to shout over the din. "Luce needs to stay on the controls with me...get up in the nose and see what happened!"

Grattan got on his hands and knees and began crawling toward the opening in front of the co-pilot. The screeching wind tore at his hair and clothing as he inched forward through the opening and beheld the nearly decapitated form of the bombardier. The appalling spectacle of it caused him to recoil backward so quickly that he barked his head on the ceiling of the cockpit. "GOD IN HEAVEN!" he wailed, sinking to his knees. Retching several times, he spewed vomit all over the control pedestal.

"What!" The pilot grabbed his arm and demanded. "What happened?"

The navigator groaned, slowly shaking his head back and forth. "It's Glow...his head's..." the big man shuddered "...*gone!*"

Shaw heard what Grattan said but it didn't register—the statement confused him. "Gone?" he asked.

"He's dead."

The A-train had fallen below the formation and was trailing off to the left. A sudden noise in his earphones snapped Shaw back to reality. It was Armistead. "Green leader to green able one! Are you o.k.?"

"Wait one, green leader," Shaw answered and quickly surveyed the instruments in front of him for any sign of malfunction. "Pilot to engineer, any damage back there?"

"Negative," Tilden answered. "Can't see none."

Shaw determined that there had been no damage to the engines and none of the fuel cells had been hit. He briefly tested the controls then called, "This is green able one...we're flyable but can't keep up speed."

"What's the best airspeed you can maintain?"

"Wait one." Shaw turned to the co-pilot. "Stay on the controls with me, Luce, and watch 'er!" He nudged up the throttles until the yaw to the left became uncontrollable, then eased back slightly.

"Green leader...looks like we can hold one-ninety."

Shaw listened as Armistead called the group leader. "Green leader to pitchfork, we've got a damaged aircraft and request we slow the formation to one-ninety, over." This would add about three minutes to their escape to the coast, three long minutes of lethal danger.

In the lead plane Spinelli, guessing the reason for Armistead's request, didn't hesitate. "Roger, green leader!" he responded, then followed with the order, "Pitchfork to all flights, reduce power to an airspeed of one-niner-zero! I repeat, airspeed, one-niner-zero!"

With both him and Clementi on the controls, Shaw advanced power enough to move *The A-Train* back into position below and behind *Friend or Enema?*. Within the protective womb of the squadron and the group, their chances of making it back to England were increased exponentially.

Although the defending enemy forces were now effectively divided by the B-17s and B-24s who were deep into the German heartland, they weren't finished with the B-26s yet. The bombers, creeping up the track they had come in on, were now only minutes away from Mons, where they would be joined again by the refueled and rearmed P-47s—*but the attackers arrived first.*

"Pitchfork to all flights, bogies incoming at two o'clock high!" The sun now was nearly overhead and gave no advantage to either side. The P-38s had used most of their fuel reserves in the fight coming off the target and would be in a critical situation if they had to maneuver again at full power. They could make one pass at the attackers, then would have to head for the coast. As the Lightnings swerved to engage them, the German fighters turned back to the east on a course to the right of the bombers. The P-38s couldn't pursue. If they did, most of them would be forced to ditch their fuel-starved airplanes in the sea. The P-47s, 30 miles distant to the northwest, were still out of sight."Turret to crew, Bogies comin' our way at four o'clock high!" Vega squinted to get a better look. "I count twenty plus 109s...but they're headin' away from the 38s." The ME-109s, estimating that the P-38s were close to the limits of their range, waited for the big American fighers to turn back to the north before commencing the attack. Vega watched silently until the enemy fighters reversed course. "The bogies are turnin' around behind us!" Vega suddenly called, his voice in a high pitch. "You see 'em, Leroy?

"Got 'em!" Rimbaud replied, rotating his turret toward the attackers. "They divin'!" he screamed. "Heah they come!"

The 109s had accelerated to 400 m.p.h. to come in below the formation, which would blank out the fire from the guns of the top turrets. Using a well-developed tactic, the enemy fighters, when they reached cannon range, would sharply pull-up and fire into the vulnerable belly of the formation. Rimbaud checked his feed belts and began tracking the approaching fighters in his sight pipper. The swarthy little gunner was now an "ace"—unofficial, of course—with six confirmed aircraft destroyed to his credit, the highest score of any gunner in the group. It would certainly earn him a DFC and probably a promotion to master sergeant. "Numbah seven," he clucked while he calculated the lead on the 109 coming into his sights. "You fixin' to die, you Nazi piece of sheeit," he muttered to himself. Rimbaud wasn't too sure what the term "Nazi" meant and really didn't give a damn. It was simple for him— they were the enemy, and he thoroughly enjoyed shooting them down. "One a' doze yella-nosed sonomabeeches," he mumbled, "uh-huh...ah got you boy...ah got you!" then squeezed the trigger on his gun handle. With a chilling absorption, Rimbaud watched his tracers twinkle around the nose of the oncoming plane and dance into its cockpit, exploding the canopy and the upper half of German pilot in a swirling pink mass of shattered plexiglas and human body parts. At virtually the same instant, a 20 millimeter round entered the bottom of the clear fairing over the gun mount, blowing off half of Rimbaud's right foot and taking the right machine gun from its mount, before exiting through the roof of the tail turret and shredding the bottom one-third of the rudder.

Shaw felt the jar on the rudder pedals and simultaneously heard a blood-curdling scream on the interphone. "Ah'm hit! Ah'm hit!" the voice shrieked.

"Who is it...who is it?" the pilot demanded.

"Ahhhh...tail!" came the anguished reply.

"Tilden!" Shaw cracked. "Take the first aid kit and get back there!"

"On my way!" the engineer replied. The tail turret was a shamble of wreckage with the tail gunner lying in the middle of it, the stump of his right foot pulsing blood. Tilden unbuckled the wounded gunner's restraining straps and pulled him onto the metal floorboard in front of the tail section. Removing the leather belt from Rimbaud's shearling jacket, he tied it below the gunner's right knee to act as a tourniquet and pulled it tight until the flow of blood was staunched. Tilden took the sissors from the kit and cut through the tattered remains of the gunner's right boot, then pulled the bloody sock back to reveal the wound. The sight of it caused him to reflexively turn away for a moment and take several deep breaths in an effort to hold back the gorge rising in his throat. Regaining self-control, the engineer crouched over the gunner's writhing form.

"You're gonna' be o.k., Leroy," Tilden crooned. "You just lie still while I fix you up...all right?" He unzipped the gunner's leather flight pants, then jabbed a morphine styrette into the muscle of the right thigh. After dousing the wound with sulfa powder, he applied a cotton compress to the end of the stump and secured it in place by winding cotton gauze around the entire foot. "Cisco!" Tilden yelled at the turret gunner. "Close the waist doors and bring me some blankets!" When he looked up, he saw Grattan standing over him with two blankets under his arm.

"How's he doing?" the navigator asked. His face bore an expression that was abnormally haggard.

"Most of his right foot's blown off, but I think I've got the bleeding under control."

Grattan pointed to his watch. "O.k., but remember to loosen the tourniquet in five minutes to see if the bleeding's stopped." Tilden looked at his own watch and nodded.

Glancing back at Grattan, Tilden asked, "What happened up front, I heard..."

"Glowgower's dead...the nose is totally wrecked."

Tilden looked at him in stunned silence.

"The 47s are back!" Vega announced. We're home free, the gunner thought. *Well, most of us.*

CHAPTER TWENTY

February 1, 1944, Great Dunmow, England.

Shaw rubbed his hands together against the chill of the drafty quonset hut. He stared fixedly at the blank sheet of paper lying on the desk before him, willing the words to come. This was something not taught in flight school or operational training—how to write a letter to parents about the death of their son. Having to write such a thing—it was part of his officer resposibilities—made Shaw wonder about the wisdom of his career choice. Flying big, powerful airplanes had been the greatest thrill of his young life. Flying combat had been the supreme test of his skills. But this—he didn't want to do this any more. Still, he wrote the letter, but the words seemed empty. He told them their son had been a brave man, the best at his job in the group. He also told them their son had been one of his best friends and would always be remembered. But he could not find the words to explain the unique bond that had existed between them. Shaw had loved Joe Glowgower like a brother, yet in a different, inexplicable way. Carefully folding the letter, he put it in a V-mail envelope.

Shaw looked again at the orders lying beside the envelope. They said: After a 15-day leave—not including time en route—proceed to Smoky Hill Field, Salina, Kansas, and report to the 472ND Bomb Group (Very Heavy) for B-29 conversion and operational training. He was surprised, had not expected to receive orders until he was stateside. The Air Force must be in a hurry to put together B-29 groups, he speculated. The pilot was ready for a change.

Another blank sheet of paper lay before him. There was much he had to say, but it could be saved for later, so he wrote:

February 1, 1944

Dear Mary Beth,

Call the preacher. I'm coming home.

Your ever loving,
Ted

Later the same day, in the large maintenance hangar, Shaw walked up to Ripley, who was perched on a work stand set up by the nose of *The A-Train.* "How's it goin', Buster?" he asked.

"Nuthin' wrong with 'er I cain't fix!" The crew chief pointed to the new, unpainted sheet metal that had been installed on the nose. The only thing left of the original red lettering was *–TRAIN.* "She'll be good as new when me and my boys finish 'er up." Shaw looked up at the bomber.

"You're still beautiful," the pilot whispered to her. He ran his hand down her flanks and noticed that her paint had been scarred by weather and time. "You have meant so much to me," he intoned softly. "But now I've got to go far away to another place, to do an important job, and I can't take you with me. I promise I'll never forget you. Good bye."

EPILOGUE:
THE FORTUNES OF WAR

June 23, 1948, Pentagon Building, Washington, D.C.

The young Major of the newly organized United States Air Force, now a separate and independent service, watched the senior officers file into the briefing room. The subject of today's meeting was the revision and standardization of aircraft designations in the Air Force's current inventory. When the meeting began, they agreed that the designator for fighters would be changed from Pursuit (P-) to Fighter (F-), thus the North American P-51D would become the F-51D, and so on.

"Strategic Air Command has recommended that we completely abandon the A- for Attack designator in favor of a B- for Bomber designator for all multi-engined aircraft designed to carry ordinance," the Major informed the seated officers.

"What aircraft do we currently have that use the Attack designator?" one of the officers asked.

"Only the Douglas A-26, sir," the Major replied.

"What do you propose to re-designate it?"

"To reduce confusion, sir, we propose to call it the B-26."

"B-26? What about the Martins, the Marauders?"

"There aren't any left flying, sir."

"Oh."

July 2, 1948, U.S.A.F. Storage Facillity, Kingman, Arizona.

She sat in the vast parking area and waited. The day was hot and there was a dry breeze blowing in from the desert, but she didn't notice it; she was only a little over five years old.

She had a name and a serial number, both so faded by time and wear that they were barely discernible. She was not alone, for she was surrounded on all sides by her sisters. They were waiting, too. Her powerful engines were now silent and her guns had been taken away from her. Her gas tanks were empty, her hydraulic lines dry.

She had been waiting a long time. She waited for the boys to come and take her away...again, for they would give her substance. Without them, she was merely an inanimate collection of aluminum, steel, rubber, glass, and leather.

Some people still thought she was pretty. Her shape and sleek lines had not changed. And her strength...she was still very, very strong. She was dressed the same way her boys had left her, though the unremitting sun had caused much of her adornment to erode and flake-off. If you walked up close to her, you could even see the remnants of the one hundred forty-three small yellow bombs that had been painted on her side. The large red lettering of her name, which somehow didn't match, was still readable, just barely.

She was ready.

The two men drove the tow tractor up the dusty road along the seemingly endless rows of parked airplanes. The driver braked to a stop and asked his companion, "Which one is goin' to the chopper?" He was referring to the large machine that chopped the planes up into scrap metal.

"Oh...it don't really matter," the other said. "Just hook up to that one...what's the name on the side?"

"Says *The A-Train*...after that old song, I guess."

AUTHOR'S HISTORICAL NOTE

A lthough Ted Shaw, his crew, and the 333RD Bomb Group (Medium) were wholly figments of my imagination, the book's account of the training and operations of the aircrews who flew the Martin B-26 Marauder into combat was based upon fact. The meeting between then Brigadier General James H. Doolittle and General Henry H. Arnold in October, 1942 did take place, my dialogue notwithstanding. Without Doolittle's timely intervention, the production contract on the B-26 probably would have been cancelled. What Doolittle astutely discovered, himself an aeronautical engineer, was that the technology of the airplane greatly exceeded the existing Army Air Force training methods. As aeronautical technology dramatically moved forward during the war, similar problems were encountered with other airplanes such as the Boeing B-29 and the Lockheed P-80.

The disastrous and ill-conceived low-level raid on the power plant at Ijmiuden, Holland was actually carried out by the 322ND Bomb Group (Medium) on the date listed in the book. Of the ten B-26s participating, one returned early due to mechanical problems, but the other nine were completely destroyed by flak and fighters in the vicinity of the target. There were no survivors. After the raid, a general standdown was ordered for all B-26 groups attached to the 8TH Air Force, and serious consideration was given to the idea of withdrawing them from combat altogether. The unnamed Brigadier General who planned the raids did exist; when he ordered a third mission against the plant, he was summarily fired by then Major General Ira Eaker.

Fortunately for the B-26 and her crews, saner heads prevailed, and the plane was finally given the mission it was designed for: bombing targets from medium ranges and medium altitudes. The transfer to the 9TH Tactical Air Force in late 1943 placed the B-26 groups in their prime, where they followed the invading American and British armies onto the European continent and soldiered on until V-E Day. Their combat record speaks for itself: the B-26 groups flew more missions, destroyed more targets, with fewer losses, than any other type of bomber participating in the European Theater of Operations. Ironically, however, the myths surrounding the aircraft were never completely lived down. I recently asked a former 15TH Air Force B-24 gunner/flight engineer what he thought of the B-26, and his reply was: "That thing was a deathtrap! Nobody wanted to fly in 'em!"

The sad fate of *The A-Train* in Kingman, Arizona was truly represented. The B-26s, all 5,157 of them, had virtually disappeared from the face of the earth by the late 1940s. A few remain in air museums and one flyable example, an early short-winged version rescued from the Canadian wilderness in 1972, is maintained and flown by Kermit Weeks in Florida. A B-26G, the last version produced, is on display at the USAF Museum at Wright-Patterson Air Force Base in Dayton, Ohio. The most notable survivor is the B-26B called *Flak Bait,* the first Allied bomber to complete 200 missions, the nose section of which is preserved at the National Air and Space Museum in Washington, D.C.

The final insult to the Martin B-26 occurred in 1948 when the Air Force gave its designator to the Douglas A-26 Invader. When I mention the B-26 to knowledgeable aviation enthusiasts, they invariably ask: "Which one do you mean, the Martin or the Douglas?" And my consistent reply is: I mean, the *original.* Although *The A-Train* and her sisters have disappeared into the annals of history, Shaw, Clementi, and Grattan will fly again.